Journeys
with
Monique

JOURNEYS
WITH
MONIQUE

Letty R. Hargrove

JOURNEYS WITH MONIQUE

iUniverse books may be ordered through booksellers or by contacting:

iUniverse
1663 Liberty Drive
Bloomington, IN 47403
www.iuniverse.com
1-800-Authors (1-800-288-4677)

ISBN: 978-1-4759-9139-0 (sc)
ISBN: 978-1-4759-9138-3 (hc)
ISBN: 978-1-4759-9140-6 (e)

Printed in the United States of America

iUniverse rev. date: 10/10/2014

PROLOGUE

This is a romantic fantasy that women and men should find interesting. We all have our fantasies and wish for certain things for our lives. Those of my friends who chose to read this will find some autobiographical connections but they will have to talk with me personally to see what is true and what is fantasy. I speak of the joy of life as a dance which I believe it is, the dance is happy, exciting, sexual, crazy or difficult but it is life. We move through it sometimes as if we're dancing be it with relationships with the "significant other" or with friends or with colleagues or just those people we meet day to day. Frequently we find bricks of all sizes in the way that we must go around or straight through. We can choose to make it happy, difficult, stressful or sad; it is an individual choice governed by our creator who if we open ourselves to him or her may direct us and then may leave us on our own to find our way. The joy of live through the artistic side, the love given and accepted of people one meets, the love of animals, difficulty of possible illness, the ageing we all face. So my dear Monique, whom I have come to love, goes for it and feels the pain and joy but at least she goes for it, many people never do. She takes a chance to go out of her realm of comfort, if in fact it is comfort, to seek a new zone. In the process she talks a lot to SELF and finds out more about herself and who she is, what she is capable of accomplishing and the choices she must make. But she remains true to herself, for better or worse, not perfect just a loving, talented human being. I hope you find some affinity with her. I hope you will understand her and enjoy her Joie de Vivre. May you all find your way and enjoy the process.

CHAPTER 1

Sometimes an offer comes, an opportunity for something new in your life but how do you make what might become a life alternating decision when you've lived so long in one place and have roots? To leave everything behind if only for a year or two and move to a foreign country, albeit one you love, can you be that brave? I had my home, friends of many years, way of life plus my dear four legged friend Serhalin to consider. He was a well built gray Arabian, had taken a blue ribbon for his 5 year confirmation. I had such a good time riding and training him and I had had him since he was 10 months old and he was now in his prime at 13. I had a difficult time imagining moving him so far from what he knew but knew how much I would miss him. Maybe I would plan to go only for a year so would lease him. Even if I got settled and decided to stay I could have him transported but that would be very expensive. But in my heart I knew it was time to go forward, to do something else but there was a lot to think about and consider. Was I considering too drastic a move ahead? Would I be lost without my friends? Could I handle all the changes? So began a long dialogue with SELF.

I had gone through a very miserable divorce, if there is any other kind. My husband had been acting very erratic for 2 or 3 years. During that time I didn't know he was embezzling money from an account he handled and when it was discovered we lost most of what we had worked for during 15 years. I was devastated by the lost monetary situation not because of things but because of security and all the sacrifices to achieve what we had. I was the one left to take care of everything and try to bail us out. He was so nervous and really out of it and seemingly not capable of coping so I was the one who had to handle the legal aspects, the sale of properties and hope there was something to salvage. I tried for 2 years to stay with him as I believed that I had made a marriage commitment and did love my home. He tuned out and watched TV and complained. I, in his eyes, could do nothing right I was always being criticized. My mistake was to think he would come to the fore. When he began to become violent towards me out of his frustration or his manic depressive state I could hold on no longer.

I had an offer from Paul Dreher, the gallery owner in Vienna with whom I had become a friend when I studied music one summer on an independent program for my Master's Degree. Several years after I worked on an art project for my own gallery bringing works from Vienna and Budapest to the United States. I met several artists, professors, media people so knew I would have some "familiar" support. He had an art gallery in Vienna and was just opening one in Budapest. He suggested I come to work part time for him. Paul of course was aware that I had started a gallery in Santa Barbara, but which I had recently sold and he sensed I was looking for something so made the offer. He said he could not pay much but thought my ability in the arts and business plus being a native speaker of English could be of great assistance to him especially with English speaking clients. He also said I could study German as I only spoke a little and this would make me even more beneficial to increase the gallery clientele list. He said he would help find an apartment, get me settled show me what he needed at the gallery. I could then study the language and under his tutelage learn much more about art. Depending on sales he would offer commissions. I knew he would be a great teacher, I would advance so much in my knowledge of the arts plus a new culture. So why not got for the opportunity even at the age of 42 it didn't have to be forever. Little did I know what the future would bring if I decided to go.

When the divorce was finally complete I felt somewhat lost and abandoned at first but soon picked up a single life. I enjoyed time to read, study, play the piano and redecorate my house with the idea of improving it and selling. I had a number of friends of many years to do various activities with. I looked for employment to see what else I could do if I sold the gallery but in a smaller city that wasn't easy especially since so many knew I still owned my own business and questioned my motives I finally decided I could lease my house that I dearly loved because it always had felt like home, I wouldn't sell right away. I had some income coming in from another property and some in the bank. I said to SELF you are only 42 and can work at something, how could I go wrong going to Vienna being part of an entirely different milieu; little did I know, in many ways. It reminded me when I left my small town at 18 to attend the University of California in Los Angeles and knew my "pigtails" were showing. Maybe I had developed a little more confidence and sophistication but sometimes that is only a mindset that you need to be aware of. In many ways the "pigtails" were still visible at least inside. I did know I was very resilient having gone through all the troubles, that I was good at planning ahead and good with people so I knew I had some valuable survival skills, SELF agreed.

Several years before my husband and I decided to do what we had talked so much about, going to live in Europe for awhile so we leased our house, put most of our belongings in storage and left for Germany. We had always wanted to spend a lengthy time in Europe, the opportunity was there as we were able to stay at the home of his aunt and uncle. We used their home as our base traveling throughout Europe. My husband's parents had immigrated to the United States from Germany. My parents were very European, my mother first generation Polish, my father an immigrant from Canada so because of that and the way they raised me I felt quite European.

Several years later we spent a summer in Vienna so I could work on an independent study program towards my masters degree. We stayed in an apartment hotel not far from the opera house walked the streets or took the streetcars, went to many concerts, dined frequently in the small coffee houses.

I had a professor friend who had been my tough master teacher when I was working on my teaching credential. He went every summer to work on a book and write articles for the music sections of certain US newspapers. He continued to be my teacher, providing concert tickets to join his wife and him at special events and concerts and showing me how to do research in the library in the Hapsburg. He said he would never complete the book but used it as a vehicle to go to Vienna and Salzburg every summer. He said I could complete it. I told him I was a vocal student not into studying brass instruments

All of this is how I came to know and love Vienna, its vibrance, intelligence, artistic standards, historical background, its total ambiance with the constant joie de vivre emanating from its inhabitants many very educated in the arts and music.

I commiserated for days with SELF and finally said YES I'm going to do this and so started putting together all the logistics. I contacted Paul and told him I was coming. He was happy and told me they would find me an apartment, help me get settled and we would get to work. I was afraid that I would become an expatriate but did that matter? Little did I know how many adventures were in store for me and how true were my concerns.

My Austrian friends found an apartment for me and even a place to board my horse if I decided to bring him along but the expense was a lot so I decided to lease him back to my friend at whose ranch he was boarded. Some people don't understand the connection a human can have with a pet, he was a best friend would I knew I would be homesick but I had to go ahead and experience something new for better or worse.

It was August in California and I decided it would take me about 3 months to get things in order so all would function, banking questions, house lease which I knew a friend in real estate could handle for me, communication plans, air ticket, 15 years worth of stuff to pack and put into storage. Believe me I had a glass of wine on evenings when it all seemed too much to go through but then the anticipation of a true adventure kept me alert. I decided to leave mid October. I had no trouble getting my house leased and all the rest organized. My friends had given me the name of the Viennese landlord so I contacted them with the details and that I would be shipping three packages ahead of time so they would know just to hold them until I arrived. So I was on my way to a new adventure little did I know many adventures and where they would take me.

At last I was ready to depart. A couple of days before my friends had a going away party with lots of laughter and some tears. They all said they would come to visit me so I knew a few who were travelers would. It would be great I wouldn't feel so disconnected from Santa Barbara. We of course would stay in touch via email and snail mail and occasional phone calls. On October20 several friends took me to LAX, again hugs and tears along with smiles of encouragement.

Leaving on October 20 I would arrive in Vienna October 21 at 8:30 am. I had the address and was told to go direct and the landlord would be there to meet me. We landed on time and since I had so much stuff I decided to take a taxi to 801 Reimerstrasse my new address. The taxi I found was actually a Mercedes sedan with a driver called Heinrich. He said he would charge the same amount as any taxi, he was trying to grow his business. So I chose him and on the way into the city we chatted. He wanted to know why I had come to the city so I told him. I asked about his family and with a big smile he talked about his wife and 2 children. By the time he got me to the apartment we were becoming friends. I took his business card and said I would call and try to send him other business. I didn't know how many times I would call him and what friends we would become.

The apartment was just on the outer ring in the section just East of the Rathausplatz so I knew the area was good but couldn't image what kind of apartment I would be greeted with a tiny studio, cramped and dingy, perhaps a one bedroom with the high ceilings and heavy, heavy curtains, one burner stove—the worry kept going—SELF was having to listen a lot. When I arrived at 801 I saw this wonderful building that looked as though it had once been the home of some wealthy individual but I saw signs of modernization outside with the typical architecture but clean and newly painted. It had been renovated with new large windows and skylights in the center section of the building. It appeared that there was a center large section and two smaller sections on either side—perhaps the apartments. I paid Heinrich and he helped me with the luggage up to the main entrance where I saw the buzzers so pushed the one for Schmidt, the landlords, and a few seconds heard a friendly voice saying "Ja, wer es ist". I answered "Ich bin Monique Stewart" and the voice with a German accent said "toll, haben wir Sie erwartet" a click and the door was available to open. In front of me was a large staircase with wide steps and railing on either side. Above was a most friendly face saying "come right up, do you need help".

"Nein I said in my broken German "Ich lasse meine Koffer hier jetzt und später abgerechnet erhalten." I was to meet Jennifer, later to become Jennie to me, who had open arms and invited me in.

"Wilkommen, Sie muss mude Sein" von die Lange Reise."

"Yah ein bischten"

I entered into their home which was quite large and open, with huge skylights above, expansive living room, large modern kitchen with all the latest equipment. I guessed someone was a gourmand.

"How was the trip, did you have any trouble getting here, would you like a nice tall drink or would you prefer tea she said in perfect English."

My mind was in jet lag and I was a bit overwhelmed by the fact I had actually arrived. I was so happy that she spoke excellent English. I was soon to learn that she also spoke her native German, plus French and Spanish. How uneducated I felt.

"Something tall, I'm so thirsty from the plane. Everything was on time amazingly. I do know a bit about Vienna so had an idea where you were located. It's so lovely the building is terrific." I was thinking I would probably have an apartment the size of the maid's quarters but I was here and ready to get started.

We sat and chatted a bit. I told her about the flight and the taxi transit from the airport. I felt right away I could talk with her and knew she would become a very good friend. She was so open for a Viennese that I was surprised how I could jabber on. I found she had studied in the US at Harvard and was an architect and designer as was her husband Peter. He was out at the moment but would soon be home. I sensed she was very empathetic. "Well let's get you settled".

"Ich werde gehen, meine Koffer zu erhalten", I said in German. I decided to keep trying some German tired or not. I went down to retrieve one and then back up the stairs.

She took me across the landing to another large door saying "This is your new home, we hope you will be comfortable. We put your boxes that arrived several days ago just inside. She opened the door and my mouth dropped open. There was a large entry space with a closet on the right, then a hallway about 10 feet long leading to a large living room all with hardwood floors. The ceilings were about 14 feet high, probably before renovation they had been 18 feet in the old style. Off the living room to the left was the large bathroom with a skylight and all new, modern faucets, toilet, bathtub and shower with tile floors of a light slate color. From the bath, going through the living room was the bedroom again gigantic with a built in closet and a wonderful old armoire, room for a queen size bed and eventually a desk and chair. Generally a built-In closet wasn't found in the older buildings, but two architects had redesigned the original space and knew what to include. It also had French doors so one could look out onto an inner court yard garden. I was later to learn that the garden was shared by the home on the adjacent street. The kitchen had a pantry and sufficient cabinets for everything plus a small round table in the corner enough to seat 4 people, large refrigerator and nice gas stove top and oven. Again there were French doors looking to the garden. I was in love with the place already.

I couldn't see how I would be able to afford this. I turned to Jennifer a little bewildered, "Are you sure the rent is correct?" She had quoted me $700 per month.

She giggled and smiled, "Yes it is correct. This is our home and we have plenty of room and don't want to rent to just anyone. Paul told us about you and said you were an intelligent, educated, honest person that would be perfect to have next door and we took his word. The rent helps us and we like to help others. He says you will continue to be a student and a colleague of his so we are happy to have you here and assist in any way we can, we remember our time in the US."

"Thank you so much." Do people like this still exist I asked SELF? "I'm sure I will be most comfortable. I will do some redecorating but will always check with you for an ok."

"Yes I know the furniture is sparse only enough to be adequate" "We do have other things in the basement storage area so you might take a look at those." Every room had just been completed and painted in a wonderful white, without the beige. It would be perfect. I just wanted to make it more my home so would add some color and wallpaper in areas and eventually some artwork.

"Right now I think you want to freshen up and take a walk and get a bit acclimated." We invite you to dinner tonight so we can get better acquainted and you won't have to shop until you're ready." I did see that she had shopped and had coffee, tea, milk, fruit and rolls In the kitchen for which I thanked her.

So I went back to my new home to freshen up and then with my new schlussel, money, ID in my purse and a map of the city in hand I went out from my new home. The air was fresh with the aroma of autumn. I decided I would walk down Reimerstrasse which was tree lined with graceful white pine trees with multi-colored flowers along the borders. Not every street in Vienna has this as the older apartments and homes often are built right to the sidewalk. The aroma was rich from the pines and their cones. The pungent smell of fall was in the air as the needles dropped, slowly decaying and mixing with the rich, moist soil.

Three blocks down my new street was the outer ring where I could pick up a street car until I came to the Kartnerstrasse a pedestrian street where I knew I could "eat off the street". The vendors are always there with wonderful ham, sausages, cheeses and an infinite variety of breads and rolls. I couldn't decide what to eat first so purchased a collection of items if only just to smell the wonderful aroma of it all. I sauntered slowly down the Kartnerstrasse munching away trying to absorb the sights and sounds from St. Stephens cathedral to the Opera House remembering how it was the summer we had spent there 11 years prior plus during the visits since that time.

That is how I came to know and love Vienna, it's vibrance, intelligence, artistic standards, historical background, it's total ambiance. And here I was again but many years older 42, with new challenges. I wanted to skip down the street, feeling so energized and free, a young student again but with a bit more wisdom maybe not a lot but some from my past.

I walked and munched until jet lag began to set in so I decided it was time to get back on the streetcar and return to my new home. I knew I would need to know all the streetcar and subway routes eventually so might as well get going. To have a car in the city, which I always had in California, can be a real pain because of the parking, there seldom is any in the area you want to be.

I got back to the apartment and sat on my new bed and cried, partially from fatigue, partially from fear, partially from anticipation. Two hours later I awoke and had to figure out where I was, I was temporarily disoriented. Then I remembered dinner so freshened up, collected the flowers I had purchased as a small token for my new landlords. I had already put mine in a container, not a vase, didn't have one yet. Whenever I am in a new place I purchase flowers, they seem to have such a wonderful calming, inviting effect.

I got ready and proceeded across the landing to the Schmidt's home and was surprised that there were two other couples. My first thought was that I was the new entertainment in town but as we all began to converse I found they were very good friends of Jennifer and Peter they just wanted to welcome me too. How generous and kind. I'm sure they were also very curious about an older woman trying to begin again or maybe they saw it was just another step of growth. The conversation went between English and German as I hunted for the words. I knew I was really going to have to study. Jennifer, an excellent cook I found out, prepared veal schnitzel, gnocchi, spinach soufflé and a beautiful fruit salad, such flavor. For dessert there was Sacher torte, my chocolate. It was a wonderful interesting evening, a great new beginning.

Back in my apartment that evening I began to look at how I would redecorate to my taste for comfort but also my statement of new beginnings. In the bathroom muted grey walls with darker grey stripes and an overlay of a low sheen lacquer, to tie in with the tiles. I would buy some new towels, some very contemporary furniture and light fixtures. I knew everything existed somewhere in Vienna. In the kitchen some marbleized painting in the small area around the French doors that lead to a small balcony and stairs down to the garden would add an accent. The phone rang, I had forgotten to ask Jennifer if it was on or not but obviously it was. I answered and heard Paul's voice. "Wilkommen" are you getting settled?

"Yes, barely. I did just come from the landlords who had me over for dinner."

"Can we come over tonight for a little while?"

"Of course" but I have little here."

"Don't worry we'll bring some wine and goodies."

"Ok come over as soon as you can before I feel like falling asleep again". They arrived about a half hour later, Paul, his girl friend Juliana, and Max a real character with a gift of gab but also an avid art collector and good friend of Paul's. He always wanted to be on the scene, seen and heard, lots of fun. Big hugs and the kisses on either cheek which is the custom. They had a couple bottles of wine and some snacks.

"What great space, fantastic to find in Vienna." said Max.

"Thanks to you and Paul. I must admit I am in a bit of awe that this exists here. I know I'm going to love it after I do a few things."

We poured some wine and began to jabber about my trip, the fact I had actually found courage to come, and what we were going to do.

"When can you come to the gallery" asked Paul.

"Tomorrow afternoon and will get started. We can set a schedule of when you need me. I want to go shopping in the morning for paint and I do need some time to go to the flea market on Friday to look for some things and perhaps somewhere else on Monday to look for furniture and other things like linens." I also told him I would be painting but could do some in the evenings and somehow work it all out. "I have to also see about German classes or a tutor so I can improve more quickly. Any ideas?"

"I think a tutor would be the best. I'll give you her name and number and you can set up a program."

While I had Max the "character" of Vienna there, who had a framing shop, I ordered a mirror for over the sink in the bathroom, about 3 foot by 4 foot with an inch bevel and very simple silver wooden frame contemporary in style, a long mirror to go behind the bedroom door and a rectangular one about 3 feet to go in the hallway.

They knew the time to leave when they saw me fading with fatigue. Another nights sleep and I should be acclimated. Now the program was to begin in earnest, very exciting. I had no time now to be homesick although I knew that would come and go.

CHAPTER 2

The next morning I asked Jennie and Peter about the painting saying I would do it and not make a mess. They said fine and directed me to a good paint store so I was off the next morning to shop. The owner was most helpful so I purchased the paint I needed, brushes, drop cloths, cheesecloth for the marbleizing then I realized, no car. How do I get this home. So I talked with him about drop shades for the windows and he showed me his selections and said he could come by to measure and then give me a price. He would deliver the paint and supplies when he came to do that. He also did some drape work so I told him what I wanted and he had a lady who could do it. The drapes that were up I would remove and Jennie could store them in the basement. He would deliver the paint in Saturday and do the measuring so I was set for the first step.

While I was out after the paint store I went to a hair salon recommended by Jenny, They cut my dark hair short in a rather French style that I could straighten or leave with my natural curl, whiffs of hair coming away from the ears, the back a hairline coming to a peak so I was becoming a new woman. I figured out which streetcars I should take to the Dreher gallery and found it was quite easily. I guess it wouldn't be so bad after all without a car and without the expense. If I needed one to go into the countryside I would just have to rent it.

Paul had a most interesting photography exhibit displayed, works from two artistic photographers from Budapest. But the gallery looked a bit dismal and not too inviting so I started making my mental notes of what we should to do change that. When he showed me the office with mounds of research papers and the desk in total disarray I knew where we would begin. His current assistant Cynthia was staying on. She was a sweet, intelligent but not a too assertive person and so didn't know how to "whip" things into shape and Paul really an artist was not the most organized. I would elicit her help and we would get everything in order.

We needed some new lighting. I wanted to be careful not to affront Paul with too many things at once but started a mental plan. So I asked Paul if we could begin in the office, I would give instructions to Cynthia, his assistant, to show her what we could achieve and he gave the ok. He was a bit reticent at first because he had his own way of keeping track of things but I assured him anything in question we would put aside and label for his attention. We would upgrade the computer system and improve our client data base and artist information. This was going to take a little doing over some time but it would show up in more success, more sales as we say. The gallery was a business not an entertainment place. We needed to work on sales for money but more important for prestige. Paul was so knowledgeable about art, way beyond my ability, he just needed someone to take care of some of the basics so he could be in order and only spend time selecting artists and planning the exhibitions. I was interested in learning from him he would be my art teacher.

We spent about 3 hours the first day reorganizing file information and relabeling setting up our own resource center. I said I would be back tomorrow afternoon and we'll continue, then we need to tackle the computer records and set up a better accounting program, one we all can use. It will be much more efficient." It was so exciting to know what I thought I was going to be a part of.

While we were working we talked about other artists in the area. Cynthia mentioned a clothing designer Gabrielle, she said Paul would not be interesting in showing her art, it was not his direction but perhaps I would like to meet her. I said of course, I was interested in design. So I took her number and planned to get in touch with her.

And so I left and went back to my streetcar hoping I would get the right one. I did but went beyond my stop so had to get off and hike back several blocks but I would soon get it down. Along the way I saw a coffeehouse and went in hoping they served food. They had simple fare but that was what I wanted at that point, I didn't want to have to go to the market yet. An older woman came to the table "war Wollen Sei Heute Abbruch?" I thought I should begin to try my broken German."

Erste Ich Muchte Ein Shoen Glas Rote Wein Bitte. Den was Haben Sie für essen." She smiled and said "Kommen sei aus England?"

"Nein aus USA".

"Nein ich glaube das nichte." Evidently she had met some impolite Americans or not any so had no admiration for or some preconceived idea of what Americans were like. "Wer haben schnizel aus scwein mit gnocci and kurken mit sahna".

"Wunderschoen, das wurde schmeck leker." So I enjoyed my repast with joy. I didn't even feel lonely as Frau Marta and Josef Hefler made me feel right at home, they were so friendly. They did speak enough English that with my poor German we managed conversation.

Walking back to my apartment I was having one of those personal conversations with SELF. It's all exciting but what am I doing? Then SELF said, "Look forward, work in the now and try not to look backward at the difficulties of the past, take from the past to enhance the now and the future. Returning I put on a Mozart CD and picked up my book and not long after was sound asleep.

CHAPTER 3

Jennifer had now become Jennie as we were on a similar wave length and knew we would become fast friends. She had told me about the local large flea market Am Hof open on Fridays. There were others on Saturday there was the Flohmarkt but I was hoping to go to the Naschmarket Saturday.

Friday morning, I figured out the trolley's to take and arrived at this huge area of vendors of all kinds. I began to browse and soon came upon one corner area with some furniture items and saw the perfect chest probably vintage mid 18 century that needed some work covering scratches but it would fit exactly where I wanted just in one corner of the living room just off the kitchen. It had a rounded front, three deep drawers. The drawers I would utilize for linens, coasters, serving pieces, candles, whatever and decanters and glasses on the top. He also had the perfect little side table that I could use in my entrance hallway. It was half circle in shape with three legs and wood inlay design on the top. It too would need some touch up but was stable and perfect where I wanted it. Then we dickered a few minutes about price if I bought both pieces and came quickly to an agreement. The only thing I wanted was a glass on top and of course now how do I get this to my apartment. I spoke with the owners who gave me the price and then I explained my quandary. The owner said wait a moment and made a call and told me he could have a man who cut glass for windows and whatever come right away to make the measurement and have the glass that afternoon. After that they would use their truck to deliver directly to me and carry it up the stairs and place it. What more could one want. So I became the proud owner of my first purchase for my new home. They also had baskets, candles and several other items I wanted so I continued to purchase I told them what else I was looking for and they gave me directions to their colleagues where I could shop until the glass for the chest would be delivered and all would be ready. I wanted contemporary things mainly, the chest and table would be my only older pieces. I continued to wander and saw much that was older sachen, dishes, glasses, etc. that I could appreciate but did not want to purchase, I was into clean line contemporary. I did find some linens; a round tablecloth for my kitchen table and napkins, a brass pot which I would use for umbrellas, and a small cloisonné based lamp to place on my new entry table. I picked up some large baskets I wanted to put at the front door for slippers which I still had to find. With the weather in Vienna I thought it was a good idea.

I wandered about and purchased of course some more flowers and a paperweight I found most interesting a traditional Italian millefiori set in a cobalt blue base. My collection of weights were all in storage so I thought this would add a touch of home. One last thing were plants, so I bought three tall fichus which would go behind the couch I planned to purchase and a grape vine to go on the top of the armoire. By the time I returned my cabinet and table had glass top properly polished around the edges and a small package they said was a gift that I should open when we arrived at the apartment. I figured he got something out of the other purchases I was making. The owner spoke with his son who disappeared but soon returned saying the truck was at the back. They were ready to load it. I paid for all and we were off. I was in the middle of Vienna with a father and son I never knew before me in the middle of the one bench truck seat and me giving directions in my broken German and lots of English. We arrived and I showed them we could park in the driveway for the time the delivery would take.

They hoisted the chest and climbed the flight of stairs and into my apartment and placed the chest where I wanted. Then they brought up the entrance table, the plants and other purchases putting them were I instructed. I opened their small gift package and found two beautiful glass candlesticks with white candles, they understood what I meant by contemporary, clean line. How wonderful. I thanked them profusely and of course gave a monetary tip which they said was not necessary. They invited me back to shop again. I guess I made their day but they had made mine also. There is hope for people being kind and helpful to each other. When they left I just sat a minute on the couch admiring my purchases and knew I was on to it, my new home. A knock at my door and there was Jennie. Having heard the commotion she had to see what I found. We opened a bottle of wine to celebrate my new acquisitions and we began to extend what would be a most close, lifelong friendship. She was such a dear person, beautiful and intelligent.

Jennie had told me we could go to an area of outlets for designers where she had a substantial discount. So we planned to go on Monday because she said I could find all kinds of things. She asked if I had a budget and I told her and she said, "Ok will shop to that. What are you looking for"? I gave her an idea. "Wow, we really do need to shop but I think we can do it."

"If I'm going to do it I'm going try to do as I want."

Monday morning we got moving. She shopped like me, knew ahead what she wanted and focused in on things. The prices were fantastic with her discount. We shopped like demons, nothing would hold us back. I had imagined an overstuffed, white couch that would make into a bed for guests and black and white geometric pillows, a small glass coffee table with only a pedestal in chrome. I wanted two non typical shaped chair one white the other a gray or black with a red pillow for each with different shapes. I didn't imagine we would find everything I had in my minds but I was surprised when we started to look.

Going to several of the stores we found everything very close to what I wanted. I had my whites, gray, black with a splash of color from red pillows. We found decanters and glasses, a small set of white dinner ware and extra pans and kitchen tools. Last we chose a television. When we got the total for everything with Jennies discount I was a little under budget amazing. I said, "Now I guess I'll have to stay longer than I might have planned to get all the enjoyment of this and I'm going to have to do several jobs to be sure I can pay the rent."

So I had spent my money but I was happy, the apartment would look great. It would be my own little show piece my own statement. I would now have to work on the artists to loan me some artwork.

On Tuesday I got up very early to tackle the painting. Soft grey with darker large strips in the bathroom, soft blue of marbleizing around the French doors. It took me the entire day but was worth it to enhance the total décor. I called Jennie to come and see and of course she was over in a minute and loved it. By Wednesday evening my apartment was going to look fantastic.

Wednesday came and delivery was at 10 am. They brought up everything and I directed them where things should be placed. The window treatment was being installed also at the same time. Now I just had to put linens away and wash and wrap up the bedding Jennie had provided, wash the dinner ware and glasses, put some books on the shelves. By the afternoon I was smiling but a bit exhausted. I had Jennie and Peter over for some wine to check out the results and they just smiled, "You did it. We are so happy you are here." And at that moment I was too, not just for the adventure, but that I was my own person with my own statement which I had never been able to make at this level before. So far my new journey was going better than I imagined.

Thursday and Friday I was ready to go back to the gallery and continue our organization. Paul told me that clients were coming to the gallery on Saturday and wanted me to be there to assist. He told me they were from the states and he thought I could have a good rapport with them so now began the real tests of my purpose of being here, could I assist Paul not only in organizing, finding new artists but also selling. The clients were from Chicago, a young couple on vacation. They had just been starting to acquire pieces. I was there and after much conversation the new clients did purchase a large oil painting quite colorful, with strong brush strokes full of vitality and imagination. It would need to be shipped so I did the paperwork and arranged the delivery time and completed the transaction.

And so I was into my new life in Vienna, working at the gallery, enjoying making new friends, learning new languages with my tutor and as well a different culture, it couldn't be better. I was becoming more European with still a bit of homesickness but that was ok, I could deal with it. I emailed to friends a lot and they responded so I had that connection. I could eat when I wanted, read, listen to music, no arguments oh what a blessing I felt very content and happy.

I contacted Gabrielle the designer and made an appointment to meet with her at her studio. Her studio apartment was across the river on Brigttastrasse. So late Wednesday I went to her studio and found some most attractive knits and fabrics ready for dresses and some wonderful designs she has completed and some she was working on. I purchased a dressy pant suit and said I would be back and bring other clients soon. She was most excited and said if I could she would provide things at a cost plus a little extra for her because she would grow her business. I agreed and so had found another new artist friend.

Over the next many days we had the office in shape and Paul was amazed at how helpful finding things easily on and off the computer was. He planned for a new exhibit about every 6 weeks so we had much work to do in the future but most enjoyable. He traveled to several artist studios, leaving Cynthia and myself in charge. I also started doing more research on new and upcoming artists in New York, Chicago, San Francisco. Any professional coverage they could find they would be thankful for. So with the gallery, studying, going to the "groups" favorite restaurant Schlau Katz to eat, talk and just relax, doing some things with Jennie and Peter there was never a dull moment. In fact sometimes I had to say no just to stay home and be quiet, read or whatever. The dance of life was going well so far.

CHAPTER 4

In April Jennie and I decided we would like a short urlaub and decided on going to Geneva and Montreux area for a few days. She had been there and loved it and there would be some musical events we could enjoy. Peter was all for it probably because he wanted a few days by himself as he had a big project he was working on. The train was a 12 hour stint so we decided to fly into Geneva and then take the train where we wanted. She knew of a charming smaller hotel in Geneva and one in Montreux so we booked our reservations and started to get ready. We spent a couple of days in Geneva seeing sights, shopping, poking around in galleries and then trained it to Montreux.

Montreux is the Swiss Rivera situated beautifully between the mountains and Lake Geneva or as the Swiss call it Lac Leman the largest freshwater body in Central Europe. There was a lovely park promenade on the shoreline. There were many art galleries, boutiques, restaurants and night spots. From the lake as you travel up the hill and mountains behind the land is filled with lush vineyards, some small charming homes and some large estates, the wineries. The light at different times of the day when not misty or rainy changes beautifully from morning glistening light to the evening mauve and reds of sunset. It seemed like a little paradise.

The second day there we decided for some reason that we wanted physical activity other than all the walking we were doing so decided to go ice skating. It had been a long time since I did that but we thought it would be great fun, not knowing what outcome it would have. We went to the rink, got on our skates and then laughingly got out on the ice feeling quite foolish. But gradually the feeling came back and soon we were racing each other and skating backwards and trying some turns. We tried one and both fell on our tutus but just laughed and got up dusting the ice off and said we were glad we didn't break anything. What fun. As we went to the side to rest for a few minutes, Jennie said she noticed a very good looking man watching us. "He's about 6'2', with blond hair, probably in his early forties, a great physic and looking as sexy as you can imagine."

"He's probably thinks what fools at our age".

"No, she said, he has his eyes on you".

"You're imagining this, I'm sure he's checking you out." Jennie was slender with beautiful facial features, blond hair and blue eyes, men were always looking her way. I was more than slender except for the breasts fortunately. I had dark short hair cut now in a longish pixie style and hazel eyes made green with my contacts.

"I don't think so, I'm sure he's noticed you."

In a few minutes she said "He's coming over towards us, be prepared.

"Prepared for what?"

"You'll see". She was always so intuitive I started to get nervous.

He came up to us smiling. "You look like you're having lots of fun,"

Jenny answered, "bien sur" et vous?"

"Oui, je trouve très relaxant." Since I was still shy about my poor French I just smiled and then blurted out "It is great fun, especially when you dance on skates".

"Well let's dance, and he took my hand and drew me out onto the ice without asking and we proceeded to dance. I told him it had been a long time since I had skated so he would have to guide me.

"Of course I will." He was such a good leader, I just hoped I wouldn't stumble and fall on my butt and look like a fool. I was worried about the image, never feeling sure of myself with men. Little did I know that was going to change in the future.

We did a simple waltz and he kept leading me to do more and the wonderful free feeling of dancing on skates began to come back again. It was great fun especially with a good looking, delicious man. The smooth movement of skating, gliding over the ice is such a graceful event.

"Are you from England".

"No, I am from the US".

He looked disbelieving. "Yes, it's true, is that so surprising?"

He just grinned and said "I just thought you must be a European your English is so clear and you have the style of here."

"Well, in my heart I am half European, the other half is American. I try extra hard to articulate English when I'm in Europe as I know Europeans often have difficulty understanding American's guttural speech, plus I learned it through my singing studies."

We continued until the music stopped and we returned to Jennie who had this twinkle in her eye. "You looked wonderful out there together so seemingly effortless better than Monique and I did together falling on our bottoms." And we laughed. We chatted a few minutes and then he said he had to leave.

"I have a restaurant in town. Would you be my guests for dinner this evening?"

Jennie immediately answered, "Nous aimerions beaucoup que". He gave us his card and we said we had seen it near the hotel. "What time?"

"Around 7:00 pm." So a date was set.

All the way back to the hotel Jennie teased me, "See I told you he was looking. Oh this will be exciting."

"Jennie, it's just an invitation, but I admit an interesting one."

"A special one, wait and see." I have to admit I was excited, there was something about this man that interested me and many in the past years had not. They say when you are not looking for things and trying to make things happen they come your way so we would see. Already I was thinking but I am in Vienna and he's here in Switzerland. Little did I know about the outcome. No matter how we try we really can't predict the actual future.

On the way to our hotel we started chattering away about what to wear, dressy or casual? We decided we would get decked out. We hadn't brought much of anything very dressy with us so needless to say we started looking at the shops and found a darling one with evening wear. We were soon in there trying things on. I found a fitted dress with thin gauze like chiffon panels, cut low in the back in black. Jennie found one in a soft green satin, one of her best colors. Then we went off to look for shoes. We now had everything together and were like school chums getting ready, doing our hair and makeup and putting on our new dresses. We were out to enjoy, ladies on the town, laughing all the way.

We walked to the restaurant Chez Janee, enjoying being admired by gentlemen along the way. We entered into a most charming atmosphere. It was already very busy so evidently very popular, must have good food and service. There were two levels of tables, not like two different floors, just four steps higher but it wasn't too large, perhaps 20 tables. On the lower level between the tables and the bar was a dance floor. At the end of the bar was a flight of stairs leading to who knew where. Straight back on the higher dining level were the double doors to the kitchen.

We were greeted and taken to a table on the upper level. Of course there were linen table cloths, gorgeous china and a charming bouquet of mostly what looked to be wildflowers. It was set for four so we assumed the owner Chris and whomever would be joining us. Not long after we ordered an aperitif he appeared dressed to the tee, silk tie and all. His charming smile melted me immediately plus the kisses on either cheek for both of us. We began some light conversation and then he said he had prepared a special menu for us, he was not just the owner but also the head chef, and hoped we would enjoy it. He spoke with his sommelier regarding wines and they were quickly brought to the table. Shortly after another most attractive man arrived and we soon learned it was his best friend, an attorney Steven Gavin. He was about 6'1", with very dark hair with just a bit of grey entering, in his early forties also, very good looking with very sensitive hazel eyes. He too was dressed to a tee. What had we gotten ourselves into? He joined us with greetings and smiles and was most attentive. As he took my hand something special happened as we looked into each other's eyes, he held my hand a little longer than some might think appropriate. Chris noticed and broke in with conversation. Steve and he had become close friends when they both were at Harvard Steve studying law and Chris business and culinary arts. Steve had lived in Europe from the time he was small as his father and mother had been involved in international law, both were attorneys. He had decided to go to the States for college. These were two gorgeous men. I think Jennie was ready to take her wedding ring off. She just looked at me with the knowing way she had and I wondered what was happening or what she was suggesting.

On the wine label it said Janee. So I asked, "The label is Janee", that is your winery? "Oui, it began with my great grandfather, grandfather, to my father and now to me the oldest of two sons." He began to explain the white and then the red, the type of grapes, the flavors that could only be found in the area. You could see he was a true gourmet of taste and my assumption was taste in other things as well. He dined with us with only a few interruptions and a few necessities of greeting other clients and friends. We had an hors d'oeuvre of puff paste with melted goat cheese inside, white fish from the lake in a wine butter sauce with a mélange of fresh vegetables and salad with a mixture of small berries and nuts on a bed of lettuce in a raspberry vinaigrette. For dessert there was chocolate mousse. How did he know one of my favorite things was chocolate.

Monsieur Gavin also interjected much to the conversation, especially about literature when I mentioned my dream of being published. Both rode horses which of course was one of my passions so we talked of that mutual interest, laughed as they both had great senses of humor and many stories of their sojourns together. Chris asked me to dance and he was very good, very graceful even without the skates. We enjoyed the evening to the utmost. As we were ready to leave Chris asked what our plans were for the next day and we said nothing definite just to enjoy. "if you would like I could take you just outside Montreux though Glion, Caux to Rochers-de-Neys a small village where there is a wonderful panorama of the Alps and Lac Leman. It will give you a sense of the beauty of our countryside. We can take a short tour of the area, the winery and have lunch at the restaurant of a friend of mine.

"Jennie answered immediately before I could say anything "Bien Sur, wonderful, what time? She was determined not to miss a thing.

"About 10 am, we will have time to tour and then lunch. I'll pick you up at the hotel.

Then he handed us each a red rose and we were off to the hotel. Jennie was so excited I had to calm her down. "This is a man you cannot avoid, I know it. He is already smitten."

"Oh Jennie," I said, "slowly."

"Not this time. This is the one".

"But it is not in my plan. I'm happy with my new life in Vienna."

"So what, plans are only guide posts they can easily be changed, new directions can happen"

The next morning at 10:00 am we were in the lobby and two minutes later Chris arrived. He greeted the people at reception, I guess he knew everyone. Jennie quickly jumped into the back seat of the Mercedes saying I should sit in front so she had the whole seat for herself to be in comfort. What a schlau lady. We drove from the city on winding roads into the hills. An abundance of spring flowers were just coming out, the grass a vibrant green, it was a bit of heaven. We drove around in the village and then he was parking the car and said we're taking a short train ride to the restaurant, the panoramic restaurant owned by his friend. The view was breathtaking of the lake on one side and the other the higher mountains. I had forgotten how much I loved looking at the vista of the water as I did in California. It was wonderful. We had lunch his friend serving us cassoulet and of course more wine, delicious.

As we returned to the car via the short train ride Chris said "We have one more stop before I take you back to the hotel."

He drove up in front of a very contemporary house, a contemporary very large chalet if you will.

"Jennie, I thought you might be interested in looking at the architecture of my house."

We walked up the few stairs to the entrance with its large double doors. The ceiling of a chalet type went diagonally from about 22 feet at the front to 10 feet at the back in the living room and there was a second story above that, structure wise how Jenny and Peter would know. There were large windows 10 feet high in two levels across the façade and then I saw they were also on the side On the right sat a beautiful ebony baby grand piano.

On the left, a couple steps up, was a dining room with a table that probably sat about 10, across was a full bar with mirrors behind to reecho the glass windows and the outside view. Jennie's eyes were trying to take it all in at once and then she began to ask questions about the architect, his plans and how things were constructed. As we continued through the living and dining room we entered the large kitchen with an island about 14 by 8 feet with all stainless steel kitchen appliances, two dishwashers two ovens and stovetops and so many cabinets that I'm sure were filled with every kitchen utensil one could imagine. In the ceiling was a skylight which gave such brightness, only a chef would think of all of this. To the left was a storage room with laundry appliances, large tables for all kinds of projects. He said he did a lot of catering so needed the space. There were also storage racks for wine plus a special cabinet for wine storage to protect it from bright light and at kept at proper temperatures for the various types. Adjacent was the garage and more storage cabinets.

Behind the dining space were the maid quarters, a spacious one bedroom apartment with living area, bath, very comfortable which we soon learned was occupied by Maria who had been part of the Janee household for many years as we learned she had started out as the nanny of Chris. She was like family, not really a maid, but as we understood assisted Chris for daily living things. Then we went upstairs where the large windows were repeated at the front. The master bedroom opened just on the landing in front of the stairs. It was a full suite, large with fireplace and large paned French doors that looked out into the forest and garden so open to the outside. It had a large king bed, sofa and chairs, walk in closet the size of my Vienna bedroom. Passed a very large linen closet there were two large ensuite guest bedrooms on the landing most tastefully decorated in a traditional manner. This obviously was his home and I began to wonder where the wife was at the time. It was a dream house very contemporary in architectural style while traditional in its décor, very elegant, yet comfortable. Some designer with a more than adequate budget had done an excellent job.

He asked us to walk outside and proceeded to the stable with an attached apartment. Inside there were two white Lipizzaners which of course I immediately went to, to greet and give them treats. He called one Saliman the other Shasar. We were introduced to a gentleman by the name of Curt. We learned he was employed by Chris as the master of the horses and this was his terrain his own apartment attached to the stables. He of course helped manage the property especially during the wine season. We stood outside and looked out over the vineyards that rolled down the hills with a view of the city and then the forest behind. It was a paradise. I would be happy staying in the little apartment and take care of the horses. Serhalin would love it but alas he was in California.

As I was enjoying all of the surroundings Chris said "You look sad Mademoiselle Monique"

"No not sad, just a bit wistful, I now miss my home and my horse in California"

"Well perhaps you will find something better in Switzerland." I only looked at him and smiled and had to think perhaps I will.

On the way back to Montreux, Chris asked us to come to the restaurant again. He promised to prepare something light after our large lunch; how could we not accept the head Chef and owner of the restaurant. He also offered to take us to Geneva to the airport for our noon flight to Vienna the next day.

At the hotel Jennie started laughing. "Thank you for getting us all this service. We're even getting transport to the airport. Now I'll get to come to Switzerland more often since you will soon be here."

"What are you saying."

"I can see what he's thinking, he's chosen you already. The rest is up to you"

"But we've just met. He's charming and talented but what else? Does he have a wife somewhere or a mistress? There's been too much hurt in my life Jennie. I won't do this on a whim."

"Forget the hurt, this man is for real and you will be with him."

In the morning we were packed and ready and Chris appeared at 9:00 am. Before we left he took me aside and asked for my card and my home number. "I have your address from Jennie's card but I want to be able to reach you directly so please give me your cell and home number." So I put it on the back of my card. He wrote his cell number and direct line at home on the back of another of his cards. So what would happen, I hadn't a clue, I am usually up for a little intrigue but also was a little apprehensive as I had been married so long and had only gone out with other men a couple of times for dinner, no relationship. So I told SELF," you came for a new beginning and to go forward for your own interests." He got us to the airport, helped with the luggage then kissed both of us on either cheek, whispering to me he would be calling. I just said to SELF, "we'll see what happens now."

Peter picked us up and Jennie immediately started explaining everything to him in German about what we had done and about the house and also about Chris. She spoke so fast in German that I missed part of it.

"We soon will be losing our Monique except for visits. She will soon be living in Switzerland."

"Jennie you are such a matchmaker," Peter just shook his head as said, "Her intuition is often right on the money."

"You just wait and see, the first phone call will be this evening and he will come up with some business thing that is going to bring him to Vienna. He has chosen."

"But what about me, don't I get to choose also? I guess I'll just wait and see and let things go as they will."

I was unpacking and putting things away when the phone rang. "Monique, this is Chris" Jennie was right on her first call.

"I just wanted to be sure that you and Jennie had a safe flight and everything is ok."

"Oh yes, Peter picked us up at the airport and I was just putting things away before I checked in with the gallery you know getting reorganized. Thank you so much for the dinners and tour, you were most gracious, we enjoyed every minute."

"Monique?

"Yes."

"I want to see you again and soon. I have some business in Munich next week and then I could come to Vienna. Would that be alright?"

"Of course, when do you think you'd be here?

"I have to be in Munich Monday and Tuesday so I could fly in on Wednesday and stay a few days. I'm considering opening another restaurant so want to decide where. I have been to Vienna but could use a tour guide in Vienna to learn more about the ins and outs, would you do that?"

"Sure, I'd be glad to but I will have to check with Paul about the gallery schedule, I'm sure he will allow me the time."

"Wonderful, I'll make the reservations and book the hotel and then let you know when."

"Ok, I look forward to it." Oh my buzzer is going someone is here so I'd better check can you hold for a minute?"

"Of course."

I quickly went to the door and there was a delivery man from the florist with a huge bouquet of tulips. I already knew who had sent them. I sat for a couple of seconds enjoying the beauty and then got on the phone. "Chris, thank you so much they are absolutely gorgeous, so many different colors, white, yellow, mauve, rose. You don't miss a comment do you?"

"Not when it comes to you. I hope you enjoy them."

"Oh yes, they're one of my favorites, I always have fresh flowers around."

So we said goodnight but then he called again a several minutes later with his flight time and hotel information. He didn't miss a step. I just said to call me when he got in and settled.

"Do I get to see your apartment and the gallery?"

"Of course. Just call me when you're ready to come over."

"Of course I went immediately to Jennie, poor thing she always had to hear me out but I think she enjoyed it. "He's coming to Vienna next week."

"I told you so. He has chosen you and I love him because he is so smart."

"Oh Jennie, it's just a fling but then at my age why not."

"It's more than a fling I guarantee you."

"How did you become so smart about things of the heart?"

"Ask Peter."

"Ok I will." I went to Peter's office and interrupted him which I didn't like doing but needed some guidance. I felt like a school girl looking for her father or mother to clarify everything. "What should I think?"

All Peter could say was "Go with the flow. I think he has his sights in a great direction, you. He can't go wrong and he knows it."

"But of it's a fling and then I'm then I'm left feeling lousy."

"So what if it's a fling and then I'm left feeling lousy."

"Did you ever think it is more than a fling. The man has been around and may know definitely what he is looking for a skinny lady and is enamored. After you're together for a few days you may not reciprocate."

"Thank you for listening, the main is I have to stay true to myself."

CHAPTER 5

So I worked at the gallery, studied my German, read and tried not to anticipate anything about his visit.

On Monday Chris called. Hi, I'll be coming into Vienna on Swissair at about 4:00 pm on Wednesday and will go to the Intercontinental Hotel. I'll call you when I'm settled and will make plans so leave the evening open."

"Plan to come by my apartment, I'd love you to see it, and we can have a glass of wine before we begin the restaurant tour, ok?"

In a soft voice, "That's just fine we'll start with that." What did he mean, "start with that." Hmm.

I left the gallery to go home and shower and dress again, I was surprised at my anticipation. The phone rang, "Hi, I'm settled in. Can I come over now?"

"Yes, are you taking a taxi or do you need streetcar instructions?" A chuckle, "I have a driver who knows Vienna well so just in case he's giving me a snow job tell me approximately where you are." I gave him directions. "I'll be over within a half an hour."

The buzzer went and my heart started pounding. What was I doing? I responded and there he was with that beautiful smile and body with yet another bouquet of flowers. "Come up". He did and then proceeded to kiss me on both cheeks in the European style. When he entered his eyes lit up. "What a wonderful, tasteful apartment, here in Vienna I'm amazed. Does it take an American to do this?"

"The apartment was the creation of Jennie and Peter, the décor is my taste."

"It's wonderful. Contemporary but comfortable, you must redo my home in Montreux." After putting the flowers in a vase I asked him if he would like a glass of wine and he asked what wine I had. How dumb of me, he owned a vineyard. I showed him and he selected a Viennese white and immediately found the cork screw in my kitchen drawer and I provided the glasses. We sipped and did small talk and then he walked through the apartment taking in every detail as though he was trying to decipher how I lived and came back to sit down saying with a genuine smile on his face. "All the details are for taste and comfort, I compliment you." We continued to talk about small nothings and then he said, "Ok let's go look at restaurants, what do you suggest?"

I said we could go first to Schlau Katz so he could see a more typisch, Viennese restaurant that I frequented often with artist friends. I thought this would be a good opening. Franz, the owner and bartender and several artists greeted me as we entered so he knew I often went there. We had a dinner of veal stew which they did an excellent job of making. He said that he had noticed that I often didn't eat that much and asked if I just wanted to be thin which I was, too thin. He said he hadn't wanted to ask me that when we first met.

"No, I just like to have tastes of a variety of foods. I don't feel well if I eat too much. I guess I'm just a horse, a grazer, nibble all day."

"I'll remember so I don't think you don't like my preparations."

"No, your food is excellent it's just me. I try to follow what my body tells me."

His comment, "Interesting." Then I took him to a Viennese Café for coffee and dessert. I told him I was offering some basics and the next day we could try a different restaurant, a typical Viennese, and then on Friday an upscale one. He would get the idea of what the gambit was in the city.

"Sounds great to me. You make the choices."

We talked and laughed on all sorts of subjects and became very comfortable with each other. Soon he saw it was time to take me home and again all he did was kiss me on either cheek, no advances. "I will pick you up tomorrow at 10 am if that is ok to go walking and we can go look at some other restaurants." I would like to see the Lipizzaners if we can and go to Grinzing. I would have to call Paul to see about the schedule but I knew where I wanted to be. "Tomorrow we can see the horses, other sights and then look at some other restaurants I know. We can visit Vienna Woods and Grinzing on Saturday. We'll need the car and driver."

Another kiss on either cheek and a smiling "goodnight".

He arrived early the next morning in jeans and a beautiful sweater looking a bit like an older collegiate. I too was in jeans and a sweater, was this an omen. I told him to let the driver go and we would do the streetcars so he could begin to better understand another part of the city. He said," you are my tour director and I will follow and experience." I knew then he was something special so I would do my best. We hoped the street car and then walked to the Hofburg for the Lippizaner training performance which I wanted him to see. Constantine the head trainer who had become a friend, since I went so often, came over to greet us and we chatted for a few minutes. After that I said "Now you must eat off the streets". He looked at me curiously but I said "trust me, you will enjoy." We went to one of my favorite vendors and there was the cheese, ham, sausage, rolls, bread with such a wonderful scent. We selected and then Herr Knoell asked if we would like a beer. "Of course" I said "yes" and he went across to a small bar to fetch it. We ate and continued to talk. He knew quite a bit about literature and certain types of music but said, "I have a lot to learn about art. You must be my teacher. How to you come to know Constantine?" This man was trying to know everything about me, a bit scary.

So I told him about how I went often to watch the trainings and struck up a friendship with Constantine. I also said I often went to muck stalls to be around the horses and the riders and then we would go for lunch and talk horse talk as well as other things. "Why do you ask?"

"He's a good looking, interesting man, I just wondered."

I let that one go.

"And where will dinner be tonight?"

"At Weiss Schwan another typical Austrian restaurant with a different ambiance."

"You're my guide."

We got a taxi and he dropped me at home and said he would be back around 7 pm.

This restaurant was more sedate then Schlau Katz, somewhere in between Katz and the Sacher. We tried Weiner Schnizel with apple puree and roasted potatoes. We talked and laughed very comfortably but things were getting closer, I could tell from the way he was watching me and very attentive to our conversation.

Kiss on either cheek and where tomorrow "the upscale restaurant?"

"Yes, would it be alright to ask Jennie and Peter to join us at the Sacher tomorrow evening?"

"Sure, I would love to see Jennie again."

"Ok we'll plan for around 7:30 and go over to their home so you can see it. Saturday we'll drive through the Woods and go to Grinzing, I do need to be at the gallery around 3pm, Paul wants me to meet with a client, hope you don't mind. So I won't be wearing jeans on Saturday."

"Ok, we can do all of that. I'd love to see the gallery and see what you do there."

I called Jennie to invite them and to be ready around 7:30 on Friday. We'll come over so Chris can see your place is that ok?"

"Sure, we'll be on our best behavior."

He arrived Friday again around 10:00 am. We went to the inner city stopped in a few restaurants just to look, he was good at finding the owner or manager and asking lots of questions. Then to St. Stephens Cathedral at the center of the city and to the magnifcent Opera House in Renaissance arched style with it's five outer bronze statues and its gold gilded foyer and hall. Finally to Karlskirche in Baroque style where a rehearsal was going on, the father invited us in and we enjoyed a mini concert of works by Schubert. A long day but eventful in getting to know more about each other.

That evening he arrived from his hotel about 7:15 pm and we went to Jennie and Peter's for a drink. Chris was very complimentary regarding their home, obviously liked it a lot and asked a lot of excellent questions about the architecture and how things were built. Peter and Jennie took him on his special tour, they were, with good reason, so proud of their home. We went down got into his car and I told the driver where we were going, to Sacher restaurant. He would see a total different scene as to dining. Here Herr Bauer knowing me from past dinners greeted us and escorted us to a very lovely table with all the attributes possible. The quiet so called "refined" were in hushed conversation and I wondered what Chris would think but he wanted to see the gambit so I was doing it. We were served with the upmost in culinary expertise much more formal. At dessert time, Chris asked, "Could we walk someplace nearby to relax and refresh ourselves? Perhaps the place we were the first evening which was so much fun and we can dance there."

I said "of course, let's go." He had just come up with lots of points regarding my taste. We walked to Schlau Katz; Franz greeted us from the bar. "You are back again."

"I have special service here from friends." They seated us and I said just for dessert and coffee and drinks. Of course Madamoiselle Monique, whatever you would like. We ordered and then Chris asked me to dance and of course I would not refuse, a foxtrot and then a jitterbug and lots of laughter. Peter and Jennie joined us so we had lots of fun. When we arrived back to our home, Jennie and Peter thanked him profusely for the lovely evening and looked forward to seeing him again.

"We will, soon I hope. Monique talks of you all the time; it's wonderful to have friends that you share so much with."

Another kiss on either cheek with his wonderful smile, "See you in the morning with the driver and go to the Forest and Grinzig and then the gallery right?"

"That's the plan, we'll squeeze it all in. Are you getting tired of all this sightseeing?"

"No because I'm with you, that's the most important thing."

Another kiss on either cheek. This man had his modus operandi down pat. Whew no decision tonight.

Jennie came over to ask what was on the schedule for Saturday. I told her I was the tour director for the Forest and Grinzing and then to the gallery. She gave me that knowing smile. "It's not going to be a flling I see how he looks at you."

The next day Chris was at the apartment at 9:00 with the car and driver and we set out for the Vienna Woods and Grinzing. He loved the area. We selected a restaurant I knew for lunch where there were no tour buses. He immediately started talking with the owner about the local wines and soon we were having a wine tasting party. He was so gregarious and knowledgeable people reacted right away so we did have a wonderful time. In between I kept checking in with Paul, he was being very understanding. I said I would be there in afternoon as planned and all next week.

We went to the gallery and he met Paul and Cynthia and was most curious about the exhibit and the gallery so soon was into a conversation with Paul. I noticed that Chris kept watching what I was doing which made me a bit nervous. I met with the clients who were from San Francisco, new collectors, who soon decided to purchase a piece. We did the paper work and I had done my job for the gallery and felt very good about it, sales kept coming in.

"Paul needs you, I can see."

"I think I need him more, he's been such an excellent teacher and friend."

We left and Chris dropped me at the apartment and asked if we could go again to the restaurant Schlau Katz where the artists went. He said he would like to dance some more or was there another place I wanted to go. "There are a few others but Schlau is the most fun."

"Ok I'll be back around 7:30 and we'll go and do some more dancing."

He came back to pick me up and we went to the restaurant. When we arrived, Franz greeted us with a special twinkle in his eye. Several artist friends greeted me and I introduced Chris to them. He asked, "Does this happen all the time. Are you the Pied Piper?" I just smiled, I didn't know how to answer. The band started playing and Chris said, "Let's dance, like we ice skated," He was remembering the day we met. The first dance was a typical waltz but then the band knowing me a bit hit on "Chattanooga" so we started a jitter bug and soon I found myself flying around the floor enjoying every minute. Then back to our table with this amazing man and dinner in front of me I didn't even want. We ate, talked and then he said, "You must come again to Montreux by yourself. I have so much to show you, things there that I know you will love.

He had said this earlier and there was no way I would not partake so said "Yes but I need to always check with Paul about our schedule and work something out because I did make a commitment to him when I came to Vienna."

"Ok, just please work it out. Let's dance again." He held me so close in the foxtrot then I knew I was in trouble, he had won. I soon was to learn that it was fantastic to have lost my battle to succumb to his attentions even if I was apprehensive.

He came back to my apartment I thought for a drink or coffee but as we entered he took my face in his hands and kissed me most tenderly. "I want you so much." I was never a seducer but he was and I wanted him to absorb me which was what he was doing. Coats on the floor, shoes off he picked me up and took me to my bedroom where we continued to kiss and caress each other. He gently removed my clothes slowly admiring as he went and softly touching every part of me, I could do nothing but shutter and whimper. He continued massaging my body, slowly and tenderly and arousing such a passion I had never experienced. From his hands he began kissing me with his mouth reaching that center that drove me into an ecstasy I had never experienced before. "You are sometimes a little girl then a very sophisticated woman and now beyond sensuous. God in heaven I just want to drink you in, my lustful lady, I'll never have enough of you." And so we made love beyond what I ever expected was possible to feel. When he entered me he took me to a height I didn't know existed and I know I satisfied him because he just wouldn't let me go. We slept and in the wee small hours he again began touching me and soon we were again locked together, unbelievable.

In the morning I awoke to see him with his head on one hand with bended elbow looking at me. All I could do was smile. He finally got up to make coffee and then we had to go to his hotel to get his things and get him to the airport at noon for his flight. He kept holding my hand and kissing me. We didn't want to let go of each other.

When we arrived at the airport he gave me another of his most passionate kisses and a reminder that he wanted me to come for a visit. "I told you I want you to come to Montreux to spend some time together. Plan to come next Saturday on the noon flight and stay for at least a week. I'll book the flight for you." This man was used to getting what he wanted. I just thought what am I getting into but I had to do this I knew, what else. I had come to Vienna after much thought to go a new direction and grow and that decision had me now making another decision that I wasn't sure I was ready for.

"I just said, "Let's talk this evening."

He called that evening and said, "I booked you on the Saturday noon flight. I'll come to Geneva to pick you up. I won't take no for an answer."

I wondered what I was doing but I said "Ok, what should I bring, will there be some dressy nights?" Having some idea of his life style I knew the answer would be yes.

"Yes, some dressy some casual plans, things change with me all the time. It depends on what I feel like doing. So bring what you want and if you don't have what you need we'll go and shop for whatever you want, no problem, I just want you to be here." He sensed I was hesitant.

Such an offer, how could one resist.

With a lot of trepidation I said, "Ok I'll see you Saturday. Goodnight."

I felt out of control but happy. We talked in the evening again, I think he was trying to convince me that he just wanted me there so we could enjoy each other. I'm positive you'll love seeing all the things I want to show you. We can ride, hike, cook, whatever."

The next morning I went to Jennie who of course knew this would happen.

"Do you love him?"

"Either I do or it's just a great infatuation."

"Then why not do it, your heart can be miserable now or later if it doesn't work."

"I guess so. I have to follow it through right?"

"I believe so. And what will you take. Oh we have to go shopping."

"I don't know what to take. You'll have to help me."

So we were off to Gabrielle's studio to purchase a new dress and then the shoe store. Jennie knew all my clothes so started putting things out and I said I couldn't take all of it, it's like I'm moving in. He said we could go shopping if I didn't have something. Typical Jennie said, "Don't take something and let me him take you shopping." Finally we got my wardrobe coordinated to what I thought would work. Then we just fell on the bed laughing like two teenagers.

I asked SELF, "what's happening? Chris called several times a day I guess to be sure it was real that I was going to arrive. We talked about all sorts of things and he kept reassuring me that we would have a wonderful time together. He had been around the bush and back and saw my pigtails and knew I was apprehensive but he wanted me there. I got the message but what about all the gorgeous women he could have or had in the past. Whatever, I was excited and I told SELF to cut off my pigtails and go for it.

I worked with Paul all week and did my language studies and then came Saturday. Jennie had to come with me down the stairs to the driver because I was so scared I said I wasn't going but she insisted and said to call when I arrived so she would know everything was ok. Heinrich arrived to take me to the airport to board the flight, I still felt like I should run but kept going. Heinrich said "You seem a little apprehensive. Just go and have a good time you know you will be coming home. Let me know the time and I will pick you up."

When I arrived in Geneva I picked up my luggage from the carousel and went out and there he was, the man with the gorgeous smile, blond hair, beautiful slacks, turtle neck, elegant suede jacket and a huge bouquet of tulips. He didn't miss a trick. He grabbed me and after a long, exciting kiss took my luggage, then my arm and moved me outside where there was the car with a driver.

"I would have driven but then I couldn't concentrate on you so had Jacque come." I soon learned that Jacque was his right hand man, his assistant, and an absolutely delightful person. I didn't know at that time that he would become one of my best friends. We drove along the scenic coastline, Chris pointing out special places he said we would visit, as he said, "I want you to see the beauty of what I hope will be your new home." This had moved too quickly for me but I decided I would just try to enjoy and see where all of it would go. We arrived at his beautiful home where I was introduced to Maria who would also become one of my best friends. She asked where the luggage should go and Chris looked at me questioningly "The guest room or master suite?"

"I said, to the master suite." I was there to begin or end something so I might as well jump in. He smiled and we went up. "Unpack, I'll get a bottle of wine and we'll talk about what you would like to do." While he was getting the wine and making some phone calls I stretched out just to relax as I felt somewhat exhausted and anxious about what was happening. He came up with the wine and we sipped and talked. I must have had a somewhat anxious look on my face, pigtails showing again although I thought I had cut them off, because he reassured me not to worry about anything. We would just enjoy. Then he said, "We're going to the restaurant tonight, there will be several of my friends plus my parents there so we need to get ready."

I then felt panic, could I handle this. I asked in my simple way "dressy?"

He said, "of course but whatever you wear you will be sexy." It will be a most festive evening. I just want you to get acquainted with some people." I guess he was testing the waters? Now I was anxious, I had to get into performance mode from my days of conducting and being on stage.

"I'll take a shower in the guest room to stay out of your way until we figure out how we work together."

Work together? He was saying live together. Oh boy I was getting in deep.

I got ready, put on a black asymmetrical topped, fitted black dress with a tulip style hem. bottom, a few sequins at the top. Jennie and I had gone shopping in Vienna deciding I needed something extra special. I took a deep breath and went to the stairs to see where he was. He was sitting on the couch waiting and when I started down he just stared and said, "Wow, my lady." I suddenly felt very shy and unsure but he came to me and took my hands, kissed me and said, "Fabulous." Sit down for a minute and have a glass of wine and wait I'll be right back. He ran up the stairs and then came down with a special smile on his face. "I wanted to give this to you sometime during your stay but tonight seems an appropriate time with what you're wearing." There was a small box which I knew was jewelry. I opened it and the most beautiful diamond laden hoop earrings set in ebony looked back at me. I'm sure my mouth was open in childish surprise

"They're absolutely beautiful but this is too much."

"Nothing for you is too much. Please put them on. I've noticed how you like earrings and these will go perfect with your dress." I put them on, went to look and they were perfect. Never before had I received such a gorgeous gift and felt a bit apprehensive about it.

"I love them, thank you so much."

"There will be many more." Oh dear I felt this plot was quick sand. I was beyond return.

We left in his Porsche for the restaurant and parked at the back of the restaurant but he said he wanted us to go in the front. All I could do was follow his lead. Hans and Jacque greeted me warmly with kisses on either side of the cheeks and then he led me to the table. He introduced me to his parents Mr & Mrs. Janee Marta and Josef, and two other couples. Steve was there also and immediately got up to grab my hand and give a kiss on either side of the cheeks saying "Welcome back it's so good to see you again, you look fantastic." The champagne was already being served and conversation began. I apologized for my poor French, said German was better but they insisted on speaking English with me although between them the French was flowing. Chris placed me by himself with Steve on my other side, I guess two bookends to hold me up. He said he had prepared a special menu for the evening so no choices and everyone seemed pleased so I assumed they appreciated his ability.

I tried to relax but Chris kept looking at me with his perceptive smiles so I felt I was somewhat on display. They were a lively group so the conversation flowed, they of course asked me lots of questions of why Vienna and why away from the US and I tried to keep it light as though it were not such a big deal. Chris brought up my apartment and said how fantastic it was and if they needed help in making design decisions they should have me assist. "She is so creative and knows where and how to get things done." I cringed a bit inside, I knew what I liked for my surroundings but for other people, I would have to get to know them.

His parents who were in their late sixties were delightful and most gracious, well educated, elegant and very attentive to me. I sensed they wanted their 40 plus son to be settled.

After we had the wonderful meal Chris had planned, although I could only eat a portion, Chris took my hand and said let's dance. The first was "Embraceable You", I'm sure selected by him. "As always everyone loves you, I can tell, especially my parents." Suddenly the musicians changed modes and a fast number came up, a good jitterbug so nothing doing, since I love to dance we were off, inside, outside, in between steps, swings and our laughter. What fun. Until we were finished and heard the applause I didn't realize we were the only ones dancing, the entertainment for the rest. Chris took me back to the table holding my hand and didn't let go of it for quite awhile. Some champagne and then dessert, which I was told was made especially for me, the "chocolate lady", chocolate mousse again this time with raspberry sauce. I knew I had to finish this. Then Steve surprised me and asked me to dance. What a pleasure to dance with him, he was very good, very musical, he felt great.

"It's nice to have you back here with us again. How long will you stay?"

"Just the week, then back to Vienna."

"Do you like it here?"

"Yes, but I have created a life in Vienna that I enjoy."

"Perhaps you can do both."

"Perhaps, I don't know right now it would be difficult. I'll see how the week goes and what I feel."

"Only you will know that."

Steve took me by the hand and led me back to the table. Chris smiled but he seemed a little frustrated. They were good friends but was he maybe concerned about my enjoying myself with someone else. I didn't want to be smothered by jealousy so I said to SELF, "we'll wait and see."

The evening came to a close and as Chris and I drove back to his house I had to ask, "Was this a validation party?" I amazed myself being able to speak out that way even though I had made a pack with SELF that I would have to express my emotions outwardly not hold them in.

"No because I make my own choices. It's just wonderful that they see the same lovely lady that I do."

When we got back, I said I wanted to take another shower to relax. I came out with a very delicate negligee knowing it would be off soon but I thought he might like it. He had opened a bottle of champagne and offered me a glass. It wasn't long before he dimmed the lights picked me up and placed me in his bed. He was most tender, it wasn't sex as in conquest, it was most loving and I completely succumbed to every caress while he kept telling me how much he loved me. Again he brought me to the height. We fell asleep in each other's arms but in the wee small hours I felt his warm hands stroking me and I couldn't believe that the joy would be again. In the morning I awoke to the wonderful smell of coffee even though I didn't drink it. I looked up and he was sitting on the edge of the bed quietly saying, "Monique, here is some coffee, it's time to see the sunshine." I had slept until 11:00 so peacefully. I stretched like a kitten and told him that although I love the smell of coffee I didn't drink it I just did decaf or tea. He apologized for having forgotten. He just sat and smiled then just drink the juice and then asked, "what would you like to do today?"

"Just be with you."

"Shall we go riding?"

"Oh yes, I would love that. Do you have to go to the restaurant?"

"Perhaps later but maybe not, I'll check with Joachim. I told him that I wanted lots of time this week. I thought it would be nice for us just to be home so you'll get more comfortable."

Hmm, home. Would it be sometime? Now the ultimate in being spoiled, I had a chef who asked, "What would you like for breakfast?"

"Anything you prepare."

So we had some wonderful fresh fruit and French toast but I ate my normal small amount, it seemed he was accepting that. We went out to the stable to get ready for a ride. I hadn't brought jodhpurs and boots along but did have jeans and tennis shoes which would do. He asked Curt to get the horses ready but I had to step in and help groom and saddle because I was used to doing all of these things, not being waited on, and enjoyed the physical part with the horses. Chris saw my moves and got involved too although I sensed he was used to having it done for him. We rode out on the trails around the property to a spot he said was his favorite. From the spot one could look over the vineyards and the city and lake in the distance, absolutely wonderful and peaceful. The vineyard covered hills ran sharply down to the city on the lake. There were a couple of small villages with their red roofs tucked here and there. I could imagine the beauty of the sunsets from this point, we would have to arrange that. He said he had come here since he was a child and still loved it. We were quiet for several minutes just enjoying the view and then he asked how I liked it.

"What's not to like, it's breathtaking and so peaceful. I can see why you come here." It's a Shangri-la.

"I come here to feel what's real and meditate but it's even better to share it with someone."

"It always is if you find the one you love."

"I have."

"How can you be so sure?"

"I just know. I've tried a lot of things but know what's real."

He was giving a clue of how much he had been around, he was too attractive not to have had been with many women.

Oh boy I said to SELF getting in deeper, the quick sand is drawing me further down.

We put up the horses together. Back at the house he checked in with Joachim who needed something so Chris said come with me to the restaurant for a little bit and will pick up some food for dinner and he asked. "Shall we get a movie and just curl up on the couch to enjoy?"

"Great, we can just be comfy but I don't want you to be bored. I know you are always active on the night scene. I don't know how you spend your time at home."

"I read a lot but I go out because there is no one here so it gets lonely, of course I work at the restaurant a lot in the evenings. Only thing is that you can go out and play around and then come back and it's still lonely. I never found anyone I wanted to be with for any length of time and just be cozy with until now. Do you understand what I'm saying?"

"I think so. You can be with yourself if you like yourself and not be lonely for a time but then you want to share thoughts, desires and space with someone who wants the same."

"Exactly. I want to share that all with you."

"But we've only known each other for a short time. How can you be so sure?"

"My heart tells me. You know I've been with many women through the years but it was only fun, games and conquest, just a male ego thing. Now being 44 I gave up thinking I would ever find my dream woman. Shows one they should never give up. There was only one when I was about 20 and in college that I thought would be the one. Then I found that she was dating two other guys and soon went off to marry one of them. I said then never again it was too hurtful, I'm just going to play."

Then he asked me about my marriage. I told him that I got caught up in what was expected of a young woman. It wasn't a great love match. We were good friends that shared a lot of things and I found some family but it certainly was not perfect. And I told him about how it ended.

"Now I understand your drive for independence. You can have it with me. I know how interested you are in the arts and how you've achieved respect in that area, I won't get in the way. I'll help you in any way I can, I just want you here. You listen, make me laugh when you are in your little girl mode, then you are an elegant, poised lady and then the most sensuous woman I've ever known and as I told you I've been around. You give me such pleasure and make life real. Does that sound stupid?"

"It's never stupid to try to find someone you can share your life with."

I was sincerely taken back by his praise and said to SELF, I want this man at least for a time. I still had a foreboding that something was going on in his brain, something perhaps a little erratic, I didn't know what. I guess it all seemed too perfect. He had a certain restlessness about him.

We went to help out Joachim for whatever he needed some special ingredients he needed for the evenings menu so we went out to shop. When we got back Chris put together some food for us to take home telling Joachim that he should call if there was anything else and then we went to get a movie. I didn't yet understand how some things at the restaurant worked but asked no questions.

We ate dinner and then stretched out on the coach to watch the movie "Seabisquit" which we both enjoyed. I'm not sure he had done that for a long time but he seemed very content. I understood that he had run on the fast track for a long time sometimes merely for distraction. Soon he was caressing me and asking to love me again which of course I could not resist and why should I and of course being such a lightweight he picked me up and carried me to his bed. I felt he needed "home" so much and that he trusted me to make it so. The love making was like the first time all over again and hopefully practice would keep it perfect and keep it exciting for both of us.

Monday we slept late and were having some lunch when the phone rang. A problem at the restaurant with a water pipe so we got going to the restaurant. He soon had the men there to repair and clean up; with a business there is always something. After he took care of everything he said let's walk around Montreux so you can learn more about the town so we did. We just wandered with him holding my hand which no one had done for a long time which again I don't think he had done for a long time. We went into some small shops and I could sense he was watching to see what I would take a fancy to so he could purchase it. I admired a leather bag and before I knew it I had a package from the shop. I had tried not to be too interested because I wasn't used to someone always wanting to give me a gift but he noticed everything. Then I said I would like an ice cream cone which he remarked, "The elegant lady has a new leather bag, the little girl has an ice cream, now the sensuous lady has me."

We went home to have dinner and then decided to read stretched out on the couch he sitting with my head in his lap until I dozed off. I woke up to him stroking my hair and just looking at me. "I'm sorry, all I do is sleep."

"Nothing to be sorry about, you must need it. I enjoyed your warmth but I think one leg is numb now."

We laughed. I got up so he could move. Who was this marvelous man I asked SELF?

Tuesday morning he said let's take a drive around the area so you can see more of the villages around and I said, "You are my guide." We drove to Lavaux area to Epesse, Dezaley, Saint Saphorin and Chardonne. All were charming and full of vineyards. Then he wanted to stop into a restaurant of a friend to say hello. Always food and wine, but wasn't that a good portion of enjoying life especially for him as a chef.

Wednesday he took me to the Chillon Castle along the lake 2 miles south of Montreux. It dated from the 13th century with its oldest section thought to be 1000 years old. Since I had read much about it I was his guide. Again hand in hand we walked and just looked around. I said I wanted to get a small gift for Jennie and Peter so we checked out various shops. I found a perfect small crystal vase for Jennie. I told him she too always likes flowers and this will be perfect on her desk or nightstand. Then for Peter I found a book on the architectural history of the area which I did not think he had. So I said "That's it for shopping but he said no, "Let's go into this shop."

They had wonderful leather items there, purses, gloves, coats, etc. We browsed a bit until he asked me to try on a lovely leather coat in soft kid leather, the style that is elegant not hard. I put it on and then said to him, in my practical way, that it was too expensive. But the rest is history he purchased it just like that. He was trying to prove something to me but he had already done that, he just could be ultimately generous. What a beautiful day, how wonderful to be so pampered and not so independent. We had lunch at the restaurant of another friend of his in Vettaux.

We only had Thursday and Friday left for my stay. Thursday we again went for a ride, walked in the vineyards with me asking all sorts of questions about the different grapes, the harvest, the process and he obviously enjoyed filling me in on all the information. That evening we went to a restaurant in Vevey owned by another friend of his. I kept forgetting that he had grown up in this area and new so many people. There we could dance too and did for a good part of the evening. Home again he was so loving as usual and I knew the web had been woven.

Friday there was going to be another party at the restaurant so I said I would like to take it easy for the day so he stayed home with me for a part of the day until he said we had to go on a shopping spree. He wanted me to have another dress for the evening. He had seen something in a little shop that he thought I would like so we went to see. It was a lovely blue chiffon with back cut to the waist, v cut at the front and a wonderful swirling skirt. "I don't have much to fill this out." He laughed," But you do. Do you like it?"

"Of course. Then I had to ask, "How do you know this shop, have you purchased a lot here. I needed to know if I was just another notch in the belt."

"Monique, don't ask those kinds of questions. We are all in business here and I know most of the shopkeepers, remember I grew up here. I looked in here before you came and saw some things I thought were perfect for you but wanted you to make the choices because I know you have your own taste. And no, I have never purchased anything here for any other woman."

"I'm sorry to be such a doubting Thomas. Thank you for thinking of me. Now I need shoes, where's that shop."

He laughed and led me to another shop and we found some to go with the dress. "Now what else?"

"Stockings. So I selected some and all was taken care of."

"One more stop before we go home. I want you to see Messieur Rosinee's jewelry store where I purchased the earrings." So we went in and I saw some of the most beautiful, not garish jewelry I had ever seen. Chris introduced me to Messier who was the designer of the pieces and then he nodded to him. He brought out three bracelets and I immediately loved one of them. It was not stagnant but had one diamond and other smaller diamonds interwoven in the twisted gold links. It was exquisite. Chris watched as Messieur placed them on my wrist and then I said simply, "They are beautiful, you have a wonderful sense of design." Both of them looked a bit dumbfounded as I didn't select one. I was a bit embarrassed to accept anything more, I had never experienced this. "You don't like any of them he said somewhat aghast?"

Monsieur Rosniee said perhaps Mademoiselle would like to see something else.

"Oh no, these are quite beautiful."

"Which do you like the best?"

"Of course, this one. The one with twisted gold links and inset diamond, it's very beautiful but I can't accept it. It's too much Chris."

"Remember I told you once nothing was too much for you. There are no buts, I won't accept that. You have excellent taste and now I understand the style you like." Then he had Messier showed me some earrings small tangling sapphires. The next thing I knew—Messier Rossnee placed both pieces in a box and handed it to Chris and we said "adieu" and we left. I became very quiet and Chris, "What is it?"

"I can appreciate you want to give me things but I feel again like I'm going to be on display. I'm just little old me. I'm not sure how to handle all of this I actually feel embarrassed."

"You are not and never will be on display, I just want the best for you, who else do I have to spoil. Please let me give you things, these are gifts from my heart. Don't make them negative." And then without hesitation he kissed me right there on the street with people watching and smiling after all we were on the French side of Switzerland.

I thought for a few minutes and simply said "Thank you." I'll try to adjust to having all of this it hasn't been part of my past life."

"This is a new life, enjoy it, and don't question so much."

So our first of many debates had occurred. SELF was trying to keep me strong, not selfish, strong. This was a very dominant man who usually got what he wanted.

So we prepared for the evening. I had my new dress and shoes. Chris came out in a tuxedo and looked fantastic, the perfect elegant man, he was gorgeous. I asked him, "What is this party?"

"An engagement party for James and his financee Stephanie."

"Why didn't you tell me. We don't have a present for them."

"Yes we do. I bought it before you arrived. It's for their home. I got the idea from you when I was in Vienna, a beautiful crystal decanter I found in Geneva. It's all wrapped and ready to go."

So we left for the party and again all the good food and wine and of course many congratulations. It was so much fun. Mrs. Janee, Gerta, noticed the bracelet and earrings and said quietly, "He does have good taste in these things this time especially in women."

Chris and I of course danced many dances. Steve asked me to dance and we enjoyed. And then I was introduced to Mr. Williamson who was about 80 years old. He had been coming to the restaurant for many years and knew Chris's parents. He asked if he could have the pleasure of dancing a waltz with me and of course I accepted. The musicians played a wonderful "An Der Schonen Blauen Donau" and we danced in the most elegant way. It was perfect, I could even caste my head to the side as the waltzers do. I thanked him so much and he asked when I would return so we could do it again. I said I didn't know but told him it was by far one of the most wonderful dances I had ever experienced. He too led me by my hand to the table. Chris was standing watching him just smiling. "My pied piper returns to me." And he invited Mr. Williamson to join us for dessert and champagne.

James and Daphne opened their presents excitedly and I saw the decanter Chris had purchased, my taste exactly. Either we were on the same wave length or he had just learned it from me. So it was a wonderful evening.

Thank you and goodnights all around and we were on our way home. When we got home I was still dancing and Chris put on the music and we danced until we danced up the stairs to bed. Then there was a different dance which was so intimate I have no words to explain.

The next morning Chris was frustrated because I I was returning to Vienna at 2:00 pm. He told me he didn't want me to leave. "What am I going to do without you please stay." I was torn between his emotion and my feeling that I needed to return to Vienna for at least awhile to think.

"I have to go now, we'll talk and see what we decide."

"I've already decided."

"But I haven't."

So he drove me to Geneva airport and I didn't think he would let go of me. Finally he did unwillingly. I was feeling mentally and emotionally exhausted. I had never felt so wanted before but felt afraid my SELF could be smothered.

Heinrich picked me up at the airport and I gave a full report, he just smiled. When I arrived at the apartment in Vienna I felt so comfortable in my own space. I talked to SELF about what had just occurred. I knew he wanted me to go to Montreux to live with him, could I do that? I knew I had to take my own time, not Chris's. Of course I had to go across and talk with Jennie and tell her what had occurred.

Her answer was, "You had a wonderful time but you need to continue your parameters and don't let self get lost in his strength and energy, don't let him dominate everything. If that happens I know you'll run and you may lose that way. Set it up at the beginning. He might balk but you will soon know if it's going to work. He is going to call you and press for going to Montreux, you already know that, only you know what is right for you."

I went back to my apartment to try to relax and the phone rang and it was Chris. "Monique did you arrive ok? I miss you being here so much somehow we have to be together." "I don't know right now, I need some time." We chatted for awhile and then said good night.

CHAPTER 6

I had been wanting to do a dinner for Paul and some my artist friends so set it up for the next Saturday night. It ended up that I invited 11 people and wondered how I would take care of it. Jenny had three card table so we could set those up. Since I didn't have enough dishes for everyone I went with quality paper goods in bright colors, red, blue, yellow—dinner, salad, dessert plates and cups. Now what to prepare. I pan fried some chicken breasts cut into thirds, placed them in three large baking pans and made my own mushroom cream sauce for over the chicken this I could complete in the oven. Also I made a large lasagna. I steamed a large mélange of mixed vegetables. I knew that some of the artists ate lots. Some of them had a hard time they probably would have enjoyed hamburgers. For dessert I had made cookies during the week and had poached pears in an apricot sauce topped which I would top with a spoonful of whipped cream cheese and a dribble of sauce over the top. I bought extra wine and I knew how they would go through it. They began to arrive several with wine in hand so we would be set. They ooed and aahed over the apartment. I put the food out on the kitchen table so they could help themselves. To help move it faster I put the salad on the tables and helped serve. The salad was one of my favorites one I learned in Montreux with currants, dates, raisins, almonds and chunks of lettuce top with a raspberry vinaigrette Lots of talk on all subjects and as always lots of laugher and teasing. As I saw some finishing I pulled out the other pan and begged them to eat more as I would not get through it in days and it would go to waste, needless to say it wasn't going to go to waste. They pitched in to clean up so I was left with just the cooking ware to clean. The phone rang towards the end, it was Chris. Right away he asked "Where are you it's noisy."

"I am home and told him what was going on." He asked what I fixed and it we were having a good time. "I'll call you later, I have something important to talk to you about." "Ok they should be gone within an hour do you want to wait until morning?" "No, I need to know something now." Ok?"

Chris called about 12:30 am asking if everyone had left. "Yes they just left."

Chris came right out with what he wanted to say, "Monique I want you to come and live with me. I love you and don't want to be without you. I'll take care of you, you can do whatever you like as long as you're here with me. You can have your office to write or whatever. I know you want to continue working with Paul in the arts and I have no problem with you going to Vienna when you need to. You won't be a hausfrau, you will be my loving companion." He put it all out before I had a chance to say anything. "Please, please." He sounded panicked."

I held my breath for a few seconds and then, "That's a very serious and important question. I'm not sure I can make that decision in a quick minute. I need some time. It would be a heavy duty commitment." I was also thinking would he abide by being just with me, I had a thing about that I wouldn't share him with other women if I lived with him. I believed in an intimate commitment between a couple.

"But we're perfect together. I don't want to be without you; I can't be without you. I'm totally in love with you."

"I'll call you tomorrow when I have some time to think."

"Don't think, just feel, let your heart go."

"I've done that before and ended up with my heart temporarily broken."

"I won't hurt you." SELF said watch out.

"I'll call you tomorrow."

"I'll call you first thing in the morning."

I couldn't sleep the whole night, I only commiserated with SELF we had a long conversation. I knew I had fallen in love but did I know enough about him, was I missing something. He had a flamboyance SELF said, would he tire of me quickly? I told SELF "You must go with your heart." He was very strong in what he wanted, when he wanted it but there was an energy in him I didn't really understand. I had committed to myself that I would be my own person no matter how much I cared for someone but I thought how he looked at me and how loving he seemed to be.

He called around 8 am and just said, "You can't say no. I want you here, please. Do I have to come there to bring you back?"

All I could say was "Yes, I will come, but I want to keep my apartment here and I want to come to Vienna at various times to work with Paul. It's part of my life". I needed to set some sort of parameters so I might as well say it right up front. "I expect a commitment to intimacy, mutual respect, no dominance and my own quiet time." I felt I should speak out to give myself some guarantee SELF would remain intact.

He was elated with my answer of yes and said, "I understand your parameters, a good way to start out with you telling me up front. I accept them all. I will take care of you, will want for nothing. I'll give you a check for Jennie for the year and yes you can go back to Vienna when you need to. I'll make the flight reservations for you. When can you come?"

"It will take me a few days to get things organized here so I think not until perhaps Thursday."

"Ok I'm going to make the flight arrangements for Thursday so you can't change your mind. I'll come to Geneva to get you."

I said to SELF, "I can always change my mind."

"Ok we'll talk again before then."

"I'm going to call you every day, probably several times a day. Now I have to be sure everything is in order for you so I'll talk with Maria."

"Your house is beautiful, don't make her do anything special."

"She will want to. I know she loves you, she even asked me when you were coming to stay. I know your artistic nature will want to make changes and anything you do is fine with me and of course we always need fresh flowers."

"It's your home and I don't want to presume I can start changing things."

"To me right now it is a house that I had built and come to sleep, shower, change clothes and have some parties. I want it to be a home. You will make that happen."

"That's another commitment."

"You just tell me what you want and we'll talk about it and we'll do it. With your taste I know it will be wonderful."

Chris called me several times a day to see how I was feeling and if I was getting organized. I think he was afraid I might not show. He even said he had arranged his clothes in a way that I would have space, his cleaning ladies that came twice a week had been there so everything was in great shape as perfect as they could make it. He said he couldn't wait.

"I don't want you to go through taking the train so call Heinrich to pick you up around 10 am so nothing will go wrong.

"Ok I will, he will want to say his goodbyes. I'm probably going to have a lot of stuff, 3 or 4 bags which I don't think will fit in the Porsche."

"Ok the Mercedes it is."

So I said to SELF, "Why should I argue with such tender loving care."

"Bring what you want or nothing will just go shop for whatever you want or need. Everyone will take care of you." What a dream world I thought I was entering, quite scary. SELF, "Am I out of control?" Life was taking me to another adventure and I could not resist. I felt somewhat out of control but happy at the same time with a new direction in my journey.

When I decided I was going to go back to Montreux I went to the gallery and talked with Paul, he seemed happy for me but also concerned that he would lose my help. I said I would be back for openings and special clients if he needed. Also I could do research on and make contacts with new artists. We were also putting together a type of catalogue of all the exhibits the gallery had organized so we would develop a format and organize photos. Also I could assist at doing the same for catalogues for each exhibit. With the computer, scanners and the phone we could do it. I would be busy with this and all the activities in Montreux. We both were excited again about all the possibilities

That night the phone rang and it was Steve. "What a surprise."

"You know I think about you all the time. I understand that you might be coming to live here."

"News travels fast."

"I am his attorney, have been his caretaker in some ways and we have been good friends for many years and Montreux is a small city so word gets around. Plus I was at the restaurant for dinner and he was so excited."

"I know, I understand that. I do care for him so we'll see how everything works out. It wasn't in my plans for a new direction when I came to Vienna but things do change and go interesting ways. He is very convincing and wants what he wants. I have to keep myself strong and be myself at all times. We'll have to see how it goes."

"Wise lady, lady always. Always stay yourself, you are so special don't let anyone take that away from you. Did you give up your apartment?"

"No, I'm keeping it for at least a year, Chris is going to pay for that. I will be coming back here to work periodically at the gallery with Paul. And I want to stay in touch with my friends and the artists here."

"Good idea. You developed a life there in a beautiful city so you should not just let that go easily."

"I won't. It's too important to me. I realized the space I created for myself here. Sorry it sounds like I don't share easily but I always have to have Monique's, space and quiet time, a small oasis. That's how I am."

"That's just one of the things that makes you so special, you realize that and I admire that. I'll help you in any way I can, you need only to ask, I won't interfere although sometimes I would like to."

"You are a very special friend. I wish you were out ice skating that day, it might be different."

"I do ice skate." I think he missed my point but did react.

"Ok, we'll do that one day. When are you coming back?"

"He made a reservation for 1:00 pm on Thursday. I hope I can get everything together by then. Maybe we'll see each other in the evening or Friday evening."

"Probably but It might be difficult for me."

"Steve, I'm sorry, am I hurting you."

"No, not you, you wouldn't hurt anyone. It's my problem. Again anything I can help with just call, you already know how much I care for you. You have my cell number don't you?"

"Yes."

"Then use it if you need to. I'll call you again this week to see how you're doing."

"Thank you. Do you think I'm making a mistake."

"I can't say who makes mistakes. Go with what you feel and as you say see how it goes."

"Thank you dear friend."

"Wish I were more. Goodnight, sleep well. I said I'd call you this week but I'll talk to you tomorrow. You know we Americans have to hang together."

Laughter.

CHAPTER 7

And so I started organizing with Paul about the gallery and we worked out our plan. We would communicate via phone and email and could scan photos and I would come back for the exhibits to assist. I would also continue to look for artists that he might be interested in. I went to see Constantine and he said, "Take care, at least you will have two Lippazaneers there to keep you happy. Remember I'm always here, you can always come back." I thanked him and we said our possibly temporary goodbyes.

Then came Thursday, I was packed as best I knew how. I had to buy an additional piece of luggage to take everything I thought I would need. I was leaving some things behind so when I came back I would have some basics. I gave Jennie the rent money, she would see that the apartment was taken care of. I told her to use it for friends or family if she wanted. She said she would keep it clean and air things out from time to time. I stood in the middle of my apartment with tears in my eyes knowing I would miss it as a special oasis for myself. Jennie had to again walk with me down the stairs because I was so scared I thought I was going to back out but she was there to support me. We hugged and said goodbye. "Call me when you arrive and can talk. I want to know how you're getting settled." So I promised I would and after another tearful hug I was off to the airport with Heinrich telling me to call anytime I needed anything or just to say hello. When we got to the airport Heinrich helped me gave me a big hug and reminded me he was there at any time to help. I was soon on the flight and wondering what was going to happen.

When I arrived in Geneva, I was a bit overwhelmed by my luggage having four suitcases. I had met a gentleman sitting next to me on the flight, Mr. Allen. He saw my perplexed look and went to get a luggage cart so I could load up. When we came out there was my delicious man who immediately kissed me very passionately. He was smiling like a Cheshire cat. I introduced him to Mr. Allen and Chris thanked him for taking care of me. He handed him a card and invited him to the restaurant for dinner that Friday. Mr. Allen said he would definitely be there.

"Stay here and I'll get the car it's easier than lugging everything."

As we drove to Montreux Chris kept his arm around me with I think affection or that he was afraid I would somehow disappear. He knew I was tired and apprehensive so we went directly home. I went up to the bedroom and unpacked a few things and then took a long hot shower and put on some white sweats for comfort. I went to the door to look for him but he came in to the bedroom and just hugged me and kissed me gently and said, "Welcome home." I must have looked or felt tense because he said, "Relax this is now home, you are the lady of the house whatever you need or want will be provided. You are to do whatever you like, you are here with me and I will take care of you. Can I get you anything? Your wish is my command, just please don't stop loving me, I don't know how I would handle that."

How could I not love him and what he was offering, it was unbelievable to me. It was too perfect, the bubble could burst and where would I be? SELF and I discussed it at length. Was this part of my journey going to be positive. "Ok. Right now I would like to just have a nice glass of wine and cuddle with you and figure out what I've done where I am and why I love you so much."

"Ok". He reiterated, "You're home with me. I'll make sure everything is what you want. Tomorrow is Friday and I do have a party at the restaurant and I want you to be there so you rest for the day and get your bearings again and we'll have some dinner at home."

I had the sense that he meant what he said about being committed to me I just didn't know if he would be able to follow through with this commitment in the way I wanted it. I just was sensing that there was something that went on inside of him I couldn't yet understand. I might be the home he was wanting but would he wander is what I was thinking. I wasn't sure and it would be something that continued to bother me.

We sipped some wine had some delicious tidbits he had made, talked a bit until he again took my hand and led me to his bed for the piece du la resistance. I could enjoy but was still a bit confused and overwhelmed.

The next morning I just wanted to sleep and I was still in bed when he came in saying he had to go shop and do preparation at the restaurant and I should just relax. "If you need something ask Maria or call me on my cell and we'll take care of it. I'll be back home around 4:00 pm, then we need to be at the restaurant at 7:00 pm or a little earlier. He kissed me and was off. I just lay quietly for awhile and then got up to shower and dress. Then I finished unpacking and tried to figure out what to wear for the evening. I would need to use the iron but of course when I asked Maria she said she would take care of it. I was not used to this service but I guess one could get used to it. I talked with her a bit about how she helped Chris and told her the things I would do so she didn't have extra chores, she was not a maid to me. Chris had two ladies come in twice a week to do the cleaning, friends of Marias. Beside the cleaning I wanted the linens changed, washed and ironed twice a week. I didn't want her to feel she had to work just be my friend, she was part of the family for years having been Chris's nanny when he was young. I asked her also if they could be there to assist if we had a party because I knew there would be some. She said of course, so the ladies would come to see me on Tuesday and begin. I figured I needed to get a handle on how to organize everything. My cell phone rang and it was Steve. "How's it going so far?"

"Just trying to get settled. There's a party already this evening. Chris's parents are coming in from Zurich."

"Yes, I know. I'll be there so save a couple of dances for me."

"That I definitely will."

"Do you need anything?"

"Right now I just need to reorganize and figure out which direction I'm going in. I feel like my pigtails are showing again."

"I know you, you'll be fine and figure it all out. That's just a part of your charm. Oh, and I dare say Mr. Williamson will be there this evening so have on your waltzing shoes."

"Actually I thought I might show up in jeans and tennis shoes with a red rose in my mouth."

"You are too much. I dare you."

"I don't think at this time I could get away with it but maybe some time."

"You're on, we'll make a bet to see how the response would be." Then we just laughed which we often did when talking together.

"Thank you for being such a friend. You make it somewhat easier for me making this step."

"I told you once or twice or many times, I care for you and I will help you in any way I can at anytime"

"Thank you and I reciprocate.

I went out to take a walk to the barn to see Curt and the horses to focus on some reality. I helped him groom Saliman and Shasar and petted his dogs and then felt totally at home. Curt gave me some instruction at first and then watched me and saw I knew what to do. "This is the real Madamoiselle Monique right?"

"Yes sir."

When I returned to the house Maria greeted me and took me around to look at things and explained how the household worked but said, "You will do as you like and I will help you." I just thanked her and said we would do it together and she gave me a knowing smile. What was I getting into I asked SELF. Did I want this commitment? I suddenly was very frightened and thought perhaps I should go back to the airport and return to Vienna but I told myself that was the weaker side of me, once again the horse wanting to run away. I had made this decision and wanted to follow through. Who knew how things would go, I certainly didn't.

Chris called me and the preparations for the party were taking longer than he thought and said he could shower and dress at the restaurant and would send Jacque for me. "I'm sorry, do you mind?" What was I to say, I didn't know how all this worked so said, "No, of course not. When will he come?"

So I showered again, did my hair and got dressed. I had on a new dress from Gabrielle with one sleeve, diagonal front, other arm bare, fitted with a little tulip flare on the skirt just below the knees in black again which I had warn, so I felt confident. My hand purse had the typical, key, money, id and lipstick and I was ready.

Jacque was on time just before 7pm and was very talkative on the way to Montreux just 10 minutes away. He told me many things about the countryside and he seemed to want to warn me of the future here, I wasn't sure whether about the land or about Chris. He said how things looked beautiful but often changed. I didn't really understand so decided I would just be alert and absorb for myself what the situation would be.

The restaurant was very busy, music going, many people there already imbibing and there was my beautiful Chris to welcome me. I felt like I did when I entered the university my pigtails were showing again how was going to handle all of this. I really had to call on my performance skills. I made a deal with Hans to put my purse and scarf in a special place under the bar so I didn't have to bother with it. He agreed and said he would guard it. From that time it was a small tradition, he even would remind me when I came in.

When I arrived at the restaurant, Chris came out in a dark, well tailored suit and just gleamed at me, "As always you look terrific." He was so warm and charming and took me into the kitchen so I could see at firsthand what it was to run this operation. I thought most creative like a dance as the chef and helpers moved quickly around each other, actually chaotic creativeness. I was asked what I would prefer for dinner and with my small appetite I didn't even know what to say but finally said "I'm a grazer, a little of many things so I can taste the wealth". They all smiled and said in French "Elle fera bien ici."

The party included his parents, James, Daphne, Steve plus the local mayor and some other government people. The Janee wine started to flow, the cheeks got rosy and soon the ambiance was delightful. Then suddenly Chris took my hand and led me to the dance floor and we were off into our own world. The first was a Strauss waltz "Frjulingsstimmen" but then the group started a jitter bug, upbeat and we were really off. I just followed his lead, laughed, enjoyed and suddenly heard applause and cheers. I just curtsied and started laughing and then Chris whipped me away back to the table and whispered more later. What was more dancing on the floor or in bed probably both.

A little later while we were still at the table, after another excellent dinner, Steve looked at me in the same way he had when we first met, and asked me to dance and I said with pleasure. The band was playing "Unforgettable" and lengthened it for us to continue a little longer. Steve was a good dancer and led me around extremely well. "Welcome to Montreux, I believe you will like it here."

"I hope so for awhile."

Then he looked at me and repeated my words, "For awhile?"

"I have my own life in Vienna so I haven't decided anything definite yet." It amazed me that I was talking to him about this except I knew I trusted him.

All he said was, "Good, stay true to yourself and your feelings. Always leave the doors open. It sounds like you've had a bad experience."

"Yes and empty ones." I realized this was a very sensitive man. I liked him and knew he would be a very good friend. I was attracted to him but told SELF I had selected and said I believed in monogamy even if not married.

"Remember I am here if you need anything."

"Thank you very much but you know I'm here to be with Chris, I don't move around."

"That's obvious, that's not my point, I'm not coming on, I'm sorry if it sounds like that. With you I would never step over that line although I've come close to it. Just call if you need something."

"Ok, I'll remember, I'm sorry I was a bit paranoid. I feel I'm a bit on a tight rope so it's nice to know someone might be there to catch me." And then we both laughed and the dance was over. And as we returned to the table I saw Chris watching very intently without a happy face. All I needed was a competition to begin. I decided I was just going to go with the flow and enjoy and worry about tomorrow, tomorrow.

After midnight we were off in Chris's car to the house. I was exhausted so he let me undress and literally crawl into bed and sleep but in the wee small hours he was there asking for love which I could not refuse. He was tender but assertive and kept saying how could this little girl be so sensuous in bed; all I could answer was that I could only express my true feelings.

He kept saying, "I can't get enough of you, I want to devour you and I don't want anyone else to touch you." So the unhappy face when I danced with Steve was explained. I couldn't conceive of being devoured, no matter what I felt I was my own person and had to have my own thoughts and life. I tensed and became afraid again and he became more tender saying he understood but did he? We would see, I would have to make my boundaries which I hoped I would never have to do again. I had here what appeared the best of the best, was I setting bricks in place? I knew I was totally in love but did I want to be totally absorbed by this and lose myself again? If something didn't work I should at my age be able to weather the outcome and still go forward.

I wished I didn't think so much but I had to be true to myself or I couldn't be true to Chris. At the moment I just wanted to think I was in fantasy land and enjoy and then fly away to Vienna where I would be back in control. I must have been a horse in my past life, first reaction when afraid is to run. I think Chris knew this so the next morning we had a relatively quiet weekend. Saturday, we had a light breakfast at home and then went to a small church in the neighborhood and walked along the lake. He was trying to acclimate me. I actually didn't think he did this mode very often but he seemed surprisingly content. He was trying to quiet me and did a good job. I hoped he wouldn't get bored too quickly with some of the basics of just living that are so important. We walked, talked, read, cooked together and took care of the horses. That may sound busy but it was so enjoyable and what I wanted. He seemed surprisingly content with it. He had had a bachelor life without any demands except what he put on himself, now he had me. We would see.

His parents were staying in one of the guest rooms but were good house guests finding their own things to do during part of the day as not to be obtrusive. They understood that I was trying to get adjusted to my new surroundings. In the evening Chris prepared dinner for the four of us and it was most enjoyable to be spoiled by a chef. After years of planning and doing meals this was a gift.

When he left Monday morning I immediately called Jennie my confident to get some direction. Her response, "Do you love him? If so, there is no question or problem. You must learn to trust again. I told you the first day at the skating rink that he fell in love at first sight and he would pursue you. He can offer you everything."

"But I know nothing of his past. I am sure that he has been a womanizer."

"Yes it is obvious that he was in the past, but now I don't know. I think he found you and won't look for anyone else. Think about it you came here for an adventure, a different life and it is opening to you. Take a chance."

"I hope you're right but it seems too perfect."

"There is nothing perfect, just enjoy and capture all you can with the experience."

"Yah, I know, but I'm sure there will be bricks in the road."

"Aren't there always?"

"I guess so. Bye and talk to you soon via email or phone."

Mr. and Mrs. Janee went back to Zurich and Chris and I got into our mode entertaining friends, doing some things around the house, reading and discussing what we read which was great and basically doing whatever we wanted to do like going ice skating or horseback riding. He took me to his bank to introduce me to the manager and we set up an account in my name depositing $10,000 and a credit card in my name with a $25,000 limit his generosity was amazing. He did spend time at the restaurant and at the hotel. I think he thought that he had to be the personality at the restaurant to keep clients coming back and I'm sure he was right to a degree but it also was for his ego. I participated in many of the evenings, of course he included me and we had great fun dancing. I enjoyed talking and laughing with the clients as much as he did. They asked for me the nights I didn't show.

So the weeks passed with me learning about my new territory. I found the Catholic orphanage where I could volunteer to do music with the children and tutor if they needed and they did so I offered my time for a couple times a week. The orphanage was taken care of my Father Joseph, Sisters Anne and Clara. There were 20 children so I would go to play the piano and teach them songs, it was great fun. There was one child that attached to me right away, Jacque who was 8 years old and brilliant, a very high IQ and inquisitive about everything. We called him Jacque 2 as we had a Jacque at the restaurant. He perceived so much which I could tell by some of the questions he asked me. His parents had died in a car crash when he was only two and there were no other relatives they had found to take him. He was so loving ; frequently, after asking Father Joseph, I would take him out to the book store or for an ice cream and of course I fell in love with him. I didn't want to slight the other children but always spent a little extra time with him. At the elementary school I did much the same with music and sometimes spent time with children who needed help in reading. It was a joy to me and a way to give back for all I was receiving in my life.

I had asked Chris earlier about setting up the extra room in the house as my office and he just said do whatever you want. It's your home now. Well I did. There was a room next to our bedroom that wasn't used except for some storage so I had it repainted in mauve, put in a berber style carpet in a soft gray and ordered my plexiglass components for books and things as well as a plexi desk somewhat like I had in Vienna and a long, narrow one for laying out photos and other information. For the window that looked out to the forest minimal treatment, track lighting and a couple of area floor lamps. Then bought a new PC and two printers, one for the PC one for my laptop and had a computer guy set it up. With my laptop and the new PC and printers I was fully equipped. I put in a flat screen TV and a small CD system. For other furniture I chose a futon in a medium grey nubby fabric and two contemporary small recliners in red. Then I got a sign from the hotel that said, "Do not disturb." to put on the door. It was my special space and no one was to come in unless invited. When it was complete I invited Chris to see. He admired all of it and just laughed at my sign saying that's my girl her own space is created. It was my need for my own space and quietude to concentrate.

I worked with Curt in the stable and of course rode the horses and had lots of time to read and write. What a life but

I still had some foreboding that it was too perfect. SELF said, "Enjoy while it lasts."

September came and the harvesting of the grapes and making of the wine. I wanted to be a part of that and said I would work in the field with everyone, including Chris. It was done in the traditional style of cutting, putting the grapes into the baskets and working a pulley system up to our distribution area for processing. It was hard, back braking work but so great to be working with the products the earth provides, getting dirty and sweaty. The aromas of the grapes were unbelievable. Dad Janne came to assist and I learned so much from him. By mid October we were finished picking and just had to continue processing the various vintages which Dad Janne taught me all about. Then we began work on distribution on which I had some ideas that I hoped I could follow through one. Our wines now we only sold in Switzerland on a limited basis. I didn't understand that, I thought we should expand our quantity and be sold in other countries so decided at some point I would speak with Chris. If he agreed I would start organizing. It would be more to do and be more of part of the winery but I liked the idea.

One evening Chris called and said the party had gone on longer than he thought and he had had too much wine and was so exhausted with the party preparations and the wine harvest did I mind if he stayed at the apartment for the night. He had done this before so I didn't think too much about it. Sometimes I was happy to have my evenings alone to do whatever.

I said, "No, do what you think is best. I don't want you to drive and have an accident. Go to sleep and I'll see you tomorrow around lunch time."

The next morning I did some errands in the morning and was to meet an artist at her studio. A sculptress whose works I had seen photos of but wanted to see in the "flesh". When I finished that it was a little early for lunch but I thought I'll just go to the restaurant and maybe he's there or I'll wait to join him for lunch. I arrived early and spoke with Hans and Jacque who seemed a little nervous but I just thought they too were tired from the party the night before. I asked for Chris, was he in the kitchen or where but Hans tried to keep me in conversation. Finally I said, "Is he with clients in the more private dining area and Hans said "I'm not sure." Well I'll just go into the kitchen and say hello to Joachim and the staff. I went in and said I'm here to see "what's cooking". So I started talking and laughing with the staff and of course tasting. As I walked past the large back window of the kitchen that looked out to some parking places I stopped in my tracks. There was Chris with a most attractive lady, expensively dressed. They were in a very intimate conversation with her hand in his where the other hand was I could only imagine. They were looking into each other's eyes and quietly kissing. Then they seemed to argue and she got abruptly into her Mercedes. My feet felt like they were in cement, I couldn't move for a few seconds. My heart suddenly ached. I went quickly out of the kitchen saying to them, "you never saw me here." I bolted up the stairs to the apartment I had never seen and saw the bed and knew the activity that had occurred. I quickly looked around and saw two pearl earrings on one of the night stands. I turned and ran down the stairs and said to Hans, "He is your employer and friend but please do not tell him I was here."

I got into the car and tears started to come and all I could thing was to call Steve.

When he answered his first words were, "What's wrong, you sound so upset, are you ok?"

"Chris has hurt me more than he knows. I'm frustrated and angry. Would you help me?"

"Anything."

"I'm on my way home to pack. I was going to leave for Vienna Thursday evening but want to go as soon as possible today. Could you or your secretary call and change my reservation for the 4 or 7:00 pm flight and get me to Geneva airport in time? I don't have time to do it. Please don't ask questions, I'll explain later." Here was the horse again running but I just couldn't confront Chris about the indiscretion face to face right now, I was just too hurt.

"Ok, I'll have Genvieve do the change, she'll call me on my way to your house. I'll drive you. Are you sure you know what you're doing?"

"Yes."

"See you in 20 minutes."

When I arrived home I asked Maria to come upstairs to help me pack.

She looked so concerned. "What has happened? Why are you so upset.

"Msr. Chris has hurt me."

"Physically."

"No emotionally which is worse. I don't have time to explain; I'll call you later. Let's pack because Monsieur Steve is coming to take me to the airport." So I started throwing things on the bed and Maria started packing.

We packed two bags, my laptop and my carry on with the necessary essentials. There were still some of my things in the closet but I had no time to pack it all, it would have to come later. I opened the safe and retrieved my passport and 5000 Euros.

From the safe II took my case with some jewelry leaving the more recent expensive pieces Chris had given me. I grabbed my charcoal grey suede coat. By then Steve was there. He gave me a big hug and without questions took the bags and went out to put them into the car. I hugged Maria, said not to worry and reminded her I would call later. I asked her if she would not answer her phone for awhile because Monsieur Chris would be calling looking for me. She wouldn't have to tell him anything until I was long gone.

I went out to find Curt to say goodbye, gave him a hug and told him not to worry I would call. I asked him to take care of the horses which I knew he always did. It was just nervous talk. Steve came to us and said we have to go right away. We got into the car and were off to Geneva. I called

75

Jennie to tell her I'd be in around 10pm as I was on the 7:00 pm flight. She asked no questions just said "take care of yourself." Then I reached Paul at the gallery saying I would be in around 10pm, a day earlier than planned. I would see him at the gallery around 1:00 pm on Thursday. Then I turned off my cell phone, put my head back on the seat, closed my eyes as tears streamed down by face.

Once we were on the highway A1 Steve took my hand. "Now tell me what happened." So I did.

Steve looked glum and said, "I hoped he would never do that to you. He was quite the ladies man and party person in his 20's and 30's, then finally settled down and seemed to find some maturity. I was a bit off the wall too in my 20's, often with him. We've been friends since we met in college. I got my fill and only once in a while could he get me to join in the party scene. Sure we meet for dinner and drinks, sometimes play basketball, soccer or ride horses and I am his attorney so I watch his legal and financial side."

"He told me that he had been a little wild for awhile but had gotten it out of his system."

"A little wild is an understatement. His parents often had to bail him out of trouble, they were always worried. They even threatened to disown him. He still is my friend and we enjoy getting together because as you know he is a very infectious guy, but you are also my good friend and I am furious with him subjecting you to any kind of hurt. He should know by now that you are real, very vulnerable and may I add sensuous as hell."

Within an hour we arrived near the airport and Steve said we would stop at café. He ordered and we continued to talk. He was a very good listener and offered advice in a very easy unobtrusive way not aggressive or dominating. As we talked he said he was sure the woman was Gabrielle, the daughter of the largest wine distributor in Switzerland. They had had a thing 2 years before and there seemed to be some sexual connection. She was spoiled and had her sights on being the

"Grand Dam of the Janee vineyard estate. I said I didn't want to know anymore and asked him if we could talk of other things.

Since Steve often came to the house and was often at the dinner parties we had talked many times before, it was not the same as just the two of us in a new setting. We told each other stories of where we had lived in our past and laughed a lot. He was good at getting me to laugh. He was so into reality of what was important; I learned a new side of him by listening also. Then it was time to go to the airport. He dropped me at the front of the terminal where I told him I would go on and check in by myself.

"No, I am not going to leave until I know you are on your way so wait there while I park the car and I'll be right back."

I thought to myself what a lovely person he is to take such good care of me. He came running back and said, "Ok let's do this." Somehow I felt he wanted to come with me. He was by my side as I checked in. He took me by the shoulders and kissed me on either cheek, looked into my eyes, and said, "Take care and I will call you tonight to be sure you arrived safely. I thanked him for being my friend and caring enough to do all of this and of course his response was, "for you anytime". I started for my gate and saw him still watching so waved and he smiled. When I boarded I felt exhausted and hoped no one would sit beside me but of course someone did and he wanted to talk. I tried my book routine where I read the same page three or four times to look occupied but he didn't notice or was unaware so we ended up in conversation. Interestingly he did go to galleries and did know quite a bit about what he liked so I gave him my card and said he should come to Paul's gallery. He said he definitely would. My shackles were up, was his interest in coming to the gallery or was he trying to do a pick up for his needs. I don't mean that in an egotistical way but just that it seemed to happen so often I was never sure of the motive. I thought SELF you are becoming a bit paranoid.

CHAPTER 8

So after 4 months living in Montreux with one visit to Vienna I arrived back to my first home. The flight was on time and I proceeded with a heavy heart but there was Heinrich with a big smile to take me to my apartment. He wanted to know the situation so I shared it with him. When we got to the apartment he helped get my suitcases up the stairs saying to call anytime if I needed anything.

In a few minutes the familiar signal knock on my door, Jennie. We hugged and then there was Peter also with a big hug. What a blessing to have become friends with these two. Not for what they could do for me, just their genuineness and our camaraderie. They came in with lots of questions. I said to them "give me a couple of minutes and I'll be over."

"Ok, we'll feed you again" Peter said jokingly. Everyone was always trying to feed me; I must have looked like a waif.

I tried to relax a few minutes then taking my schlussle and cell phone went across the landing to their entrance. They had eaten but there was my plate and our glasses of wine to enjoy. I explained to them what had happened and Peter said, with a bit of a chagrin, "men will be men, male ego thing." But Jennie said, "He degraded her. All the staff loves her and they knew. Is he on a self-deprecation mode, out of control or just pushing away what he really knows is happiness because he doesn't think he's worthy." Jennie always the self made psychologist.

My cell phone kept ringing but it was Chris and I would not answer I needed time. I again felt I made a huge mistake in trusting. I trusted Jennie and Peter and told them what I saw and that I felt like a puppy who got dropped off at the pound. Peter did say again, "Men will be men. Their sexual drive and ego keep going."

"Maybe I should let my female ego go as a free spirit and see what would happen, maybe I shouldn't always be a goody two shoes."

"Now you're talking junk, that won't get the kind of person you are anywhere."

"I know, I'm just hurt and angry."

"So be angry and go on."

Jennie spoke up and said, "Peter you know it is not that easy, that's being irresponsible to self. He has degraded her by his actions. His staff knows and some of the people at the restaurant I'm sure observed something. She needs to see, if possible, if this is going to be a reoccurring event that will give her more heartache. It's like being cuckold and she shouldn't have to accept that. She is not a gold digger or manipulator she is real and should maintain her self esteem."

Peter responded with, "You're right, I guess I'm just as angry at what he did. Monique doesn't deserve it."

They were as always intelligently supportive with so much empathy. They made me eat something and then said go and rest. While talking with them their phone rang and guess who. They said they had not seen or talked with me and expressed their concern of my whereabouts. So I had their support. I called Paul and said I was in Vienna and what did he need from me and he said everything so I said I'll be there tomorrow. He asked no questions another good friend. So I said, "SELF, let's get on with it. There are many things we can do and enjoy and keep busy." A good avoidance tactic I would have to face it and eventually deal with the situation but not right now. The phone kept ringing but I would not answer my child said let him suffer for awhile and see what he finally does.

My cell phone rang. This time it was Steve starting out with a simple "hi" and then "did you arrive ok, are you at your apartment, what is going on? I was somewhat amazed at the concern in his voice.

"I'm just fine. I'm with Jennie and Peter and they are trying to feed me trying to ply me with wine so I will relax and they are doing a good job. I'm going to go across in a few minutes so I will call you back ok? Cell or home?"

"Cell, I'm at the restaurant and we've already been arguing."

"Give me about 10 minutes."

"I'll be waiting. If I don't hear from you I am going to call back,"

"Ok, don't worry. I will call then we can talk."

"I miss you already and so do several other people here."

"Give me a few minutes."

Jennie asked right away, "Was that Chris"

"No, it was Steve. I'm not taking any calls from Chris. I'm going to go home and call him from there so I'll say goodnight." Jennie gave me one of her what is going on special looks. I didn't say anything. She might have been thinking that I created something myself by being friends with Steve.

Peter refilled my glass and said, this will help you sleep."

I called Steve back and he said, "Hold on a minute while I go outside. Are you a little more relaxed?"

"Yes, Peter and Jennie are great friends. It's nice to not feel alone right now. Why are you arguing with Chris?"

"I'm glad you have them. We're arguing because Chris gave me hell for taking you to the airport but I gave him hell back for hurting you and told him no matter what he did or didn't do I'd always be there for you and I mean that. He'll get over it. If he doesn't shape up his act I will take you away or come to Vienna. Remember I'm an attorney used to arguing and negotiating. What's your schedule for tomorrow? You know he's going to come to Vienna to try to bring you back. That's one of things we were arguing about because I said he should just let you be for awhile but he's obsessed."

"Yes I know he will come but I need time alone right now so. I'm not a bed hopper or a conniver for things. When I care I care. In this instance I may be entirely wrong, it may just be a dream."

"Hey, stop it now. I don't often get angry but I will with you on this. Obviously you are not a bed hopper you go with your feelings not what is judicious to gain some wealth or play games. That is not you. You are going to be the one to decide. My arms and heart are wide open for you but you need to know what Monique wants or needs."

"Why do you always make such good sense but I sometimes can't follow it."

"Because you're you and that's why I love you so much. I just keep hoping you'll find your way and it will be at my doorstep."

"Do you know when he's coming here? I hope not tomorrow because I want to go to the gallery in the afternoon to help out with the opening and then go out with some friends to catch up."

"He has a large group coming in tomorrow night so it probably won't be until Friday. I'll see if he'll tell me and call you to let you know. You know I'm going to call you at least once a day. There's a large party Sunday night so he won't stay more than a couple of nights but you know he's going to put the pressure on you to come back with him."

"I know but I'm going to stay here to work, relax and do some serious thinking about what I'm going to do. I don't know right now. I just have to have time alone."

"I understand but I've been thinking that I've never been to Vienna and would like to visit. Would I get in the way of your quiet time? Do you know a good tour director there who could personally take me around?"

I laughed and said, "At your service sir and very inexpensive."

"But you said you wanted time alone. Are you sure that a visit from me is Ok?"

"Of course, I would love it. I would have fun showing you around. When would you like to come?'

"As soon as possible. What about next weekend? Let me check my schedule. How about Wednesday evening on the 7pm flight; I have appointments Monday, Tuesday, Wednesday, I can clear Thursday afternoon and Friday. I have to be in court Monday morning so I would come home on the early afternoon flight Sunday. Does that sound ok?"

"Perfect. Make the reservations, don't rent a car it's so hard to park here, just take a taxi into the city. If we decide to do something that we need a car for we'll just go rent one. I don't know what kind of hotel you like. It's not necessary to stay in a 5* unless that's your preference. I know of a small hotel in a great location, Hotel Schilling It's charming in an Austrian way, very comfortable, nicely decorated, has all the amenities. They have a couple of suites which I would suggest as some of their 14 rooms are a little small. I know the owners so they will give you special service above the norm. They also have a breakfast to die for you won't have to eat until dinner. I've been invited there several times when we have other gallery owners or professors staying there. If that sounds ok I'll make the reservation right away."

"If you recommend it, it will be perfect. Let me make the plane reservation and then I'll call you and you can go ahead."

"Wonderful. I so look forward to it. I can show you my other city."

We chatted a few more minutes and then said good night. I said to myself, SELF this is a very nice man, should have met him first. Then talked to SELF again, "don't get yourself in any deeper"

As I dozed the phone rang. It was Steve again. "I can come in the 4:00 pm flight on Wednesday so make the hotel reservation please."

"Wonderful, I will right away. I call you and give you all the information, I don't want you to get lost."

"If the hotel is not available, remember I have your address and I will be ringing the bell."

"I don't think that's a good idea yet. I'll call you with the hotel information. I'm so looking forward to you being here, we will have a good time. Oh I was by Gabrielle's studio today and I bought you a gift."

"From Gabrielle?"

"Of course she does things for men and women and I saw something I liked that will look great on you. I will hand deliver it to you when you arrive for your visit."

"I only want hand delivery but the best gift will be being with you."

"You are making this more and more difficult for me, you know that."

"It might be part of my ploy. I just want you to be happy and make the decision right for you but I'm hoping I can be part of that. You know if you need someone I am always here. Take the joy you can have today; sometimes it isn't with your intellectual side but with your heart. Whatever, make the time invaluable and remember I am always here, you must understand that by now."

"Oh, great philosopher I think I'm making a mistake by not coming back directly to you. Thank you for validating my thinking. I do understand that you are more than supportive. I miss you so, when I come back we will have long talks."

"Well that's a start." Where had I heard that before. "I'll just repeat I am here for you, you have to decide what makes Monique complete. Have you definitely decided to come back?"

"Although I just said when or if but I'm sure it is inevitable if I'm to solve anything but I'm still going to take my time for self."

"Wise lady; always a lady. If my sword were sharper I might get in the way but I will not step in no matter how much I care for you. I leave it to you. I can wait."

"Steve, am I being unfair to you?"

"Not at all. The situation is what it is. Just know I am here for you for anything at anytime and leave it at that. I will never make it awkward for you. You don't have to respond just keep me in your best friend category and we'll go from there."

"Thank you. I don't deserve you."

"Yes you do. I told you I won't interfere, it is your heart and life. I won't get in the way."

I know shazt. I thank you for your understanding."

"If he ever hurts you again I will interfere, understand? I will take you away."

"Yes I understand. Bye for now. Please call me."

"You know I will.

CHAPTER 9

The next morning at the gallery I spoke with Paul and asked him and Cynthia to screen my calls as I didn't want to accept any from Chris. As understanding friends they didn't ask any questions. I knew he would eventually arrive at the door but I didn't want to speak with him before that. I wanted to focus on the exhibit and try to stay calm.

We re-hung a few of the abstract photo work from the artist Joesph Gaton fantastic black and whites some with two or three photo overlays, quite dramatic. Then we rechecked our catalogue numbers with the system I set up as sometimes pieces were entitled, sometimes not, so we kept track more by specific number codes relating to the work and the specific artist. Paul went out to purchase some more white wine and Cynthia and I made sure all the glasses were clean. Although exhibits are party atmospheres we had decided several months ago to no longer offer food as the purpose was to discuss the art and of course for us purchase art. We always had quite a group at the openings, many other artists come to be in on the scene but also clients. When the artist came by to inspect and offer his suggestions he was too nervous to come up with any so we all left to have dinner and relax.

While we were at the restaurant my cell rang and I checked the ID and it was Steve.

"Bonsoir monsieur."

"Bonsoir my charming lady. It's noisy so you're at a restaurant."

"Yes and having a good time. We worked hard today to prepare the exhibit so were out to relax."

"Wish I were there with you."

"I wish you were too. It's really so much fun and intellectually enlightening. But you'll soon be here for your visit and we'll enjoy it all. I just love this atmosphere."

"I know you do I can hear it in your voice. Where are you now, it's quieter?"

"Oh I just stepped outside. It's a beautiful night here. Hopefully when you come the weather will cooperate."

"I can't wait. I have my own personal guide who is a love so what more could I ask for."

"A lot. You are so special to me you are always in tune and ask about what I'm doing and seem to enjoy when I tell you but I have to go through my life process I guess. Maybe my time away will show me the correct path."

"Is there a correct path?"

"See you respond to what I say and what I'm feeling. I don't know if there is a correct path. I do know I'm happy and full filled here in a special way so maybe I have to stay and forget the rest."

"Only your heart can tell you that."

"Yes and it frequently gets me into DS."

"You're going to find that path and you will be fine and I'll be there to help as I've said many times."

"Merci beaucoup monsieur, vielen danke. What would I do without you?"

"You tell me."

"Monique come inside and dance with me."

"I heard that, who is that?"

"My crazy friend Max, you'll meet him when you come here. He's fun and harmless, he makes me laugh, teases me all of the time."

"Ok as long as he's harmless."

"He is, he has a new girlfriend every few weeks but always calls to talk with me about them. All my artist friends are just bon vivants, free spirits."

"A bit like you except for your practical side."

"I guess so and that's what makes us interesting to everyone, but many don't understand us. We're not really crazy or deviant we just have this immense curiosity and desire to experience all that life has to offer."

"Now you are the philosopher. Have a good time and get home safely. I'll call you in the morning or maybe even this evening to check on you."

"Ok papa. Don't worry I'll be fine and when I'm at home I have Jennie and Peter who watch over me."

"I'm glad they are there for you. Monique"

"Me too, they're great, loving, intelligent friends."

I got home late and was getting undressed when Steve called again.

"Just checking."

"You're lonesome. I'm fine, ready for bed and going to sleep in tomorrow if I can because tomorrow evening is going to be a long one."

"Has he been calling?"

"Yes, but I won't answer."

"He's definitely flying in tomorrow so be prepared."

"My sword is drawn at least with verbiage and my feminine ire."

"Keep it drawn. If I were there my real sword would be drawn. You know I haven't interfered but if he hurts you again I will, my sword will be drawn for battle."

"My knight in shining armor."

"Talk to you tomorrow."

Friday morning I was trying to sleep in for a little while when the buzzer rang. When I answered it was the florist not with one bouquet but two so he brought them up. One was a dozen gorgeous white roses from Chris the other a very artful fall bouquet of sunflowers, pussy willows, orange roses, wheat and cattails from Steve. What a contrast in their choices. I know he meant it as a gift but I talked with SELF, "Do you suppose he thinks Chris will be in the apartment and that he'll notice that someone else sent flowers? Hmm Well I'll just enjoy them because Chris will not be in this apartment this time.

Before I left for the gallery I called Steve, he was with a client but excused himself. "Hi lovely lady, how can I help you."

"Thank you for the beautiful bouquet, it's perfect for this time of year and I am enjoying it. I wanted to let you know that right away. It's very special."

"It is my pleasure to give you what I can at this time. I'm with a client so I'll call you later."

I got dressed for the nights exhibit in a slinky red dress that Gabrielle said I definitely needed for my spirit or my bon vivant attitude. I didn't know, I just liked it and said ok be sexy. I wondered why I needed all these dresses I was accumulating? In Europe and NYC most everyone comes in black or dark colors to exhibits, some sort of statement I've never figured out.

Before I left to go back to the gallery Steve called.

"Hi, ready for the exhibit."

"I think we're ready we worked on lots of details this afternoon. I'm in a slinky red dress and ready to hop the streetcar and go to the gallery. I'll even put a red rose between my teeth."

"Hey, you won't go on the streetcar in a red dress. There will be a line of men behind you. I thought everyone wore black or dark colors at these events."

"Usually they do and I do sometimes, I just feel like doing something else tonight. I don't know where the dark color dress came about, the exhibit should be a celebration full of color. The dark is some sort of esoteric comment. As far as the line of men, they can follow me and I'll get them to buy some artwork."

"You are lovingly incorrigible. Seriously, Monique, please take a taxi and go direct, do it for me so I can relax."

"Ok, I will, just being facetious. I have to lighten up the evening, I have to work and then there will be Chris."

"Ya, a tough night but you'll do it. The most important thing is to be your best at the exhibit, that will give you the pleasure you want and deserve."

"Thank you. OK, I'm going to get off now and call Heinrich my taxi guy."

"Another friend?

"Bien sur monsieur. An absolute love, I know his wife and kids now."

"You are a pied piper."

"I'll call you later."

Before I could leave other calls came in. The first from Jacque to say Chris was acting crazy hollering at everyone and they weren't sure what they would do. "Please come back, we need your help, you make our lives happy." I had to tell them I was sorry but didn't know when or if I would be back but that didn't mean I didn't love them all. I said I would try to tell Chris not to take out his frustration on them.

Maria also called and was most upset but I tried to keep her calm and let her know something would be worked out. I was ok and she shouldn't worry and that I would call her to stay in touch but she should not tell Msr Chris. I asked about Shady, Serhalin and Sasha. She said that it was obvious that they missed my attention but they were otherwise fine.

I called Mom and Dad Janee because I knew they were probably confused by the situation. Dad answered and I said I wanted to stay in touch no matter what my decision was about Chris. I told them that I understood that he was their child and knew that connection.

Dad Janee of course said "but you know about men and their weaknesses. I don't condone them but you know we think of you as our daughter and don't want to lose you."

"Thank you that's why I call you Mom and Dad. Whatever Chris and I decide I will always be in touch if you want."

"Of course we want that. So now when can you come to Zurich.?"

"Let me see how I do here in the next few weeks and then I will be in touch. Perhaps I can come from Vienna to Zurich spend a few days with you and then to Geneva if I decide to go back. Will you be my tour guides?"

"Absolutely, we would love it. You know you have your own room here with us?"

"Yes Dad I know so we will do it, just let me figure out the time, ok?

"Ok dear heart. Calls us anytime you wish, we love you."

"I will call, now take care, know I'm ok."

Heinrich arrived and we left for the gallery. He came in for a few minutes to look around and said he would come back to get me when I called.

Paul told me there was a couple from the US who had called wanting directions to the gallery, evidently collectors who search for small galleries, also someone from Munich. Perhaps we would have some sales, that would make everyone happy. The gallery was down a side street where there were no other shops so we worked with email, regular mail and the phone to find good ones. We also advertised in art journals we could afford. The locals of course new us it was the new clients we were looking for.

People started arriving around 5:30 pm and soon within an hour the gallery was packed with artists, friends, and a few art collectors. So I was on to who were the collectors while being friendly with all the other people who were there just out of interest. I was working with the couple from New York City who were very interested in two pieces when Paul came up to me and said I had a visitor. I knew who it was. I excused myself and Paul took over the conversation.

As I went to the reception area I kept talking to self, "how am I going to handle this?" In 4 seconds SELF answered, "confident, not afraid, strong." There was Chris standing in the reception area. He smiled, just said "hi" put his hands on my arms and kissed me on either cheek. I said "Hi", then blurted out, "Why are you here?"

"You know why. Since you wouldn't answer my calls I had to come here to talk with you, I had no options. I want you to understand and come back to me."

"I didn't want to talk with you because I was too upset about what I saw. I have to go back to my clients and I probably will be here until 8:30 or 9:00 pm where can I meet you, what hotel?

"Oh no, I'll stay, I'd like to see the exhibit and watch you work, maybe even purchase something and then I'll wait and we'll go somewhere you choose. I don't want you slipping off somewhere I don't know and have to call the police to find you. That dress is smashing on you. I thought they always wore dark to these openings."

"They do but I'm me and often get into my own space. Alright, take a look. The artist is the one with the long green scarf, Messiur Gaton. You might like talking with him about how he creates his images since you are interested in photography. Here's your chance to have a primer lesson in art."

I returned to the clients and they had decided on two pieces so I put up the red dots and asked them to come with me so I could get all their information. This started some more interest. It always takes the first purchase while others are talking about it and then they decide their taste has been validated and more sales usually come. I saw Paul put up another red dot and came to reception to do paperwork also. Chris was talking with the artist concentrating on two pieces and then he looked up and motioned me to come over. He was going to purchase two excellent pieces telling me I knew exactly where they would be perfect. I ignored that, just put up the two red dots and noted the choices.

I could do the paper work tomorrow I would just need to know the credit card he wanted to use. I smiled and thanked him saying nothing about where they were going to be hung. The couple from Munich also selected one so I did their paper work. The artist was becoming ecstatic. There was still

Max who I knew would purchase and there would be 4 more weeks for more possibilities The first evening the gallery was bringing in $12,000, half to the artist, half to the gallery out of which would come a bonus for me

Just then in came my energetic, a bit crazy friend Max who came to every opening he was an avid collector. He immediately swept me up in a big hug twirling me around laughing. "You did it again, red this time." You look wonderful come to dinner and whatever with me."

"I would love to do that but I have some other plans. Ask me in a few days. I can wear the dress again. Self was being a bit of a green eye female as Chris watched with a tight look on his face, he was taking this all in.

"I will do that most definitely." said Max.

Then Cynthia handed me the phone and said, "It's for you, very important."

I answered and heard Steve's sexy voice.

"How are you doing? Did he arrive" What are you going to do?"

"Whoa, you sound like an attorney friend of mine doing a deposition."

He laughed, "I'm sorry I just want to know if you are ok."

"So far so good." Talking softly, "wish you were here." Again the green eyed female because I knew who was trying to listen."

"I do too. As I said I would come in my armor with my sword drawn. How's the exhibit going?"

"Packed with friends and other artists but there are some buyers and I need to get back to them so we need to cut this short. I'll call you later tonight, hopefully not too late."

"It's never too late."

As the crowd began to dwindle Max was still talking up a storm. He had his arm around my waist when I introduced him to Chris as just a friend. Paul got in on the conversation I think to hopefully keep Max directed. Then Cynthia and I cleaned up a bit and said we'd finish the next afternoon when

I came in. I got my coat and said to Chris, "Let's go. Do I need to call a taxi?"

"No, I have a driver waiting outside. Just decide where we can go to talk, your apartment?"

"No, not my apartment." I knew how convincing he could be. "I know a small café we can go to. If you're hungry the food is quite good, not up to your gourmet standards but they have good wines.

Before we go I have to call Heinrich to let him know that won't need his services."

"Ok, just give the driver the address."

While we were going to the café he said, "You know everyone misses you and they are complaining that I am impossible. I'm sharp with Maria and Curt to the point they avoid me, Joachim tells me to stop hollering at everyone all the time or they're all going to leave, it's because you aren't there to love me and keep me even."

"I know I have spoken to them on the phone. You have to keep yourself even. You shouldn't put your problems on to them."

"I know, but that's how I am." My first thought was spoiled brat, what was I getting into. If I didn't act or do what he wanted would I get the same treatment? I would have to test that to know.

We arrived at café Heiderof and Frau Heider greeted us saying she hadn't seen me in such a long while. I quickly explained but said I would come in the next few weeks. We were seated and she gave us the menu for the day.

To Chris I said, "I'm not very hungry but you go ahead if you are."

"I'm just hungry for you."

Then he asked Frau Heiderof they had a rot wein from Grinzing by a certain winery and she turned to ask Herr Heider and he said surprisingly, "yes". He opened it and

Frau Heider served us. I asked her about her soup of the day, "Minestrone".

"That will be fine with some of the very good bread you make." She turned to Chris and he said, "The same please."

She brought the wine and did the tasting bit with Chris and he shook his head that it was fine so she served. I began immediately sipping so I would stay calm, so far so good.

Chris started in, "Where do I start to explain?"

"Just start talking I said stiffly and tell the truth.

He cringed.

"The party went on much too long and I was exhausted what with the wine making and preparation at the restaurant and I had too much to drink. She is the daughter of the biggest wine distributor in Switzerland. We had a "thing" 2 years ago for about 6 weeks until I knew she was all over the place with different guys. She never let go of her idea that she could bide her time and get back with me, she's very spoiled and very seductive."

"Obviously."

In the midst of this conversation Frau Heider brought our soup and bread and I suddenly felt I had to eat something but I also I needed to get tipsy so had some more wine as did Chris.

"I've never seen you drink more than a half glass of different wines before. What are you doing."

"Doing what I feel like doing, myself changes from time to time." I was trying to send a message I hoped he would comprehend.

"That night was crazy. When I started up the stairs to the apartment I thought she was with one of the other men there who were after her but when I got to the room she followed me right in and one thing led to another. I was drunk. In the morning I kicked myself."

"Good. Hard I hope."

"I told her it was all wrong and she started to cry and then got angry and that she was going to tell her father that I had forced her. As I said he's the largest distributor in Switzerland."

"He's also a business man who makes money distributing wonderful wines. He didn't become the largest by listening to his spoiled daughter."

"But I panicked so I tried to console her before she left."

"I think you were doing a great job of that."

The look on Chris's face was pathetic. I almost thought he was going to cry.

"I told her that it was final, that I was with someone I loved and wanted to be with me forever. She just smiled and said she didn't believe me. I've always been able to appease women before by being seemingly kind and consoling at the end and I hoped it would work again. My hope was she would keep her mouth shut with her father and find someone else."

"What an opinion you have of women. You may have hurt her too, did you ever think of that."

"I'm not sure she can be hurt."

"Everyone can and sometimes are but this is not the time for me. I want someone who loves me for who I am and commit to that. I can put up with a lot of things disagreements, flirtations but not on the intimate side. I can't do that. I wouldn't do it to you. I have to know my own feelings and be my own person not an available thing you can love when you want and give gifts to. I want to share someone's life, someone I can trust and come to with anything. Don't you get it?" The wine was kicking in but so was SELF.

"And I want to share my life with you. I can't say anymore than I have. I love you and want you in my life forever.

After a long sigh and another sip of wine I said, "Then why look elsewhere? I can't commit to anything or anyone right now. I need my own space, time to work on the things I love, time to think. I can't say when or if I'll come back. I have to work through my own feelings and see what choices I'll make."

"Is there someone else?"

"Ha, you mean Max? He's just one of my crazier friends. When I first came to Vienna I was the new lady in town so we had a short fling but it went nowhere. He's just a man about town with lots of girls."

"What about Steve?"

"Steve is a dear good friend in the category of Jennie and Peter, he's always there for me."

"Am I in that category?"

"Not at the moment. Maybe it's your time to hurt and think about changing your mind about some things."

"You've already changed me. I love you and I want you with me all the time. I am miserable without you, I can't sleep. Joachim told me to grow up and calm down and stop hollering all the time. They all miss you."

"I've spoken with them all, they've told me and they want to know if I'm coming back. I was honest with them, I said I didn't know. And I don't know. I told you long ago about my thoughts on intimacy and how I couldn't or wouldn't share you with anyone nor would I go out looking, but you did and I think it's part of what you think you need."

"No, I won't see any other women, this was a dumb mistake and it won't happen again, I only need you. All I know is that I love you, you are my life, everything I have is yours. I don't want to be without you. We never talked about marriage except when you said that you didn't think you could ever marry again. Will you marry me?"

"Not right now until I am more sure what time brings. Seeing you with that woman hurt too much Chris, I felt violated. If you want her, go to her but don't come home to me after, I just can't accept that, it's cheap and tawdry. I can't make any commitment now, I just don't know. The wonderful things you purchase are beautiful but they are not what I want for a life style. I can't be purchased. Time is a healer of sorts so that's why I have to have my own time just to be Monique, to have time to do what I like and do a lot of thinking. I need to do a lot of talking with SELF and have a lot of time alone. I guess I have to be selfish and just get along with myself. That's all I can tell you. If you can't wait then do what you want to do, see who you want to see."

"Then he paused, looked miserable and said, I don't want to be with anyone but you."

"But you were and someone from your past so what should I expect for the future."

"I just lost my male head and did a big goof, I'm so sorry. Maybe I guess I was testing myself."

"At my expense. You were intimate with someone else, how do you think that makes me feel, think about it. You've already asked me about someone else so what if I did this to you? Wouldn't you feel abused?"

"I don't want anyone else touching you. Please try to forgive me."

I didn't know if I could. "How long are you staying here?'

"Just until Sunday. I have a big party I have to take care of. Do you have anytime tomorrow for us?

"I have to be at the gallery around 2 or 2:30. The clients from NYC are bringing another couple arriving tomorrow morning and Paul wants me there. Also some other client, I'm not sure who but business is business. I need to sleep in a little so we have time for an early lunch around 12. The NYC clients also invited Paul, Cynthia, myself and the artist and his wife to the Sacher for drinks tomorrow evening around 7 pm, then we'll leave them and go for dinner. Of course you are welcome to join us." I thought it would be good to have safety in numbers.

I sipped some more of the wine and said we had to leave so I could get some sleep. I thanked Frau and Herr and started a bit precociously towards the door, somewhat teasing Chris to accompany me or I would be gone again—at least that's what I told SELF. He paid and was right there and looking a bit confused by my behavior. I was doing a good acting job of the devil may care. Isn't that what he had always thought of himself? My sword was drawn. The driver took us back to the apartment. Chris took me to the door and asked if he could come up to talk some more. It wasn't talk he wanted.

I said, "No, I need to get some sleep to be up for tomorrow. Are you going to come by at 12 or should I meet you somewhere?'

He just shook his head, "You know I will always come to get you in a proper fashion. I'll be here at 12 and will go from there. Where would you like lunch?

"I know of a charming place by the Hapsburg that has quite a "grazing" platter. I'll direct the driver tomorrow." I was now the one in charge. I realized I didn't want to go through this battle but he needed to know I was self sufficient; not from money but from myself and who I was and contacts I made out of friendship. I suppose it was a bit of a crush to his ego but he had to learn I would survive in a wonderful way with or without him. Maybe not as happy without his loving but I would be fine—so I told this to SELF. I had a feeling that he didn't think it was going to be this difficult to convince me. When he had property and money and could give me anything why wouldn't I just say yes and return. I wasn't ready and wasn't sure I ever would be.

He kissed me politely on either cheek and said goodnight.

The next morning I dragged myself out of bed to be ready by 12 pm. I had this wonderful new outfit Gabrielle had made so I decided that was it for today. It was silver soft silk wide leg pants and a top with a blouson collar. Over that was one of her wonderful sweater creations of multicolor yarn, some iridescent coming midway thigh length scrumptious. The buzzer rang promptly at 12 and I answered not inviting him up. I just went down to meet him. My check list schlussle, money, id, lipstick in my purse which I always did methodically so I could always take care of myself and down the stairs I went.

Chris was there in wonderful gabardine slacks, silk shirt and soft, brown leather car coat, looking smashing although a little tired around the eyes. I loved this man with so much style and joie de vivre although I knew there was something going on underneath but wasn't sure what. I knew I had to protect myself and let him know my parameters so far so good.

We went to lunch and of course he wanted to taste everything too so two grazing platters of rolls of cheese and various sausages, ground meat mixture wrapped in triangles rich pasta dough, tips of asparagus, raddichio salad, slices of fresh fruit and of course some delicious fresh baked rolls. In all a delicious blend of flavors.

At the gallery Chris and Paul started a conversation and I knew Paul was enjoying it. Cynthia and I finished cleaning up and prepared for the few clients coming in. The clients arrived and introduced us to their friends and we again went through the exhibit. We also had many artist works in the adjacent room on moveable panels I had Paul install. He and Chris went there to peruse the works of other artists. I had given Paul "heads up" on one particular piece that would work perfectly in the restaurant so he would take care of that part. The other couple from NYC told me of their collection and how they looked for new artists from all over. They were definitely avid collectors. Now some become so due to their own perspective and some due to "keeping up with the Jones" which every city has. These were definite collectors so I tried to be my most erudite self in talking about the works. The artist did arrive and they were pleased with him because they asked specific questions of the creator. In the end they purchased two pieces. I was so proud to be a part of promoting his work, giving the purchasers great pleasure, supporting the artist and Paul. Paul and I just beamed at each other. I spoke to SELF it is wonderful to be in this milieu of intelligent, responsive individuals. What a joy. All the mundane dissipates.

We came into the reception area to do all the paper work and there was Chris watching every move. The clients commented on my outfit and I told them about Gabrielle. They asked if it was possible to go to her shop or studio and I said of course. They only had Sunday so I said I would call right away. I called and Gabrielle said absolutely so I asked the clients if 4:00pm would work. I asked her if she had any wine or champagne and she said no but would get some. I said, "no I'll arrange that. And any glasses?" "Some." "Ok I'll take care of that so don't worry just have the studio in order, one of your assistants there and your portfolio and I'll take care of the rest." The clients would have the rest of the day to do what they wanted and they would be back at the hotel to get ready for dinner or whatever. I turned to Chris and said, "what time is your flight tomorrow?"

"2:00 pm departure."

So I thought he is off to the airport, I can meet the clients around 3:30 and be back around 6 and collapse. I asked Cynthia if she would like to join us I all ready knew she wanted to.

"Fine, we are all set. I'll meet you at the Sacher Hotel between 3:15 and 3:30 pm and we will go to Gabrielle's studio and spend an hour or two while you shop and see the beautiful clothes she designs. And remember there is no obligation on your part but do remember this is very special, not everyone is invited."

"If she has other garments like what you are wearing we're sure we'll find something we love. Thank you so much for arranging this we're really excited."

As they left I said we would see them at 7:00 pm for drinks. "May I include my friend indicating Chris."

"Of course, we always want another good looking man around."

Chris smiled and thanked them. Then he asked, "you need champagne and glasses?"

"Yes, we just need to see when and how we can get that done."

"I'm going now. You want it back here at the gallery."

"Yes so we can take it to the studio tomorrow."

"Ok. Paul where is a good wine shop nearby and will they have glasses available?"

Paul gave him directions and he was off. My knight was coming to the fore without a request and helping with what I was all into what I was about.

With two more sales we were now at $15,000 for our two day effort. Beyond the necessary money we were proud of the acceptance of the artist and for ourselves that we had selected this artist for an exhibit.

In about a half an hour Chris was back with 6 bottles of very good champagne and the glasses. He had a little boy grin on his face as though he had done his good deed for the day, he had. I thanked him and Cynthia and I went to wash the glasses and then rewrap for transport to Gabrielle's studio. Cynthia would pick up the champagne and glasses tomorrow and bring to the Sacher. Then I called Heinrich about the cars. I told him I need two cars at Sacher Hotel at 3:30 pm returning around 6:00 pm.

As everyone left, Chris asked, "What now" This is a bit of a new world for me."

"It's like organizing things for the restaurant." I need to go home for a little a quiet time and to change and then we have to be at the Sacher by 7pm. We'll have drinks with them and then excuse ourselves and go for some dinner to laugh and relax with my friends. So if you could take me home now I'll meet you later at Sacher and will join in.

"You will not meet me. I'll be at your apartment before 7 and we'll go to Sacher and I'll follow your lead, whatever your program is."

"Do I sound like I'm programmed? That's not me. Yes I need things somewhat organized so everyone's happy, but programmed?"

"I don't mean it in a negative way. I see how you work and you a do a great job of pulling everything together. I want you to do that at home. I'm not that organized all the time. I need you there, I need your special touch with everything."

He was really trying in every way to appease me.

I was getting so tired I didn't quite know how to respond so just thanked him again for his help and understanding. He just beamed. I said to SELF, "I think he does understand something more about me or more importantly about other people."

He dropped me at the apartment saying he would be back just before 7. I went up to sit and think for a few minutes then got up to get ready. Chris was back as he said and we were off to Sacher Hotel. I had on one of Gabrielle's knit dresses in emerald green. Chris just stared and then took me in his arms for a big hug saying even if you are thin you fill that out beautifully. The clients were in the lounge and had the restaurant set up lovely hors'deuvre platters and of course had the bartender at their beckon call. They commented on the dress and I of course said, "it's one of Gabrielle's and they said "We can't wait to see what else she has." These people knew what they liked, how to entertain and yet were most open and friendly. Chris was his charming self. We enjoyed the typical chitter chat and when ready to leave I reminded them of the next day, that I would be there to accompany them to Gabrielle's. With smiles and hugs, we left to go for a more relaxed place.

We walked to the restaurant and were met with all the usual enthusiasm. A large table was set up for our group already artists were there talking and laughing. We no longer sat down when Chris asked me to dance. Oh, oh SELF. It was an easy tune for a good foxtrot but I knew they would soon go into something special mainly because I saw Chris had spoken to them when we arrived. So we danced quietly close he whispering in my ear how much he loved me and that we could partake of both my "homes". Then it started, "Pardon me boys, is that the Chattanooga Choo Choo" and we started in. I couldn't resist side steps, insteps twirls, dips, you name it. We always came together with the dance, smiling and laughing all the way. When we finished there was only the applause and I knew we were made to dance. I still needed my time and would take it but I saw a little more where I was going. We enjoyed dinner and then I was literally "pooped" and said to Chris please take me home to my apartment. Lots of complaints of us leaving early but I said, "I have to sleep sometime."

At the door I knew he expected to come up but I was being very strong and still a bit vindictive. If I had suffered he would have to too. I said, "No. I'll see you early for coffee before you have to leave for the airport. I will just take the street car to the hotel, don't argue, that's what I want to do."

His response, "I can't stand this." and he immediately kissed me most passionately which I responded to but SELF said "no later." I repeated I would see him off to the airport in the morning but nothing more was going to happen tonight. He just shook but said ok, kissed me again and went to the car. I had to do it to know if I was that important to him. He would have to understand what might be the depth I wanted him to go otherwise I was not willing to give up the small world I had created.

The next morning I hopped the streetcar and was at the hotel just before 11. I went in and asked for him and he was there waiting in the lounge. He had not slept well but neither had I. We had coffee and talked around things and then he said he had to leave. He wanted to take me back to the apartment before he had to leave for the airport so I acquiesced. When we arrived he said he would await my decision, he would call everyday to see that I was ok.

Tears came into my eyes and I couldn't conceal them.

Then he smiled and said, "Find trust in me again, we'll have a wonderful life together."

I was getting so tired I didn't quite know how to respond so just thanked him again for his help with the Champagne and his understanding of my feelings. He just beamed so maybe a light bulb had illuminated. I did have a question about his sexual drives. I knew how he was with me but was that enough for him, it frightened me. Was he capable of accepting intimacy as love, did he understand the fragility of intimacy? I didn't have an answer only the question.

I wanted to go with him then but SELF kept myself strong. All I could say was, "I love you, we'll be in touch, please give me my space now."

He shuttered and said, "You are true to yourself in a strong way for such a sweet thing. I don't know what else to do, I just don't want to be without you. Then he asked the driver to open the trunk and he retrieved a small gift bag. "This is something special for only you, it might need some alteration so just go to the shop and get it done. "He kissed me and was off to the airport. I could hardly make it up the stairs.

CHAPTER 10

Then I realized I had to go back to the Sacher to meet the clients and take them to Gabrielle's studio so I pulled SELF together, changed clothes and got on the streetcar again. I arrived and Cynthia was there with the champagne and glasses and I just said let's go and she was happy. Heinrich was there with the two cars so we put in the goodies and said we would be back in few minutes. The clients were waiting in the foyer so I greeted them and said let's go for something different. I gave Heinrich the address and directions and we were there in 15 minutes. Heinrich and the other driver would wait for us. Gabrielle was dressed in one her own outfits and looked fantastic. She too was thin, quite tall and had beautiful long golden hair. She was very much a model for her own designs. Her assistant helped me with the champagne and we were ready to serve which of course we did. Gabrielle had her portfolios out to show what she could show about her process and the inventory she had in her studio. The ladies were most excited and found some things for themselves and their husbands soon had new sweaters. Also their grandchildren would have special gifts of knit sweaters, caps and mittens. And then the ladies had Gabrielle take their measurements and ordered other items. They were most happy knowing they had come to something out of the ordinary.

When we arranged everything, the payment and shipping addresses the ladies had their packages with them. I just asked if they had room in their luggage or wanted to ship it." Oh no we want to wear these on the remainder of our trip so we will find a way to carry it aboard the flights. They were very pleased and said they wanted to receive more information from Gabrielle and they would send her more clients. Quality does somehow achieve this reaction with many people.

We went back to the Sacher and I said "au revoir and I will see you again perhaps in New York."

"You are welcome anytime. Just give us a call and let us know your plans." Little did I know that I might take them on their offer.

Heinrich waited to drive me home and as always I went to see Jennie and Peter who came to the door, "So how is it going?

"I had a good time with my clients at Gabrielle's studio. Gabrielle is happy. My heart aches and I don't know what I am going to do."

"You have to know what you feel and go with it. There will always be, as you put it, bricks so you have to get through them.

"How did Chris take everything?" Jennie asked.

"With difficulty because I made it difficult for him. I told him I was going to stay to work and do a lot of thinking that I couldn't make any commitments right now about our relationship."

"I agree you have to take time and search out your feelings. My intuition wasn't right on this time was it."

"Oh Jennie it takes time to learn about someone, it's not your fault. Oh he gave this to me when he left but I had to go to with the clients to Gabrielle's studio."

"Jennie got excited "hurry and open it."

I opened the package and found a beautiful gold watch, the style like a bracelet with the watch face covered. "Now I understand why he put his fingers around my wrist the other night, measuring the size. He never misses anything. He wants what he wants."

"Well wear it with pleasure. At least he still wants to be generous with you."

"I guess but I need time before I decide."

We said goodnight and I went home to collapse.

I continued working at the gallery and doing my studies and then realized it was Wednesday that Steve was coming in so went home early to get ready. He called around 6:30 pm and said he found the hotel fine and was ready.

"Great. Give me about a half an hour and I'll be there and then we'll walk to the restaurant for dinner."

"Are you sure you don't want me to come and get you?"

"No, I'll get on the streetcar with no problem." I took the streetcar and walked the few blocks to his hotel and he was waiting in the lounge so after the typical greetings we started our walk to the Schlau Katz Hans greeted me as did several artists and we were directed to a table. Steve said, "You obviously come here frequently."

"It is a kind of hang out for artists so we come a lot to relax and just have good conversation and we can also dance."

"I see that. Are you going to dance with me?"

"Of course, right now." So we did and enjoyed.

After dinner we walked back to the hotel hand in hand. "I'll meet you around 10 am tomorrow morning and I'll start my special tour for special people."

"I'm looking forward to it. I'm concerned about you going alone to your apartment, let me get you a taxi and I'll ride with you.

"No, no it's not necessary, it's my city and I'll just take the streetcar, I'll be alright." So a kiss on either cheek and I was off for home. I was trying to keep things in control, not too intimate. I got home and immediately went to bed to get ready for tomorrow.

In the morning I arrived at the hotel just a little after 10 and then Steve and I set out on our tour. We walked on the Kartnerstrasse and to the Hapsburg to go through the museum and to check about seeing the Lippanzers. I asked at the ticket window for Constantine and she said they had started training but let us in. We were the only observers there. Constantine waved and signaled he would speak after the training. I explained to Steve that I had made friends with him and often came to muck stalls as he knew the horses trusted me and he would always treat me to lunch and great horse conversation. After the workout Constantine found us, I introduced Steve and we chatted. He asked when I would come to do my mucking and I said not until Monday. "Fine, 9 am." "Ok, I'll be here. Now will you come to lunch with us?"

"I wish I could but I've got an individual training session right now so no time."

"I understand, see you Monday morning." Steve and I went out and began our walk to eat on the streets again.

Steve looked at me and said, "How do you know Constantine and what's this about mucking stalls."

I just laughed, "I went so often to see them work out the horses because I miss mine and Constantine noticed. We got into conversations and I asked if I could come into muck stalls, I've had lots of practice. He said he would try me out. He wanted to see how I worked around the horses which I knew would be no problem. Then he told me he would pay me by taking me for lunch whatever days I came to work. I told him fine because anything helps with my small budget and it was fun talking about training horses."

"Are you short on money? You know I'll help you anytime."

"I'm ok. When I decided to come to Montreux I told Chris I wanted to keep the apartment for at least a year and he paid the rent in full so that's set for awhile. I had spent some money I had set aside for all the décor and with Jennie's discounts as a designer I did alright and I do love what I did in the apartment, the contemporary feel I created. My plan was to be as comfortable as possible for whatever time I decided to stay. I have some income from the States, then I barter a lot like with Constantine, play the piano at the restaurant a couple of nights, work with Paul who can't pay me much but when the sales are good he gives me a commission. Then I ride streetcars, no car. I also have a couple of clothing designer artists where I can buy unusual clothes and they give me fantastic prices so I manage. It's a whole new world with Chris and you too, I have things I'd probably never would be able to have but I've never been into a lot of things in fact sometimes I'm a embarrassed by the gifts and living situation. It's a different life here for me and my goal is to always know and be in tune with myself, in fact I talk a lot to SELF to work things out all the time. Even when in love with someone I couldn't give up certain dreams I have mainly about the creative world. No I can't be a kept woman, I have too much pride. If I run in to trouble I'll let you know."

Steve looked very thoughtful, smiled, said "I would love to keep you at any level you chose." Then took my hand and we started seeing the sights. With him holding my hand I thought how lust, as I was beginning to realize was with Chris, often gets in the way of a true love which could be lustful but full of tenderness and understanding. SELF told me to watch out, a new decision is coming.

Steve was a bit in awe with Vienna, absorbing everything. I was surprised he had never been here before. We did the typical sights after the Hapsburg. We visited St Stephan's, walked Karnerstrasse to the Opera House, then across to Karlskirche and finally the open air market. Finally we were both tired so I said let's hit the trolley and go home. When we got to the apartment he was amazed at the building. I said I lucked out via friends. Inside I took his jacket and showed him the slipper routine.

He just stood and looked at the interior, Will you do my apartment? This is fantastic, contemporary but comfortable, I love it. "So I put into my head that I needed the catalogues from the shop so I could order anytime once I saw his apartment and knew more about his taste. From our conversations I realized it was very close to mine.

I put him in the kitchen to open some wine while I changed into some nice sweats to be comfortable. When I came out of my bedroom, the wine was open and he was perusing some of my books and had also found the CDs and had some good jazz on Stan Getz. We relaxed and chatted and then I said I needed to start dinner so into the kitchen. He watched everything I did which wasn't so much. I had prepared some veal stew in the morning so it would be that with rice, a mélange of fresh vegetables and salad, after some fresh fruit and cheese. I had made a special pudding for dessert and after the first dish he asked if he could have seconds, so my new child had two desserts. I knew it wasn't difficult to please him. I sensed he just wanted to be with someone he cared about and be content. At the end of the evening I said he would probably get lost on the trolley so I would call a taxi to take him to his hotel. I would see him the next day with a rent a car and go to the Vienna Woods, Grinzing and Schoenbrunn. He wanted to take me somewhere special for dinner so I suggested Restaurant Walden.

We did all of it which he thoroughly enjoyed and then returned the car before returning to his hotel. I hopped the streetcar to go home to shower and change and then meet him at the hotel because I had tickets for the Musikverein the center of Viennese musical culture. The program was heavy with Mahler but he loved music and the best was performed here. After I took him to a café Heiderhof and after meeting Frau Ruth and Herr Hans and hearing the menu for that evening he was all smiles. "You're showing be the best that can be offered and not always at the 5* places. It is absolute enlightening and fun; you try to taste everything don't you and I don't mean just food."

"What's life all about if not to taste and find what you enjoy the most. I like trying all types of restaurants and activities. Of course I'm partial to music and art but also love reading. I decided awhile back that life was a dance with steps in, out and around and you keep moving to your own tune. If you're lucky you find someone to share it with you who has the same rhythm and can sing a similar song, if not you just go your own way and make do the best you can." I could begin to see how Steve and my dance was very close. In the current situation that frightened me and I was confused.

"I would like to share your song and dance with you through life."

"Thank you for such a thought. Give me some more time."

"Since I see a glimmer of hope, take whatever time you need. I'm here waiting."

We went back to the apartment but he didn't push me, always a gentleman.

Saturday I took him to the special shops for furniture, lighting, glassware, etc. so I could learn of his taste. I also took him by the gallery to meet Paul and Cynthia and see where and what it was. He spent some time pursuing art and talking with Paul, my "teacher", they seemingly got along fine, interested in what they were discussing. We got on the streetcar and back to the apartment. Steve was very relaxed with me so I said go on the couch and soon he was fast asleep with a book in hand. What a lovely, comfortable, but interesting man. I woke him and said time for dinner and he apologized for falling asleep. I said it was a compliment that he was that comfortable. He just smiled his knowing smile, such a patient, relaxed, generous, loving man. In the evening we had dinner and great conversation with Jennie and Peter at their place, they were very receptive to him. I helped Jennie in the kitchen while Peter gave Steve a tour of their home. He loved it and asked both of them very interesting questions about different architectural styles. I could see why he and Chris had been good friends for such a long time they were so erudite in many ways. Jennie gave me some knowing looks which I continued to ignore.

He thanked Jennie and Peter for the evening and then asked, "Please be sure Monique is always ok and call me if she is not."

"Of course we will." Jennie just cocked her head to one side like she did when trying to understand something or come up with an idea or some thought.

Throughout this time he only kissed me on either cheek and made no advances but I knew he wanted to I just didn't give him the opportunity. I now felt sometimes I was between a rock and a hard place. I said to SELF," Wouldn't it be great if I could mingle the two men's qualities together." There is no perfection and if there were it would end up boring and I knew I was not perfect. After dinner, a hug and the typical kiss and he returned to his hotel.

The next morning he called me before leaving for his flight thanking me again and I then I felt lonely. Around 4:00 pm my phone rang and it was Steve driving back to Geneva. "Thank you for the tour, all you shared with me and most of all your wonderful companionship. I would have liked to stay for a much longer time and I have to tell you I tried to stay on my best behavior until you decide what you're doing. It was so much fun and I loved being with you."

"Thank you for being so understanding. I enjoyed your visit and I'm grateful that you didn't push on me. I have to tell you I now feel lonely so you must come again."

"I will or you can arrive here at my doorstep and I'll welcome you."

"Ok I won't forget that."

"Monique I told you several times I am here for you but I won't interfere unless he hurts you again and then I'll be there full force. Remember that because I will be there for you once you decide."

"You are so special I must be brain dead not to just come to you."

"I'm here waiting, the door is open.""

"When you speak to me that way, that's when I get more frightened and have to go into myself and try to know what I should do."

"Just know I will always love you and I will do my best to make your life comfortable and without any kind of fear, I would love to share the joys with you. You have to decide if that is what you want."

"I'm sorry Steve, now I'm totally emotionally confused and just want to run.

"Don't run anywhere unless it is first to me and we'll figure it out. Will you promise that?"

"Yes, I promise."

"Ok, scout's honor baby?"

With a laugh I responded, "yes scout's honor."

"Moni, we're joking a little but you know I am serious. You can come to me or I will meet you anywhere you want."

"Moni?"

"Yes that's my diminutive for you."

"All I'm going to say right now is that I will call you tomorrow morning, how early can I do that?"

"Anytime you want, I'm at your service, remember no one else is here with me."

"Ok, it will probably be early."

"Not a problem. Sleep well."

"If I can at all."

Jennie and Peter wanted to know how the visit was,

"The visit was great fun, he was a total gentleman, a loving friend that I was becoming so attached to him which confused me even more. Any choices I make are going to affect my whole life pattern."

"All choices have that possibility. Be wise and do take time to do a lot of thinking and listen to your heart. You'll find your answer and it looks like it might be a different choice of men."

"I'm so confused I don't even know if I want a man. I just didn't think I would have to be going through more choices. It's difficult."

"Life is difficult frequently, you'll find your way. Know we are here for you."

"Thank you dear friends. How did I have the luck to come to your home."

"Through another friend, so think about what you create by your person. You pull us all together."

"But you shouldn't have to be my support system."

"And why not. When you love a true friend you help out anyway you can. You would do the same for us."

I hugged them both, thanked them and exhausted went across the hall to fall into bed and think. SELF and I had a long conversation. SELF thought I was being overindulgent but I needed time to try to put together my direction. Everyone needs to have that.

The next morning I called Steve around 8:00 am just to hear his voice again.

"Hi, I'm just out of the shower and was thinking of you and if you were sending over breakfast."

"I'd rather have you here so it will be prepared perfectly."

"I'll cook for you again sometime but remember I will never be a hausfrau again. When I want to do it to please someone I do but not every day."

"With what you do once a month would be just fine."

"Oh you're too easy. I could manage maybe twice a month."

Laughter. "I would just like you to be here with me, for food we can figure it out or starve to death together."

"I just wanted to hear your voice. I'm on my way to muck stalls and then later to the gallery plus I have a German lesson, plus . . .

"Sounds like too many pluses but go and enjoy, I didn't hear a plus for some man that you want to see so that's good, I'll talk to you later in the day or this evening."

CHAPTER 11

So for the next week I got into my routine of the gallery, studying, walking, mucking stalls, talking with Jennie. It was a great respite, I guess I could easily be a recluse with books and things but I did love the exchange between people. Both Chris and Steve called each day, Chris still asking when I was coming back. He told me that he was so sharp with Maria and Curt that they avoided him, Joachim told me to stop hollering at everyone, to grow up and get it together, even Jacque and Hans avoid me. I'm miserable. I need you here to love and keep me even. I told him he needed to keep himself even. I figured I would have to test this one to see how he would react if I didn't do or say what he wanted. I would have to test it to really know what life with him would be.

When Steve called we talked about music and books we were reading, what things we enjoyed and he always brought up how we shared it all. He said he had gone to the museum and was frequently perusing the art galleries. I said good and that he should keep looking and he would learn more about the art that spoke to him. Again why can't you find one that has all of it. One packaged man needed with all the attributes. I was really confused at this point.

Saturday we had an opening at the gallery beginning at 5:00pm. Paul had the eye for selection and I had been learning so much from him. My background was more in the historical images up through the impressionists, he was leading me into perceiving the abstract, installations, contemporary photography. That's what his gallery was all about, that was his direction and I was loving it. I would miss my almost daily lesson when I returned to Montreux but we would be able to scan photos of art and we could discuss over good old email or just get on the phone, not quite the same but workable.

He of course sold works but I had become his prime person for selling especially with American clients. So I decided I would be at all the openings which meant flying to Vienna every 4-6 weeks depending on how many exhibits he decided on. I was trying to put what might become both of my worlds together. We would have to see how it would work out, eventually a decision time would come.

The gallery was packed on Saturday as often happens with openings. We usually didn't do exhibits so close together but momentum was up and the new artist had things in his style complimenting the one we had just displayed. The work consisted of acrylics on very large canvases of bright colors in abstract done in bold, definite strokes of paint with lots of brush texture. It was extremely expressionistic. We did well and sold two pieces to two, young Austrian couples just beginning to collect works. Considering they were $5000 each, this was terrific for an opening. It also was important to the artists who of course needed sustaining money but also needed acceptance. They were not the type for the old idea many people have of "won't that look good over the couch. This was for the work itself and what it had to say. The old routine in galleries is the red dot means sold, the blue dot it is on hold waiting for a decision. So in addition to the sales we had several blue dots which was hopeful. We knew which blue dots we had placed for the ploy of creating an interest because someone else was interested. Afterwards Paul, Cynthia, myself, the artists and other friends went out for the customary celebration. Even when we didn't sell at an exhibition we went out to talk very esoterically about the art and the lack of insight from the viewers, it was part of the art scene which I have to say I enjoyed.

I got up Sunday and decided to take a long walk and do some thinking, I had now been back in Vienna for 6 weeks and did enjoy the city and my friends but I could not get Chris off my mind. I meandered and when I got home didn't go to Jennie I just read and thought and then about around 9pm called Chris on his cell. "He sounded busy but when I called he always took time. "Hi baby what's up, how was the exhibit, are you ok?"

"The exhibit was great lots of people and some sales. Paul and the normal group with the artist went out and we had a good time last night and I'm fine. Been walking a lot of the day and went to see Constantine and the horses and ate off the street. Can you talk for a minute?"

"With you anytime, the soup pot can boil over, nothing gets in the way, what is it?"

"After a lot of soul searching I've decided to come back to Montreux." I knew if I was ever going to have peace with myself I had to be with Chris again to see what we really had.

"What, say it again."

"I've decided to come back."

And then he broke loose, "My baby, my baby Monique is coming back, she's really coming back. He was yelling so I knew everyone in the restaurant would know. It sounded as though he was dancing around. When, tell me when, tomorrow? I'll make the reservation right away."

"I have some things to get organized here so I don't think until Friday. I still want to keep the apartment and come back to Vienna to work with Paul and I want you know how important this is to me."

"Keep the apartment, and go back as you need, I understand it is important to you. I'm trying all the time to understand you and I think I know more now. Do you know how important this is to me? Monique I am miserable without you, I need to hold you, love you, laugh with you, buy you things. Then he gave the phone to Jacque who said, "We are overjoyed you're coming back, our lives will be back to some normalcy, we all can't wait, we miss your energy so much."

"Thank you Jacque, I look forward to being with all of you too."

Hold on here's Hans."

"Hi Hans, I'm not sure what you miss but I will come back and be my old self with all of you."

"We will love it."

Then Chris was back on the phone and still yelling, "My baby is coming back. I can't wait." Then I heard "Champagne for everyone to celebrate. Baby I'll settle down and call you a little later ok?"

"Ok. I didn't think I'd cause such an uproar."

"You know yourself in some ways but you don't have a clue how everyone misses you here. Oh Monique you have made me so happy. I've got to call Mom and Dad to tell them, they will want to be here when you arrive."

He called about an hour later and said the reservation was for Friday on the 12 pm flight. Please don't take the train, call Heinrich to take you so I know nothing will happen. I'll be in Geneva, to pick you up."

"I'll probably be coming with more luggage than usual so know which car."

"There's no problem, we'll be talking everyday so you just tell me what you're bringing and I'll be sure we can handle it."

"I won't bring my whole apartment, just a lot of stuff I want with me."

He just laughed, "You are too much, so much into what you enjoy, you are my girl but most of all my sensuous lady. I'll take care of everything most of all you, not to worry, I will try to make it your dream."

"I do have dreams, so I hope you can understand them and I'll try to understand yours."

"I'll do everything I can to be sure to meet them. I can't wait until you're here, I wish it could be earlier."

"Just remember I am myself and I have definite ideas about certain things."

"Yes, I know and I will try to respect all of them."

"I'll talk to you tomorrow."

Monday morning I lie in bed contemplating what I now had to do starting with packing clothes for the trip to Montreux I would leave on Friday so had a lot to organize. I also had to work everything out with Paul. It was difficult to concentrate on what I was doing as I kept having the same conversation with myself. SELF are you sure? SELF you are crazy? SELF you are frightened. SELF you are excited. SELF answered "yes" to all the above. What a mental turmoil. I planned to spend some time with Jennie and Peter and at the gallery Tuesday, Wednesday and Thursday getting my last "taste" of my life in Vienna which might never be the same even though I would be returning every so many weeks, I knew I would have to keep SELF alive.

So Friday came and again Jennie had to walk down with me because I was again afraid. Heinrich was there with his wife and children to see me off. I hugged Jennie so hard, it is so difficult sometimes to love people in many places, you're always going to be missing someone. "You know we are always here for you just call anytime or email and we will respond right away. Remember you have Steve also who is there for you."

"Thank you. I won't say good bye just au revoir"

"Au revoir."

We arrived at the Geneva airport and Heinrich said, "Is this what you want?"

"Right now yes, I only have to see if it will continue to be what I want. Please come with the family to see me in Switzerland."

"You let us know when and we will be there."

Hugs and kisses as always and Heinrich went in to help me with the luggage and make sure there was no problem with my check in.

So I was on my way back. On the plane I got my book out so I could read a page four times or more if I didn't want to talk to the person sitting next to me but amazingly Mr. Allen came aboard and changed his seat to sit next to me. We had some champagne and chatted about many things. I told him I was returning and had lots of luggage and he said not to worry we'll take care of it. So on the carousel my three pieces of luggage arrived and the large package with the artwork. He got the carts while I stayed with the luggage and he helped me load everything on it and we went out and there was Chris pacing like a new father waiting for his child to be born or a horse waiting for his feeding time. He came directly to me put his arms around me and started to kiss me as he always did. Mr. Allen waited and was smiling then Chris noticed and grabbed his hand and said thank you once again, "I can't believe this has happened twice. You know where you are most welcome, please join us at the restaurant tomorrow evening there will be friends and family."

"Thank you, I will take you up on that. May I say I am envious that you have this lady. May I have permission to have a couple of dance?"

"Mr. Allen, you do not need anyone's permission except mine and I will say yes."

"Thank you. Until tomorrow night."

"Yes tomorrow, tonight I just need to get home right now and relax."

We went out and there was the car and another driver so I asked where Jacque was?"

"I had something else I needed him to do so hired a car. I would have driven but it's the same as the last time, I would be a mess if I couldn't just hold and talk to you. Are you tired?"

"I feel exhausted."

"We'll go straight home so you can rest."

We talked a bit as he held me and when I put my head on his shoulder I fell asleep and he let me be. I only awoke when we arrived at home and he awakened me. I just asked SELF to let me do this. We went in and Maria came right away and we hugged and she said everything is in order so you can just go and relax. "Thank you Maria, it is so wonderful to see and be with you again. Shady was right there tail wagging and right foot up. How is Curt?"

"He's fine, waiting to talk to you about the horses and other things."

"Ok I'll get into my jeans and go visit him." Chris just stood back smiling and then said he would take the luggage up and asked Maria if she would help me unpack. He said he would be needed at the restaurant but he would be back as soon as possible and would take care of dinner, I only needed to take it easy and get reorganized.

Steve called me to see how it was going. And I just said I was trying to get reorganized. We chatted a bit about Vienna and then he said he wanted to see me to go over some business things he thought I should know about so we set a lunch date for the next day at the Chillon Castle as Chris said he had to be at the restaurant most of the day. I wasn't sure what he wanted to share with me but my horse ears were up.

I went to the stable to see Curt and the horses and really felt at home then. Curt had everything in order and clean as always and the horses all nickered and I had tears in my eyes when Curt came out and for the first time approached me and gave me a welcome hug without reservation. "I'm so happy you're back, I hope it can work with Msr Chris."

"I do too, I will try my best because I love this place so much. It feels like I was meant to be here."

"You are happy here with the land, the horses, it is a question if you can be happy with Messieur Chris."

"I understand Curt, I'll have to see."

I went back to the house and showered and put on some sweats, laid down to read and fell asleep. I don't know how long it was but then I felt someone holding my hand and saying baby wake up it is dinner time and saw Chris with that fantastic expressive face, the blue twinkling eyes, the huge smile and I thought I was in heaven. I asked SELF, "Why do I question anything about this man?" But SELF said, "Be careful of the big bad wolf." I stretched again as I do like a cat and said wonderful. "What are we having?

"You'll see.

"Ok, let me splash some water in my face to wake up and then I'm ready, I'm actually hungry."

Joachim and Chris had made my grazing platter, how spoiled could someone get. The grazing platter had a lot of vegetables prepared in different ways, aubergine with parmisan cheese, tomatoes and cucumbers in vinagrette, a few mushrooms, some beef with a wonderful béarnaise sauce, some pork with apples, a little pasta, all in tiny proportions to taste, a beautiful plate which I knew they had prepared for me, wonderful. Dessert was a special very chocolate cake and ice cream, what a delight.

I enjoyed it all.

"Wow, we might put a few pounds on you if we keep this menu going."

"Oh you want me a different way?" I was testing the waters.

"I want you as you are, I just want you to be well."

When we were finished Chris said he had a movie he wanted me to see so we cuddled on the couch upstairs and again I fell asleep, not out of lack of interest, just shear exhaustion. He carried me to bed and tucked me in. It wasn't until many hours later that the hands began to caress me, first a back rub, then my feet, then my legs and then the remainder until he knew he had me and entered and I was once again lost in him. In the early morning I stretched as always and reached for Chris but he wasn't there so I went in to shower and dress and then went downstairs and there he was reading with a half empty coffee cup and he just smiled, "I didn't want to wake you, I know how sensitive your are so I know how difficult this new homecoming might be."

"Thank you for understanding." And then I just went to cuddle with him and see what he was reading, it was Yeats. I said to SELF "What have I found?" I looked at him with what I'm sure was an amazed look on my face.

"I told you I read a lot and of many authors, are you surprised?"

"Yes a bit because people often tell me they read but it's often what I call airport books and not past historical, wonderful, artistic authors."

"Well I didn't pull this out to impress you. When you were here last time I couldn't slow down enough which is not good but now you are back because you decided and I am satisfied and comfortable and I have your companionship and this house is now a home because of you so I can relax and read or do what I want."

"But I haven't done anything."

"Oh yes, everyone is happier that you're here, Maria, Curt, my staff, my parents, the horses, I even think the grapevines, everyone and everything is smiling."

"Don't put such a big burden on me. I'm not everything but I do have a lot of love to give so maybe it exudes."

"Oh it exudes and it is wonderful, I cherish it."

I wanted to say something about the other woman but I couldn't go there, not now, or maybe ever. I would just accept what he was saying and see, hopefully he meant it. I would have to wait for the future and see where we would go. At the moment I was extremely comfortable and happy so why rock the boat.

"What would you like for breakfast?"

"Anything you want to prepare but you know . . . ."

"Yes, you won't eat much but you will taste everything."

"Yes." I could get very spoiled with this man.

Chris sensed that I was apprehensive so he took over, we had a light breakfast with Maria at home and then went to a small church in the neighborhood and walked along the lake. He was trying to quiet me and did a good job. In the afternoon we took a drive to Vevey and walked and talked and I knew I had found a new home at least for awhile. That evening we would be going again to the restaurant.

CHAPTER 12

On Saturday afternoon he had to go to the restaurant and the hotel to do some things and that we would be going to the restaurant in the evening so he just wanted me to rest and relax for the day, sounded fine to me.

I didn't tell him that I was meeting Steve to see what it was he wanted to tell me. He was there when I arrived and greeted me as always and then said leave your car and we'll go in mine to the restaurant. We just talked about things for awhile and then he came on like a competent attorney but in this instance my friend also saying he wanted to be sure some things were put into place for me to ensure my security.

"There is a lot of wealth involved and you are giving yourself to this person and should be protected. I know you may not think this way but I care too much for you to not have things organized for your benefit. Do you understand?"

"I understand and appreciate your concern."

"I want to set up the contracts so you will be the manager of the hotel and the vineyard distribution on a salary. I know you can do it."

"It all makes sense to me how do you think Chris will react?

"I think fine without a problem."

"So do the contracts and call him when you want to see us. I think he'll accept it and you know I'll do a good job at both."

"I know you will do a great job and it will protect you financially, but of course you could just come to me and I will take care of you at any level you want."

"Steve I can't respond right now."

"I understand."

"Why do you understand? Maybe you should just get your sword out and fight."

"Watch it, I might just do that because it is difficult to love and protect you but not have you. But it is interesting that you said that because you're coming closer aren't you? Remember in my profession we work to get what we want."

My emotional side was getting so confused, I was in love with two beautiful men, maybe I should just go back to Vienna and start over. All I could do was take his hand and smile and talk to SELF that I was crazy not to take this man. So he called Chris while we were sitting having lunch and said he wanted a meeting at the office on Monday, he told him why. It was set for 11:00 am.

When Chris came home I was ready but not yet dressed. He came up with a bottle of wine and we sipped and talked for a short time. He said it would be a festive evening with friends. I must have had an anxious look on my face because he took my hand and said, "Don't worry I'll take care of you and you'll have everything you need and be comfortable. He showered and was ready to get dressed but when he came out he just stopped and stared because since I had assumed it was to be a dressy evening I selected the new dress Gabrielle had just completed for me and was sitting waiting for him. "Another one that is spectacular, what taste."

It was a softer look, draping silver lame silk sleeveless with a cowl collar, lots of fabric in the skirt with an asymmetrical hem. I had never had so many dressy dresses, I had no need before but l now I did.

I had on the earrings Chris had given me when I visited the first time and with my hand purse and a shawl that was it. He asked me to show off the dress and I did, I got a hug and he got dressed in a tailored dark suit with a great silver tie so we were together even in colors selected which I appreciated because I understood he did it on purpose. We were ready to leave but then, "Wait a minute I have something for you." I thought now what. He produced what I knew was more jewelry. I opened the small box and there was another diamond bracelet not of the typical garish, overstated style but very simple to show off the stones. Again my mouth was open and I didn't know how to respond. He just looked and smiled and asked if I liked it.

"What is not to like, I don't really know what to say except thank you. I don't expect all these gifts."

"Your eyes tell me that you like it and that gives me so much joy." I would have to find the special time to tell him that he didn't have to buy me with gifts. Maybe that was wrong thinking, he was just wanting to please and give to someone he cared about. So with my new bracelet and new dress I felt more confident.

When we arrived Jacque and Hans greeted me with a kiss on either cheek what always seemed obligatory but both genuinely welcomed me back. I said good evening to Mom, Dad and Steve. Then Chris said, "Let's go into the kitchen so you can see Joachim and rest of the staff. Again they were all very warm in their greetings. They asked what I would prefer for dinner and with my small appetite didn't even know what to say but finally said "I'm a grazer, a little of many things so I can taste the wealth". They all smiled and said in French "Elle fera bien ici."

I left the kitchen because he was talking with Joachim about something so I thought to myself get out of the way. I went started talking with the musicians and of course was at the piano enjoying myself. He came out in a little while and looked at me but not in a happy way. "What are you doing, we have guests here you should be talking with."

I just said, "Well excuse me I thought you were busy and I was just having some fun here and everyone seemed to be enjoying it"

"That's all you think about. You look beautiful as always, I love that dress, I would have liked to parade you around and show you off but you had other ideas." This was a new attitude.

"I am not some sort of prize you parade or wear around your neck. I am myself and enjoy people but don't need to be paraded." I could not believe his egotism but I guess I would gradually learn more about that. I just went to our table and started chatting with Mom, Dad and Steve. Chris followed and introduced me to some other people that were joining us.

So my strong feminine side went to Steve and asked him to dance. It's that kind of thing you think, SELF said show him you're independent, don't let him tell you what you can or can't do.

He looked at me, smiled, got up and said, "Now we'll both be in trouble."

"Fine. He's out of line and I'm not going to get into an argument, I can enjoy myself too. Whatever bee is in his bonnet is his problem." He just laughed and we started dancing. Now Chris was glaring at me. I had not a clue what was with his attitude but made up my mind I was not going to worry about it. If he had some sort of problem he should tell me. Maybe it was male menopause.

The Janee wine started to flow, the cheeks got rosy and soon the ambiance was delightful. Then suddenly Chris took my hand and led me to the dance floor and we were off into our own world. The first was a slow piece but then the group started a jitter bug, upbeat and we were really off. I just followed, laughed, enjoyed and suddenly heard applause and cheers of more, more. We started laughing and then Chris whipped me away back to the table and whispered more later. What was more dancing on the floor or in bed probably both.

A little later Steve came over and whispered in my ear "Let's live dangerously, let's take on a Viennese waltz. I just smiled and said let's do it.

No one there knew that he had been to visit me so it was our secret. We danced and then he asked me to play the piano so I did while he sat at the bar watching smilingly and then Chris arrived to retrieve me, I knew he was unhappy about something. I decided I was just going to go with the flow and enjoy and worry about tomorrow, tomorrow.

After dinner I was ready to go home and was debating what to do since I had not driven myself to the restaurant so I went to Chris to ask if he was ready and he finally looked at me, complimented me on the dress again and said no we haven't danced enough and then I found myself on the dance floor. What was going on I didn't understand. He was not the loving, fun, relaxed Chris I knew from our past dancing. He acted somewhat possessed. We danced and then said he said ok we can go home now. Something was in his craw and he wanted to be in control which I hated.

I didn't understand his problem it was really an over-reaction. Finally we started for home but he continued to pout and have ruffled feathers. I simply didn't understand and he was not being conversant so I kept quiet. I guess as we go we keep learning about our partners, sometimes we wish we didn't. I was just bewildered about what his behavior had been. My main concern was what was underneath this wonderful charm he exuded.

I was exhausted so he let me undress and literally crawl into bed and sleep but in the wee small hours he was there asking for love which I could not refuse. He was tender but assertive and kept saying how could this little girl be so sensuous in bed. He said he adored me and just wanted to devour me, which I could not let happen. Then he crossed the line and said, "Do you have something going on with Steve?" I immediately tensed and was scared.

"Steve is our mutual friend and I enjoy his company and help."

"But you enjoy dancing with him don't you. I don't want anyone but me touching you in any sexual way."

"He doesn't, we just dance, laugh and have fun."

"I don't see it that way."

"Well I am very sorry but there is nothing going on. Is there with you somewhere?"

"Why would you ask that?"

"If you can ask so can I, don't forget that. And if there is I will be going back to Vienna, I won't stay. We discussed this once and you must know that."

Then he was very angry so I had a new clue. I didn't like where this was going, I was not a possession. I was a loving, giving human being and I would not accept less than a commitment on his part. I couldn't understand this other side of him. I picked up my purse, cell phone and a book and went to the guest room.

The next morning, while I was still in bed, he came in and just gave me a kiss and said I'll talk with you later. I think I had found the Achilles heel. All I could do was to go work in the stable with my friends and then go to the orphanage and school and do what I did best. It felt good to visit with Jacque who was now known as Jacque 2 as we had Jacque at the restaurant. My phone didn't ring except for Steve.

"Hey, good looking what are you up to?"

"About 105 pounds."

Laughter.

"What are you doing today?"

"I am just leaving the orphanage. At home I'm staying out of Chris's way. I'm in the guest room for awhile. He asked if we had something going on and I questioned him the same way, did he have something going on with whomever. I hit a male ego brick so I decided the guest room would be my place."

"I'm sorry. Be careful how much you confront him, he can get erratic."

"Right now I don't know what else to do, I think he'll get over it but maybe you should be careful too. After all the years you've been friends you may know him much better than I do."

"Maybe." How about lunch and we'll talk."

"Ok, is now a good time?"

"For you, anytime is a good time."

We went out to a small restaurant out of town so everyone wouldn't notice us and he asked me what had happened. He was concerned and said be careful which obviously frightened me.

"What do you know that you're not telling me?"

"I told you he can get erratic and I don't know sometimes what he's possible of. I can't know how strong your feelings are for him I just want you to be aware to be careful. I don't want anything to happen to you."

"Has he been terrible with women before?"

"A couple of rough instances have occurred in the past, I won't go into them. I do know he truly loves you, you are his princess but I do know how his behavior can change if he gets something in his head that you are always there just for him whenever he wants. Neither of us are doctors so we don't have an idea."

"You're telling me I should get out."

"Maybe, I can only tell you things and you have to decide."

"Thank you for being so straight forward with me. You know I may just run."

"Monique you can't always run, you have to make a decision. I'm here and I'll help you."

"Ok, I have to give Monique time to think. I wish I didn't think so much but I have to be true to myself or I can't be true to anyone else." At the moment I just wanted to think I am in fantasy land and want to enjoy and then fly away to Vienna where I can be back in control. SELF and I had a long conversation.

We met at Steve's office on Monday as planned at 11 am. He had drawn up contracts for us to sign giving me the responsibility of the hotel and wine distribution on a salary. He explained to Chris that it protected me financially should anything happen and would have some positive tax benefits. Chris was all for it and gave no argument which surprised me since he had been so angry this might be his way of making amends.

He said where do we sign. We left and I knew I would no longer be in the guest room.

When I got home I had to call my confident Jennie.

"Do you love him? If so, there is no question or problem. You must learn to trust again. I told you the first day at the skating rink that he fell in love at first sight and he would pursue you. He can offer you everything. Look you're now set financially with the hotel and vineyard which is great."

"But I really don't know anything of his past. I do know he has been a womanizer."

"Probably but think about it you came here for an adventure, a different life and it is opening to you. Take a chance."

"But it seems too perfect"

"Nothing is ever truly perfect so take the best and be happy."

"Your right. Bye for now we'll talk via email or by phone soon. I'll keep you posted on what's happening."

CHAPTER 13

Chris and got on with our lives he at the restaurant and playing soccer a couple times a week. I was busy with the horses, orphanage, gallery communication and lots of reading and writing and of course the evenings spent at the restaurant, always busy. All was good between us.

With all the projects I had talked with Chris about doing a cookbook with all the special dishes he and Joachim had created. We would come up with a theme, I would put it together with all their input as to what dishs and accompanying wines and use the photographer I used with the artist studios. Joachim had also developed over the years a combination of various seasonings he liked to use for lots of dishes and I said we should package or bottle that and have it ready at the same time as the book release. Boy, I sure created projects for myself but it was the creative side of me and I loved it. We could use the proceeds for a foundation which could benefit a lot of children and maybe even animals.

"I'll think about it" was all he said.

I just thought, well thanks a lot for all the enthusiasm and support.

I was interested in the property adjacent to ours and called Dad to talk with him about it. Chris and I had walked down to it but his idea was we had enough acres and enough to control. Dad and Mom came up to the house so we could go and look. I trusted his judgment because he knew so much about grapes having learned from his father and had built the Janee vineyard up to such a high level. I had so much to learn. He thought it was a good idea and perhaps we could be partners in the purchase. So I laid out a plan to talk with Chris about it again. At first he said, "I told you I think it's more than I can handle we already have enough to take care of." Then I thought maybe I'm only here for awhile as his doll so he doesn't want me involved after all we weren't married. I kept telling him of the possible plan and soon he started to listen and his business ears went up so he said, "Ok, let's look closer at this." Now I knew we were on the right track. It wasn't what I could accumulate for us it was for my foundation that would help others, that was part of my dream. We had more than enough, we had the wear withal and intelligence to create something to help others, not just party animals or takers.

And then one of those bricks came into the road. We were asleep when the phone rang. Chris bounded out of bed and said the restaurant was on fire he had to go right away. A feeling of panic came over me but I said ok you go and I'll be down right away. Evidently there was an electrical problem that sparked the fire in the kitchen. The firefighters were there and they managed to put it out before the entire building was engulfed. The kitchen was gone, the rest of the building was totally smoke ridden so we were going to have a lot of work ahead. We had to rebuild or Chris would be lost. Steve was there and said after the investigation he was sure our insurance would cover most of the cost of rebuilding. My mind started and I said ok we have to move Chez Janee to the hotel so we have work to do there. Chris just looked at me as if I were crazy. I said, "it can be done". We'll do a quick refurbishment which we've been talking about and everyone will just come there."

Dejected Chris said, "it's too much."

"Not if we work together and pull in all the staff and the people I know here. We can do this, believe me, let's get moving." Steve said the adjusters would be there around 3:00 pm. I went to the hotel and looked over the kitchen and dining room and made my notes

"Chris give me a list of what you need in the kitchen and I will order it and have it here tomorrow." Someone had to take charge. He started with the negatives and I said assertively "get off it, I want your restaurant functioning again."

There was a room adjacent to the kitchen which had only been used for storage so I decided we could install another cutting board table in there and storage cabinets so added that to the list. I got my man who had done the painting and redecoration for his parents condo over immediately and told him what I wanted. I went with him to purchase the paint. White wash the storage room and the kitchen area. Mauve over the wallpaper in the dining room and I said, "It has to be done by tomorrow even if you have to work through the night." Then I called the florist and told him what plants I needed for instant décor. I called to have a large mirror done for over the mantel and said I needed it the next day or wouldn't order it. Everyone needed to work and earn money they just needed to produce quickly.

Chris had his list together so I called the kitchen supply place we dealt with in the past and ordered everything; they said they would deliver at 8 pm that evening. Amazing how money and drive can do wonders. Next we had to create a sign saying where Chez Chris would be and I had to convince Chris and Joachim they could do a special limited menu for the evening. For all that he had given me and shared with me I knew I had to be strong to return this to him that's love in my book. I gave each of the staff specific chores for scrubbing, polishing, whatever to get things in order. I sent one staff member out with all of the linens to be washed, pressed and returned by the next day. The fireplace would be cleaned, checked out and extra wood brought in. I knew the hotel needed renovation so here was the start. I was keeping track of the euros we would spend and knew that would be back to us if we opened as soon as possible and it would also keep Chris's spirits up.

Next was the meeting with the insurance adjustor at 3:00 pm who with lots of questions gave us the resolution. Almost everything would be taken care of so we could start rebuilding in a couple of days. I just kept telling myself to keep up the energy I knew eventually I would crash. We went back to the hotel and the painting was partially done and was going to look great. The art that had been hung was so trivial so I thought about pieces we had at home that we could use temporarily in the dining room until we bought new things. I saw it as an art gallery so I would also have to pull on the local artists to share with the concept of exposure for their works. It would be a long evening and a long day tomorrow but I knew we could do it and Chris would be ok.

The next morning we went to the hotel and found everything in order; painting done, floor lacquered, plants delivered, kitchen in order although they would have to arrange everything as to how they worked, mirror and art hung. To help keep up their spirits I had also ordered knew aprons and working towels so they were ready. The creative spirit has to be in everything but it sometimes needs a good boost. Chris looked exhausted but I told him he needed to keep going through the first night and he would see how it could work until the old restaurant was restored. We went home to rest and then dress for the evening. He left early to help with the cooking, I said I would be down later. I called Steve to discuss the insurance again and he assured me that we were ok and we would be reimbursed for almost everything. Steve said, "I've heard what you're doing, it's all around town. Is it going to work?"

"If I have anything to say about it, it will work and it will help Chris from going into a down side."

"When you love, you love don't you."

"Isn't that what is all about, loving, sharing, supporting."

"Would you do the same for me?"

Without any hesitation I said, "Yes, without question."

"You don't make my side easy do you."

"I can only be in one place at a time and since I've chosen this path for now, right or wrong, I have to go through it and try to figure it out. Chris has problems I don't completely understand but in his way has been good to me and I need to return that."

"Your choice."

"Yes for now and knowing you I would expect you to respect that."

"I do and I'll support in any way I can."

By 6:00 pm I was dressed and ready at the new restaurant. Chris had been there working with Joachim on the food so I just brought his clothes to him and he showered and changed in one of the hotel rooms. He was so nervous because no one was there yet. I just said wait they will appear. 7:00pm still no one but at 7:30 the flood began. People began coming in and very excited about a new ambiance, after all it was a small community so anything new had to be checked out. By 8pm we were full with a waiting line and Chris was smiling and wondering how he would feed everyone. The band started playing and and he knew he had to dance and found me and swept be onto the floor and we started as always to enjoy ourselves. Often when we danced no one else would participate so we were the entertainment, this night we were and in great form. Our dancing enlivened the entire group and soon others joined in. At one point Chris just held me in the middle of the floor in a big hug as his thank you. We were again a success and knew all these people would be back at sometime until the old restaurant was functioning again. No accolade to me, just the message that many things are possible you just have to go for it and work hard at it and it can come to fruition.

When everyone had left we just sat for a minute in a kind of disbelief of the evening and then started to laugh. I just went "whew, how did we bring this off? Chez Janee at the hotel was a success and would continue to be until we rebuilt the original and then the hotel restaurant would be an enhancement to the hotel for the future as we renovated the entire place. We went home totally exhausted from the day and half of work and the evening but that didn't keep Chris from caressing and wanting love. I began to think he was insatiable.

We started the rebuilding project for the old restaurant, Chris was very excited and eager to get on with it. It would take awhile but he could now have a chance to make some changes and be sure the building was in excellent condition while having the other restaurant going. I was hoping this would keep him so busy he wouldn't become restless which he was sometimes and I knew where that restless nature would take him. I kept up with Paul and the gallery and the vineyard and helped in whatever capacity I could with the rebuilding.

And finally at the end of August the new Chez Janee was ready and so we planned the opening celebration which would be a black tie event, as special as we could make it. Chris and Joachim had planned a new menu which included the "grazing platter." Chris was so excited and I was happy for that. He kept asking me what I would wear and I just said it is a surprise and it is not about me it is about your restaurant and what you love. "But I love you and want to know."

"You know I will be in something special so don't worry about that, worry about the food and the service, I'll be there and do what I do." I had a special dress to wear from Gabrielle in a wonderful raspberry color with some satin and chiffon, fitted at the top but with lots of fabric in the skirt to look great for dancing. I intended to do a lot of dancing with whomever.

Chris called me around 6:00 pm and sounded frantic, "When are you going to be here?"

"Just let Jacque come or if you need him Curt can bring me down, I just don't want to have to drive back late at night. I'm dressed and ready." Always a sense of panic and pressure.

"I need Jacque so please ask Curt."

"No problem, don't worry, I'll ask him right now."

"Do you need anything from home?"

"I brought everything with me I just need to go shower and dress."

"Relax, it will be great. I guarantee it."

"Keep me on course Monique, I need you so much."

"I will, it's just another performance. It's going to be such fun, just make sure the food is good. I'll be there in just a few minutes."

"Hurry."

So Curt drove me down the hill saying he would come back later with Maria. I wanted everyone I cared about to be there so had definitely included them.

Curt dropped me at the front. I took a minute before going in and talked with SELF, "here I am in this wonderful, romantic part of Switzerland with all this excitement. Did I ever dream I would be living in Montreux, flying to Vienna to be part of an art gallery, having two wonderful men to take care of me, I had to pinch myself to know I wasn't dreaming. When I walked in everyone was running around checking everything. The task master had them moving. Hans saw me and just stared and smiled and then Jacque went right to the kitchen and Chris came out looking wonderful in his tux and he too stared and then I began to wonder if there was something wrong. Chris just came to me and said, "Wow, that dress, I love it and you, took me to the dance floor and whirled me around. "Thank you for everything. We are going to dance the night away."

I asked if I could help in some way and he said, "Just be your special self, please play the piano. I have to do some things still in the kitchen but I will hear your music." So I started to play and sing and worked with the musicians. Then people started arriving so I became the hostess, greeting, chatting being my smiley self. I was talking with some people when there was a tap on my shoulder, Steve, whom I turned to and greeted with a big hug and he said right away let's dance so we did. He was so handsome in his tux I was starting to really get confused with these two gorgeous men

both of whom I enjoyed for different reasons. Then more
people started arriving so I had to continue my greetings;
finally Chris came from the kitchen and started in too. Then
he took my hand and said we have to dance and we became
the entertainment once again. It was so much fun because he
had to start out with "Rock Around the Clock", Chatanooga
and then he grabbed a red rose from the bouquet on the
bar, handed it to me, "Madamoiselle Monique please we
must do the tango which we had never done before so I just
followed his lead sexy beyond words. He took my hand both
of us laughing while he escorted me to the table for dinner. I
greeted everyone but was somehow frightened about where I
was going. Steve was seated next to me and under the table
he just took my hand and looked at me with that knowing,
loving look. Dinner arrived I did my typical nibbling because
Jochaim had my special plate with a variety of things. "Pour
toi mademoiselle Monique. As always we ate, talked, laughed
with Chris, Steve and James telling stories and jokes. I felt it
was a bit of a show on my part but I would follow through.
I loved our friends, dancing, food but sometimes it became
a little superficial since it happened so often but I realized
tonight with the new restaurant it was very special so joined
right in.

Steve asked me to dance again and we did to some slow
numbers. "I know you are intelligent, loving, intuitive but I
will tell you to watch out."

"With Chris?"

"Yes."

"I will try be careful with my heart."

"I know you will just know I just don't want you hurt, I
love you and will always take care of you. I keep hoping when
you're ready you'll understand and come to me. I want you
more than a friend."

I just looked at him and couldn't say anything. I was
lost, I just wanted to go back to Vienna or the States and get
back to simplicity but how could I pass up these two men

who were wonderful in their own ways. I had to have a long conversation with SELF. How could I be in love with two men at the same time.

Mr. Williamson arrived and I had a respite from the seriousness. I was so happy he had come and we immediately did a waltz, it was so elegant European stylish. He joined us at the table for dessert and then asked if I would join him again and I did. He was the crème de crème and I asked nothing at this point but to dance. I loved it. So the evening was successful, enjoyable, a bit confusing for me but that was sometimes a normal state of affairs with me lately.

When everyone finally left it was over and we were going home, I just wanted to sleep but Chris did not have that on his mind and so a late evening of love making.

So the original Chez Janee was functioning once again and becoming even more popular which kept Chris busy. I often went in to assist with food preparation or sometimes just shopping at the market for what they needed and then I often had to play the piano, dance and be the hostess. I had more than a full time job but it was exciting. I did often get very fatigued so I put in the back of my head I needed to check with Dr Bovet sometime. Now that the restaurant was functioning it became time to begin renovating the hotel so it would be up to date. I as always started making plans.

One day I was relaxing on the bed reading when Chris called and said the ambassador from Belgium for Switzerland was arriving for dinner that evening and of course he needed me there. He needed his tux and shoes and wanted me dressed to the hilt so I said I would be there by 6pm. Duty beckoned. We often had so called celebrities at the restaurant. So I got ready with his things and dressed in a wonderful dress Gabrielle had designed for me a long very slim black dress, smashing if I do say myself. I drove down the hill and parked in the back. When I entered all I got were stares "is something wrong?"

"No you look fantastic, I love that dress, another Gabrielle."

"Yes"

"We must have a shop for her here."

"I don't know, right now she is my designer."

"But she will always make special things for you. Think of what we could do to create a business. My Chris had great ideas but how many projects were we willing to take on. Maybe it would be good for Gabrielle, I would think about it.

So I talked with the musicians and played the piano for awhile until Chris came down looking absolutely suave. If ever a tux was made for someone it was Chris. Then we heard the cars arriving outside with the ambassador's entourage and so got ready to greet them. Once I saw them I said to SELF we need to do something to help them lighten up and fly right. Chris saw my expression and shook his head. I ignored it. Introductions were made. The ambassador was soon talking about places in Belgium I had been to not Chris and soon we were getting a little livelier. The band started a great song "Let's Do It" so Chris said let's dance and we did in our style. It was sometimes sex on the floor. When we came back to the table the ambassador and wife were laughing and tapping fingers so I said "Sir may I have the next dance." He smiled and said, "But of course" That left Chris to take care of the wife. He was a relatively good dancer and we conversed a bit. Chris was working hard had being his charming self. When we returned to the table she had a change of attitude and was "getting with it." Then came dessert, a special chocolate cake Joquim had created and she was in awe. We had found her Achilles heel. She started babbling about how wonderful it was here, the best restaurant, the most delightful people, etc. They even went out to dance too. I spoke a bit with the ambassador about horses and his eyes lit up as I guess he was quite a horseman. As the wine flowed he complimented us on the selection and asked questions about the winery. This gave me the opening to say we were trying to distribute outside of

Switzerland. I immediately clarified everything for him and he gave me all the information I needed, distributor name, phone, email. He said he had a contact and would have him get in touch with me and I could follow through.

After dessert they graciously said they were ready to return to their hotel. They had been to Geneva on business then wanted to visit Montreux and the next day would be on their way to Paris.

Chris thanked me for being so hospitable with them, they had seemed to enjoy themselves. I don't know what you did but they were out there dancing and I think from the look on your face you made a deal."

"A deal to send him information and some wine. He has a distributor in mind that he will contact and then in time will contact me. He was also interested in the cookbook, so we'll see if he is full of bull or is a follow through man."

"You are a tough cookie under all that sweetness."

"I've been taught that if you're going to do something do it right and to the utmost. I'm thinking about how many kids and animals I might be able to help so I'll work on it. Chris, I could be happy riding, reading, writing, working on art projects. I took this on as an opportunity to help a lot of children and animals, that's where I see part of the proceeds going. I'll find the energy to do it."

"Will you have the same energy for me tonight?"

"Haven't I always? Right now I don't want to stay around much longer, I would like to go home."

"Ok, I got the message." Within a half hour Jacque was driving me home. I took a long hot shower and put on the new negligee that Chris had purchased and crawled into bed.

Maria knocked and asked if she could get me anything. I said I was very tired, which seemed to be more often lately, and would love some tea. Several minutes later she brought up the tray and I invited her to join me. We chatted for awhile and then I said I needed to sleep and so crawled into bed. A couple of hours later Chris was home. He came to bed and of course reached to cuddle me. I generally could not resist him but tonight I was nonresponsive. The next morning I got up early to go work the horses. Chris was slumbering fine.

While working out Sasha I saw Chris with Curt watching what I was doing. When I brought him in Chris came over to me for our morning kiss. I didn't know if Chris felt the way I did about the horses. Were the horses just here prepared to go for a ride, did he not get into their personalities and empathize with their needs. I had so many questions. SELF and I we're talking a lot.

Chris walked back with me to the house saying he had to go to the restaurant, the bank and meet with Steve but would be home early and cook us some dinner. I went up to read and relax but the devil said I should check in with Steve which I did. He said no he had not called about getting together, maybe he meant to but hadn't. Steve said don't worry, he runs sometimes like a rabbit and forgets what he planned. But of course my mind started in and I had to talk to SELF. As I was commiserating about his whereabouts I heard his car in the driveway. He came in with a large bouquet of flowers and a big sack with what he would do for dinner. So I kicked myself and told SELF "stop being so worrisome. He was home as planned, he had a right to do what he wanted, as did I. It was just that little question always sitting on my shoulder, it might be there forever. Little did I know that something was beginning there would be more times when I wasn't sure where he was or what he was doing and with whom.

We had a lovely, homey evening with a new pasta dish he wanted to try, mixed salad and for dessert a apricot sorbet they had made at the restaurant. He was mine for the evening. We watched a great Astaire and Rogers movie "Shall We Dance" and even found energy to try out some of the dances, laughing all the way. It was so wonderful to be with him, so much life, though I sensed something restless in him. I said a very simple thing to SELF it is so wonderful to be loved and loved in return, nothing else matters. Then he wanted to watch a western movie and I soon fell asleep in his arms. Soon all was quiet and I was being caressed and once again more love making. I knew eventually this would diminish so was enjoying it while it was new.

CHAPTER 14

The next morning over breakfast Chris said, "I want you to apprentice at the restaurant so that if anything happens to me you will know everything and can take over."

I'm sure my eyes got wider, "nothing is going to happen to you."

He said, "One never knows. I just want you to know so you could manage well. Will you do it?"

I said, "of course, I've always wanted to know more about cooking so when do I start?"

"Anytime you want." "Ok tomorrow morning. What do I do learn how to wash dishes first?"

Laughing he said no you will start with the vegetable preparation, how to chop, etc."

"Ok, I can do that and we'll even have more time together." He smiled,

"Now you have the picture and you can keep track of me."

"I don't want to keep track of you, we have no leashes."

"Well I need one because I get curious and stray. You're the only one that keeps me on track."

"I don't want that job, you have to be who you are."

"That I will be but it might not be what you expect or want. Will you always think first that you love me with all of my faults before you do anything strange?"

Which meant would I run away. "I will try to remember that." So some sort of another level of understanding was met, I thought, without either of us knowing what would come in the future, I already had a sense what it might be but didn't want to think about it now.

I went to the restaurant around 12 and Joachim put me at the vegetable station. I told him to treat me as an employee and I would produce. I washed the vegetables, drained them and then began to learn to chop very quickly and efficiently. It was fun I was in the midst of this great activity. The others just looked and shook their heads at me as if I were crazy but Joachim understood. I washed and chopped for 3 hours and then said now what. They looked at me in amazement that I was enjoying myself. It was drudgery work for them but they did get to eat the results so what was the problem. I would keep working and eventually find out. Joachim said that was it for the day, I had done a great job and he would put me to the next step tomorrow and so I began my job for several weeks at the restaurant along with all the other things I tried to do. As I left the staff were still shaking their heads I knew with a question, why does this lady want to do this. Little did I know that it would help in the future.

As I was leaving Chris arrived and asked me how the first day was. I said fine and that I was going home. He said he had some people coming in from Zurich and would I please come back for dinner. I said if it was important I would be there. He said he needed to come home to shower and dress because it was very important. I asked is it formal? How shall I dress? He just answered beautifully as you always do. That gave me a lot to go on. I asked him who the people were. All he said was business people. That gave me a lot to go on. So . . . . later I got ready and decided to go smashing and selected my long black dress again with the slit up the front to the knees. Chris didn't offer for someone to come for me so I just got in the car and started down the hill.

My cell phone rang and Chris said, "Are you ready?"

"I'm on my way half way down the hill."

"I was going to send someone for you." "Well I guess you forgot. I'm fine I'll be there in a few minutes."

"Be careful."

I arrived at the restaurant, parked in the back but walked to the front to make my entrance. Hans and Jacque just smiled and shook their heads with appreciation. Jacque came to take my wrap and purse as always to put it in my special spot in the bar and escorted me to the table. Chris was at the table and almost reacted with surprise staring at me with admiration but then quickly introduced me to everyone. I was in my acting mode so I knew I could pull this off, not really knowing what I was "pulling off". They were business men interested in the local property and other commercial ventures. I really did not like them but conversed civilly with them. They were the types that wanted to buy up property below market level and build new condominiums and other high rise hotels. I was against this because it would destroy the beauty of the area, it was such a charming small city, there was already a few taller buildings but a comfortable level of population. I knew Chris's father would agree. I guess I was of the old generation but it was important to me if this was to be my home. So what was I to do. Chris saw the dollars. We had dollars and didn't need to assist these people. So I said to self how do I keep them from doing this. If I were to contact the real estate people they would rub their hands and do anything to sell no matter the consequence. Perhaps it would be up to me to give a negative picture. Up all the prices, talk about the traffic, unwanted growth in population. I was thinking.

We went through dinner, eating, laughing while Chris kept his eyes on me. Finally he asked me if I would play the piano, what a relief from these jerks. I excused myself from the table and greeted clients on my way to the bandstand. Talked with the musicians for a minute and then started to play. I was going to send messages out don't consider helping these people. The band piano player and I often did great duets mostly with rock and jazz and we got going, me doing boogie bass sometimes and sometimes the treble. We just improvised and had a great time as did the listeners. I must have played and sang for a half an hour before Chris came up and motioned for the hired musician that he wanted to dance with me.

While dancing he said" you are against this right?"

"Right. I don't want my home desecrated by these jerks."

"We could make money"

"We have money and can make more with good management of what we have and live in a beautiful atmosphere."

"So what you are saying forget these guys?"

"Yes don't work with them it will be awful." They are going to rape the area, don't you see."

"It always takes my baby to put me in the right direction. You are right. Ok we won't help them and forget what their kick back might be."

"Chris as I see it we don't need their money. Now it's how to prevent them from going ahead anyway." If they come in to develop I'm out of here."

Chris stopped in our dance and said, "You mean that and I said "Yes."

"Now you just gave me fighting words, you're not going anywhere without me so there, that's the answer. I will make it impossible for them to proceed."

"Thank you. Pull all of the strings."

"I will."

We refused their offer and in the next few days talked with many of the store owners and other businesses even the real estate people explaining what the developers wanted to do and how it would be so negative to Montreux and they agreed, they would not work with them. We had one the battle.

With all that was going on I still found time to help at the orphanage with the children's studies, activities including music. Of course I continue my special time with Jacque 2 who was such a love. I wished I could be with him more often.

CHAPTER 15

Chris asked me one evening about Serhalin and I said I had been in contact with the lady leasing him and he seemed ok but was being a bit obnoxious and I knew why. He was mine and he was unhappy. He said, "I want to bring him to you so I need the contact information." I just said it would be very expensive and I didn't know how he would take the trip, perhaps I should just go back and sell him. "No, we're not selling him, he should be here, he'll make it ok."

One late afternoon I heard a truck coming up the hill and wondered what it was so went out and saw "horse transport." The drivers asked if they were at the Janee vineyards because they had a delivery to make. They opened the doors at the back of the truck and led out a very thin, nervous grey Arabian horse who started bellowing, my Serhalin was here. I simply thanked the drivers, gave them a tip and took the lead line and I had a big head on my shoulder. He was shaking and scared but I soothed him. Curt came out to see and just smiled, "So he has arrived."

"Yes, one of my babies. Please I'm sure he wants some food but will take it easy until he settles down. I will stay with him for awhile and then lead him around so he gets more comfortable, he's had a long journey."

"I will help Mademoiselle Monique, we will take care of him and fatten him up a bit."

"I called Chris at the restaurant."

"Hey, good looking what can I do for you?"

"You already have. He arrived a few minutes ago and we are trying to settle him down."

"So we have moved a part of your home to your new home. Is he ok?"

"Skinny like me and quite nervous but Curt and I will settle him down. I can't thank you enough, you don't know what it means to me."

"I think I do and if it gives you pleasure I am happier. When I get home you can introduce him to me."

"But of course said the horse."

"I'll come up about 5 and then I need to come back and hopefully you will come with me."

"OK, whatever, I just want to enjoy him for awhile and make sure he is comfortable."

"Now I have competition."

"No, you don't but I would suspect I might."

"Monique, what are you saying?"

"Nothing, I'll see you in a bit."

He didn't get home until around 10:00 pm with excuses of people dropping into the restaurant and he had to stay as they were important clients from the past. But why hadn't he called me I asked SELF. That question on my shoulders reared again. Even though to some I was living like a princess I agreed except for this foreboding over the intimacy question.

We waited until morning for him to see my Serhalin since he had settled down and I didn't want him to get anxious again. Serhalin I have to say reacted to him quite well because he was a horse person. That evening we got ready to go back to the restaurant for whatever was happening there. When we arrived I found it was a group of some crazier friends of Chris who loved to party. I went to the restaurant to have fun with people who wanted to be merry, eat, dance and enjoy. These were really partiers and a couple of the men came on so strong to me that I began to understand some of the women that had been involved before. I just kept smiling, avoiding, going into the kitchen and finally went to the piano but that even turned them on more. Eventually I just said "I'm out of here and asked Jacque to drive me home. Chris was so in to it that he eventually saw I wasn't there and then my cell started to ring. "Where are you, what's wrong?"

"I couldn't take anymore of the come ons I'm not a party girl, I have fun but I'm not superficial, sorry, so I came home. Do what you want."

"Monique, why didn't you say something when you were here I would punch them out."

"But you were there Schatz and should have seen. I expect more from you. I told you beware, I am a free spirit and when I feel something I will be a horse. Thank you for bringing me Serhalin but no thank you to tonight's party." And then I hung up and would not answer his calls after.

He arrived home about two hours later in an obvious angry state so I just pretended to be sound asleep and when he reached for me I did not respond. He kept trying to get me to react and I finally said I cannot. He got very angry so I just got out of bed, put on my robe, took my phone and purse and went to one of the guest rooms.

In the morning, he came in to apologize and say they just got carried away, that I should have said something and he would have told them to lay off, that I was forbidden territory.

"But why did you put me into this position? Why didn't you anticipate it."

"I once told you that men will "sniff you out", you are so sensuous, and you will have to be aware of that. You didn't like when I said I needed to put a leash on you, not to prevent you from doing things but to protect you, but if you are to be mine alone I may have to do that."

"No leash thank you, I just expect respect for my feelings and my qualities as a woman." The whole thing disgusted me. "I want to be by myself for awhile, I'm going to ride, walk, play the piano and I don't want intrusions."

"So you're shutting me down."

"For awhile yes until I can regroup and see what Monique wants. I would appreciate if you would respect my declaration."

"Done, not happily, but done."

I called Steve and told him what had occurred and that I had to figure out if I would stay or be on my way.

"I remember the party times I spent with him. I got over it I had hoped he had too but maybe not. If you think you are on your way you have to come to me first, don't just disappear. I am no longer a partier and I care about you too much to let you go where I can't find you. I will come and get you now and put you into an apartment until you decide what you feel and want. Just tell me."

"I'm here for now but I won't put up with the junk, it's just not me or how I want life to be. I may take you up on the offer just give me a little time to see what I decide."

So we went through a week of my being in the guest room, I didn't pick up on Steve's offer just kept doing what I wanted until Chris came begging to see if I had done my thing and we could be together again. With his charm and my feelings for him I had to succumb and once again be his lover. After all he had brought one of my babies to me.

Around the end of October Mom and Dan Janee expressed the interest in moving from Zurich to Montreux. They were getting older and I think wanted to be closer to us even if it meant giving up their roots and good friends in Zurich. I said the friends would come to visit and I would help them make new ones.

So I shopped for a condo by the lake and found a 3 bedroom one that I felt would fit their needs. It would need renovation but I loved doing that. They came for a visit and loved it said to go ahead and start in. We went shopping before they were to return to Zurich to look at colors, carpet and lighting. They left it all in my hands. When they came back they stayed at the hotel until there furniture and other things arrived from Zurich. When it came we placed everthing plus I added some plants and flowers on the balcony. It was another show place. Chris was very pleased and I think glad to have them close by. He had seen the condo but hadn't been by to see the finished product so when ready I called him and he came over with a bottle of champagne to toast in their new home. I spent time getting them oriented to their new city and to new activities so they would remain independent.

We were now at the end of November with Christmas in the future. So I started making plans for gifts and decorations. Chris's Mom and Dad went with me to Geneva for some shopping. Chris left it to me to decide on everything although I did get him out to pick out the tree which Curt would pick up and help me put up. Mom and Dad wanted a tree for the new condo. Jennie and Peter said they would come as their children had other plans, Steve of course would come, Mom and Dad, Curt and Maria, maybe even Paul and Juliana and for Christmas Eve I invited our winery manager and family, Father Joseph amd the sisers so I needed several gifts. I wanted it to be a very special Christmas Eve and Day for all. Perhaps even Joachim and Jacque would come over for Christmas Eve. I could find gifts for everyone except what do you find for the man who has everything Chris?

So doing some research for Paul, my own writing, the horses and Christmas I kept very busy plus Chris wanted me frequently at the restaurant as, I guess, as a type of hostess. Very soon it was December 20th and Curt had the tree up and the ladder to put the upper decorations on the 12 foot tree while Maria and I started decorating the lower portions. Then the outside lights and the bows for the stable doors. I ordered poinsettias from our florist Herr Robinette which he delivered because I wanted 10, some quite large. When finished I just sat back and enjoyed. What a wonderful house to decorate. I finished wrapping all the packages with the most gorgeous paper and bows. It was the first time I had the opportunity to do something on this scale so I was going to enjoy. I had special ribbons and decorations for the dining table. At least I didn't have to worry about the menu, Chris would take control of that. He suggested we go to the restaurant on the 23rd. he and Jacque would prepare something special. He asked what I wanted for dinner and we decided on roast beef tenderloin and all the extras for Christmas Eve and he insisted on Turkey and a goose for Christmas day saying he knew I had missed the American Thanksgiving. Once in awhile he amazed me about how in tune he was to my needs without me saying anything. So now I could relax, everything was in order. Jennie and Peter were arriving on the 23rd at around 2:00 pm at the airport and then around 4:00 pm they would be here from Geneva so I could just enjoy being with them. Paul and Juliana would get in a little later on the train.

Chris came home the evening of the 20th and saw the tree and just sat down to enjoy. He wanted to hold me while we looked at the tree and he was very wistful. "Only with you here would we have this and I love it." I asked him if he was sure. He just looked at me and kissed me and said. "don't ask those kinds of questions you know the answer."

Jennie and Peter arrived around 4:00 pm on the 23rd saying traffic was heavy so they were a little delayed and then the holiday started. They brought their packages in and we added them to the many already under the tree. I settled them in one of the guest rooms and said when ready to come down. Peter was already checking out the house for all the architectural qualities, both were excited to be with us. An hour later Paul called that they had arrived so Chris asked Curt to go pick them up, they were soon settled in our hotel. We all then proceeded to the restaurant where Mom and Dad, James and Daphne and Steven joined us. Chris and Joachim prepared scampi for hors 'oeuvre, veal scaloppini, pasta and a delicious vegetable salad, excellent food, conversation and of course the Janee wine. For dessert flambeed crepes, another lovely evening. All were weary to we turned early as tomorrow was the Eve and we still had things to do and enjoy.

In the morning after breakfast, Chris went to get some things he needed from the restaurant while we went out to the stable to talk with the horses. Peter also wanted to walk a little in the vineyards which we did. Jennie looked at me and saying that we had a paradise. I said as long as the master continues on the current path and she understood what I meant. Chris returned with his parents and the festivities started. Maria was so happy and joined in to assist. We were all in the kitchen probably driving Chris crazy as that was his domain. He gave us all a task and we listened to the master. He had prepared "nibble" platters for us for the afternoon saying dinner was the most important for this festive evening but he knew from breakfast until the Eve we would want something but not a full lunch. We all took a little quiet time and then prepared for the Eve. There were Jennie and Peter, Paul and Juliana, Steve, Chris's parents, Maria and Curt, Jacque and Joachim and even Jacque 2. Later our vineyard manager and his wife would come for dessert and to share presents. I loved their two little girls so it would be a lovely, giving, festive evening with a whole mixed family.

I had decorated the tables with long ribbons and small poinsettias, the music was on so the ambiance was set. I smiled and said to SELF if only once in a life time, this is perfect, everyone should enjoy. Now everything would be wonderful. Chris excused himself and said he needed something from the restaurant a pot or some ingredient but wouldn't be long. I questioned it because we had such a complete kitchen but I didn't pursue with questions but SELF was giving me a bad time. His cell phone had rung several times during the day and he excused himself to take it in another room. Also the home phone had rung a couple of times and he just said let the machine pick up, I'll check it later. Since most people called me on my cell I seldom picked up on the home phone. I just decided to enjoy my friends and not worry. Soon we were together talking and laughing and then Chris returned with Jacque who brought out the champagne and we started to celebrate and soon dinner was prepared. A beef tenderloin cooked to perfection, several vegetable dishes, fruits, my favorite gnocchis, a real banquet.—my man did it again. I had cooked before for friends but this was an artist who could put this together and then sit down and enjoy with us. We dined and of course kept sharing talk and laughter and then I said Mrs. Claus is ready for presents so we all gathered in the living room near the tree.

I sat on a pillow on the floor by the tree and started to figure out how to best disburse the gifts. I passed them out and everyone got something special that they seemed pleased. There was a very big box for me from Chris. I was afraid because it was being disguised and inside was an engagement ring which I was ready to accept considering the current situation. "Wait a minute before you open that." Curt had gone out and when he returned he had an animal sleeping basket and there was my wonderful little golden lab puppy. He was adorable, I looked at Chris and he just gave me that wonderful smile. He had a little diaper on because they were afraid what might happen as I picked him up and caressed him. Chris said, "watch this, he will cling to her." And he did right away, he was so precious. They asked what I would name him and I said "Shady." I wasn't sure why it just fit.

Then Chris said, "With all that dinner we need to take a walk." Everyone just looked at him thinking leave us alone to be in comfort. "No we have to go as far as the stable." So everyone got on jackets and started the short hike. I wondered what this was all about. When we got to the stables I heard another whinny, a new whinny and then I saw a young Arabian colt in the stall next to Serhalin. I couldn't believe it. Before I even reacted with Chris I went in the stall with my white Christmas Eve pant suit on and hugged him to welcome him and of course I was then a mess. I immediately said hello Sasha. Where these names came from I didn't have a clue. I went out and put my arms out to Chris for a hug and thanked him for such a wonderful gift. Now I had Serahlin, Shady and Sasha, a whole family, such blessings plus Shambar and Schambalie, Chris's two Lippiazaners, all my ss's were in a row.

Then he said, "what about the big box?"

"I said too much tonight, let's wait until tomorrow so we have something special on Christmas Day."

He looked disappointed but agreed.

So was Christmas Eve.

The reason I didn't want to face the "big box" was that I had an idea what was in it at the bottom and didn't want to face because of the phone calls. Chris's cell phone had rung a couple of times during the day of Christmas Eve, he took it into another room and just said it was a friend. Also he had excused himself on Christmas Eve in the afternoon saying he forgot something at the restaurant and needed to go but would be back quickly. He actually was gone for 3 hours. I knew he was the artist in the kitchen, but our kitchen had everything. My horse ears were up checking things out. On the holiday why this behavior? SELF and I were having quite a conversation.

During the day the home phone also rang and he said just let the machine pick up saying he would check it later. Then Steve gave me a long look and I began to wonder if I should know something. Most people called me only on my cell number so I seldom picked up the home phone. Then in the evening the home phone rang and he said again just let the machine pick up I'll check it later. It wasn't making sense to me, I hoped I wasn't jumping to negative conclusions.

Later in the evening everyone was tired and so we all said goodnight. The manager went home, Jacque and Joachim would be with their families tomorrow and we would be at home. Chris left to take his parents home and Jennie came to my room to talk and to tell me it was wonderful. I still had trepidations.

I talked briefly with Jennie before she went to her room about the phone calls.

She said, "do you love him."

"Absolutely,"

"Then go with it, it will be fine."

"I'm not sure, I think he is seeing someone else."

"Are you sure? You know what is in the big box?"

"Yes I think an engagement ring packaged to keep it a secret but I'm not sure now."

"Oh, Monique maybe you're imagining all of this."

"Jennie I've learned much from you and one of the things is intuitiveness. Something is not right. I don't know what I'm going to do about the big box, I don't want to spoil everyone's Christmas with a problem." SELF was telling me I needed to wait because there is a problem, the phone calls.

"Can you listen to the messages?"

"That's what I'm going to do."

"Do it and record it, I want to know."

We said goodnight, I got into my PJ's and waited for Chris's return which took quite a bit longer than what was normal for the time to get to his parents home and get back. In the meantime I was going to listen to the message on the home phone, he had his cell phone. I went up to our bedroom and said to SELF, let me check, Chris may have forgotten. A sexy female voice came on, "Hi Baby, thank you for coming by for such a little stay today but I'm glad you did, please find time for me tomorrow. I called you on the cell phone as you told me. Now I'm trying this number since you aren't always picking up your cell hoping you are going to get away on Christmas Day so we can be together for whatever time you have. Don't be mean to me on Christmas Day. Please come over and we'll enjoy." Again my feet were in concrete. I got my little portable tape recorder and recorded the message. Chris came home in about an hour and a half, I was tucked into bed and pretended to be sound asleep so no confrontation. I didn't want to ruin my friends Christmas over this, I would figure it out.

Before Chris returned home as always I called Steve. He responded, "Hi sweetheart, the Eve was beautiful, thank you so much. I'm surprised you're calling since we'll see each other tomorrow."

"Steve you already know don't you."

After a few seconds of quiet he said, "I knew it would take you awhile, I didn't want to be the one to warn you."

"It hurts so much. I don't want to spoil everyone's Christmas Day so I need your help in keeping my spirits up."

"I'll try but I would like to punch him out in any way I can. I wish I could be there to take away the hurt. Know I have your positions on contract so you are financially ok. I don't know what I can do about your heartbreak but time will heal that. Try to make it through Tuesday, we'll talk in between and work out a plan. I have an apartment in one of my buildings that you can go to. So when everyone has left for home I want you to pack some things and we'll get you out. I'm afraid you will have to get out of the house because once we confront him with the affair he will be very angry."

"I'm angry too but that won't help anything. I just don't know what I'll do tonight. What do I do in bed to keep him from knowing I know something?"

"Fain fatigue, headache or whatever and try to get through it and I'll try to help tomorrow unless you want me to come to you tonight and we'll break it all apart but you will be unhappy because of Christmas."

"No, I'll be strong and get through it I just need your help."

"You know I'll be there to help you always."

"Steve he is your friend, are you going to get into the middle of this?"

"I love you more than you know, and I will be in the middle to protect and provide for you. Has he ever gotten violent?"

"No, not with me. Sometimes very short and a bit erratic about some things but personalities are personalities. Why are you asking me this?"

"Let's just say he's gotten very rough at times. Monique, I know he truly does love you, I think he even worships you, it's an obsession and he believes he's giving you all the best but he can't always maintain. He has some sort of streak in him where he has to play so hard and prove something. I'm not a psychiatrist so I don't know the answer but I've been through some times with him."

"Why did you stay friends with him so long?"

"You already know how gregarious and fun he can be and he is generous and we've had some great times together, plus I am his attorney, but I'm not the woman. That's something totally different."

"Yes, I'm not a doctor either but from past experience with my ex husband I think he is manic depressive and the cracks in between the behavior can start to get wider. I'm sure she will call again tomorrow. I recorded today's message and I will try to do the same with the new calls. Of course I'm not married to him but at least I can confront him with it."

"I don't want you to confront him with anything if I'm not with you so keep the recordings and will do it in the office."

"What are you saying?"

"He won't take it well and I don't know what he'll do so I want to be with you for protection."

"Steve you're obviously a man, how can he do this when he knows what I said that I can't accept lies about intimacy. I can accept a lot but not that. I'd rather be alone."

"He has a bigger problem than just male ego. I'm not sure what it is, a need to prove himself, a sex thing or a mental thing. I'm an attorney not a doctor. He does need help or he's going to self destruct."

"His moods seem to be fluctuating more and more. I just want to get through tomorrow and the next day, I just don't know what to do about the big box."

"I don't like manipulate women but this time I'm going to give my advice that you should be one tomorrow. Open the box and accept and we'll deal with the rest a couple days after Christmas. This will keep him satisfied. I'm sorry to give you this advice but I know you and know how important it is to you to get through Christmas and keep everyone happy. Otherwise you can confront him tomorrow and blow the whole thing up. Any other messages come in tomorrow I want recorded too, ok? Make excuses to do it. Hopefully the woman doesn't show up at the house."

"I hope she doesn't but who knows. The only positive out of it would be that everyone would see and it would be in the open. I think she's at our hotel, I could call and invite her but don't know her name. Just be with me tomorrow. The bubble has burst, I should have stayed in Vienna."

"No, then I couldn't have been around you as much and I really want that. Stay strong, do an academy performance and then everyone will go home and we'll take care of it quickly. I'll be available at all times, you know that."

"I know. I talked with Jennie about the phone call so she will try her best too. Why am I in this mess?"

"It isn't by any fault of yours, it's just how it is. Together we'll work it all out. You can tell everyone later so heed my words."

"Ok I'll try to be strong."

"I'm here for you. I'll come over a little earlier tomorrow so maybe I can make you feel more comfortable, alright? If you have any problems tonight call me or call the police."

"Now you're scaring me."

"I don't mean to, I just want you to be aware and react if you need to."

"Alright. Between you and Jennie I should be able to make it."

CHAPTER 16

In the morning I was up early and went to the horses, including my new Sasha, to give them their Christmas carrots and apples and to enjoy the wonderful aromas in the barn. They had no idea of what it was all about but they enjoyed. Curt was leaving to see what family he had so I wanted to be sure the feed was all ready. He was up and ready to go and I said, I'll muck the stalls and he started to laugh. Cur

"It keeps me humble and tied to the earth and what is real."

"You are always happy when you come here. Do what you have to do."

"Well I have lots of real and steady friends in the stable and it gives me pleasure to be around it all. It will be fun. Have a good time with your family I'll take care of our friends."

Chris came looking for me with his parents in tow and just shook his head when he saw what I was doing and then grabbed me and said, "I will do anything to make you happy. You keep me straight. I don't understand you all of the time but I'm trying. Please come back to the house, our home."

Christmas Day was a most beautiful day; blue sky, no rain, crisp and cool with lots of puffy clouds. The morning sun glistened over Lac Lehman and over the colors of the buildings in the city casting a rainbow of color. There was that aroma that comes with the winter, most of the trees dormant, accept the Palms but the earth settling in to get ready for spring in a few months. Chris made one of my favorites for brunch, eggs benedict which we all devoured. I actually had hunger. Then the big box appeared and Chris was in a performance mode. I carefully opened all the boxes he had had the jeweler do one inside the other to conceal the inevitable to hide the "prize" which was a most gorgeous diamond ring. It would have been fun, exciting and a prize if not for the phone calls. When I opened the small box he asked me in front of everyone to do the honor of marrying him and I followed through with a bit of hesitation and said yes. Everyone applauded and acted so surprised. I just looked at Steve and Jennie and they saw what they needed to see in my eyes. It was all an act, I was saving Christmas for everyone, I did not want the ring at that moment but I would do the ploy to get through what I needed to do with everyone else being happy.

We took a nice walk through the vineyards. I talked a lot with Dad again about my ideas of purchasing more property adjacent to ours and expanding. I told him I needed his expertise to learn more about the wine business and he was so interested we made a date to discuss it some more after the holidays. I began to know what I had to do and once that realization comes about you have to follow through but now it might never be an option for me but perhaps I could work separately with Dad.

We all took a little respite in the afternoon while Chris was doing his preparation for dinner. His job was never done but it was one of his lusts. The home phone rang again but I did not pick up, the message machine did. Then I heard Chris's cell go off again. She was trying her best to get in touch, very brazen on her part. During the day the home phone rang several times and he again just said let the machine pick up saying again he would check it later. He did make a couple of phone calls so I knew to whom he was speaking and it hurt but I tried not to let on. So I excused myself and went to check the messages and it was the same sultry voice asking Chris to come to the hotel sometime Christmas Day even saying "I know where the house is so I might come by." I recorded them as Steve and Jennie had asked me to do so there was a record.

Chris was in the kitchen and seemed even more intense and I wondered if he had listened to the messages and wanted to go out; perhaps he just returned her calls. Then his cell phone rang again and he excused himself to another room and when he returned said he had to go to the restaurant for some problem with the building. He just looked at me because I'm sure I could not hide my expression. Everyone was taking a nap or quietly relaxing so I tried the same. Shortly after he left saying he wouldn't be long, the home phone rang and I did pick up and there was that voice. "May I speak to Chris please."

"Who's calling please?"

"Oh a very good friend."

"Mademoiselle it is Christmas so I suggest you not call again because my family and friends are trying to relax and enjoy. Perhaps he will join you shortly. I do not wish to speak to you again." And then I hung up, what was I to do, I was angry and hurt but I would not give in.

Chris returned home, saying nothing about my conversation with the woman so I assumed she had said nothing. He then went back into the kitchen to complete dinner. I provided late afternoon drinks for everyone and went to the piano so they would come and sing some Christmas Carols which we did and chatted and reminisced over other Christmases. We laughed and they even danced a bit then they asked me to sing some of the standards like "White Christmas" which I did and "Chestnuts", but I had a hard time keeping the tears out of my eyes so Jennie came to sit next to me.

I told Chris if he needed my assistance to ask and I would help serve. I began to think he knew that she had spoken with me but I would do the old thing "rise above", the dam may break again and then I'd figure that one out. Find a way to get around the bricks in the road. Steve stayed close around me. Then we heard a car or van outside and the wonderful sound of carolers with candles in hand in the traditional way; they were from a local organization that had sing fests sometimes. So we went out to listen and enjoy. Quickly I asked Maria to help me and we put a lot of the cookies and candies we had purchased and packed everything into a basket with a couple bottles of wine as a gift. They would collect along their way and have a bounty for their evenings works.

Chris called for help so I went in to help set up the serving cart, Steve stepped in to do the wine and soon we were at the table devouring again the next sumptuous meal, turkey with all the stuffing and trimmings and a goose with all the accouterments one could ask, completely beautiful and delicious. The turkey was for Steve and myself being Americans. We dined or should I say stuffed our faces, told stories and shared memories of past holidays and laughed with each other. I kept up a good front deciding to just enjoy and go the next step the next day or two. Then the dessert, Buche de Noelle so special and delicious. I kept helping Chris serve because as a chef he wasn't always in to that part of it, he prepared the food but someone was always there to assist. After dinner and coffee everyone was exhausted so we said our goodnights and with tummies too full they went to their places. Chris still had to take his parents home and Paul and Juliana to the hotel because there was no one else to do it so he left with them and I went into the kitchen to clean up. Steve was still there and helped me and told me I deserved the academy for the night.

"But tonight I don't know what is going to happen."

"Do you want me to take you away now?"

"No I won't do that to my friends. I won't disappoint them."

"Jennie and Peter already know and I know Paul has a clue, he knows you quite well."

"Well then they will understand why I did it."

"Give me the recordings now so I can take them to the office. I think you will be fine tonight except for your hurt. What's planned for tomorrow?"

"Jennie and I are going to go into town and Vevey to browse around and just be together. I think Peter was going somewhere with Chris. They all have your cell number so they know how to contact you. I think Chris is going to want us all at the restaurant tomorrow night for the final celebration and that way also Joachim and the sous chef will do most of the work. Everyone is leaving on Tuesday am so then we can meet on Tuesday pm?

"We need to confront him right away."

"I agree I don't want to prolong it in any way." If I never had another Christmas I would know that I tried to make this one perfect, although obviously it wasn't.

When Chris and I were alone again he thanked me and wanted love so I had no choice. He said, "You have taught me what is important and I enjoyed every minute. Now my dear come here" and of course I had no way out so went to him and there is nothing else to describe, you must use your imagination. I just kept trying to remember that this was farewell. "What's wrong, you don't seem yourself?" I just said with all the preparations and confusion I was a bit out of sorts and he said he understood. The next morning I went downstairs to see what mess we had left and Maria was already busy so I pitched in and soon everything was back in order. I planned to go with Jennie for the day to Montreux and Vevey to look around and enjoy. Peter would be with Chris doing whatever. I just wanted her company so much. So we all got ready and took off to who knew where. Puppy Shady would be in the hands of Maria and Curt. I had never had this kind of life before so I decided to live it to the ultimate while I had it. There was always that foreboding with me that it somehow couldn't last and now I knew it wouldn't. I tried to put that in the back of my mind and just enjoy the moments but knew it would soon be over with Chris, I would have to confront him the next day when everyone was on their way home.

We went through the day with everyone wanting to do something. Jennie asked me about the phone calls and I said there had been more and I had recorded them and I would be meeting with Chris in Steve's office to confront him.

That evening Chris insisted we all go to the restaurant for dinner as it would be the last night for everyone together. I had even asked Joachim to invite his wife. I decided to put on my slinky red dress and get into performance mode. I would be the femme fatale to hide my true feelings. All our usual close friends were there so I said to SELF, "a lot of dancing is going to go on." The first was a waltz with Mr. Williamson, we enjoyed as always he even said you are dancing even with more flair tonight. After I asked Dad to dance with me and he just beamed. Steve asked me after that and he asked if I was doing ok.

"I'm hanging in there, just going to have fun and show off."

"Everyone enjoys you so just be your energetic, artistic self. Remember we'll meet in the office probably on Wednesday."

"I know, don't remind me right now."

Then the musicians gave me the high sign and I went over to play the piano, first by myself. I chose "Memories" and was urged to sing it also, I thought it was appropriate. I could feel Chris's eyes watching my every movement. Then I thought maybe "Bewitched, Bothered and Bewildered" was appropriate. Our piano player sensed my mood, wanted to lighten things up so said let's jam so we started in as we often did. I was on the base line playing the boogie while he was on treble trying to follow my rhythm and then as we always did we switched with me on treble, he on base and really went at it smiling all the way. The base player, drummer, the guitarist and woodwind gal followed our lead and we had a great time. By then it was time for dinner. Joachim joined us at the table sitting next to his wife so others were serving and of course I got my great grazing platter. I tried to stay as jovial as possible. After dinner I did another waltz with Mr. Williamson, danced with James and then told him to get Daphne out there. I also got Dad and Mom up to join and pretty soon everyone was out there, including me with Chris.

"What is with you tonight?"

"What do you mean?

"You're acting a bit differently,"

"In what way?"

"Like it's your last night to enjoy everyone."

"Well it might be."

"Never. You're going to be with me."

After everyone sat down I excused myself to Joachim's wife and asked him to dance.

"Is everything ok?"

"No but don't concern yourself about it right now."

"I know how he can be and what he does so I can suspect. They have been brazen enough to even meet here at the restaurant. Listen to Messieur Steve."

"I will, we meet tomorrow or the next day. Don't let on. I just want to enjoy all of you tonight and hope that I will have the opportunity again."

"Well then Jacque and Hans are dying to dance with you, will you?"

"Of course. So first Jacque and then Hans who as a bartender was assertive but on the dance floor was scared so I just tried to put him at ease. And then to my surprise came young Heinrich with his girlfriend and asked if I would work with them again on the jitterbug. "Sure come here and then your parents can join us." The musicians played what I wanted and I danced with Heinrich and then said Susie get up here and you try. I grabbed Jacque 2 again for my partner and we started in with me being the teacher. We were all laughing and having a great time. He asked me if I would come back to the school to do more dance lessons and I said if the young people want me I will be there, I'll call Father Joseph. Then I felt the piano drawing me again so I told the piano player to watch what I did and maybe he could play it so my friend and I could dance again and I went into "Edelweise" and sang it also. Mr. Williamson got up from his chair and walked to the piano and just stood there beaming with such a wonderful smile. The piano player took over and Mr. Williamson and I danced. It was lovely to give an 80 year old man something special, no strings attached just genuine appreciation of each other. The dance of life for all reasons, it can be wonderful, loving, sexy but difficult also.

We went back hand and hand to the table and I could see that Chris was in a temper. Suddenly he said, "Is it finally my time?" So possessive or guilty.

"Of course sir."

And we danced again with him saying very little because as we danced the woman who I assumed was the caller had come in with another man. Chris tensed, we finished and went back to the table. I was not going to be thwarted by anything this evening so went back to the musicians, played the piano for a bit and I was ready to return to the table when this other man asked me if I could do a tango. I said of course and asked the musicians if they could play one. We proceeded to do a very sexy tango. After the dance he said perhaps he should learn the jitter bug was I up to it. I said, "Bien Sur messieur." After he invited me to join him for a drink and I said no I had friends I must return to. "But who are you?"

"I'm certain you know messieur. Your friend must have told you and what is your game?"

When I returned to the table, she came up and put her hand on Chris's shoulder saying, "Bonsoir, Cherie. Where have you been? I've been calling and calling, but you have so little time for me over the holidays." She was going to try to embarrass me and everyone at the table.

Chris tried to get out of it by saying, "What are you talking about."

"You know what I'm talking about. I've missed you so much. I feel hurt that you are no longer responding. Is it this little skinny slut you have on your mind? What a shame when you have had a well rounded woman."

Chris immediately got up and grabbed her arms to take her down the stairs and wherever, I was concerned he was going to hit her. Another brick in the road, a big one.

I just looked at Steve and he was up in a flash and taking me away. He told James to call the hotel and tell them we need three suites for one night, penthouse for me with two bedrooms. By then Chris reacted confronting Steve saying what in the hell are you doing? Steve just turned around and slugged him in the jaw and he was down. Steve started organizing. He gave Jacque the car keys and said bring it to the front and in a few seconds I was inside. He also asked Jacque to make excuses to the other clients. He told Jennie, Peter, and Paul that Jacque would take them to the house to pick up their things and they would be staying at the hotel for the night. "I called Maria and she's packing some things for Moni and will be there to assist you, we'll deal with the rest of her things later. Please bring her computer too and phone charger Jennie she will need you and Peter." He called for a taxi for Dad and Mom. He just was concerned because he didn't know how Chris was going to react. They wanted to know what they could do and all he said was, I'll get her settled and then you can call and speak with her, we'll get together in her suite. "Paul I think it would be best if you flew home so I'll make the reservations tonight. He told them that I had known from Christmas Eve that there was a problem but didn't want to ruin their Christmas so hung in there. Tonight was not expected but it happened and now we'll deal with it. He had the basics all in control, now he just needed to deal with me.

Steve came to the car and I immediately said "Don't leave me alone tonight."

"I told you if he ever hurt you again I would take you away and my sword would be drawn so I'm taking you away to have you safe and so you can regroup. I want you to just follow my instructions and we'll work out everything together."

Again how could I refuse this wonderful man who I knew loved me and would protect me. We are frequently as females independent but when you find someone who can take care of things in your behalf with your cooperation why not work together.

We went first to his apartment to pick up some clothes and his briefcase and then to the hotel. "You are the manager of the hotel, Chris is the owner, but I want you to tell the staff that he is not to have a key for your room. I have notified the hotel security and called the police to put them on alert. I just don't know how angry he will get.' All I knew was that I was scared. "He said that's why I'm going to stay with you, you will not be out of my sight." When we arrived I told the staff, my friends would be arriving and they should have the best service and that Messieur Chris was not to be in contact with me in anyway. I also told them I would stand up for them and to not worry. They looked concerned but seemed to understand from the trust I had built with them.

Steve and I got settled and then Jennie called. Everyone came to my room bringing my things from the house. We talked for awhile and I explained that I had known but didn't want to spoil Christmas. The phone calls and Chris's absences had told me. I told Paul our arrangement was still valid so not to worry and to Jennie and Peter that I still wanted the apartment and that we would take care of the rent. They were not concerned about that, they were concerned about me. I said I am healthy and I have Steve, who was holding my hand so I will be fine I just need some Monique quiet time. Now you guys have to get some sleep. I told him that I would order breakfast for the next morning and then the drivers would be there to take them to the airport soon after.

"How can we refuse our pied piper?"

"You can't or I won't "pied" for you anymore."

After they left to go to their rooms, Steve and I talked for a little while and then I said I needed to try to sleep if possible. I didn't know what to tell him about the sleeping arrangements. There was a king bed and the other bedroom and he said "You know what I really want but I'm going to take the other room and let you rest. I have some phone calls to make. We'll talk about the future tomorrow." Knowing his feelings for me I was amazed he was being so thoughtful of me. I just thanked him for everything.

"I will have a surprise for you day after tomorrow."

"What?"

"It is a surprise."

"Ok shatz."

Around 2:00 am there was a lot of noise outside our room and then someone pounding on the door. Steve was up in a second. It was Chris yelling for me to open the door he wanted to talk. Steve immediately called the hotel security who were out there but didn't know how to handle it, so then he called the police. He had me go into the bathroom and lock the door and then yelled back at Chris to get away and go home or he would have legal problems, I also knew he had his pistol ready and that frightened me. They kept at it for several minutes and then the police arrived since Steve had forewarned them and took Chris away for that night. I was shaking and scared to death but my hero was there and finally quieted me down and said it would be over for the night. We would face it all in the next few days.

The next morning we were all at the dining table for 8:00 am breakfast and didn't tell them about confrontation with Chris. What would be the purpose of that. I didn't want them to go but it is the way when you have friends in many places. We got them in cars by 9:30 am to go to Geneva airport and again I assured Paul that I would be there in three weeks for another exhibit. Hugs, kisses, quick positive words and they were off. So I was now in the hands of Steve. He wanted to go to his office first to talk to me about something. He wanted to explain his financial situation. He had a trust fund of 10 million dollars which because of the way it was invested and his age he could draw dividends on or take money out as he wished. Through his legal practice which he liked doing he did another $400-500,000 a year. He owned the office building he was in, the apartment building he lived in and another with condos which he had just purchased and was considering moving into. "I have something else I want to show you and get your feelings about so that's where we're going now." We drove up into the hills and I said I didn't want yet to go to pick up my other things and he assured me we were going near but not to Chris's house. He took me nearby to an adjacent vineyard, there was one house there but I saw the foundation for another house higher on the hill.

We walked around, a man came out of the house and greeted Steve. Steve immediately introduced me to him and I found out he was the manager of the property. So I looked at Steve and said, "How many acres of vineyard?"

"250 acres of vineyard and 20 acres of the forest and areas to build on. The wine produced was bottled under the name G rather than his whole name and most of it was sent out to other countries. The Janee brand had been so strong for so many years he didn't want to compete with that so thought it best to have it go elsewhere. It could be found in some parts of Switzerland but he had never promoted in strongly in the local area.

I stood there in disbelief. There was a fantastic view of the city and the lake at a different angle then Chris's home but equal in its beauty. I asked him why he didn't he make a home here?

"Because I get immersed in the law and I'm a bachelor so why should I have a big home. I have a manager with whom I work to keep track of everything. I also like to come and work during harvest and production time. I always wanted to build a special house here but I've never had anyone I wanted to share it with until now so it didn't have much meaning to me. Will you share it with me?"

I just turned to him put my arms around his neck and kissed him and said "You are the most forgiving, loving man I've ever known. I've just come from an affair and you're asking me to share all of this with you. I don't understand."

"We all have history. From the first time I met you and held your hand our eyes met and there was already a connection and communication, do you remember? And since then we've become closer and closer."

"Yes, I do and wondered why I didn't change paths right then."

"You had to go through what you did. Now it is our time if you'll have me."

"Have you, what a thing to say. Such a good looking, sensitive, intelligent, loving, generous, sexy man who can dance, who likes to read and discuss books with me, loves my lousy piano playing, understands my need for space every so often and is the man I have always loved dearly but now want as my lover, why would I not want to share. I love being with you in all ways. I've been naïve or rather stupid."

"You are anything but stupid and you play and sing terrifically so don't put yourself down."

We took a walk around the property looked at the beauty and talked about what we could do and then he said he had some appointments he needed to take care of so I'm going to take you back to the hotel and you can just rest. Little did I know what he had in store.

Steve said he was sorry but I was not to leave the hotel unless he came to pick me up. So I stayed at the hotel tried to rest and then went to the employees to talk with them and try to do some work as Steve said no matter what I had a valid contract as manager of the hotel so I had that control. I had my computer so emailed Paul and Jennie and hoped for a quick response. Steve called to tell me that Chris was out of jail and I should not go anywhere. I felt like a prisoner, what had I gotten myself into, just be patient and all will be ok. My impulse was to run away but I knew I wanted to stay with this man that was helping me, so I stayed.

Steve called again and said he would be over about 7 pm. I was so happy to see him. We went to a small restaurant in Vevey. He wanted us to stay at the hotel for another night until he had things set up for me as he wanted. I just followed his lead.

The next morning he took me to a building across from his apartment building which was his condo building he said he had thought he would move into if I decorated for him.

We went up the stairs to the second floor and we entered into a 2 bedroom condo. All was painted white except the bathroom in lavender and some blue in the kitchen. There was new gray carpet, it had that wonderful new aroma, new plush furniture, beautiful comforter on the bed with wonderful linens edged in embroidery, great towels in the bathroom, a very large shower and old style bathtubs in the baths in both bedrooms, some basics in the kitchen enough to do something, several green plants and of course fresh flowers. There was even a TV in the living area and the bedroom and a small CD player like I had in Vienna. I just looked at him and asked what are you saying. "This is yours or ours whatever you decide to enjoy."

"You must have just refurbished this."

He just smiled and held me. He told me I had to thank Genvieve, Ruth, Daphne and James and the painters for helping pull it all together so quickly. "I was a very bad task master. They ran around like demons."

"You had them do this in two days?"

"Yes and everything is prepared for you. So I will get the few things Maria put together for you from the hotel and your computer. I'll try to get more tomorrow perhaps via Maria. You will stay here tonight with or without me, that is your choice."

"I want you with me, absolutely. I'm too frightened to stay by myself. How wonderful you are, such a friend. I can't thank you enough. I will repay through kindness of friendship. I have to ask why you did all of this, I'm sorry."

"Oh Moni, don't ask why. You've already know in your heart since we first met I've been in love with you. Don't think you're getting away from me again?"

"For once I don't feel like running away." I made the wrong choice didn't I."

"No you made the choice when you were in that time frame. Don't beat on yourself. Will this do until we can build our home?"

"This can do forever if you are here with me, but build our home?"

"Yes on the vineyard and you will have to be the top manager of the vineyards and take care of the horses but not be the hausfrau."

All I could do was hold on to him. "Thank you for understanding and loving. What a blessing you are."

"We are to each other."

We spent the night with me in the bed and Steve in the other bedroom poor man. He knew he had to let me get through some things before we would be free to love completely.

They had held Chris overnight at the police station but the next day Steve called him and said he needed to see him at the office. Chris I guess was a bit repentant and in need of a friend so Steve said ok, he wanted him to hear the phone tapes and discuss behavior towards me. He didn't know I would be there and didn't know about the recordings of the phone calls. We were not trying to gain anything from him other than my freedom from fear. So at 11:00 am he arrived and when he saw me just grabbed my hand and kissed me on either cheek and said "I'm so sorry, I never wanted to hurt you."

Steve was the conductor and started with the recordings and said this is the problem, you have hurt her and neither I or her friends will accept it. We love and respect her too much.

"You know me I get into my moods and get carried away. Monique I love you, I've given everything I can think of that would please you. That woman was seductive and I had to try."

"But never at the expensive of Monique's feelings and loving."

"And how many times will you try. I won't accept that even if my heart aches. I'm done Chris. Yes you have given me all the material things and lots of words and lots of caresses but all that we thought we could enjoy and create you've destroyed because, I guess, of your instability. Where Is the truth and your commitment which is the most important entity when you love someone. We talked of this long ago and it's important to me. I can't be just the entertaining, well dressed lady that makes you feel good about yourself or bolsters your ego while you're out screwing other women that in the end don't mean a thing to you. You need to figure that one out. It isn't that I didn't give you everything in bed like some men say about girlfriends and wives, you know I did, you said it yourself. You have to decide how to satisfy yourself obviously, I'm not doing it so I want to be on my own.

"No, I want you at home with me, I'm not going to give you up. I have no real life without you."

"But you have part of life with these other women so go and enjoy but I can't be part of that. I told you long ago I can put up with attitudes, bad moods, flirtations, whatever because I go through that too but not intimacy. I won't because I think I offer enough to satisfy any man. If I don't he should talk with me about it and we'll see what the problem is."

Steve stayed quiet through all of this but watched me the entire time with a most thoughtful look on his face. Then he spoke up. "Chris I suggest you go to a counselor but in the meantime you are to stay away from Monique. James has issued a restraining order and she has other lodgings.

"Oh so you can have her, right? Isn't this fun and games, you two."

"No we have never had fun and games, you have. We've been friends and she has never played games, she's never crossed the line. She gave herself to you out of love and you must see that you've really got lots of problems I just want to be sure she is protected. I'm speaking as your attorney and still a friend, get your act together. Monique has her own attorney."

"And if I fire you as my attorney?"

"You can do that but Monique's contracts stay in order, they are legal documents and Monique is ready to follow through with them. She is manager of the hotel as well as the distribution of wine from the vineyard on salary. She has a right to retrieve her personal things from the house and ownership of her horses and Shady. It's up to you. I am professional so I'm not going to do anything that would cause a problem to me as an attorney. You can keep me on retainer to follow through as I always have or decide differently, it is up to you."

Chris just looked totally dejected and I felt so sorry but something had to be done. He just got up and walked out saying he would be in touch.

I was exhausted so Steve said let's go take a walk on the water and get something to eat and then I'll take you to your condo. I was in his hands, I was a basket case. We walked, ate a sandwich and then he took me to the condo and said he had to go meet a client but would call and we'd do something in the evening. I went in to try to get my bearings, so I unpacked and put things away and looked around and then took a book and lied down and was gone in a few minutes. My cell rang and I checked the number and it was Chris so I did not answer. The next call was Steve and he asked how I was doing and I told him I had been sleeping and that Chris had called but I didn't answer."

"Good. A lady we'll be over in about a half an hour. Her name is Antoniette and she is going to be your protective companion. I don't know what Chris will do and I can't be with you all the time. You will like her and she's most capable of taking care of any situation. She was once a police officer and now is with a private firm. You are not to go anywhere unaccompanied. If Chris shows up call the police. I already have a security guard outside the main entrance.

"What do you think he'd do?"

"I don't know but I won't take any chances so just stay in and wait for Antoinette and if you want to go out she will be with you. Remember I told you Chris can get erratic. After I leave the office I'll go to my apartment and shower. The apartment is just two blocks away. I should get there by 6pm. We'll go somewhere new and laugh a little. Maybe they'll even have a piano there."

I took a shower to revive myself. I still had to figure it all out, I just felt emotionally exhausted. I put on some cords and a pullover sweater,

"Now I think you're setting me up. Just let me be. I'll eventually get it all together. Oh there is that little charming restaurant by the Chillon. Can I go casual?"

"Sure. That's a good idea, I know the place, they have good food, not as good as you cook."

"You are such an attorney, you select your words very carefully, and I don't mean that in a negative way. When I'm more organized I'll cook for you again, ok?"

"Absolutely, you've only done it once and it was excellent."

"I will miss the restaurant, Joachim and the staff."

"Well maybe you'll have your own restaurant at some point."

"I don't know about that, to have it full time is a lot of work."

"I guess it is. Just get ready, I'll be at the condo in a couple of hours, do I get a welcome.

"Of course."

Laugher.

"Don't run away again."

"Well I was thinking I could do with a night on the town so I might consider that in my red dress."

"Not without me or there will be real trouble."

"I know. I'll just sit tight and see what the next step is. I can always go back to Vienna, I have a home there."

"Call me when Antoinette arrives."

After we hung up I thought for a minute and decided something much faster than I thought I could ever do so I called him right back.

"Is everything ok?"

"You may think less of me when I say what I'm feeling right now and have for quite awhile but I don't want to lose my courage. I'm afraid I might lose you when I suggest what I'm thinking."

"Monique, just say it."

"I have to get away for a few days, it's the horse in me but I don't want to be alone for once in my life because I found the best friend ever in you. I need to get to know you even more than I think I do now. I don't want you to think I'm some stupid willy nilly woman who jumps around. I just made a huge mistake with my feelings."

"Yes, keep going."

"Hold on to your hat. Will you come with me to Paris for a few days, not just as friends?"

Silence for at least a minute. I held my breath. "Are you serious?"

"Yes. I've known and loved you from the first but now know I made a wrong choice and the choice is not for me, it will end up in total confusion and misery. If you say no I'll just go by myself."

Silence again, my thoughtful man.

"You'll go with me?"

"Do you think I'm stupid? Would I not accept an invitation like this from a beautiful woman? You just tell me when, soon I hope"

"I was thinking the weekend after this one, going Thursday morning and coming back Sunday late or Monday morning depending on your schedule. I will get Madame

Gigande to take care of Shady and call Curt to be sure the horses are ok."

"I'll change my appointments and make the plane and hotel reservations and we'll go, simple as that and you can lead me around, shall I bring my halter?

Laughter. "No halter just your good looking self, walking, talking and laughing with me."

"What hotel?"

"Can we stay at the best since this will be so special?"

"Absolutely, with all the special service and whatever."

"Ok, the George Cinque or the Inter are in a great area but they are expensive." I know some other smaller boutique hotels too.

"I don't care, whatever my baby wants."

"Are you ready for this?

"I've been ready for a long time."

When he arrived we hugged but I had decided we were waiting for Paris for the rest. We talked for awhile and I said, "I guess Chris is just in a funk because he thinks we have something going on. Maybe we should. I feel like he wanted me as some prize to always have me available to show off and entertain. I am concerned that he is getting more erratic and don't know what he might do. I just need a new space for a few days."

"Well there are two ways to look at this, either you finally have a clue of what he might continue to do or you decide if you want that we should get something going together."

I spent the next few days trying to do some work and relax too then came the following Thursday. He had made the reservations for Paris. I was packed, he had ordered a car for us and we were off to Geneva early Thursday morning to the airport. We arrived in Paris in an hour, transferred to the hotel and got settled. The suite was gorgeous in wonderful soft colors, a step out balcony on the quieter side and marble bath, of course a fresh flower arrangement. In a few minutes room service came with a chilled bottle of chardonnay and wine glasses on a tray so by 1 pm we were celebrating

My cell phone rang and I didn't check the ID, it was Chris. When I heard his voice my first response was why is he calling

"I understand you are in Paris."

"How do you know that?" It frightened me that he could find out where I was.

"I still know who to call to find out things. Are you with Steve?"

"I'm here by myself doing work. I've already been around the city a bit and am now taking a nap and then maybe I'll have some dinner." Steve was ready to grab the phone but I motioned him off otherwise it would be another confrontation.

Then he gave me a list of restaurants to check out and I said I would, ha ha. He started in with an apology for his behavior, and that he loved me and wanted me back with him but asked me again if I was there with someone. I said I am here to do one of my businesses on my own. He already knew I'm sure that Steve was away. Sorry more than two can play a game. I didn't like games and knew Steve didn't either; he was my stalwart and I would try to please him and not let him go. Chris asked me to call him the next day so he would know I was ok and I said I would but I wouldn't.

Steve was watching and listening through the conversation. When I hung up I just said, "He won't give up, he thinks I'll come back to him."

"Are you finished with him?"

"Absolutely, how could I go back when I have you, I hope you can believe that."

"Do not call him back. Together we'll work everything out but let's get on with Paris art, shopping, food, let's get going."

First was lunch although it was late even my Parisian standards. Before we left Steve asked the Concierge about some shops the area and got all the information, plus he had a small package he asked to be put into the hotel safe. I didn't ask what it was. We had something to eat and then he started looking for these shops, found one which we went into and he wanted me to try on some dresses. I was not the shopper but knew he wanted to buy me things so two dresses later, one very sexy black in silk, spaghetti straps, very minimal. I just thought I'm glad he's here to take care of me with this dress on. The other was a lime green with a fitted bodice and a soft chiffon, draping skirt, great for dancing.

"I don't have shoes for these."

"Ok, next stop" and my eyes lit up because I love shoes. Black, simple but elegant and for the other dress another pair of a sandal strap style.

"Now what for you?"

"Nothing, I have you."

I insisted so we went to a jewelry store and I found onyx cufflinks I liked and purchased them as his gift. He just smiled and shook his head like he did when he was surprised or amazed at what I did. "I don't even have shirts for these." "Well let's find some.", so we went to a men's boutique and bought two white shirts and also a beautiful blue silk shirt he admired. He seemed pleased like a little boy who just received the bicycle he had been admiring.

Then to the Louvre for just a small taste of what it offered, a walk along the Seine on the quai des Tuilleries where I found old books for Jennie and Peter, across to the Ile de la Citie to visit Notre Dame and the Ile de St Louis. There was so much to see and enjoy but we finally decided to return to the hotel. I told him I was so tired that if he wanted a good dinner partner I would need a nap, he fell asleep too. He had checked with the concierge about a restaurant I mentioned and made reservations.

I put on the new black dress and the shawl he had also purchased and paraded for him, he just smiled. He dressed in a dark suit with the new shirt and cufflinks and looked so gorgeous I wasn't sure I wanted to go out, but we did. As we were leaving he went to the concierge to retrieve what he him put in the safe. We literally waltzed out of the hotel, while the staff just smiled, and got a taxi to the restaurant. I had been there once before and loved it so hoped it would still be excellent. He ordered champagne and I said another celebration and he answered I hope so. We ordered and then he said let's dance which we did, and I knew he had talked to the musicians or the owner about what he wanted, very sexy, love songs. Something was going on.

We had dinner and then Steve reached into the upper pocket of his coat and to my surprise got down on his knees in front of me, obviously other people were watching. He took my hand and said I love you will you do me the honor of marrying me as soon as possible, then the ring. A gorgeous Ceylon sapphire 4 or 5 carats cut in an unusual oval shape with a few diamonds around to enhance the stone, a work of art, my new student had been so perceptive. I hesitated, "Steve you have been a bachelor for so long, doing what you want when you want, eating or sleeping at different hours, I don't know about you having a woman in your domain, it will be different. Can you handle that? Also it's only been three weeks since we've been together and I've just finished with Chris. Am I such a loose woman?"

"Moni, I've known you as long as Chris and the first time I met you I fell in love and said this is the woman I want. I had to let you go through your time with Chris, so I waited for a year but was always there for you. I've told you I've been with lots of women but not one did I want to share my life with and I haven't been with anyone since I met you. I only want you. You are a free spirit and you can do anything you want with me as long as I know what you're doing, I'll give you your freedom. I just want to be with you, to take care of you, to provide for you, to have all the joy of sharing, I'll never hurt you."

Hmm, I've heard that before about hurt.

"Yes, you've had two bad experiences but you should know me by now, what have I done."

"You've always been there for me and helped and supported me, so I want to trust you."

"You can. I know all the things you love to do, riding the horses, cooking, working with the children at the orphanage, the art in Vienna, the quiet time you need, your writing, you can have it all. I just want to know that I can enjoy some of all of that with you. Can you imagine what we can do together. It's so much fun to spoil you. I love my legal work so I'm busy, I won't get in your way. I just need you so much, you make things so exciting and interesting. I want a home and you are the only woman I've found I would share everything with, it's taken me a long time so I won't let it go. Believe me you won't be a hausfrau tied to that kind of restriction. You are set financially but you will keep that and I will provide for you. Please, please, marry me, it will be so special."

"You want this skinny minny?"

"I don't care how skinny you are the breasts are beautiful, it's you as a person I want. Maybe we'll fatten you up a bit if you're content."

All I could do, with tears in my eyes, unbelievably said "Yes" very loudly and then applause. So we danced for everyone a slow one to start, then a fast one and kept going for several other dances until others joined in, our first big celebration, just the two of us with a few strangers.

We returned to the hotel holding hands and dancing into the lobby. As we entered the staff at the desk applauded smilingly. Steve had told them what was in the package, that it was a big night. In our room there was a bottle of champagne from the hotel for congratulations, two glasses and two red roses. I said I was going to change; I had brought a delicate negligee, I planned to do this right. When I came out of the bath Steve was in a robe and stared at me and just sighed. He poured some champagne and we toasted each other. I went to look out the balcony, we were quiet for a few minutes. Then

I felt his mouth on my neck kissing me, one arm around my waist. We finished the champagne he took the glasses and then picked me up to take me to bed. I only needed this man to be complete, I was amazed.

"I've waited so long." He started kissing me, gradually removing my gown, caressing me on my entire body, looking so lovingly at what he saw and then I did the same with him, taking off his robe, caressing as I did. We continued until we reached such a passion level we were both frantic and then he entered and in seconds the fireworks were all around us, continuing for a long while. After we were both spent but stayed intertwined. I realized what I had missed by my other attraction this man was fantastic, so tender and loving, we were soul mates. What a fool I had been with this at my doorstep. I couldn't understand myself going from one to the other but knew it was right.

"God, Monique I have never experienced this with anyone, such sensuality, I can't believe it. All that came before is fool's gold. I'll never get enough of you, I may just have to stay home to satisfy you. I feel so content and happy and know I love you completely, I will never let you go."

"I feel the same, I realized long ago how much I loved you but felt immersed and couldn't even explain it to myself. Now I feel free. Please don't get tired of me.'

"No way could I ever get tired of you, I am just going to enjoy all of you every day until the time when we have our mutual canes."

Tired but so excited with each other we laughed and said we couldn't waste good champagne so the glasses were again full. We talked about building a new home on his property. I said I we could put together our ideas, scan it to Jennie and Peter and ask them to come up with a plan, one of course for the stable. He just chuckled and said, "Yes my baby will take care of it but do it as soon as possible because there is going to be a wedding in between. You have a lot to do."

"To be with you I'll do anything I have to," I looked at my engagement ring it was beautiful I cherished, it was so unusual.

We finally both fell asleep in each other's arms until very late in the morning so Steve called room service. It was 3pm before we decided to go out. We went to the D'Orsay and then just wandered the streets observing all the different people.

On Saturday we were going to Versailles and we would be able also to see the performance of the Equine school. It was fantastic, I think Steve watched me more than the performance. He seemed so happy. We went to the little village nearby because I wanted to get some presents for Jennie, Maria and mom. Steve asked the concierge about restaurants and we decided on one for dinner so out again.

Sunday we went out walking and decided to take the elevator up the Eiffel tower again to look at the city. Our flight was at 7pm, the hotel was gracious to us so we didn't check out until around 4:30 pm to go to the airport, our flight was 7 pm. We arrived in Geneva and the driver was there for us and we were soon home in Montreux and as always after a trip a bit let down but it had been fantastic. Now Steve would be off the couch and in bed with me at the condo which of course pleased us both.

Monday Steve had to be at the office. Antoinette came just before he left. I got on to it and even called Jennie to tell her what was up. She said, "I goofed with my so called intuition this time but I think you have made the best decision. Can you forget Chris?"

"No. I still love him it's just that he has a big problem and I can't solve it. I've always loved Steve too. I guess I'm a terrible lady, loving two men at the same time."

"No you are not but Steve is the right one. He is so even and loving."

"I didn't come to look for a man and then I got caught up with all of this. I really don't understand myself."

"You are too loving not to be with someone it was inevitable."

I told her about Antoinette my new protector and the necessity of the security guard outside.

"Listen to Steve, don't be naïve. Chris will do anything to get you back."

"We'll look at the plans for the house right away and get back to you tout suite." She asked me if we had been ice skating again and I just said "Bien Sur Madame." Then we laughed and did our other chitter chat.

I went to my computer to do some things and then looked at the calendar and realized the date, it was my birthday. I didn't want to know I was getting older but then began to think Steve had something up his sleeve so told Shady I have to shower and do my hair and decide what dress I should wear. I knew he wouldn't forget. When he came home Antoinette left. He had a lovely new bouquet of flowers but didn't say anything. No present, no card so I said to SELF, "maybe he did forget." He went in to take a shower and said get dressed and we'll go out, wear something elegant. So I said to SELF, "I will and put on a new dress that Gabrielle had sent me as a gift since my clients had purchased many things from her. It was a slinky silk dress in a raspberry color with again in what she had decided was my style, low cut bodice when I had not much to show off and open at the back to the waist and a lovely flow of fabric in the skirt, as she said for dancing. It was lovely and very sexy. Steve came out of the bath with his robe on and saw me and just sat down and said, "Model it for me." I did and then he said, "Maybe I won't take you out anywhere."

"You must. I have to show off, maybe find new clients for Gabrielle and tonight I am hungry for food."

"Surprise, you hungry?"

"Yes I forgot about lunch."

He got dressed and then I knew something was going on because he had on his tuxedo. He just said don't ask just come along with me. I was surprised when we arrived at Chez Janee.

"Don't worry I had a long talk with him and knowing it was your birthday he said he would behave and that he accepted your choice. I think he is getting better but knows you are with me now. Am I right?"

"Have no doubts. You are stuck with me forever."

"I'm happy to be stuck with you and my partners."

"Partners?"

"Shady, Serahlin and Sasha."

Then I really laughed and thought now I do have a family.

He led me up the stairs and then said close your eyes and when we entered there was applause and people saying "Happy Birthday. There were balloons and a big banner saying Happy Birthday and so many people. I just gripped Steve's hand even harder and asked, "What have you done?"

"They love you so what is a better way to celebrate your creation."

I just smiled and started my rounds, the musicians, Jacque, Hans, Joachim, Mr. Williamson, Mom and Dad all beaming, people that I had met in the restaurant, and they were all ready to dance. Of course Chris was there too and just smiled, gave me a hug and a kiss and said you deserve it all. I was needless to say overwhelmed and told SELF, "We will enjoy." Then a special surprise, Father Jose[h, Sisters Anne and Suzanne and the 20 children from the orphanage arrived. They all ran to me and were all talking at once until I had to say "shush one at a time." Father and the sisters tried to help to control the children because they were so excited they didn't know what to do. They finally calmed down a bit as did Shady who had come with Curt. And then the party began. Dancing was only one of my loves but a most passionate one because my parents had always done it in and out of our home, so I was ready to dance the night away, be it a waltz, fox trot, tango, jitter bug I was up for it, there were so many partners to enjoy and I got to choose. First was Mr. Williamson and another waltz, next came Joachim in a tux also, Jacque, my shy Hans and then Dad and even James. Then the most difficult was Chris but we did our thing and he seemed to take it well especially when we did a "Chattanooga." Steve watched it all and finally came to retrieve me and we danced to "Unforgettable" and I thanked him for it all. He just smiled and said, "For you anything, you should know that by now."

Then the group started with, "Monique play the piano and sing for us," so I put on a different hat. Steve just took me by the hand to the piano and said, "Enjoy and give your love, we'll hold dinner."

And so I started in with the children who finally had gotten seated at their table but now I brought them to the piano and had them sit on the stairs. "We are having a performance so do the best you can."

"Oui Madamoiselle Monique, we will said Jacque2, still my favorite of the group."

We started with "Dite moi" and they were as charming as could Then I asked them for father and the sisters to sing "Panis Angelicus". "Mais oui." They were like angels, father and the sisters had tears in their eyes.

Then I couldn't resist and started with "One for the money, two for the show, three to get ready so go man go, we're going to rock around the clock." And there was no keeping them on the stairs. They were on the dance floor singing and jiving and having the best time. They even dragged father and the sisters and Jacque 1 to join in. I looked up at Steve and then over at Chris and they were both just smiling and shaking their heads. Steve just put his hands in the air, threw me a kiss which meant go for it. After we had to settle the children down for dinner which was another project.

After the children's performance I knew they wanted me to perform. I had to really think what I would play so asked the piano player to join me at first. We started our jamming with "It Don't Mean a Thing If It Ain't Got That Swing and "That Old Black Magic". After that he looked at me, "Do your own thing." I had to think for a minute and then started with "Memories", then "Bewitched" for Mr. W. "Edelwiesse" and then for Chris "Embraceable You". Then I just got up, I could do no more, on the way to the table Chris came to me and gave me a hug thanking me and then I turned and went outside to cry. Soon Steve was there with his arms around me and said it is your birthday, all these people want you to be happy. As always he calmed me down and we went inside for dinner, me with a smile on my face. We dined, or should I say the others dined while I picked. I felt very sad. Then Chris spoke to Steve to ask if I could dance again with him. Steve just said if she is ok with it I am. The musicians knew to do "Embraceable You." Chris held me closely and whispered in my ear that if I could ever trust him again he was there for me. We danced elegantly and he took me back to Steve and even thanked him. I understood why I had protection, he did not want to let me go.

Next there were presents so I had to get up for that. The staff had pooled some money for a gorgeous crystal vase, Mr. Williamson's gift was a great book on Indian spirituality, from Mom and Dad a beautiful book on wines and vineyards with a loving note saying they were there to help in any way they could, another book from James and Daphne about cooking. I guess the message was out that I was a book person, they wouldn't tackle my style in clothing. The children had a huge card they said father and the sisters had helped them with. Each of their pictures was on it and each had written a special wish poem for me, how beautiful. I told them I would cherish it forever. And then a very special, most thoughtful gift from Chris, a white orchid plant with a most special note saying that I was as fragile as the orchid and he hadn't realized that but it represented what I was.

Then Steve handed me his gift with a Cheshire grin, it wasn't jewelry because the package was more like an envelope size. Everyone was looking at me as I opened it and inside were travel documents for Portugal. I got so excited "When?

"Look at the dates and if that doesn't work we'll change them. You have wanted to go for a long time and now is the time. Now you can be my tour guide and once again my pied piper.

At that moment I knew I would never leave this man who listened to me and knew what I needed and wanted to join me in my dreams. He was my best friend. Then he took out his cell phone dialed and handed it to me and there was Jennie. "Happy Birthday, I hope it was grand. We wish we could be there with you but when you come in a couple of weeks to Vienna we will re-celebrate."

"Oh, Jennie, it has been grand, a wonderful evening and we will re-celebrate when I'm in Vienna. I'll call you tomorrow, ok?"

"Ok dear heart. We'll all get together, we miss you so much, can't wait until you're here. When will that be?"

"Second weekend in March, Paul has another opening."

After came a special birthday cake by Jochaim, of course chocolate with too many candles and I did my thing. The children had to come to see me blow them out. Joachim had made several cakes so everyone would have birthday cake, even Shady. We enjoyed and I went around to everyone to thank them all and then I took Steve's hand and looked at him and he knew it was time to go home. Jacque helped us pack up the gifts and get them into the car. What an evening.

At home I just wanted to get ready for bed and fall in but Steve said, "There's another small present you must have."

"You are my present. I don't need anything else."

"I think you will like this one." So I opened the package and there was a very large, contemporary crystal paperweight in multi-colors. He had even remembered what I told him about my collection that was now in storage. He never missed a thing. Perfect for my desk.

And then we gave each other the best present possible, love in the most sensuous way one can imagine.

In the morning I was still enjoying my birthday and stretched like a cat again, my dear Steve wouldn't let that go unnoticed so I was loved again needless to say with great enthusiasm.

"You are going to wear me out, all I can do is think about you and what you're doing, my clients are going to suffer.

"Take care of them like you take care of me and they will be most appreciative. You know where I am and what I'm doing so not to worry. I will always be here for you. Come here so I can kiss you again."

"Moni, don't start or I'll never get out of here."

"I just want to kiss you."

"But if you do I'm done for."

"What an attitude, ok no morning kisses."

But of course then I got several and we could cuddle for awhile before he had to leave.

"What's your plan for the day, if you're going out call Antoinette. Granted Chris seemed ok last night but I'm not sure what to expect, he still wants you."

"I thought I might stay in for the most of the day to do some writing but I do want to take Shady out for walk and I may want to go by the orphanage."

"For awhile I don't want you doing that on your own, listen to me please. So call Antoinette and don't go out without her or call me and I'll go with you."

"But you have court today don't you?"

"Yes but I don't want you out there on your own for awhile, understood?"

"Understood but is she always available to me?"

"Yes just plan what you want to do and call her this morning."

"Ok master."

"Come on Moni you know what I'm concerned about."

"Yes, I do and I appreciate your concern, I will be responsible. Will she take a walk with me and Shady?"

"Of course but realize he knows what you like to do and he knows where you go."

"Now you make me afraid again."

"I don't want you afraid, I just want you aware."

"Alright, I understand no freedom for awhile."

"Not for awhile, it will change. I don't want anything to happen to you, then I have nothing, you are my life. Do you understand that?"

"I think I understand, it's just that no one has ever been there for me the way you are."

"I am and if I had to give up my practice to be there to take care of you I would. I can't be without you. Remember you said we are soul mates and when one soul is gone so is the other, that's how I feel."

"Now you just gave me another birthday present, an unbelievable one. I love you so dearly."

"More than Shady or Serhalin and Sasha"

"Bien sur messieur. You are my first love and always will be until we have canes. Do you understand?"

"Oui mademoiselle."

When can I go riding?"

Go any tme as long as Antonette is with you"

CHAPTER 17

The next morning Steve called from the office, "When is the wedding date.

"Do you really care what they think? Remember were in the French side of Switzerland not puritanical America."

I laughed. "I was thinking the first part of or mid May. I want to go to Vienna mid March to assist Paul with a special exhibit. You know I want Jennie here so I need to check with their schedule and we have to decide where to have the ceremony. Father Bauer, although I love him isn't sure he can permission from the diocese to do it because we are not practicing the faith but he wants to so he is trying. If that doesn't work I was thinking of the small chapel with Reverend Leon. It's lovely and then we can decide where we want the reception, probably at the hotel since people will stay there. I don't want to go into the typical wedding planning, I want it simple so we should talk about it. I want your thoughts. I'm thinking May1."

"Sounds good to me. Over dinner tonight we'll talk about it and make some plans, remember this is all new to me. What do you want for dinner?"

"You know me. Tonight I'd rather stay in but don't know what I feel like cooking."

"Well as you said cooking is not for you every night."

"Why not call Joachim and say you want for pizza choice and a salad and he'll prepare it and you can pick it up on the way home. Would you mind that? I know it means going to Chez Janee. I could also have Jacque bring it over."

"You call him, tell him I can come by around 6:30 to pick up and we'll have our feast. What movie do you want tonight."

"I have no idea, if you want one pick it up or we can just read together and listen to some good music."

"We really need to get the house built so you have your piano. We could get a small one now if you want"

"Let me think about that. I have some ideas. However long it takes to build the house, remember I am completely content in the condo if you are here."

"You always do have ideas. If we get the piano will you have the whole group over?"

"Maybe sometime, only if you will dance with me."

"I will always dance with you on the floor or in our bed."

"Go and take care of those clients, win the court case, get on with it so you can get home and don't forget the pizza and salad."

Laughter.

Steve arrived about 7:00 pm with Joachim's offerings and looked worn out so I told him as always, hot shower and then we would relax awhile before eating something. Shady gave him his right paw to say glad you're home because Mom is now happy. If he gave his left paw it meant he needed to go outside. Chris had been calling me again but I decided not to bring that up for the evening. I would have to deal with it myself and possibly with Antoinette's help. We ate our pizza and salad while Shady just lied on his rug obviously content as could be. Steve had a detective type movie so we cuddled on the couch to watch. He made it through about the first 15 minutes before he was sound asleep. I watched and then tried to awaken him to get him into bed, checked his date book to see how early he had to be in the office and then the phone rang Chris.

"Why are you calling so late?"

"I need you and I am going to fight to get you back."

"If you care for me at all you will stop this. I am not coming back. Then Steve was behind me and took the phone and started in. "Leave her alone, she is with me and I will do anything to protect her, do not call her."

"I will get her back no matter what I have to do."

"Don't push this Chris, I'll repeat she is with me and I will not let her go. Find a life and let us live ours. Go find one of your ladies of the night and enjoy. Monique is too precious to be treated badly."

"She had everything with me."

"She has everything with me including trust and tender loving care plus consistency. You are too selfish to have her. I thought you had come to terms with this and would not stalk her but it's obvious you haven't so I we'll be sure she is protected. Leave her alone and that is final."

"Has he been calling you?"

"Yes a couple of times but he always was very calm and nice so we just chatted. I guess tonight he's in a manic state."

"Why didn't you tell me?"

"Because you would get upset as you are now."

"Monique I don't want anything to happen to you and I can no longer trust him. Do you understand?"

"Yes and I know you are right. Now what am I supposed to do, be a prisoner. I think it's best if I just go back to Vienna."

"Other than your times for the exhibits with Paul you will not go back there to stay unless we both go there to live. I will not do without you. We'll keep you protected and eventually he will get over it all it's just going to be a change but we can do it. It won't be forever."

I just put my arms around him and said please take care of me, I can no longer do it myself.

"You know I will, just listen to me. I know you want to be free but right now I'm thinking of your safety so please take my advice."

"I'm totally in your hands. Why are you so wonderful to me?"

"Moni you know why, I want you to be mine, I want us together. It's what you taught me, it's all about love and I know there's nothing of importance without you. We'll work all the rest out as we go."

And so I was once again with Antoinette which was ok but I felt constantly cautious and not free. I started working with Shady to see if I could get the idea of attack across to him. He was a lab so he knew about birds but that was just a retrieving built in mode. He listened and seemed to get the idea but in a pinch would he have it down, he was too young. I really didn't have the concept that Chris would try to hurt me but I did trust Steve and his knowledge so did listen. I think he was more concerned about Chris taking me away somewhere where he couldn't find me. So Steve would call every couple of hours to check in, wanted to know my schedule and who I was seeing. What a bummer but he was right, he had to watch over me.

Things quieted down, there were no instances. But I did sense that Steve knew more than he told me about past history. He was always on the alert and carried the pistol in the glove compartment and brought it into the condo when we returned. Typical of me I kept asking SELF, "what did I do to create this mess, this tension?" SELF just said really nothing it is just happening.

Steve called from the office one night and said let's go ice skating. I just answered great shall I meet you there. "No I will pick you up, remember, not on your own for awhile."

So we went ice skating, déjà vu but with my Steve. We skated dancing away, laughing and just enjoying, wonderful. What a joy to be with him. "What is the date? I guess I'm afraid you will change your mind or run away."

"No I'm not going to change my mind but I have some other things I need to work on and I need to see what Jennie and Peter's schedule is because they must be here, I want her to be my matron of honor. Also I need to go to Vienna in March for the special exhibit Paul has planned for the American artist so I have lots to do. I still have in my mind that it is so soon after my living with Chris that it might not be appropriate but I told you all ready May 1."

"I wanted to be sure you hadn't changed your mind. What do you mean by appropriate?"

"Moving from one man to another so quickly. I may seem like a free spirit but I do think of other people's opinions."

"The ones that are close to us know that we've known each other as long as you've known Chris and know we've been close."

"It still makes me look like the loose woman so I take the burden of scrutiny. We're together now so let's take a little time to decide on everything but the May 1 date seems to work for everyone.

I went to see Father Joseph. "Have you selected a date?" I told him May 1. He just smiled, "You and monsieur Steve are so special to us with all your help, energy and most of all love that we want to share this union with you. We will do it here in the chapel."

"Thank you Father, I feel like I'm again at home. Steve is such a good, generous person and here we are two Americans in Europe that found each other, God works in interesting ways."

"Yes my dear, he does."

I called Jennie who got so excited. "Absolutely just let us know when we should come and as a typical woman said right away, "What do you want me to wear?"

"I'm going to talk with Gabrielle and ask her to send some sketches and then I'll let you know. When they're ready Gabrielle will bring yours to you for fitting if necessary. Know it will be something beautiful because you are beautiful. We will make the plane reservations and you will stay In one of the guest rooms."

"Fantastic. Steve is so wonderful and helpful to you, you will have a good life with him."

"I think I am just worried that I come out of one relationship and now I want to marry someone else."

"But you've known Steve just as long and I saw when he was here how you two got along and enjoyed each other. I know he loves you and you seemed more comfortable with him and it seems that Chris is too obsessive and getting more erratic."

"Yes he is. As I said to you before, I came not looking for a man and ended up loving two of them but Steve is the one for me, I know that now."

"I can hear it in your voice and I am happy for you. You finally found your soul mate. Wonderful, just keep me posted on the dates and of course will be there." Then we just did our normal chat about things going on with her and Peter, their new projects, and the Vienna scene.

I called Paul, told him the plans, invited him and Juliana and he said of course, just to keep him up on the details. I said we would take care of the plane reservations and the hotel.

Then I called Gabrielle about the dresses and she said she would start right away and email me some ideas and yes absolutely she wanted to be with us. I told her the same as Paul about reservations but of course she would stay in the hotel with a guest if she wanted.

CHAPTER 18

I had to now find out about dwell citizenship, if it was possible or would I have do the green passes as I did in in Vienna. I figured Steve could help with that.

Steve called from his office to check on me which he always did I told him fine and what I had been doing. After awhile I called him back. He said he was with a client but I came first. "Hi lovely lady, what can I do for you?"

"Hi, are you ready, are you ready to get stuck with me, nows your chance to run."

"I've decided, getting stuck with you is perfection. I have to ask what are you going to do about a dress?"

"I told you I talked with Gabrielle about that for me and one for Jennie. It won't be white so we'll see what she comes up with it will be beautiful, stylish, different and of course sexy."

"I want to buy a special wedding present so I need some idea."

"Well you know the kind of dresses she designs for me so use your imagination. I have to watch it a bit because Father Bauer is doing the ceremony, sisters Anne and Clara and the children will be there. But Steve you've given me so much you don't have to do more. Will you wear a wedding ring?"

"And the children and all your friends want to see the Monique style so it has to be special. And yes I will happily wear a wedding ring."

"Then we have Mr. Rosinee to see about that and the ring will be my gift to you. Now that I've done all of this planning are you sure?"

"I decided long ago, I've just never been through this before so put the halter on and lead me. What am I getting myself into, I've been a bachelor so long I just meandered."

"With me you can't meander anymore so decide."

"I'm just teasing, I already told you what I decided. Moni, life isn't worth being in if you're not with me, believe that. I don't want to be a bachelor anymore, I just want you next to me."

"Do you mean for sex or for everything. Since you've lived alone so long are you ready to have a woman around in your domain?"

"Moni sex with you is wonderful but that's not the prime issue, I want it all, I just enjoy being and doing things with you and thinking about our future. It's not that I need any woman in my domain as you call it, it is you otherwise I guess I would have chosen someone earlier in my life. Being with you makes me feel complete."

"That is beautifully put, thank you."

"Is there anything I should be doing or planning?"

"Give me a list of people to invite, I know some of them but there may be some I don't know about. Also I want a carriage ride from the chapel to the reception. Show up in your tuxedo with James who will do your buttoner and have the ring and be your ever charming, even self and remember we are dancing down the aisle after the ceremony. We have time to work on it."

"No more orders? I'm on my own?"

"You are on your own."

"I'll take care of the carriage and decide on the reception place but you have to do the food planning, you are the gourmand."

"So we have a special date?"

Laughter.

"You know Chris may show up."

"I'm sure he will and we'll deal with that if it occurs. I'll have Antoinette with you and alert some of my police friends."

"Whatever you think is necessary. I'm not going to worry about it. No one will spoil our day, it's ours. When will you be home?"

"About 6:00 pm."

"Ok, then I have time to go to the market so I can cook dinner for you tonight. Any requests?"

"I get spoiled tonight like the other three? No requests, whatever you prepare will be wonderful. Wow another home cooked meal but you can't go to the market by yourself."

"You caught me on a good day, tomorrow who knows."

"Let me repeat, you are not to go out by yourself."

"I can put on a disguise."

"He'll know the body."

"Antoinette is here so she'll go with me and pick up some things for Maria and himself, will that work?"

"Ok, but just the market.

"I understand. Come home with an appetite." I we went and shopped and but I saw her looking constantly around for Chris so I shopped quickly so he could go home and relax. Everything went fine so we made it through another day.

I did some small spareribs with my own sauce, a special coleslaw and some beans with french bread. When he arrived home he had to ask what smells so good and I said just change and relax and you will see. He soon had barbecue sauce on in his face with a smile that was like a child. "My baby is spoiling me. It was so delicious it reminds me of home."

"Perhaps we have to go to the States soon to enjoy some special treats."

"I agree, we'll plan a trip for fun although home is where the heart is, right"

"Yes, home is where you make home and it is here but there are things that I miss, so let's do it. But first we have the Portugal trip."

"What about the last week in February for Portugal that would give me time in between before I go to Vienna."

So things seemed to be going fine until the next night when Joachim called us and said he needed help, Chris was in the restaurant and causing problems "What problems?"

"He's ranting and raving at all of us and started throwing things, he's out of control."

I said talk to Steve to see what we should do so handed him the phone.

Steve said he would call his connection at the police, that Joachim should not confront him just let him do what he was going to do and we would be there in a few minutes. We got dressed and went to the restaurant. People were confused and leaving except for some of Chris's friends, the partiers. When Chris saw us he came to me and said once again, "It would be all ok if you would just come back to me."

"I can't Chris but I will help you so we'll call Dr. Bovet, you can go to the clinic where you can get help. I got him to sit down and motioned for Steve to leave us and just thought how one controls a horse. I held his hand and talked quietly with him trying to calm him down and relax and he gradually did. I said I would take him to the clinic and there he could talk with the doctors who would help him. He quietly said ok whatever you think is best. Steve called the doctor and the clinic who said do not drive him over because there could be another outburst on the way. They sent an ambulance van and I convinced Chris I would ride with him, no lights, no sirens, he agreed if I would come with him. I was really putting Steve in a difficult situation but he seemed, as always, to understand how I did things. Steve called Maria to put some things together for him, PJ's, notion bag, change of clothes and said he would pick them up. Steve followed us to the clinic, they got Chris into a room and then Steve and I left to get his things from the house. Maria was so confused and scared, had a few things in order, then I did the rest. We went back to the clinic and they had sedated Chris so he was calm but a bit out of it. They would have a psychologist come in to talk with him in the morning.

The next morning I went with Antoinette to the clinic to see how he was doing and as I entered his room there was the woman who he was seeing before and during Christmas time. She was sitting on the bed and he was stroking her thigh and she was kissing him and I'm sure whispering sweet nothings in his ear. He saw me and pushed her away. "I'm sorry I intruded, I just came to see how you were doing and obviously you are doing just fine. Goodbye." All I heard as I left was him yelling "Monique." I walked out and walked to the condo and told Madame Gigande that I would take Shady for a walk at the lake. I took my cell phone and keys and the three of us left with a frisbee to enjoy some release. We played and I said I am free of that one, I can no longer worry about him.

While we were playing I heard "Moni" and there was my loving Steve. "You wouldn't pick up on your phone and I was worried, what happened." I told him.

"I'm so sorry Moni, you don't deserve that kind of treatment."

"It will never happen again. It's very clear to me now that I have a special gift, you. Please understand that." He just held me and said, "Let's go home and get on with our lives. We have our wedding and our new home and lots of things to enjoy."

One evening we went out for dinner with some friends and Mom and Dad. At one point I excused myself to go to the ladies room. When I came out there was Chris obviously very angry and frustrated. He said he refused to give me up, and that I was going to go with him whether I wanted it or not.

I of course said no I am not going anywhere with you and then got scared because he grabbed my wrist and in the other hand had a pistol.

"You are mine and I'm taking you away now."

I said no again and then he slammed me against the wall and I hit my head and back and then started screaming for

Steve for help. By then Chris was trying to drag me toward the door but I found out later that Steve bolted with James right behind him and slugged Chris, got him to the floor and put his foot on the wrist holding the gun and he dropped let it go.

"Moni, kick the gun away don't touch it and then James was on the phone to the police." I was panicked and of course having an anxiety attack and having trouble breathing. The police arrived and took Chris away again. Steve insisted we go to the clinic for the doctor to check me out. The doctor said I would have a big knot on my head and bruising but thought I would be fine just for me to come in the next morning or call in the evening if I had any symptoms of nausea or pain.

By the next day the bruising was very visible on my wrist, my back and I had a terrible headache. Steve took pictures to document in the legal way. What had I done to cause all of this mess I kept asking SELF. Steve said this was what he had been concerned about, he didn't know how erratic Chris could get. It seemed his episodes were coming more frequently. Basically he was stalking me now so I would have to continue having protection. Another brick in the road, was I to go around, over or through the pile. I wasn't sure.

Chris did get out on bail but was to be under psychological care. But after a few days he started calling me again. I told Steve, he was furious. There was a restraining order but that wouldn't matter to Chris if he wanted to get to me. I was to go nowhere without Antoinette or Steve but I was concerned about Steve. What if Chris came after him? With my kind of brain I could imagine all sorts of things. Steve had again contacted his friends at the police department so they would be on alert. We had to have surveillance at the condo and at his office. After a few days things seemed to settle down a bit with no incidents so we were feeling more comfortable. Steve still insisted Antoinette or he go with me for shopping or to the orphanage. We were hoping he was getting help and would leave us alone.

One evening just after New Year's Steve wanted to go to Vevey for dinner at Chez Phillip. I said fine but can I drive your "baby". He just handed me the keys saying I'll find out what kind of driver you are. So we were off in his Porsche. He said I was a good driver for a woman and of course I had to respond, "Just say good driver or I'll turn around and really burn rubber."

"Ok, ok, just joking."

I noticed a car in my rear view mirror and told Steve that we were being stalked. Chris is two cars behind us.

"Are you sure?"

"Yes I know there other silver Porsches but I can sense him breathing down our necks. What do we do?" I started to feel panic again.

"Watch in the mirror to see if he moves up. You just keep driving and I'll give you directions where to turn and go, I will say them at the last minute so be prepared."

"Now there's only one car in between."

"Ok, take the turn off for Vevey and you know we're on a straight road for awhile so get a heavy foot like I know you've been dying to do."

I turned off, lowered the accelerator until we were doing 70 but he was still behind us.

"Slow down and I'm going to give you some right and left turns, we'll try to lose him or get in front of the police station." So I slowed, "right here" a few blocks and "hang a left", a few more blocks, "right down this alley at the end a left, watch out it gets very narrow." We kept doing this through the small city like a jigsaw puzzle or if we were in a maze we were trying to get out of, which we were.

"Why are we doing this?"

"To see if he will give up and know we understand he's following us. Straight here" and voila the police station with Chris right behind us. Steve knew the direct way he was trying to avoid another scene. "Go directly in and ask for officer Fontaine or whoever you can get." I ran up the stairs and told them of the problem outside. I knew Steve would confront Chris and I was afraid. The officers came with me and the two were already physically fighting but no pistols thank God. They separated them and took them both inside for questioning, I just sat telling SELF, we're going back to our apartment in Vienna, this is not worth it. Steve came out and signed something shaking the hands of the officers. "Let's go." and we left to go home, he driving not me I was too upset. Steve was so angry, I had never seen this before, not at me, I'm sure at Chris his friend so we didn't talk. Near home he asked if we had anything to eat.

"I can fix something."

He went to change, I just took off my shoes and started the omelet trick with some small sausages, some fruit and a baguette from the day. He opened a bottle of wine and was still quiet. He ate, I nibbled. "You shouldn't have to go through this, I won't let him do this."

"Perhaps it's just better if I leave for awhile, to Vienna or Paris or home then he would stop it. I'm too much of a problem for you, you don't need the mess and confusion of this."

"Moni sometimes I think you don't get it. My life would be miserable without the joy you bring me. No, it will take time, going away won't solve it and I don't want you away from me. Perhaps after we're married he'll decide to stop. But from today, I'm sorry I know you'll feel like a prisoner, you have to go only with Antoinette or myself when you go out. I can't take a chance. He really is obsessed and needs help to accept the situation."

"Is he in jail again tonight?"

"No they're only holding him for awhile so we could come home and hopefully he will go home. Enough, thank you my chef for dinner, you make great omelets. Is there dessert?"

"You get two. Give me a few minutes for the first one." I had some light custard in the frig, so whipped some cream, mixed it with the custard, some fresh berries, a drop of liquor and a dribble of chocolate on the top and put it into a large goblet. It was gone in seconds and a smile started to appear again. "I don't know if I can take the second desert." I poured him another glass of wine.

"Right now I need to go to bed and watch something inane or interesting on TV, come with me." So we had had a difficult night and wanted to relax and be content with each other. He didn't get his second dessert because he fell sound asleep. About 3 am someone was pounding at the door and we knew who it was. Steve got on the phone to call the police again, he was creating a record of the pattern of behavior and trying to protect both of us. "Go away Chris. What did you do to the security guard downstairs?"

"He's out for the night. Open the door, I want to talk to both of you."

"No Chris we want no violence, just accept the situation and get on with it. We don't mean any harm to you, why are doing this to us?" Steve kept on talking through the door.

"Because Monique is mine."

"Monique is herself, she belongs to no one, her life is her choice. Let it go Chris realize she is not coming back to you, you lost her. You have lots of other ladies to turn to."

"Of course I do but not my special Monique. I'm miserable without her life around me."

"I understand but she is now afraid of what you might do."

"I won't hurt her, maybe the others, but not her."

Finally the police arrived and Chris was once more taken away. I felt so sad, sorry, empty. I wanted to help him but he needed professional help.

We just went back to bed but I could not sleep until about the time Steve had to leave. He just told me to stay in bed or do whatever, but that Antoinette would be over soon to stay with me until he could come home. What a mess. I was a prisoner in all this confusion and crazy behavior.

So I had no time to be free. Fortunately I liked Anotinette and she seemed to enjoy what I wanted to do with my days.

When I read, she read, when I was on the computer she read, and enjoyed listening to the music I frequently had on. She loved going to the restaurant with me, to the horses and even the orphanage. She walked with me on the lake front along with Shady and it was comfortable but I had no time to be alone which is something I always needed. I felt we were always looking over our shoulder which I knew she was. But she was there to help and in the process became a friend. So the next few days went, when she went home, Steve was home and we would go out or I would cook something. We all kept hoping it was at an end, that Chris would be taken care of, calm down and just look elsewhere.

One day Antoinette had to leave a little early, Steve said he would be home in a short while. Someone knocked at the door which was strange since we had a buzzer system at the main door but I thought perhaps Anoinette hadn't completely closed the door when she left. I was expecting a delivery so when the man at the door said "delivery" I without thinking opened the door and there stood Chris with a look in his eyes that frightened me. He obviously had been watching, stalking our movements since he knew the exact time to come to the condo. I asked him what he wanted and he just said "You" and pushed right in. "Pack some things, you are coming with me."

"I'm not going anywhere with you." I told him I wasn't his or anyones and said, "No I'm not going with you."

He pulled out a gun and said "You will come with me or I'll do us both in and we'll meet somewhere else."

I tried to calm down and tried to get him to sit and quiet down thinking that Steve would soon be home but he refused. "We need to go now, so get going."

I went into the bedroom and started putting some clothes into a suitcase. As I went into the bathroom to get my notion bag I picked up my cell phone hoping I would get a change to use it. I also left my engagement ring which I never took off so Chris wouldn't take it and as a signal to Steve. He grabbed my things and my arm and literally dragged me out the door,

down the stairs to his car. "Get in and don't try to get out."
He spun out the parking area much too fast and started for
highway A1.

A1 so we were on our way to Geneva. "I won't let Steve
or anyone be with you, you belong to me, my life is nothing
without you." I tried to talk calmly to him hoping I could
convince him to stop but he would not listen. I tried to speed
dial Steve so he would hear the conversation but couldn't do it
without pulling out the phone, I might have a chance later.

When we arrive in Geneva we went to an apartment area
where he stopped got out and then literally pulled me out. I
didn't know he had an apartment in the city. Inside he started
babbling about how he wanted only me and couldn't stand
what had happened. He was sorry for everything and asked
for forgiveness saying it would never happen again. I began
to realize that he was probably a manic state and it had gone
beyond his control. After a short while he wanted to go to get
something to eat and warned me not to try to signal anyone or
run or there would be trouble. I couldn't eat much of anything,
I was too frightened. We went back to the apartment where
he wanted to make love and I said no I could not. "You will,
you are mine. I will have you." He started in. I fought as best I
could but he would not stop and had his way, literally rape. I
was beside myself, how was I to get away. He said he needed to
get some sleep and so I wouldn't try to escape handcuffed one
of my arms to the bed. I couldn't believe what was happening.
The next morning I wanted to shower and thought perhaps I
could get to my cell phone. He told me to keep the door open
so he would know what I was doing. I turned on the shower
and got my cell but he was listening and came in grabbed the
cell away. "Don't even think about it."

When we were dressed, back into the car and I figured
out we were headed for the French border. He had told me he
had a small house in Provence but I had never been there so
didn't know exactly where. He calmed a bit but still had that
erratic look in his eyes so I just stayed quiet. Steve was smart

he would figure out hopefully in time before anything more terrible happened.

Steve had gotten home and saw the outer door open went into the condo calling for me, saw food out for dinner, closet doors open and the back French doors open and my ring so he knew right away. He called the police to report it giving them as much information as he could. They immediately put out an alert for the car and our descriptions. Since he knew all of Chris's business I figured he would know of the French house although he had never spoken about it.

We drove for hours only to stop for gas and a break. I was getting exhausted. I was trying to think how I could getaway but the gun was on my mind. We finally arrived in a small village and small house with a stone façade. I really wasn't sure where I was but knew it was France. "Get out we'll by staying her for awhile." He relaxed a bit and tried to talk more civilly to me, trying to appease. "Let me go Chris, this is not going to work, it won't do either of us any good. I can no longer trust. Take me home and I won't press any charges, believe me, just take me home please. I love you but I can longer share life with you, there is something wrong, you're so erratic."

"I'm not erratic just frantic because you're no longer with me. I can't stand it. There's no life without you. You're the only one that keeps me on a even keel. I don't think I can live if you're not with me."

"You need more help than I can give you. If you love me why would you make me so unhappy and try to hide me and give me no life?"

"I'll give you anything you want"

"It's not about things Chris they're meaningless it's about sharing life together, trusting and loving each other. I can't do that if I'm always afraid or on guard. Can't you realize that you're giving up everything each of us has by being too obsessed."

"I'm not obsessed It just hurts too much to be without you."

"So you'll hurt me to posses me. That makes no sense."

Then he came at me again to make love and force himself on me until I thought I would be ill or pass out. What was I going to do, I had to get out.

This went on for a week and I didn't think I could survive, the idea of what the gun could to seemed almost good. I thought maybe if I just walk out the door and start yelling and hope someone would come to the fore and help. Maybe he wouldn't use the gun on me but I couldn't be sure in his state of mind.

Steve and the police finally decided by asking various people that we were somewhere in France. Steve found out that Chris had a house but wasn't sure where but figured the south. They scoured the area but didn't know which house. He went into a café right in the town we were in and had a beer. He asked the bartender if he knew a Messieur Janee, he was an old friend and he was trying to locate him.

"Oh you mean the Swiss man, yes he is comes to the village, has a house here." "Could you show me where.?" "Bien sur, I will have my son go with you and show you." So Steve now knew which house but was cautious enough to go back to the police to get their help.

On the 7th evening of my captivity I heard something outside, someone walking, then another set of feet. Then it was quiet so I thought it was just people passing by. The gun was on the table behind where we were sitting. Chris was trying to talk with me once again how good it could be. He would take care of me and we would have a great life together. I couldn't begin to fathom how terrible it would be.

I heard footsteps outside again and then a man's voice saying he was with the police and demanded Chris to come out with no weapon. Chris grabbed the gun from the table put it to my back saying they wouldn't take us. "You are going to tell them we are coming out but that I have the gun on you and will shoot if they try to take us. I panicked and said they will kill us both. "No they will let us go so you won't get hurt. Yell out at them and tell them we are coming out and they are to give us an hour to drive away." I did as he said. They answered in the affirmative so we edged toward the front door. I opened the door and we were hit by the lights of several police cars. They said to drop the gun and let me go but Chris backed to the car and had me get in. As I got in one shot rang out. Chris yelled and went down dropping the gun. They had been able to get a shot off to his right arm. I got out and ran not knowing where I was going just getting out of there. The next thing I heard Steve's voice and him running after me telling me to stop as it would be ok. I turned and fell shakily into his arms and started to cry

Somewhere in my fog he was telling me he was sorry it taken so long to find us. He had figured it out as a last resort knowing Chris and that he would not stay in Switzerland where he would know the authorities would have an easier time finding us. They found no plane or train reservations so decided he had taken me not too far away. Steve didn't know of the French house but did a lot of sleuth work to finally get the general location in Provence. He had put that together via comments the staff of the restaurant and friends had made. Then he had gone to several cafes asking for Chris Janee saying he was an old friend but wasn't sure which house was his. The owner of one café knew the house so Steve called the police and they came with several cars. It was almost like a movie, the problem was we were part of it, not happily so.

The police took Chris away to the hospital. Steve took me to the police station so they could interview me and take down my statement. We were not far from Cannes so he decided to go to a lovely hotel to help me calm down before returning to Montreux. When we arrived he took me shopping for new things as I felt so dirty plus I needed makeup as I had a black eye from where Chris had hit me. I was once again safe. I was still shaking but he provided wine and talked to try to calm me down. "Let's go for dinner I think it will do you good rather than staying in with room service." He was so gentle and caring. I didn't know that Chris too would show his caring in the future even after what he had done to me.

Chris would be charged with kidnapping and possibly rape if I testified to it. This time he was in for jail time or probably psychiatric time. He was wealthy enough to get out on bail so we would still have to be careful. The next day we started back with me sleeping most of the way. We stopped in Mont Blanc and then the next day to Montreux. I was so happy to arrive home. It would take me many days to try to relax and get back to some normalcy. Steve was very loving but understood I needed time before we could really be together. We had missed our trip to Portugal but he said we would plan another date, not to worry. Chris did get out on bail so I had to go only with Antoinette or Steve if I went anywhere. When would this be over? I felt like I was locked up and the key had disappeared.

Two weeks after we had gotten back Steve called from the office. "Moni please sit down I have some news I need to give to you." "What's wrong, are you ok?" "I'm fine." Chris was in a car accident last night on his way to Geneva." "Oh no, what happened, is he alright?" "No Moni he didn't make it, he's dead." I was stunned, even with what he had done I still cared. "Was he alone?" "No, Stephanie, the distributor's daughter, was in the car." "Did she make it." "No. We don't know what happened, there were no skid marks and the car is in such bad shape they don't know if they'll be able to determine if it was mechanical." The tears began to flow, it was all too much. "Are you ok, you want me to come home?" "No I need to be alone right now to sort it all out. More bricks in the road that one couldn't get around but had to go straight through. I'll see you tonight." I went to the lake to walk and think, I was overwhelmed with emotion. I had come to have simplicity in my life and here was all this complication and confusion I had the feeling that I should just go back to Vienna and start over and once again be in my own control.

When Steve came home he told me Mom and Dad Janee were ordering an autopsy mainly to see if there was any problem on Chris's brain such as a tumor that caused his erratic behavior. That would take a few days so as he wanted to be cremated the memorial service would have to wait, he understood their need after all they had gone through with him. "We're going to have a few long, emotional days but it will pass and you will at last be free,"

But at what cost freedom.

The next morning Steve talked with me about some things regarding my financial situation. The reading of the will wouldn't be until the day after memorial service which I knew I would have to be at but expected nothing. Chris had taken out a $1,000.000.00 life insurance and listed me as beneficiary. There was insurance money coming for the car and Steve said there was cash available if I needed it. Steve had always taken care of most of Chris's financial concerns with the help of an accountant. He had explained that all to me much earlier. I was again in a numb state that Chris was taking care of me; that I would have something to work with. So I began to think he had planned the whole episode and Steve just looked at me and kept quiet. "I don't know. But at least he wanted to take care of you. Steve told me he also changed his will in October when I had returned after the first episode but couldn't discuss it with me until the reading of the will. I just wanted you to know you are going to be ok and give you some peace of mind."

The autopsy was completed and they found nothing, no tumor or other obstruction so said it was mental probably manic depressive with lots of confusion in between so the memorial service was set for the day after. Steve arranged everything. He had done all the preparation for the cremation plus contacted family and friends to tell them of the situation so I had only to sit and be miserable. Regardless of the difficulty of the last few months I knew that Chris had loved me, was always generous and kind until the end when his behavior changed drastically. My solace of course was always the horses so I went to the stable and talked with them and Curt and found some peace.

Steve came to pick me up, always at my side. We went to the chapel where Chris and I at one time had planned to be married. The memorial service was held there. Again I sat through everything in a numb state talking to SELF about what I really felt. Then we went to the restaurant for the typical get together which I've never understood but somehow seems necessary and went vaguely through everything until Steve said, "I'm taking you home now; no more of this." We went home in silence. Maria, both Moms and Dads came with us and we had some tea and commiserated. I could only think about my past with Chris, wonder if we had been able to be together how would it have been. I felt terrible thinking that way when I had this wonderful person who would soon be my husband, Steve. I just had to think it through as to how it would have ended up. When you've lost someone to death you have to mourn and find your own way. Steve understood that and didn't interfere. I wondered what my future was really going to be.

The next day was the reading of the will, Steve was the executor. Chris provided for Maria and Curt for their lifetime which I would have done.

He said his parents were fine with their estate, as was his brother who had received what Steve had from his parents. Joachim was to receive $250,000, Wachter, the chef at the hotel, $100,000, Jacque $100,000, to Herr and Frau Gottlieb currently the managers at the vineyard $100,000, to Hans $50,000. Then Steve read from the will "To my beloved, loving, intelligent, sensuous Monique, the love of my life, who I hurt not willingly, I leave the house which is paid for, the vineyards, the stables, the restaurant and the hotel which have mortgages but provide enough revenue to maintain that and still realize a profit. She has all the capabilities of taking care of it much better than I. Also my investments and money in the amount of $10,000,000 which she may use anyway she chooses. I want to make amends for all the grief I have given her. In the will Chris said," Steve help her through the trusts set up. I entrust lovely Monique to you, you must be her guardian, personal attorney and take good care of her as you love her as much as I." At the end was a simple "au revoir, God bless you all". He had left letters for his parents, Steve and myself which made me wonder again if the accident was just an accident. It seemed so well planned. I would never know for sure.

I had to excuse myself and go outside by the lake because I was overwhelmed. I thought I guess his manic side tried to take care of whom he loved. I wouldn't understand until years later how true my feelings were. So I began my new journey; one I had never anticipated, wealth with lots of responsibility with the vineyard, restaurant and hotel when I had come looking for simplicity. Where does life take you. I would find the strength to do it somehow with lots of assistance from all the wonderful people around me. I had to go ahead to meet the next bricks that would inevitably arrive.

Steve came out to retrieve me saying not to worry he would be there to help all along the way. "You are now a wealthy woman with lots of responsibility but I guarantee I'll be right at your side to assist. You know I'll help you with the businesses, you won't be on your own so don't be overwhelmed." We went and walked on the shore of the lake asking ourselves if it had been an accident. At this point what did it matter except to maybe leave us with some guilt and more grief. Maybe we had pushed him to the brink.

After the reading of the will everyone went their way and Steve took me to the condo. We just lied on the couch with Shady by our side and I wept, I was totally emotionally exhausted. He just held me and said, "Let it all go, it is over now and you and I will go on." What a gorgeous man, my soul mate. I had always managed to take care of myself in some sort of fashion even while giving to others and hadn't expected anything from Chris with all that had transpired. Needless to say I was in a state of disbelief. I had always been a working girl and now I was being handed wealth with a lot of responsibility. Could I take care of it all. How life can change in an instant without one doing a thing but going through it. I had never been interested in wealth, just a fulfilling life. But now I would have access to a lot, but a lot of work too. At least I knew that if I lost it all I would survive I always had worked and could do it again. I was not the type to just sit around and have her nails done so I would be now more that super active. So I said to SELF, "Dust yourself off and get on with it."

My parents were deceased but now I had two sets of new parents one of which said I was like a daughter to them, the new ones I would soon have via marriage, Maria so loving, Curt so helpful and Steve to keep it all together so I would have to take on the challenge and still do the special things that I loved, the art, music, horses, the writing. I had to make it all work for the sake of all the people I loved. Fortunately Steve's parents decided to come over for the service. They had known Chris since he and Steve were at Harvard and felt like he was an adopted son. I enjoyed them and their visit provided a needed distraction from the sadness I felt plus getting to know more of his family. They now lived in Connecticut semi-retired both being attorneys who during Steve's childhood had been in international law in Geneva the reason Steve and his brother had grown up there.

The next morning Steve and I discussed the house and decided I should move in right away to start taking care of things and so the next day I started packing my clothes, books and papers, looked around at the condo which had come to be so comfortable to me, said au revoir to Madame Gigande saying I would visit, organized Shady and his food and we were ready to take on the big house. We knew we couldn't get everything into Steve's Porsche so Curt was there with the truck to take care of everything. The house was beautiful but how empty it felt now without its creator but I had lived here for awhile and would try to make it home. Maria, Curt and I just sat there for awhile until I said "We have to get on with it, remember his life and all he offered." So Maria and I changed the linens and then went to the market to pick up a few things. I started moving Chris's things to a storage area in the garage for later donation. Mom and Dad Janee came over to look at photos and any other things they might want as remembrances. We talked, cried again but then agreed that we had to get on with the future. They wanted to stay close which I was glad of. A loved one dead and those who remained had to go forward and try to hold on to only the good memories.

I told Steve that I wanted a few days by myself in the house to think, meditate and get rid of some ghosts. He wasn't happy but said he understood and would go to the condo. Would I at least go out to dinner with him. The first evening I walked up to the point where Chris and I had often gone. The view was stupendous. The sun was just going down so the colors were rich yellows and golds shining on the lake which was so still it looked like a colored mirror. The aroma of the earth, the grape vines, the evergreens were all around me. As the sun gradually went down the colors became even richer with some vibrant reds until dusk was there, the sun was gone and the lights of the city came on like stars. It was magical and so peaceful not a sound except for the crickets and occasional nicker from one of the horses in the stable. The solace was much welcomed. I went in to the kitchen to get something to eat and then to my oasis of a room to read, contemplate and try to think toward the future and what to do first

The next morning I got going with some plans. Since Chris had me work in the kitchen I knew how things functioned so I immediately made Jochaim head chef with all the responsibilities of a manager with an increase in salary and he was to hire another sous chef to assist. He exclaimed and gave me a big hug. He would of course always be in touch with me, I would check in and even help in the kitchen if needed. Regarding the hotel, our new chef there was doing a great job but I knew as a woman in the situation I had to assert my authority which I did and he accepted that. So I would be governing over two kitchens with European men but they seemed ok with it. My kitchen at home would only be in occasional use. Next I had to go over all the financial situation with Steve again who had taken care of Chris's finances for years. I knew I was now a wealthy woman but needed to manage everything well. I would pick up reports from the restaurant and hotel each month to go over everything to keep up with the finances and progress. I trusted Steve implicitly so he would guide me through the investments and trusts.

I went to Mom and Dad Janee to talk to Dad again about purchasing 100 more acres adjacent to ours and he agreed to come and look it over and we would talk and see if it was feasible. He had so much knowledge in the winery business I wanted his involvement in my idea. He was a young enough man and really needed to be involved with interesting adventures to keep him alive and well.

He looked over the land, we walked the property and he got so excited gave me a big hug saying, "Hello my new partner. You have a great idea to keep the Janee legacy going and I want to assist and be part of it."

I called Steve and asked him to do a search on the property and to organize the necessary financial papers to purchase. He was quiet for a moment, then said "So you will stay here and work the property and not run away from me."

I responded, "You asked me to marry you and that is what I want most there's nothing without you no meaning to anything. I will need your help in organizing and keeping everything going, we'll do it lovingly together. You'll be part of the winery business too."

"I'd like nothing better to be totally with you I agree there is nothing if we're not together. Ok I will get the information on the property and we'll talk tonight. I'll be there about 7pm".

"Wonderful. Oh, Steve would you do me a favor and pick up some fresh flowers so I don't have to go out? Also there is very little for dinner here and I don't want to go out. I'll call Joachim and see what he has and Jacque can bring it up. I know you'll be starving.""

"I'm already hungry."

"Also I would like to drink some wine and I know you will and I don't want you to drive when it's dark if you imbibe so bring some things to stay for the night if you're comfortable being in the house. We have a lot to talk about.

"It's just a house Moni, I've been there so many times it is a bit like a home to me. Don't worry I'll be fine anywhere as long I'm with you."

I told him that all Chris's clothes were now in the storage area until I found an organization that could use them. All the linens are changed so I'm trying to think it's my home or hopefully our home. Mom and Dad have already selected what they wanted. I just don't want to be without you. I'm going to make a few changes here to erase the past and you will feel more comfortable then we'll decide if we really need to build."

There was one thing that might be difficult and it would be for Steve, the reminder of Chris his house, his property which was now mine but still all the remembrances were there and I had to understand and take care no matter what he had said about it. I decided first to ask him outright how he felt about living in the house. He thought it was just a structure so if we made it ours via redecorating to our combined taste he might be more receptive. I was anticipating another brick in the road. His response was that he had known Chris for so many years he was family but did want me to redecorate. The new decor would make it our home; another project. It was time to let Chris go and move forward to another world. I got thinking that we would probably never build the other house, it seemed like too much when we had this one.

Steve arrived and we ate and talked at length. It was too soon to go the next step emotionally so he slept in one of the guest suites. At breakfast I told him I still needed some time alone and he seemed to understand although not happily so. Even though I loved him and wanted to share everything I think I still was craving my single life, the one I had had in California for awhile and Vienna, fewer complications.

I decided to start redecorating right away to try to erase some of the memories and make Steve more comfortable. The big project was the bathroom. I called the man at the paint store and the one from the carpet store to come up and measure starting top would be the basins in marble in pearl like finish. The shower would have floor to ceiling 6 inch tile also to be used on the splash and top of tub, white marble on the floor. It would be terrific. The cabinet maker started, the painters were ready to begin. I selected a wall paper in cobalt blue with metallic sections, paint with just very small hint of blue for around the white cabinet and one wall. I decided on a very light grey berber style carpet which I would use throughout the house. I got in touch with the electrician to put track lighting over the bed and in the closet with small cans and on a dimmer so we could adjust the effect. By the third day the lights were up, the painting and wallpapering complete. The tile man was completing the tile work and the marble flooring.

For furniture I wanted an overstuffed, comfortable look so Mom and I to Geneva where there would be more selection. We found a coach in medium grey and a overstuffed chair in my shade of blue with an ottoman which Steve had been hinting about. It would come after the carpet was laid. I did not like standard drapes so did accordion style fabric shades for the windows then long ones in a nubby white linen fabric with a simple cord tie back mostly for a softening, finished look along the sides. The furniture arrived with special floor based reading light and a nest of table. I had been able to finish it in 5 days with lots of organizing and a little elbowing.

Saturday morning I called Steve who sounded down. "Hi, would you come home tonight to stay?"

He sighed "I began to thing you were never going to say those words."

"I have a surprise for you. Pick up some things and come home. What time can you get here?"

"I'll go drop things off at the laundry/cleaners and come up about 4 pm ok? I want to take you dinner to Chateux Chillon.

"Wonderful. See you soon."

He arrived with more fresh flowers and nearly smothered me with his hug and kisses. Like a kid he asked where the surprise was. I took him upstairs to show him.

His face lit up when he looked around, immediately he went to his chair. I showed him the track lighting and how they could be dimmed. He went into the closet and said, "Now you can really see the colors when making a selection and you organized everything so we can find stuff." Then he went into the bathroom and just said "fantastic." I love those kinds of bowls, the tile and the marble. Perfection. Now I understand why you did all of this, you wanted to make it our room to help fight the past . . . you succeeded." He understood my thoughts and ideas.

He went back to his special chair and ottoman I knew he wanted and sat immediately just sighing.

"I'm going to keep going throughout the house, ok?"

"Whatever you want. Your interior design talents along with all your others, are amazing. You get even better with practice. You just go ahead and do whatever you want. Send me all the bills because I can include them in the hotel renovation you're going to start and it will help a little on taxes." So I would get busy continuing to plan the rest of the renovation. I needed to continue redecorating because I see that it in fact did erase some of the memories and make Steve more comfortable. He was always so appreciative, helpful and loving it was the least I could do for him and I admit for myself too. And after the practice I was having to keep coming up with new ideas. I really hadn't been able to be open to self expression at this level without conflict from my ex-husband.

So I got started with painting the living room in white, because of the high ceilings would require a lot of work, scaffolding and all, but by Monday I had the painters there and getting started. Next they would do the adjacent dining room in a tint of green. I would use emerald green for seat cushions and pillows for accent. When it was time to put the carpet down I wanted them to wrap the base of the bar in the same carpet for an effect. In the guest rooms I selected soft blue for both but would find different spreads for each. So things got underway and would continue through Maria's apartment, the kitchen and Curt's apartment. I got his opinion of what he might like. Of course it was his apartment so I didn't want to force my style on him. I wanted it all clean and new.

I talked with Steve about going to Vienna mid March now that the Chris's problem was settled for good. He knew how important it was to me, that I had the comforts of my apartment and Jennie and Peter to watch over me so he relented. I was off again to Vienna feeling quite free wondering why I needed to feel that way when I had so much at home. I left definite instructions with the contractor and how to reach me if he had questions, otherwise he was to go ahead as planned. Maria would be there to watch over the crew and report the progress to me as would Steve.

Paul was having an exhibit of an American artist, the opening was to be on Friday so I was scheduled to leave Thursday at noon. Steve drove me to the airport Thursday giving me all sorts of instructions and staying with me through check in and looking like a little boy. I assured him I would be fine, not to worry. I was off to Vienna once again planning to spend only 4 nights. My flight arrived at 2pm and I Heinrich was there to pick me up. When I got to the apartment I just smiled and some tears came. I loved this place and wanted always to be able to come back. At the same time I had been homesick for California but couldn't do it all. Perhaps in the near future Steve and I would travel to the states. I called Jennie and said I was in so she came right over and we were again like school chums jabbering away. She told me about her new architectural contract to redesign three historical buildings keeping the outside authentic but creating a modern inside which took a lot of research. It was a huge project but would be most rewarding for her. She was really excited.

Peter came over saying that they had to feed me again. What wonderful friends I had found in them. We spent some time together that evening,

I went back to the apartment, put things away and fell into bed and the cell rang again, this time Steve. "Is everything ok?"

"Everything is fine, I've just come across from having dinner with Jennie and Peter. Tomorrow I'll be at the gallery to be sure everything is in good order, then come home to change for the exhibit in the evening and of course we will go out for a late dinner with everyone talking and laughing."

"You love it don't you."

"Yes, it is a different world but it is wonderful that I can experience this one and the one in Montreux. Just remember you are the most important part of all the things I do. You must tell me if I ever slight you, I don't want to, you are my center. The rest really doesn't in the end mean anything if I'm not with you I don't want to be selfish and do only what I want."

"You just humbled me and made me realize I can be selfish too. Ok, we keep the apartment in Vienna and you go as you need to, no questions asked. Do what gives you your joy."

"My dear, loving, generous Steve, thank you for being so understanding and wonderful to me. You know by now I would do it anyway."

"Sure, but this way I look like the good guy."

Laughter.

I went to the gallery Friday morning. Paul had not done this kind of exhibit before with the work of an American so he was anxious for my help so we had been busy weeks before sending out emails and brochures to everyone because we knew this might be a difficult sale exhibit in Europe. The work was collage of drawing and fabrics and papers in very bright colors. I assisted with organizing everything, the positioning of the art pieces and the cataloguing. When everything was in order I went back to the apartment to change and get ready for the evening. Steve called to see if everything was ok so I filled him in on the days activities. "Please call Heinrich, no streetcar."

"Heinrich will pick me up and Paul will bring me home after dinner and Jennie and Peter will be here so I'm well taken care of, so don't worry."

"Moni, you know I always worry about you, I have nothing without you"

"I'll be fine. My friends always watch out for me. I have the exhibit tonight and perhaps I have to go in tomorrow for other clients, Jennie and I want to go to Gabrielle in the afternoon to see about the dresses and we will go somewhere for dinner in the evening and then I'll be home Sunday afternoon and be with you. Everything is planned."

"Ok, but call me in between so I can hear your voice and know you are ok"

"I will, night and day, you will have no rest and no looking around at those pretty blonds.

"I'm not looking don't worry I won't have rest until you're home. I have my list for the invitations so we will take care of that when you return. I can't wait to do this. He sounded so excited like a bride should be."

"Ok we'll take care of that when I'm home. Be sure you have everyone on the list. Did you call your mom and dad?"

"Yes and they're so excited. They never thought it would happen and quite honestly I didn't either but then came Monique, the love of my life."

"They will stay in the house as will Jennie and Peter, everyone else in the hotel, I've already blocked the suites we just need to make their plane reservations."

"Genevieve can do that. So it's Jennie, Peter, Paul, Juliana, Gabrielle, Max and friend, and my parents."

"Right."

"Done"

"Are you happy with all of this?"

"Ecstatic."

"Perfect. I have to get dressed now for the opening so goodbye."

"Bye. I hope the exhibit goes well and you sell a lot. Knock their socks off."

"I'll try for Paul, the artist and myself. It's just so exciting to be a part of it."

"You can do the same here too you know."

"Yes in a different way, not like in Vienna but I have thought of it especially when the jazz festival is in full swing, we'll see."

"Enjoy love but don't overdo. Go to sleep to get your rest, think of me here alone missing you."

"You're not alone, you have Shady, I don't."

"Oh, so Shady is my real company."

Laughter.

"Don't dance with any new men."

"Promise I won't."

"When you go out tomorrow with the group, I want a report on your crazy friend."

"He probably has another new girlfriend, don't worry."

"But you'll go to that great restaurant and dance with several guys and I'll be sweating in my office worried about you and wanting to be there, maybe the next trip."

"Don't worry, here I can take care of myself and there is no one like you here, their just friends and I know how to handle them if they even try to come on. Remember Paul watches over me much like you do so I am in good hands. He and Juliana will drive me home tonight and Jennie is here so I'll be fine. Don't you go down the streets in Montreux and let some voluptuous blond pick you up, they are always looking your way. They wonder why you have a skinny little thing next to you."

"I see them look and cross the street and ignore them, not interested. I have had enough of their type in my past. I only want you."

I got dressed and called Heinrich to pick me up to go to the gallery. At the opening that evening we made a couple of sales and of course I had my friends who were always there; fantastic people. After a group of us went out to our hang out the Schlau Katz to celebrate and give me a chance to catch up on all the activities. Steve kept calling to check up on me in a loving way. He said he was having trouble sleeping because I wasn't there. I said he had to keep understanding my need sometimes to just do my own thing, not with another man or men, just me being alone or with my other friends.

I was on the move the entire time Saturday. I would have to be at the gallery again as other people were coming in. First Jennie and I went to Gabrielle's studio to see some new things and of course to purchase something. Jennie found a couple of hand knit sweaters she couldn't do without and I found a knit skirt and top with a diagonal pattern in shades of blue. By Saturday evening I was tired and wanted to spend some time with Jennie and Peter so I didn't go out. We just cooked together, had some wine and talked about a lot of things. Sunday morning we went for a walk in the Vienna woods and to Grinzing for lunch. In the afternoon Heinrich picked me up for the airport with his wife and two children along. I had some gifts for them since they were always so hospitable to me with dinners at their home and Heinrich's driving me wherever I needed to go. Delightful people.

I returned to Montreux on Sunday in early evening, Steve was lovingly there to pick me up. We went to Chez Janee for dinner and then home to cuddle and talk about the happenings in Vienna.

The next day I stopped by the office to ask Steve a question about something with the renovations, Genevieve and Ruth looking a little sheepish said he was with a client and it might be awhile. "I'll wait a few minutes and if he's not finished come back later." The girls talked with me I think to cover some strange noises coming from the office. In a little while the door opened and there was Steve with his jacket off caressing the arms of a very attractive woman who was looking so intently at him. I heard the words ok "later at the hotel." Big brick in the road. I was up and out in a flash, déjà view Chris. I ran down the stairs jumped into my car and heard Steve yelling behind me "Monique, stop." I didn't want any explanations or confrontation, I was a horse and I was getting away.

CHAPTER 19

I called the travel agent and asked her to book me on the morning flight Tuesday for JFK and she was not to share the information with anyone. I then called Bob and Susan Sanders my clients in New York and asked if they would be home that I had a last minute business trip. "Of course. What's your flight. I said I would let them know. "What nice hotel is in your area?" "You don't need a hotel you will stay with us we have a lovely guest suite and you are most welcome." "I don't want to impose, I will be staying until Sunday." "No imposition, we insist. Let us know your flight and our driver will pick you up." I ordered a driver to go to Geneva at 1:00 pm so rushed into the house, got Maria and started laying out clothes for Maria to pack, my jewelry in order, got my computer and my manuscripts in their case. I gave last minute instructions to the contractor and by 12:45 pm was ready. I asked Maria to make a couple of sandwiches and give me a bottle of water and told her not to worry I would be fine and call her later. The driver arrived and I was off to Geneva where I would stay at the hotel Intercontintal overnight since the flights went out in the early am. I knew I was once again a horse running away at the first smell of confusion or danger, it was my survival kit, not confrontation. It allowed me to feel I was holding on to SELF. I decided to get away quite some distance to lick my wounds but accomplish something at the same time. I had learned that this was the way I could cope, I hated immediate confrontation and needed time away to clear my thoughts and feelings before facing it. I was once again a horse running away but I would find that was fantasic one of my journeys.

I called Bob, gave him the flight number and time and said also that I wanted to meet with the wine distributor and a couple of publishers for my book entitled at the moment Mysterious Feast, who knew if the editor would come up with something else for more appeal. This was a brand new area for me so I would have much to learn. He said he would start arranging the meetings plus dinners and other entertainment. He would send a car and driver to pick me up at the airport the next day. So one of my journeys was beginning.

I had some wine in my room and got organized for the next morning. I decided to just have some dinner at the hotel rather than going out by myself although I did take a little walk in the afternoon before dinner. The next morning I was up and out early to catch my 9:30 am flight out of Geneva to New York. When I arrived in JFK the driver was there but we were in a lot of traffic so I didn't get in until about 4:00 pm. Bob and Susan were waiting and seemed please I had come for a visit. Their penthouse was fantastic, large, bright, well decorated and with an unbelievable art collection. They were so warm and friendly, I was happy to be there. They took me up to the guestroom suite, it was most tasteful also.

"Get freshened up and when ready come down for cocktails. We're going out for dinner with Alice and George tonight to one of my restaurants."

"Great, I won't be long. Dressy?"

"Yes."

So I showered and then put on my black dress with the one sleeve and tulip style skirt and went down to oohs and ahhs from Susan about the dress." With your taste we have to go shopping, perhaps on Friday." "I'd like that, I do want to see some interesting shops and I have gifts I want to buy." It was going to be a very busy few days. She gave me a tour of the penthouse especially their art collection. They had oil paintings, pastels, lithographs and etchings, and sculpture pieces of different artists and different times. They were now focusing on the contemporary so we had lots to talk about.

There intercom rang and Bob said come up we want you to meet someone. A young, very nice, well dressed man appeared. It was their nephew just dropping by, I think. He joined us and then Bob invited him to join us for dinner. He looked at me and said, "with pleasure." Alice and Stan arrived and we all enjoyed cocktails and discussed their art collection. As we were getting ready to leave the phone rang, Bob picked up and motioned to me. "It's a man for you, I think your Steve." He had found me already.

"Moni, what are you doing."

"I might ask you the same."

"She's someone I was with 3 years ago, came into to talk to me supposedly about legal things and was so seductive I fell for it. I am so sorry it happened, I have no other excuse except that I'm a man and easily swayed."

"I guess so, but you were also making arrangments to see here again, you can't deny that. If that's what you want do it, I told you my parameters of intimate faithfulness. If you don't accept them that's your prerogative. Go ahead and see her don't expect much from me."

"Don't be angry. It won't happen again. I'll make it up to you."

"I'm more than angry, I'm very hurt and you know what I do when I feel that way. I don't know right now if you can make it up to me."

"When are you coming home so we can talk about it?"

"I won't get in until Monday morning."

"I'll come and get you."

"No I'll come with a driver and I want to be in the house by myself for several days so I suggest you go to the condo until I figure out how I feel and what I want to do. I have to go now, they're waiting for me to go to dinner."

"Ok. I'll call you tomorrow."

"Everything ok?"

"Not really but don't worry about it."

Bob's restaurant, "Chez Roberts," was very large and elegant well laid out with various dining areas rather than one large room. We were led to his special table and of course then the wines appeared. They were most gracious and most friendly in a more relaxed American way, fewer formalities. We talked and laughed and then ordered dinner. Bob said he had made an appointment for lunch with the wine distributor for the next day and also one with Rand House at 4:00 pm. He knew the owner whose arm he twisted to get the appointment. He was also trying for the day after at Mariner Publishing where again he knew the owner. If this didn't work, I guessed it would be very difficult in the publishing world. His nephew Larry asked if I would like to dance so we did. He was most attentive but I said to SELF, he's wasting his time. I will be going home.

On Wednesday Bob and I left for lunch and had a long conversation with the distributor. Bob had saved a couple of bottles of Janee and G wine so we tasted. The distributor said he would like me to send a bottle of each variety of Janee and G wine, which I said I would do so he know the entire gamut. Bob ordered 8 cases Chardonnay and Pinot Noir two of each blend of both Janee and G wineries saying he wanted it now until the distributor made his decision. I couldn't ask for more support.

After lunch we went directly to Rand House where we met with the owner who immediately called for a reader who was to complete it that night and have a report by the next the morning. I began to understand what a strong business man Bob was with many connections. I was in second heaven.

On the way home Bob got a call from Marineer. We could meet at 12 the next day, the owner had made some time. I started crossing my fingers, something had to come out of this.

That evening we went out for dinner again to a different restaurant owned by a friend; Larry joined us again. Bob said he wanted me to experience different ones so I might find ideas for my two. This one was highly contemporary in décor and offered a more Japanese flare with sushi and open grill cooking. The food was delicious. I was having such a good time with them I had forgotten how upset I was when I departed from Montreux.

On Thursday we got ready to go for our 12 pm meeting. On the way Bob got a call from Rand House asking if we could come by at 4 pm the only time the owner had and of course he said yes. The reader had done a very approving report on my book and the owner was making an offer. Bob being an attorney said he wanted to talk with me in private. He said he wanted to negotiate as we had the other meeting also and see what would be the best deal. I put it into his hands and I thought he knew much more than i. Rand was offering $150,000.00 up front and 10% of net book sales. Bob offered back $200,000.00 and 15% of sales, all expenses paid for book signings and anything else regarding marketing the book. The owner accepted the offer and immediately called in a couple of his editors to talk with us. One seemed most interested so I selected David to work with. I said with all I had in Montreux to take care of the editor would have to come there, I wouldn't be able to be at length in New York. I would be available for book signings but that was if everything went well. I could offer the hotel at no charge, they would foot the bill for his transportation. He could have stayed at the house but I felt being near the town he would have more activity and I wouldn't have him around every minute. It ended with Bob saying we would go to the next appointment the next am, find out the offer and he would get right back to Rand with a definite answer. I had to pinch myself to believe this was all happening. I had been extra nice and helpful with them in Vienna and now it was all coming back my way. They had to do the same with a reader so we wouldn't know until Friday. It was going to be a long night.

Once again dinner out at Bob's other restaurant Hickory Tavern just the 3 of us which was nice since we could talk easier. It was much more relaxed with lots of wood and comfortable décor plus a very good musical group. As we were dancing, Bob said please play the piano, these musicians won't mind, they've been with me so many years. So I sat with the piano player and we did a little jamming and then he said, "Time to do your own thing." I was nervous, this was New York, not my little Montreux but I started and played a couple of things, even sang one. Back at the table Bob and Susan both said "We should get you here with your cooking ability and music skills you could run another restaurant for us."

"What an offer, but I'm afraid I'm tied to Montreux and Vienna, can't bounce around forever."

"We really must see more of Geneva and Montreux, your hotel and restaurant sometime."

"Anytime you wish, you will be my guests."

On Friday Susan, Alice and I were off shopping. They took me to Soho and Greenwich to shops they knew rather than all the larger department stores. Since I hadn't brought a lot with me I picked out a couple of dresses done by young designers one for evening one for day wear, and a pant suit all interesting unusual designs anything but the typical department store look. Susan and Alice got carried away themselves making their purchases. Then we went to a leather shop they knew where I found a buttery leather coat in a style I had been wanting and also a suede jacket for Steve although I wasn't sure he deserved it. At other shops I found a beautiful blouse for Jennie, a book on local architecture for Peter, scarf for Maria, shirt for Curt, vests for Genevieve and Ruth. I then needed more shoes so with all of this we had to buy another suitcase or I wouldn't make it home. Somewhere in all of this we found time to squeeze in a quick lunch at the deli. While at lunch Bob called and gave me the offer of Mariner, good but not up to Rand so we decided Rand. The owner wanted to meet at 5pm to do the contract so we girls had to move fast. They dropped me off and went home with all the loot. Bob went over the contract and had me sign so I was actually going to be published after having worked on my novel for two years. The owner wanted to start as soon as possible so

I said I could begin on Thursday. I got on the phone to the hotel and talked with Emil about blocking a suite for at least two weeks, gave him the editor's name saying to reserve a suite and a note that anything he needed regarding food or services were to be included. I would explain everything when I got home. The owner was impressed. We were all pleased that the contract was completed and soon editing would be on its way.

After we returned to the penthouse Steve called just to see what I was doing.

"Well I have a contract with Rand House and will be working with an editor soon. I'll tell you all about it when I get home. We'll talk. Right now I have to get ready for dinner again. We were out shopping most of the day, even had to buy another suitcase to pack it full. Tomorrow I'm going to cook for them so will be shopping during the day, there will be 8 of us so I'll have to put together a menu tonight. They have wonderful kitchen, fully equipt so it will be fun."

"Fantastic about the publishing contact. All that work and you call it fun."

"It's a way of creative expression, I love it.

It was time for dinner again. We were going to a French style restaurant know for its fish dishes. I thanked them for all this entertainment. The food at the French restaurant was suberb. I wished I had the access to such variety of fish in Montreux. We had another lovely evening. Returned home to a nice brandy before settling in. They told me they had tickets for Sunday night on broadway would I stay and go with them. I immediately said yes and said I had to change my plane reservations for Tuesday, call Steve and let him know.

Tomorrow evening you will dine at Chez Janee.

"You're going to cook for us."

"Yes, It's the least I can do as a thank you. I'll have to take one of you or one of your maids with me to show me the nearby places for food, I'll have quite list of things. How many should I plan for?"

"I know Alice and Stan would love to come and we have another couple, very good friends, plus I'm sure Larry. He's been wanting to get you away just the two of you but I did say I thought you were spoken for and did love Montreux plus we had so much to accomplish."

"Ok so 8 for dinner at Chez Janee. I'll make my list tonight and go shopping in the morning and get ready. One thing I did want to do. I saw a piece of art in one of the galleries we went in that I would like to purchase so if I get going in the morning would we have time to do that?

"We'll make time. Remember which one?"

"Yes in the Soho area, I know exactly, in fact I could just take a cab if you have something to do."

"No we'll go with you and see what's there and what you purchase."

I purchased the piece I wanted a wonderful pen and ink drawing of a standing nude and had it packed for travel. I was really going to be loaded on the plane. Bob and Susan found something they wanted also and they always purchased.

They told me they had tickets for Sunday night on Broadway would I stay and go with them. I immediately said yes and said I had to change my plane reservations for Tuesday which I did. Then I called Steve who was in court so left a message with Genvieve.

In the morning I went grocery shopping with the maid in tow. I bought a lot of fresh vegetables including small artichokes for an appetizer. I had decided on Cornish game hens with a wild rice, fruit and nut stuffing. I also made a tart fruit gelatin platter for color and compliments to the hens. In between my preparations we went to Soho to the galleries. I purchased the piece I wanted and had it packed for travel. I was really going to be loaded on the plane. Bob and Susan found something they wanted also and they always purchased

When we got back I prepared a mixed green salad including arugala, hearts of palms, cherry tomatoes, sliced green beans and topped it with a vinaigrette dressing. For dessert I did a swirled chocolate and vanilla pudding flavored by grand marnier and topped with a little swirl of whipped cream with some chocolate wafers I made. We served, they oohed and aahed, talked, laughed, drank some excellent Chardonnay and thoroughly enjoyed.

Bob interjected again that he should get me back to New York to run a new restaurant for me called Chez Monique with unusual dishes and lots of art. "I' m afraid I have almost more than I can handle at home and now with the book I will be back. I'll give your cooks some of my ideas on my return. How's that?"

The next morning Bob and I went over the wine and publisher deals. We relaxed most of the day because of the theater and a late dinner at Chez Roberts. When Steve called I told him I wouldn't be in until Tuesday because of the broadway production. He responded that I didn't miss a thing. And I said why should I.

Monday afternoon I had everything packed and ready. I told him I couldn't thank him enough both of them for their kindness and generousness in accommodating my every need. Dinner this evening was to be at Chez Roberts again. They promised to come to Montreux soon which would be fun.

Tuesday morning we all lugged my paraphanelia to the elevator with the help of the driver and loaded it all in and with hugs and goodbyes I left for the airport. The flight was on time and I began to think I was going to have fun at the airport but the driver said he would help take in the luggage and I would get checked in. In Montreau I had to enlist some help getting everything out to meet the driver and finally was all settled in the car and on the way home. When I got there Curt and Maria helped get everything upstairs and then I was pooped. Maria was going to make some tea and snacks while I showered and changed.

CHAPTER 20

The phone rang and of course it was Steve wanting to know the situation.

"I got in fine with too much stuff have had some breakfast and now am going to take a nap before unpacking as the trip has done me in."

"I would like to see you for dinner, are you up to it?"

"Ok but don't come around until about 8 pm, I should be in good shape by then." I wasn't sure I was really up to hearing his explanation but we had to do it sometime. I had done a lot of thinking even though busy in New York and new I cared so much that I had to find out what he would tell me and how I would respond to it. I wouldn't know until I confronted it head on. I still felt angry and hurt but that seemed to be a part of life that never was guaranteed not to happen. Maybe one has to realize that and go ahead and jump in, not however, without reservations several times in your life, you just go through it.

Steve arrived around 8 pm with flowers in hand and a bit of a shy, anxious look on his face. I wonder why. He kissed me on both cheeks, finally smiled and said "let's get going." I'd like to go to the restaurant by Chillon, the intimate "Le Chateux which we liked so much for its ambiance and excellent menu.

After a few sips of wine and some tales of my trips to New York he started. "She was someone I used to see about 3 years ago, we did have a steamy but short affair. She came in to see me, she said, for some legal work but kept going back to the time we had spent together. She is very much a seductress and before I knew it she made her play. She totally surprised me approaching me the way she did in my office. I would have thought she wanted to go somewhere but she came right on. And before I knew it we were hot and heavy. That is not to excuse me but I am a man and my ego was right there. All I've felt is anger with myself and grief since that day. I am so sorry, I would never want to hurt you. I know and understand how you feel about commitments of intimacy and trust and I broke them in a moment of lust and weakness. All I can do is ask your forgiveness

"But in your office and when I saw you were caressing her arm and obviously making arrangements to see here again that evening how do you think I would react. I wanted no part of it and the horse came out, I just wanted to get away and lick my wounds. I have lust and an ego too."

"Soon as I saw you going out I knew my mistake and was scared to death you would take off. You did it so quickly I couldn't catch up. I did not see her again except to return her legal papers and tell her I had arranged for her to meet with another attorney. She was livid and said she would cause problems. I threatened her with a harassment suite so have heard nothing again from her. I created a mess for which I'm so sorry. Please try to forgive me."

"It may take me some time to be home again and see what I feel. I did a lot of thinking in New York but I was also very busy so I need to get back to my life here and I need to do that for awhile on my own."

Steve just cringed. "I don't want to lose you, I can't, I'll do anything."

"Do anything just don't grovel or constantly apologize. It may take awhile but I have to work that out for myself and know for sure I want what we can have."

He took me home. I made no commitments but we would talk and see what time and healing brought. I told him the editor would be coming on Thursday so I would be busy working with him while taking care of things at home. The renovation was continuing Maria and Curt were there to help out as needed with deliveries or whatever. I would work the horses early in the morning then work the entire day and maybe some evenings with the editor depending on where we were in our efforts. We would talk and go for dinner that would be it for while. Maria said she could prepare the dinner when I needed so again I was taken care of without my efforts.

With whatever bricks were going to come into my life I had some sort of direction, hopefully with a good outcome. Better to get acting then sit around in the doldrums. I slept long I guess from shear exhaustion. In the morning I was revived and ready to get on with things so made decaf coffee and prepared some breakfast. When Maria didn't come to the kitchen right away I went to the stable and got Serhalin ready to ride in the arena, a way to be free and clear my mind. Coming in Steve and Curt were at the fence looking, they had been watching me for awhile I'm sure. By the time I cooled Serhalin down and put away all the tack, Steve said he had to be at the office and would call and we would do something for dinner later. I said that Maria was preparing dinner for me and wanted to stay home as I was still tired. I reminded him about the papers for the property and he said he would go over it all tomorrow with me over dinner so I said fine. I knew in the future something was going to happen, it was too early for me right now to comprehend what.

CHAPTER 21

D ad and I talked more and made a decision after we went over the property papers and price being asked. We finally purchased the other land, Dad was now definitely my partner as we shared the cost and the future responsibility. I began my "studies" with him about wine and vineyards. I felt like I was on to another life, little did I know how it would go; I knew only to go forward. So I started walking in the vineyards looking at the plants and talking to them to try to understand how it all worked. Strange I know but necessary to me for understanding. Through Dad we hired the extra experienced workers we would need and help us through the harvesting and processing of the grapes. We started the addition to our winery processing area and also the enlargement of our distribution section. I was totally into it now and enjoying it. The Janee legacy would continue along with a new label which I had designed and Dad agreed to. And so the processing time came and I was with the workers plucking the grapes into baskets in the old style and they would go to be processed. And so I would have to be there to supervise that portion too but it was exciting. I felt like I was doing 24, 7 days a week but that kept my mind busy. Chris had tried to give me so much I would try to carry on his family's legacy and Steve would have to live with that.

On the following Thursday the editor arrived and I got him organized at the hotel and then we went out to look around in Montreux and went up to the house so we he could see the set up and know how to get there. We planned to start first thing in the morning around 11 am each day.

He mentioned that it was a big place to be living in alone. I told him just that I hadn't been alone before and maybe wouldn't again it was just a respite. He didn't push for more information. Steve kept calling but I admit that I was so busy and preoccupied that it was working out to be without him for the time being. The editor and I worked diligently and got a lot completed. He had good ideas and made his criticisms so I had to keep a tough skin but we gradually worked out a lot of details and improvements. Dave returned to New York for some R & R saying he would be back in a week and hopefully we could finish and have a completed novel.

Then I was alone and started missing Steve very much. He had been calling constantly but I could put him off because of the work with the editor and no decision. He did come up a couple of times to go riding. We walked the vineyards, I cooked a couple of times and we went out. The feelings all were still there just as strong. One night after David went back to New York Steve and I went for dinner. Arriving home I invited him in for coffee but instead we opened a bottle of wine. He soon was sitting next to me on the coach caressing my face, soon my arms and we embraced and kissed and soon were up in our bedroom. Our love making was even more passionate and filled with love then even before.

The next morning I told him to gather his things and come home to stay.

"I was afraid I was never going to hear those words again. I'll be back around 6 pm."

He came as always bearing flowers and this time a big smile many kisses and very happy. "I will be true to you, I never want to lose you again."

All I could do was believe his sincerity.

The wedding date was set for May 1. The invitation list included Steve's family, Mom and Dad Janee, Peter and Jennie, Paul and Juliana, Gabrielle and friend, James and Daphne, our many friends, the staff from Chez Janee and the hotel, plus Father and the sisters and all the children.

Then I wanted to take care of the horses and Shady so went out to relax in the fresh air. Steve as always called me during the day and said not to worry about dinner he would take care of that. I went by Mom and Dad's home as promised and they tried to feed me lunch and were most supportive.

The ceremony would be in the small chapel at the orphanage with Father Joseph doing the ceremony. The chapel was small, quaint, and had beautiful stain glass windows, it was storybook like. I had talked with the musicians to give them my requests and that we were going to dance down the aisle after the ceremony. So we decided on a 4 pm taking of the vows and then directly to the restaurant in a drawn carriage led by the lippizaneers. I guess I was going to feel like a princess. Since Chris was now gone and I owned the restaurant we decided to have the reception there even with the memories. I could work with Joachim, Hans, and Jacque and put it all together. So we were set for our wonderful celebration. I had worked with Msr Robinette the florist so he knew exactly what I wanted for the ceremony and the restaurant. Gabrielle would get Jennie's dress to her so she could do shoes and would send mine to the house for a fitting so we just needed to get the invitations out.

Steve asked was there anything he I needed to do for the wedding. He wanted to help in someway.

Be sure your parents have flight reservations, have them come as early as Monday so they can spend the week. Be sure your brother knows the time, have them come on Friday because we will have a special dinner that night. Your Mom and Dad will stay in one guest room and Jennie and Peter in the other. Everyone else will be at the hotel, I've already blocked suites for them. Be sure you have the flights for the Vienna group. Check your tux, the buttoners will be delivered to your room, I'll send Genvieve up to pin them on you. I will give you my ring which James should keep in his pocket, Jennie will have yours until they put them on the pillow that Jacque 2 will carry down the aisle. Be sure the carriage and horses are ready and be your handsome calm self. All the same things I already told you. You have the easy part."

"Just remember my lovely lady I have never done this before and I want to do everything right.

"It will all work, just come with all the love you show me every day, don't worry, we can talk over dinner tonight to calm you down. Are you thinking of changing your mind?"

"Of course not it's just my legal brain at work, things have to be in order."

"Trust me, they are. It will be simple, elegant and beautiful."

"I should know, that's how you like things."

"Absolutely. Now get on to work."

With all the anticipation of the special day I still had a foreboding feeling that In the future something was going to happen. It was too early for me right now to comprehend what it might be. Maybe that everything seemed so perfect right now perhaps the boat was going to be rocked in some way. I just didn't want any bricks in the way.

The editor returned as planned and we got to work again. Within a week we felt everything was in order so he could return to New York and we could communicate by phone and email. If anything major arrived he would return and we would work it out together. Soon we would have to talk more about the cover and the actual publish date and then the book tours. While Dave and I were working Steve just kept occupied.

After Dave had gone back to New York Steve took the day off. We nibbled on some lunch and decided we were so comfortable we would read for awhile and of course we did and then took I took a luxurious nap in the late afternoon, with my head in his lap while we were sitting on the couch. It was Friday evening and we decided to go out but not to a restaurant in Montreux but to one in Vevey he knew well. We met some people there he knew and enjoyed conversation, laughter and dancing. A couple of people who had been at my restaurant recognized me and asked me to play the piano which I didn't feel like doing and looked at Steve and he just shrugged his shoulders saying I know, do what you want to do, So of course, I played a few tunes. Being together with him was most warming and it was great playing the piano again.

At home he was so loving, not in a demanding way, just loving but with great passion. I had found the best and SELF agreed, he was the ultimate. Besides all his loving qualities and evenness he was so handsome. I told him half the women in Montreux must be after him and he admitted he thought it might be so but told me, "But I've only had eyes for you since I first met you, I haven't even been with another woman." I wondered about this handsome man, how no woman had gotten her hands on him, enticed him into at least a temporary relationship, but he said he didn't want any part of it he wanted it complete and that meant me. So different from earlier relationships, Chris had made me feel this way but not in the terms of monogamy. Steve was offering it all.

So the days went with both of us working and looking forward to the wedding. I had all the plans complete as were the dresses and the suit for Jacque 2 who would be the ring bearer.

Steve's parents arrived the Monday before the wedding, we were there to meet them, they were as comfortable as when I met them at the funeral. We talked on the way to Montreau and went to the house. We went upstairs to the guest room and they were most impressed and said they would be very comfortable. "Everything is here that you might need, and if not just let me know and we'll get it. Why don't you get unpacked and we can have some tea or coffee and later some lunch, take a walk and then you can rest before dinner."

Steve had to go back to the office for awhile so just said, "I'm leaving you in good hands, Monique will help you with anything you need. I'll be gone so you can get better acquainted."

So I would be left alone with my in laws to be. We chatted about a lot of different things with me asking lots of questions about the US since other than New York it had been awhile since I was there and I was still a bit homesick for California. We were going to the restaurant for dinner, I suggested we go to Montreux the next day to look around, go shopping at the open air market and other shops. They would also want to see the hotel and Steve's office which had also been refurbished while we were having work done on the house.

When Steve got home he asked how it went and I answered fine I like them very much. I just wasn't sure how they would take me maybe some strange bohemian woman.

"You are not, you are uniquely Monique and they think you are so sweet and talented they are most pleased so we have it all. How could they not love you. Let's get dressed and go have a wonderful dinner. Will you cook tomorrow for us?"

I said I would to the restaurant tonight and I'll cook tomorrow evening. It would be fun to take them to the market and have a look around Montreux. They may want to do some shopping so we can make a day of it, you should meet us whatever part of the day you can.

"I think they will follow wherever the pied piper wants to lead them. So do it all, I'll look at my schedule and see what time I can take."

"Please it will be fun."

We had dinner at the restaurant that evening, Joachim prepared to the limit. To my surprise father arrived with Jacque 2 in tow and they joined us for dinner. Jacque 2 spoke with me and then went around to introduce himself and greet everyone even calling James and Daphne uncle and aunt. Then he came to sit between Steve and myself and I had to tell him to calm down, "setz dich" like I did with Shady. We starter dinner and he asked me about all the forks and knives so I explained and he listened and did everything right. What was most interesting was how he could keep up and offer comments to the conversation. After dinner Steve wanted to dance so we did and I know James said watch this they are Fred and Ginger. We danced as always with flair but more importantly with love and joy. When we came back to the table they couldn't say enough. Then Jacque 2 stood up and said Madamoiselle may I have this dance but you will have to lead me because I don't know really what to do."

"I will I dance with my little gentleman you'll learn quickly." He was so sweet on the dance floor and tried so hard. He of course especially liked it when I showed him the jitterbug steps.

Jacque 2 asked me to play the piano some ballads and then to jam.

"Where did you hear that?"

"From you one night"

"So I started in with few melodic pieces and then the piano player joined and we improvised and jammed for a few minutes. Then for my new Mom and Dad I played "Fur Elise" and after for my husband to be "Besame Mucho". After the applause which I never expected, Jacque 2 took me by the hand back to the table. Little did I know that Steve said there is my son and that everyone looked at him with surprise. They are two of a kind and they love each other it's just a matter of time. Father I will have to speak with you about that.

Also James said you should make a CD of her. Steve told him he thought I would shy from that. She does it for her own expressiveness and for others she cares about.

"Then find away to get a recording for whatever she is supporting and she'll be comfortable with that."

They were plotting all sorts of things I didn't know about.

We had coffee and a little breakfast in the morning and of course they asked me lots of questions. Why did I leave the states for Vienna, what was my education, how did I get to Montreux. I just talked with them about the whys, my honest reasons. To my amazement they just smiled and told me there son had chosen well. We took a walk to the stables and the vineyards and kept talking and I knew then I liked them so much and told them because of them Steve was what he was. When we got back to the house they asked me to play the piano for them and of course I said yes. I played a few classics and then onto some ballads while they enjoyed a glass of wine. Steve called during this time and asked how everything was going and I said just fine. He asked to talk with his dad and he was just smiling, so I assumed I had approval.

I will do dinner which will be at home tonight so we have to do some shopping so we we went to the market and I started ordering. Messieur Koellhe cut one tomato so we could all taste. Deux kilo please and a few in the another bag, some for the restaurant and some for home. Oui Madamoseille. I need onions, cucumbers, peppers, the very small new potatoes and champignons. Oh I also need lots of lettuce some for the restaurant again and some for home. Oui. Now who has aubergine and the small little red onions? I think Messieur Thaler has so Michelle would go to see. He came back and I gave him money and told him how many of each, telling him they must be the best. Normally I would go look for myself but since I had my entourage I thought do it the most practical way since they were always honest at the market and wanted me always to return. I had them running all over and being very happy to assist. Now I need fruit berries, apples, bananas, anything that looks perfect. I saw Steve and his parents looking at each other and he just smiled and shook his head, "She does this a lot so knows what she is doing." We had so many bags and Steve said "Now what."

Don't worry. "Michelle we need to get this to the car as always are you ready. Oui Mademoiselle. He got a cart and loaded it and was ready so I said let's go. Everything went into the trunk, I gave Michelle a tip once again. Mercie Madomoseile Monique, until next time. Then I said we have to go to the butcher store, the one that supplied the restaurant frequently. Four beef tenderloins, fork pork tenderloins, lambchops, several sausages. They just seemed amazed but it was a normal thing for me. We have to take part of this by the restaurant, just park in the pack and I'll whistle so they'll come out to pick up everything. We went to the back I whistled and they came out to pick up. Joachim came out to greet everyone and gave me as always the last minute instructions about preparing the meat, etc. and I always accepted that, he was my teacher.

We walked around Montreux so they could get acclimate and they did a little shopping and bought a few gifts for home. They said they found the place very charming and said they would come again sometime. We said anytime and mentioned Christmas festivities.

My dinner of lamb chops, au gratin potatoes, mélange of vegetables was well liked plus the dessert of cream cheese cake with fruit on top.

We had another day before everyone else arrived for the wedding. They said that they would just relax and take a long hike.

Gabrielle's dresses were beautiful. Mine was in a silver almost like a lame fitted to the mid calf with a flounce of chiffon around the hem, cut low in the back and at the bodice. Jennie's was a similar style but not identical in soft lavender which with her golden hair and blue eyes was spectacular. We both were doing just a small arrangement of flowers woven in our hair, no hats, no veils. We just pranced around in our new shoes admiring each other and enjoying like two school girls ready for the prom. What gems Jennie and Gabrielle were.

And then came the day for our wedding. What was I doing. I guess I could say the long walk of life was bringing me to something so special I couldn't resist. Steve came home and I would not show the dresses to him just said they were perfect and in his way he just smiled at both of us and said "I know."

Then wedding day. Steve had gone to the hotel to dress and I guess commiserate with James who was the best man while I got ready at the house. Jacque arrived at 3:00 pm to pick us up. Madame Gigande was coming with the dogs via taxi. Of course they had to take part. I was sure Shady and Dachsy wouldn't know what to make of it all but I wanted them there. The driver picked Jennie and I up and we went to a special little room. Jennie and I hugged and she asked me if I was ready. Jacque came to the door and had a small package for me. Jennie as always said, "Open it right now, it is your wedding present, I know." I opened it and there was a most beautiful necklace with a single oval cut diamond and earrings to enhance, it was perfect elegant simplicity. I replaced the earrings I was wearing with the new ones and Jennie put on the necklace and we both just started to cry, tears of joy. She handed me my bouquet of white tulips and took her's of iris, smiled at each other and went to take the proverbial walk down the aisle. I put my arm in Dad's and we started.

I heard the musicians doing their thing, playing my selections and then it was time for that long walk down the aisle, Jacque with the rings laying on a pillow, Jennie next and then me with Dad at my side. I just smiled at everyone and it was wonderful and then I saw the look on Steve's face of total awe. I had found a gem for sure. Father did all the basics of the ceremony but not of course in the Catholic tradition. Jennie picked up my ring from the pillow and handed to Steve then James did the same for me. In a few minutes we had done our vows and were blessed by father, kissed and then surprised everyone. I looked over to the musicians and we danced to "Unforgettable" down the aisle. The children could not contain themselves and started applauding and of course the adults got the message and joined in. The carriage was outside with two white horses, the confetti came quickly and we were off for champagne and our reception.

At the restaurant all the staff had returned quickly and were preparing the "goodies" for everyone. The reception was fantastic, everyone enjoying, laughing, eating, sipping champagne. Most of the people we knew and cared about were there including Shady and Dachsy. Then the musicians arrived and the dancing started and of course we were the attraction but everyone joined in too. What a wonderful day. I excused myself and went outside and tears came but Steve came and covered me with a hug, "Are you alright."

"Yes, I have you and it is the best. I love only you, I want only you and I will do my best to be a good wife, bear with me right now, some memories came to mind about the past."

"Moni, one of the reasons I care so much for you is the depth of your feeling and I think I understand how much that takes from you. You're thinking you might have been doing all of this with Chris. I think we will have the best of lives more than you can imagine. Just know I love you and will be here for you for whatever you need."

"Will you dance with me messieur, right now?"

"Bien Sur Madame."

So we went in after he wiped my tears, took me in his arms and danced until I could smile again. I know everyone especially Jennie was wondering but we didn't have conversation about my exit we just returned like everything was fine.

He was so gentle and loving I had every confidence all would be well. Then the festivities really started. Even Mr. Williamson arrived, my waltz partner with congratulations and a request to dance with me. We enjoyed a lovely Viennese waltz "Der Tanz ein Leben" and after had him join our table. He had been coming in for weeks to dance and at his age did an excellent job but I knew we would soon lose him. Then it started, "Monique play and sing for us please" and I just looked at Steve and he said give them pleasure. So I started with the piano player and we jammed awhile with some boogie and some jazz and then he said take over. So I had to think what do I perform here on my wedding day. I started for myself "Memories" and then went to "For the Rest of My Life". Since the children were there but I didn't have the energy to be my normal exuberant self, I just play "Dites moi" and they sang from the table but soon gathered around the piano to ask for more so I continued to play until Father and the Sisters got them under control back to the table.

I went to the table and gave the signal to Steve about being tired he had already intuitively understood. So laughingly he told everyone we were departing they could stay as long as they liked but he had to take care of his bride. They could take that anyway they chose. We went around thanking everyone for celebrating with us and of course before leaving Jacque 2 came to give each of us a hug. When we got home we were both "pooped" but Steve said he was getting a bottle of champagne for our own personal toast. We just looked at each other lovingly. So I now was Mrs. Gavin. I was pleased and so happy and I said a prayer it would continue like this. Then he took me in his arms carried me upstairs and we made love more passionately than ever before.

The next day we were to have brunch with our closest group around 11:00 am and then do something in the area. They had come all this way to celebrate with us so we wanted to enjoy them a little longer. We showed them our property and how far the house refurbishment inside had come and told them about our plans for the winery with more distribution of both wines. They walked through the vineyards asking lot of questions. Although they enjoyed wine they had never spent any time in the fields. They wanted to take us for dinner that night as their treat so we selected another restaurant in Montreux. So a full long day of almost too much celebration but it might never happen again with all together so we just enjoyed.

Sunday morning we slept very late and then had to be sure everyone got off ok. After we looked at each other and said now what do we do. We went for a long walk, then came back to read for awhile, worked on the computer as I had some things I wanted to send to Paul and Steve said he never had time for learning on the computer but wanted to know more about it. So we did productive things in each other's company. Then I said are you doing dinner tonight? He said ok. So we checked out the frig and then he changed his mind and decided we should go to another place he knew in a small village nearby owned by some people he knew that were his clients, I didn't know. I said ok if I can go casual and have a grazer plate. He laughed and said of course.

CHAPTER 22

Monday morning I awoke and cried out "Steve" several time because he wasn't next to me and then I called for Maria. Something was going on inside me, fear of loss, fear of doing wrong, I didn't know. I just felt panic for some reason. Steve came out of the shower with a towel around him somewhat panicked and then Maria was at the door. I was totally disoriented and was frightened that no one was there. Steve came to hold me and Maria said she would get tea and asked if she should call the doctor. Steve said no not right now let me just calm her down and we'll decide later but get the tea. I was so apologetic, but was shaking. I didn't know how fragile I was. Steve calmed me down and soon I relaxed. Then he called the doctor and said he would come by around 4 pm. Steve had to go to his office because of some court situations but asked Maria to stay close to me and he would call as he could and the doctor would be there to check on me. I felt really dumb causing them so much trouble but accepted the assistance. Steve called Madelaine to come to do my hair because he knew I would feel better. He left but called an hour later to check in with me and I of course said I'm doing ok.

I'm sorry to cause you so much stress.

"You are no stress, I just want to take care of you, just relax and rest. I'll be home as soon as I can."

"I'm ok, don't change your schedule for me."

"I will give up everything for you."

"And so would I."

"So we are on the same track."

"Of course. Can't wait until you're home."

"It won't be until between 6 or 7 pm but I'll keep calling."

"Ok, I love you." Doctor Bovet came and took my temperature and blood pressure, listened to my heart and lungs and said everything seemed fine but he wanted to take a blood test to check, he was concerned I might be anemic because of my weight and lack of interest in eating. He prescribed vitamin pills, B 12 complex, multi vitamins and said I needed to eat more. So I said ok. I called Steve's office and gave Genevieve what I needed and asked if she could get Steve to bring it home and she said she would take cares of it. I had never done this type of thing before to ask others to take care of this but Steve had instructed me to do so and not try to do it all myself so I said I'm too tired, I will do it.

And so we went on with the daily, me working with distributors, the new one in New York via my art clients, a new one in Switzerland, a new one in Belgium. I would probably have to travel to NYC at some time to discuss some parameters but I was building the winery business step by step. I was including the G wine along with Janee. Steve was busy with his practice and doing very well but always attentive to me and what was wonderful was his loving kindness and acceptance of me. It was mutual.

The next morning he said, "let's take the horses out for a ride". I was up in a minute and we were soon out at the stable with a smiling, knowing Curt. We saddled up and were out into the beautiful day looking at our vineyard and the wonderful view to the lake. We returned and took care of the horses and then hand in hand went back to the house to shower and change. Before I knew it Steve had me back into bed and it was the ultimate love. We slept and when we woke he said he would do dinner or did I want to go out. I said I wanted to stay at home. We went to the kitchen he started to prepare dinner, he said he couldn't' do what Chris had done and I said you can do better for what I like. A smile and he continued. After eating we went upstairs to watch a movie and just cuddle and be together, he seemed so content as was

I. There was nothing better than the closeness we felt for each other, no complication just loving acceptance. I thought he was willing to forget the past as was I; we would move only forward and create our own "heaven."

The next day after our short respite would come reality and we would have to move on again, Steve at the office and me with the various businesses we held. We planned to take a honeymoon trip a little later I was thinking of Christmas coming again and would try to make it a happy one so started making plans. I still had the work I had to do with the properties, winery and the art exhibits with Paul. It would all come together if I stayed well.

Steve had his legal work to take care of but called several times a day, while I was doing all the other things. No "hausfrau" stuff, he knew I didn't want that. I wanted to use my talents in my own creative way and he agreed. We had Maria to assist in whatever we needed and we continued to have two other ladies to come in once a week to house clean and do the linens, it was too much to ask of Maria. We sometimes cooked, sometimes went out and all of the time enjoyed each other, talking, laughing, sharing and of course loving.

Steve went with me to pick out a Christmas tree even a taller one then the previous year. It was too big even for Curt's truck so he borrowed a friends large one to get it home. Curt and I again put up the tree and he decorated the top as we had last year and Maria and I did the lower parts. This time we thought there would not be as many to join us as they had been with us for the wedding but Peter and Jennie, Paul and Juliana said they wanted to join us so there would be several again. It would be festive and special. Other friends would come by and we would all share. I just wanted the holiday to be for Steve since he had to set on the sidelines before but now would be one with me.

I didn't know what to give Steve but finally settled on a new watch, some special cds he wanted, an artist etching from the gallery and the sculpture piece we both admired. I would have to enlist Curt's help in hiding it and bringing into the house. I pondered what he would find for me, I had so much already I felt like I needed nothing.

I decorated as always with all the poinsettias, lights outside, wreaths and table cover and ribbons. I also had lots of candles of all sizes. I enjoyed doing it so much. I certainly was no designer just knew what I liked just like my music and art interests. It was a time when I could be as expressive as I wanted which for years I couldn't because of the criticism I received during my first marriage. I wasn't perfect I just had some God given talents I was not able to express to the fullest and as I did it the practice made me grow in my ideas Everyone should be allowed that freedom to express themselves without a lot of negative input. That was one of the things I tried to draw out of the children at the orphanage.

Those from Vienna arrived late on the 22nd, I was so please they had come. The next day we went into Montreux as they said they had a little shopping to do. After we hike on the property in the vineyards and the woods. They took us out for dinner to Vevey, the next evening we would go to Chez Janee which I knew they enjoyed.

On Christmas Eve I heard two cars drive up so went out to see who it was but saw nothing so was a bit perplexed. Steve took awhile to come in and then I heard Curt leave with the truck and was really confused. I asked what was going on, he just smiled and said you will find out soon. Strange I thought but just kept preparing our Eve diner. Mom and Dad had arrived so we were in conversation.

Steve said, "I'll go take a shower and change and come down to enjoy the Eve. He came down and we sat looking at the tree with a lovely glass of champagne and I heard Curt arriving. Maria came in and asked if she could help and I said in a little bit to sit and enjoy the Eve with us. And so we dined with roast beef, roasted potatoes, several vegetables, a traditional cranberry mold and some bread I had made that day, my day to be the "hausfrau or the chefess. Dessert was to be of all things a plum pudding which Maria made. Now present time. I was always like a child with the presents, I couldn't wait. As Mrs. Claus again, I handed out all the presents and realized there were only presents for me from Mom, Dad, Curt and Maria. Where was one from Steve? Well they all said lets go out to see the horses and take them there gifts of apples and carrots so I said ok. Outside by the garage was a black Porsche with a huge red ribbon and a big sign saying for Monique. My stupid dream of having that kind of car or myself was realized and I was overwhelmed, my loving Steve always attuned. His facial expression told me everything, things are not the most important in life but if we have the wherewithal to achieve it why not enjoy. I was a child that had just received a new bicycle. He said he would do anything for me and I now believed that he would, not for things, just for my dreams, he was totally in tune with my wants. I of course sat in the car and he said we would go for a ride Christmas Day and test it out. Jacque and Joachim came by with more presents and greetings and so it was a wonderful, giving Eve. Everyone came around the piano to sing Christmas carols and feel the content and joy the holiday should bring.

The next morning Steve and I took the new car out for a drive, of course with me behind the wheel; it was terrific and he could only beam and of course as a man tell me how to drive but I could handle it. It was Steve's turn to do the cooking for Christmas so as a good American he had planned to roast a turkey with stuffing of course and Maria and I would help with all the other accroutments. We all relaxed for awhile, took a walk and then started in to help with dinner, all a joy.

Steve said, "I have never had such a wonderful Christmas before with all the trimmings, thank you." We went to our room after we got everyone organized and just enjoyed the evening lovingly.

The next day Jennie and Peter, Paul and Juliana were flying back to Vienna. They had brought the architectural plans for what was to be our new home but I began to think it was too much, one was enough and if we built what would we do with the old one. We both liked it and it had been refurbished inside. I would talk with Steve about my thoughts and we put away the plans or the time being.

Then came Monday and we started again with the workings of the world; Steve to the office and court, me to do my planning. Next would be festivities at the restaurant for New Years, I had a lot of organizing to do with Joachim, so I was off to take care of that. The restaurant had been getting even more popular after all the renovations so it would be a busy and long but festive night. Besides acting the hostess I was pushed into playing the piano and singing a couple of songs never a problem for me. Everyone showed up even Mr. Willamson so we had a fun evening if long evening.

In February we took our 6 day Portugal trip to Lisboa and up the coast to Oporto excited about all we saw and experienced. We ordered some beautiful tiles in large picture formats thinking we might use them in one of the restaurants or hotel, walked the beaches around Lisboa and the vineyards in the north. When we returned home I felt very tired, more than usual after a trip. The next two days I was dragging and finally Steve was concerned and called Doctor Bovett who came out to a check up of temperature, blood pressure and a blood test. He said I was still too thin and wanted me to agree to rest more which I always fought. In two days he had the blood test results and he told me severe anemia showed so was put on a diet of B Complex, multiple vitamins and calcium, iron tablets as he had earlier and a list of foods I should try to consume, none of which appealed to me. Orders were given to rest and in a week he would do another test and if the results hadn't improved he would contact Dr.Egger from Zurich again.

I didn't need this curtailing of all the interests I had but decided I had to do something other than drag myself out of bed each morning and feel so depressed. Steve hired another man to help Curt with the horses and made sure the two ladies came once a week to do take care of the house as we didn't want Maria to feel she had to do more. In a week I was not feeling much stronger so the specialist Dr. Eggef was coming agai to Montreux to do some testing. My thoughts were, we have so much, I don't want to be an invalid for Steve to take care of but he tried to keep up my spirits. He cut back on his cases so he could be home more to talk, read and be with me to keep up my spirits. The tests showed I had the sort of virus again they thought was causing the anemia but they couldn't really define it yet. The Dr.prescribed some new drug he thought would assist. He had been doing special research on different drugs in cases of anemia. The virus was still a mystery.

He wanted to hospitalize me but I fought that so they brought in a nurse to be with me during the day to administer the drugs which came in shot form which I hated but did it, They would keep evalulating my progress. We went through this for two months they thought the new experimental drug was helping and wanted to continue finding no side effects. I agreed of it was helping. I started my routine of walking each day, working at least one of the horse, trying to eat several times a day and taking the natural vitamins and iron. I read a lot about natural medications and meditation. It took me a couple of months but I gradually started feeling much better with more strength and energy. It was a kind of mind structure only I could create in myself to know I had to be with and support Steve. He got happier everyday and by June I was back on my feet thinking I had gone around another brick once again and was able to be a strong, loving wife again to my dear husband and friend.

One evening we were talking and he brought up Chris and our relationship which for me was part of my past. He seemed to be comparing himself in some way and thinking about the intimacy he and I had had when together for that short time. He had done this off and on and this evening it really got to me and I got angry which didn't happen very often. "Why do you keep talking about Chris and my relationship when it is over. Yes obviously I was intimate with him and yes I was infatuated with him. He was a very strong personality and had won me over and yes we had many goods times and yes he provided for me very generously but he also could be very erratic. I thought I loved him and in many ways I did but not like you. I've loved you all the time I've known you. It was inevitable I had to go through that stage until I realized you were the man I wanted. If you can't realize that by now I don't know what to do."

He looked at me bewildered saying, "I don't think I've ever seen you get so upset with me."

"Well I am. I just don't understand why you can't let it go. It's though you're comparing yourself with him regarding our relationship. I just don't want to hear it anymore."

"I'm trying not to compare but it comes to my mind often. Maybe it's a male thing, maybe I'm jealous or doubting myself."

"All you can do is get a grip and stop it. If it's this house that Chris built but we've redecorated to make our own is on your mind let's sell it and everything else and move somewhere."

"No I just have a difficult time imagining you with other men. I'm sorry I'm just expressing my feelings.

I was so angry I got my purse and went out to the car. I just had to get out. "What are you doing, what did I do?" I couldn't believe he didn't understand. Was it a male thing? I knew it was an overreaction on my part but I couldn't help it. When you hear comments and sense innuendos and don't react at the time it builds up and then the cat is in the corner with claws out. Where would I go at the hotel I would create a scene so decided to go to the apartment at the restaurant.

I laid on the bed and cried. In the morning I surprised Joachim by being in the kitchen. I just said I had a problem and need to do something to clear my mind, how can I help? He handed me a knife and said vegetables and then I want to show you a new sauce I'm trying. We were working on the sauce when Joachim said "Good morning Msr. Steve." I shut down immediately. I knew I was always oversensitive to words but this shook me. He had often made comments about Chris and my relationship and I had tried to pass them off and not get upset but now I felt degraded like I had been around so much that I was like a toy to play with or even worse a whore. I pushed him away and got up and got dressed, grabbed my purse while he was saying, "I couldn't believe he didn't understand. Was it a male thing?

I started down the stairs and he came after me saying, "What are you doing?" All I could do was shout "Stay away from me, I just want out of here." I had given myself to him and it didn't seem to be enough, I was still being questioned. Where would I go, it didn't matter at that moment. I thought about the hotel but that would create a scene and he would look there right away. I couldn't bother Mom and Dad at that hour so I went to the restaurant. There was the apartment upstairs so I went in and locked the door and just layed on the bed crying and saying it is always the same. I talked with SELF and said what do I do to create these problems, it must be me. Finally I did sleep a little got up and went to the kitchen to wait for Joachim and the other staff who usually arrived about 10am to start preparing for lunch. I just said, "Joachim there is a personal problem and all I want to do is work in the kitchen so tell me what to do." He just looked at me without asking questions and directed me to the chopping block to prepare vegetables. I just needed to do something productive. Then he wanted me to learn a special sauce he made and as we were in to it he said, "Bonjour Msr. Steve. I looked up and then went back to the sauce making. Steve took me by the arm and said, "I want to talk to you know."

"I'm busy, can't you see."

"Now" and he lead me out the front of the restaurant where he had parked his car. He started in and I turned and went to my car and drove off. I went to a small chapel to be quiet and think. The Father came out to greet me and asked if he could be off some help. I just said I had a problem and wanted somewhere serene to be quiet and mediate. He said you've come to the right place. Come to my office if you need anything. I thanked him and said I would soon feel better. Then I drove home.

Genevieve called me later and said, "Someone got you upset, right? He came in with a look only a mother would understand, slammed his door and is quiet right now, no normal chatting with us."

I tried never to share our close moments with anyone but was still upset so said "Yes I am a bit upset."

"Well he's trying to make it up today. He came in and gave me morning orders which are generally about business but this time it was, "Please order flowers for Monique, call Maria and ask her to chill a bottle of champagne, check with the bookstores if they have these two books she wants, package up some printing paper and cartridges for her printer and then call Joachim and ask him to prepare something she would like for dinner with a special dessert and I will pick it up to take home or better yet have Jacque deliver it."

"Well I guess I got my point across. You're telling me this will make my day a little easier. What I'm going to do is go work with the horses and get grubby and feel free."

"Go for it Monique. We have to show them how it can be."

So the flowers arrived two dozen red and white roses which I had put into our bedroom.

"I'm sorry just get this image of you with someone else I didn't mean to get you so upset"

"Well you did. You have to get over it. I'm all yours I don't think of anyone else believe that."

"Forgive me, it won't happen again. Ju

Jacque from the restaurant came around 6 with dinner to be warmed. So I showered, dressed in a gorgeous lounging outfit and sat in the living room reading with the jazz CD he liked so much and waited. He came home around 7 pm looking totally beat, with packages and brief case in hand. So I just hugged him and said "hello my dear loving husband, took the packages and briefcase. "There is some wine upstairs. Take a shower and get comfortable and we'll have some dinner." He immediately relaxed, kissed me so passionately so I knew he was really home and I had calmed down.

That night was one of the most passionate. We slept in each other arms and in the early hours we were one again but no more discussion about why I got so upset. So the morning came with sunshine. He had to go to the office early again. He was working on a special liability case of $3,000.000 and today he believed the judgment in court would come soon. Steve was defending someone over a business problem he was having with the so called big men from Geneva. We figured they were part of the local mafia scene there. I was hoping if Steve won there were not going to be some kind of retribution. His payment from this case he wanted to put away for security so that if anything happened to the winery or our other holdings it would take us through anything we wanted to do. I reminded him of my dream of a foundation for helping orphans and other young people. We had so much to share.

Now was June and we were working in the vineyards. Dad and I would go out every day to inspect the growth of the vines and beginning development of the grape also to be sure the workers were doing what we asked. It was so great working with him enjoying the beauty of the natural growth, the delicate colors, the aromas and knowing if we did it right we would have a terrific product. I was already talking to other distributors so if all went well and the harvest was strong we would be grateful.

CHAPTER 23

One night I awoke and called to Steve that I smelled smoke so we immediately got up and started searching. Looking outside I saw where it was coming from—the North vineyard. Curt was already up and coming to us and we called the firefighters. It would take them a while to arrive so all we could do was to out with hoses and canvases and anything we could get our hands on. The firefighters arrived and started with their equipment and managed after an hour or more to put the fire out. We had lost at least half of the North section some of the best vines but had not lost everything. We went in exhausted and knew the next day we would have to regroup, another brick, they seemed to keep coming as they often do in life. The next day we ascertained the loss and began making plans of what to do. Other vineyards would help supply us new cuttings but they would not produce until the next year if we were lucky so we looked at what we had. We would have to optimize our production and limit the distribution so a loss but not all was a loss, we would make it work. Steve suggested we try to buy another 100 acres adjacent from a private owner who did the same as the owner of the other property we had purchased, The current owner did not manage it well but we knew we could with a lot more work. I was concerned we would have too much to control and too big an investment so Steve and I had one our few arguments about this until he convinced me the return would keep us in good shape. So we would be larger landowners did I want this, I wasn't sure. I really just wanted to be content with what we had but I went with his recommendation and we purchased the additional 100 acres. He said this would allow us to satisfy the distributors and next year we would be in better shape. Maybe we wanted to be just vineyard and restaurant owners and forget the hotel or just get a better manager. We had lots to think about. All the while this would take a lot of time and effort and I didn't see how I could keep my dream of writing and art career alive. But I thought about the old adage the busier one gets often the more one achieves. I hoped that was true in or case.

And so I trusted his judgment and we purchased the next 100 acres. He was taking more time away from his clients and working with me on organizing all of this so we went ahead. By late September all of us were in the field working with the workers and the grapes, actually it was very invigorating. We became a type of peasant and one with the earth, sweaty, grimy, exhausted but laughing and singing while picking the grapes and loading them into basket in the old style. We put the baskets in the truck and took them the short ways to our processing facility. A big job but most rewarding. The men in the processing plant had much to do, I would be there to supervise with Dad's help We would be able to take care of the orders from the distributors and were pleased with the monetary outcome. We had a great celebration at the house for everyone who had participated in all the hard work. All the while Joachim kept the restaurant going extremely well and fed us frequently because we were too tired to do it ourselves. Many times I thought about Chris and if he was looking down and seeing what he had created and we were building even stronger. He would have been pleased, after all he had left all of this in trust to me to take care of and his best friend was with me to assist. Mom and Dad were great and it kept them young in spirit so the entire effort was a family affair.

Finally end of October I could return to Vienna to assist Paul at the gallery. He had a very important exhibit he had been working on for months for a Hungarian painter who did very large abstract oils and he wanted my help. I couldn't resist the opportunity so convinced Steve that I must go. I went a few days ahead and he said he would arrive later for a few days and insisted I come back with him. I was so happy to be with Jenny and Peter again in my own apartment. It was a bit of a respite. Although I loved Steve so much I still had the drive to sometimes just to be alone on my own doing my own thing. Paul, Cynthia and I worked on the hanging of the works and the cataloguing and of course I went out with Viennese friends for the evening meals and laughter. The day of the exhibit Steve arrived and went with me early to put on the last minute touches, he was ready to help out too. How much he was a part of everything I did and vice versa. The opening was packed with people and it went very well. The New York clients I had assisted quite awhile back, not Bob and Susan, but another couple were there once again and did purchase. Several other pieces were purchased so we had again a success for the gallery and the artist. After, Steve and I went back to the apartment and just relaxed, cuddled as we hadn't done for quite awhile made love as passionately as always and renewed our vows to each other. With all the bricks that come, find happiness in the moment, it's the only way. I worked the next day at the gallery while Steve just walked and relaxed, the next day we went on our inevitable shopping jaunt for special items like clothes from Gabrielle and some glassware we were interested in. That evening we went to restaurant Hof Heiderman with Jenny and Peter, saw lots of people I knew but had not seen for awhile, enjoyed dinner and the local wine, danced and laughed. The next morning was a sleep in day just to be and enjoy the setting of the apartment. We went out to the Lippizaner stable to see Curt and then out with him to "eat on the streets." Home again with one more night before returning to Switzerland so we asked Jenny and Peter to come over and we cooked the fresh things we had purchased at the market. The next day off to Switzerland again with me feeling torn about where I was supposed to be. I just had to keep up strength to do it all and not be selfish to the people I loved. I knew in my heart I couldn't do it without Steve who was always there to help with the work and the financial.

Steve called in the afternoon. "Should I go shopping at the market?" "No, Maria and I will take care of that. Why not get a couple of movies you would like to see, maybe we'll have an inclination to lie on the couch and enjoy."

"I will do as you ask my love. I should get to you between 5 and 6."

"I'll be here with a big hug." "More I hope." "Of course, that goes without saying. Come as soon as you can." "Now how am I to concentrate on my next client?" "Well, that's your problem, no problems here."

Maria and I went to the outdoor farmer's market in Montreux and purchased some fresh vegetables; eggplant, tomatoes which the farmer was good enough to let me try to see how sweet they were, zucchini, mushrooms, potatoes, a salad mix, some fresh basil ad thyme which I usually had in my garden but hadn't right now; everything looked so delicious. Then to the butcher for some lamb chops, I thought we could cook everything on the outdoor grill. I always purchased more so Maria and Curt would partake also. And I thought what for dessert so bought some apples for an apple flan which I new Steve was partial to. I wanted to get some fresh flowers but Maria said no, she knew something I didn't. When we returned home Curt came over with a big bouquet of fall flowers from the florist who had delivered but didn't want to leave them outside the door.

After we took care of putting away everything I went to work in my office. I had to send some photos and information to Paul in Vienna so he could look them over and give me his comments via email. I was determined to keep up my connections there and work on the exhibits so I needed to produce. I then went to an appointment at an artist studio in Vevey, an artist who did hand blown glass like paperweights, goblets and also glass sculpture. They were full of color and extremely well created I loved his sculpture the best so took photos and would send that to Paul the next day. I also wanted to purchase one but wanted to see Steve's reaction to the work first. Home again and time to shower and dress and start with dinner. I started the grill early so we would have wonderful coals. Used some virgin olive oil to baste the meat and vegetables and seasoned them of course using some of the fresh herbs. I then had to make the dough for the flan and cut up apples and bake the creation. Thanks to Chris and my internship at the restaurant I could whip out some good things.

At 6pm Steve came dragging in from a hard day. I just hugged him said grab a shower and relax. The wine is open and I can start anytime. He gave me a hug, smile, kiss and said it's great to come home. But I reminded him I was not the hausfrau. He only would find this on special occasions when I was in the mood. He laughed and said, "I accept the terms of the negotiation." Once an attorney always an attorney but an understanding one I hoped. We relaxed and talked and then I started the dinner and we kept talking. I wondered if we would always have so much interesting things to share, one never knows.

I went to the catholic chapel to be quiet and pray and try to figure out my feelings. The priest came out and greeted me, seeing me distraught he asked if he could be of assistance. I just said, "I just came to pray father and be quiet." Looking concerned he said, "I'm in my office if you need me." After some time I went and knocked on his door to thank him and he said, "Please come anytime and if there is anything you want to talk about you need only ask."

Then I was once again a horse and felt the need to run away from what I was upset about. I suppose I was doing the adolescent thing of "I'll show you what I can do." I just hated confrontation. So I got on the phone and called Bob and Susan the clients who had purchased from the gallery and Genvieve said I wanted to come to New York for business reasons that had just come up, would they be home. They were surprised but seemingly very happy and said of course come. I said I would make the reservation and give them the details. When I asked what hotel they suggested they said none, you will stay with us, we have a lovely guest room and you are most welcome. I said I didn't want to impose but they insisted so I agreed. I said I wanted to visit their restaurant and possibly talk to the wine distributor they knew and also wanted to go to a couple of publishing houses. They said just come and will arrange everything even to their driver to pick me up at the airport. I made the reservation for Tuesday morning on Swiss Air, ordered a car to take me to Geneva Monday evening. I would stay at a hotel by the airport since I wouldn't have to argue with Steve again. I went home to pack. Steve kept calling but I wouldn't answer. I didn't know if he would come home and knew he had appointments and court in the afternoon so decided I would be gone before he returned. I would not tell him where I was going or what I was doing. I was repeating a pattern but that was my way not to confront, just to get away and then face what would come next. I left him a note just saying I would be away for a few days not to worry, I didn't say where I was going. I told Maria I would be away but would not tell her where so she could be truthful with Steve. I told her not to worry, I would be ok and that I would call her. I would only go for 6 nights and be back and see what could be solved. I told Curt the same and said goodbye to the horses and left. My typical Modis Operandi, when hurt get out of town. Not the best thing to do but it was what Monique did. After all I understood horses didn't I, when in doubt the wind or fear run.

I arrived in New York around 4pm and the driver was there to pick me up and take me to their home. They seemed so happy to see me, they were lovely people and I was already feeling better. We chatted and then Mrs. showed me to the guest room and said to come down when ready. She said she would send the maid to see if I needed anything pressed which I did. I was so spoiled by now. What a contrast to my earlier life when I was the hausfrau. When I came down they told me that some friends Mr & Mrs. Wright would be coming by and we would all go out to dinner early so I could get some rest later. Their home was fantastic, beautifully decorated with art of all types everywhere. Bob had already made an appointment for lunch the next day for us to talk with the distributor. Before dinner he made a call to a friend regarding the publishing houses and at dinner got a call back that he had made one for 3:30 pm after we had lunch the next day and would work on the other for the following day. I began to understand how much I migh accomplish. We met with the distributor on Wednesday. Bob had a couple of bottles of red he had saved from their trip. The distributor tasted and was most interested in the Janee/Gavin wines. The distributor ordered two cases, one of white and one red. If he liked what he recieved we would make a deal for delivery for the fall. Mr. also wanted some before for his two restaurants so I said when I returned home I would ship the two cases. Bob said let's start with 12 cases and go from there. He wanted them for his private home wine collection also for the restaurants.

I slept well for the first time in two days, peacefully. I joined them for breakfast and then got dressed for the days appointments. I had a very nice grey suit with a slim longer skirt with a slit up one side and of course Susan wanted to know where I had purchased it. Again I told her it was made for me from another designer artist and she said she now had to come to Switzerland. I said I hadn't brought too many clothes and would like to some shopping as they had planned a party for Saturday evening at their home. She said, fantastic, let's plan for Friday and Saturday. We thought you might like to see a show while you're here so we're seeing what tickets we can get for Thursday or Friday evening. They were being so great and I think enjoying it. They did get tickets for Jersey Boys for Friday so we were off that evening for the show and then a late dinner. I missed Steve and we would have to work some things out but I was having a great time and accomplishing a lot.

After lunch we had an appointment with the publisher at 3:30 pm, a business friend of Bob's so we were able to get in He called in one of his readers and asked for a critic by the next morning since my time was so short. Bob had also made an appointment with another publisher for the next day at noon.

He did the same and had a reader come in. Late Thursday Bob got the call the Random was most interested and could we come to the office immediately by 4:00 pm. Immediately shopping ended. They offered $150,000 and 10% of the book sales. Being the lawyer that he was Bob took me aside and told me he was going to ask for $200,000 and 15% of the books sales, all travel costs taken care of. The publisher smiled and said you have a good attorney. We accept. But Bob told him we had another appointment Friday at 12:00 pm and wanted to discuss that offer. I was scared, maybe Random would change their minds. Bob assured me they had made the offer in good faith he just thought they should know there was other interest. They offered the same beginning offer and Bob couldn't budge them so immediately called Random and said were on. They said they would draw up the contract and we should come over by 4:00 pm again to sign and talk with the editor. We had done it. We went to their home and the champagne began to flow. I was going to by published, I could only pinch myself. What a power house Bob had been to accomplish this in record time. I couldn't thank him enough. He just beamed, he obviously liked getting his way and getting things done.

Friday we were off shopping. Although they often shopped at the typical upscale stores they knew of other ones which they thought I would prefer. I was looking for a dress for that evening's party since I had not brought a lot with me and in one little shop of a beginning designer, we found it. It was perfect in a gauze like fabric with ribbon design, open in the back to the waist, covered in the front, asymmetrical skirt with two layers of fabric in a variety of the color of lime green. Then shoes and they knew where to go. While looking around I saw a coat to die for in black cashmere in an A shape with a throw shawl around the neck and since I was here to please self I purchased it. I also wanted a gift for Steve and found a great leather jacket and of course a couple of special things for Maria, Jennie and Peter. My friends were all smiles. We poked around in other stores and they found some things but I realized they were returning what I had done for them in Vienna—give and you shall receive. We managed to grab a bit of late lunch at a small café and then returned to their home to relax and get ready for the evening. But I got the idea to cook dinner on Sunday so said direct me to the closest best butcher and vegetable market and I would go shop. They were a little lost until Mrs called Mr and he told me where to go so he sent the car for me, not even a taxi and I went shopping. At 7pm everyone started to arrive for the evening party. I was dressed and ready to perform. They had a catered buffet which pleased me because I could graze and no one would see how much or how little I ate. They had presented me as some sort of art critic or connoisseur so I was on deck to talk about their art collection and other artists' works I knew—delightful. Then Mr. _____came to me and said I had a phone call and I asked who. He just said, "It sounds like an international call and it is a man so it must be Steve." He had found me some way.

"Hello."

"Finally I found you. What are you doing? I have been crazy with worry. Why did you do this?"

"Thank you for asking how I am. Your words hurt me and you know I am a horse and don't like confrontation. My first response is always to run away and find solace somewhere else."

"I know I was an ass, some sort of male ego thing. I'm so sorry."

"You've been fighting my connection with Chris for a long time and I can understand why but I tried to explain to you the situation but you won't let go. Until you do and come to terms with it we can't go ahead."

"Monique, I have no life without you I'll try harder maybe talking it through together will help. Sometimes I just can't stand the idea of you and him together."

"Well we were. But what you said degraded me as if I were a woman whose whims changed all the time. We either find trust in each other or there is nothing. You've always been there for me and loving but what you did the other morning I won't accept."

"I don't know what to do."

"Think about it. Think about what you said. I don't want to continue talking internationally about this now and I am expected to be a part of this party. We'll have to deal with it later."

"When are you coming home?"

"I'm scheduled to arrive Tuesday morning unless something comes up that I want to do here so I may change that. I'll call you when I'm sure."

"Call me and I'll be at the airport."

"I'll call you but don't come to the airport. I've already arranged for a car and that's the way I want it. I'll call you when I arrive home."

"Monique, I love you so much please be careful and please come home. We'll work this out."

"I have to go now. I'll call you when I know when I'm coming home. I've already called Maria and Curt and will keep in touch with them so they know where I am and what I'm doing. I'll call you when I know when I'm coming home. Take care, I love you very much, bye for now."

And I hung up, bad person that I am.

I went back to the elegant party and decided to just think about being gracious and enjoying myself. Bob asked if everything was ok and I said no but I wasn't about to let that get in my way of enjoy his friends and the evening. He gave me a big hug and said, "You will always come around to be on your feet, and I will help you do that."

I relished his "hug" with a quiet "thank you"

During the festivities someone mentioned some art exhibits opening in Soho on Tuesday evening so we would have to shop during the day. I said I would love to attend and we made a plan to all go and enjoy with me as the leader. I asked if it was ok if I stayed another night. "You can stay as long as you like." The party ended with plans for Tuesday night art event, what fun, exciting and most interesting. So I would stay Monday and Tuesday and not leave until Wednesday evening.

On Monday I called Steve and told him about the plan and said I would not be back until Thursday morning. He was most upset and said I was just trying to hurt him. I said, "No I'm not, I'm just being myself and doing what I want while I'm in NYC. I have lots of good news to share with you when I get home. I said I was sorry but I felt I needed this right now and was enjoying my holiday from my responsibilities to the business and to him.

"I guess I have more to learn about you than I thought."

"I guess that's true. I'll call you Thursday morning. Bye."

We slept late Sunday and then planned to walk in Central Park, have lunch and just relax and talk. We all took a little siesta. Then I started to prepare dinner for what would be 7 people. They seemed surprised but I said that I had apprenticed in the restaurant and did know how to cook and it was my gift to them. The menu would be _____

At 7pm the friends arrived, Bob took care of the cocktails. I had everything under control and with the help of their maid found all the proper dishes. I instructed the maid in how we would serve the 5 course meal and she was most willing to participate. So I planned a very delicate recipe for lobster bisque which Chris had taught me, a crown roast of lamb with a rice of a combination of wild rice, seasonings, almonds and dates, a mélange of fresh vegetables, a salad of mixed greens with a vinaigrette dressing, a cheese platter with french bread and some fresh fruit. (I usually made the bread myself but this was a time thing so found an excellent bakery), and for dessert two mixed, fresh fruit flans with whipped cream. I selected a red wine of _____ and a white of _____ to go with the courses. I, along with the help of their maid, served each course. I did sit with them and nibble. It was a wonderful evening of enjoying food but also most intelligent conversation about many topics. The maid earned an extra something from me for all the clean up. There was no little man under the counter, the one I always joked about as I washed dishes in my apprenticeship at the restaurant. They all seemed happy, said it was an excellent meal and I was happy to have given them something for all their kindness. Mr. said I think we'll keep you here for my restaurants.

And what we were we to do with Monday? I decided if they didn't mind that I wanted to just go on my own and walk the streets. I went to MOMA and just browsed in other shops. I had to purchase another suitcase for the extra clothes and gifts I had purchased, what fun. Monday evening we relaxed and ate leftovers that were in the frig and I went to bed early. I tried to not be in their way all the time, so just said I had phone calls, etc. to take care of. I called Maria and told her I would be home Thursday morning, to not do anything special, I would be tired and just rest. I called Curt and asked how the horses were and he said fine except that they missed me. I told him, "I miss them more than you can imagine but I'll be home soon." I had called Jennie when I first arrived and hadn't returned her latest call so did. "Guess who?"

"Monique, are you ok?" "I'm fine having a great time, just what I needed."

"You are one of a kind, I wish I could be with you."

"Next time I come here you and Peter have to come too, we would have so much fun."

"And Steve, will he be included?"

"We'll have to see when I get home. We have some work to do. Why do I make everything so difficult?"

"You don't, you just don't want to accept anything less than what makes you and your partner happy. I think you're doing the right thing. It's difficult I know but it will be worth the effort. You've come to a time in your life when you want it true"

"Thanks Jennie as always you put things in order for me."

"No, you have to put them in order for yourself. Now you have the monetary safety so you can be freer so go for it."

"I'm trying Jennie. Oh, I brought you a present, I'll send it to you when I get home or keep it until I come to Vienna which I hope will be soon."

"Wonderful. Just take care of yourself. We want you with us."

"I will, can't wait to hug you."

On Monday I called the airline and changed my reservation to Wednesday night for my return to Geneva, then called the car company to change and all that was settled. I didn't know what to expect when I returned but felt stronger and knew we could deal with whatever. As to Steve, we would see how that would work out, I loved him dearly but I guess sometimes I just had to do something dramatic because that's how I sometimes functioned. I guess in my female brain I thought it kept him on his toes, not to take me for granted. Whatever, it had to be what we both wanted or I would make my way to be alone. I guess it's called choices.

And so Wednesday came and Bob had the car to take me to the airport. I hugged them and thanked them so much for their hospitality and all I had experienced and once again invited them to Montreux which I was sure they would soon decide on doing. The flight was fine even but with my extra luggage I wondered how I would handle it all but did manage with a cart. I seemed to be accumulating when I really wanted to simplify. The car was there, no Steve which I was glad I just wanted to get home first. I arrived home about 11am and of course Maria was there. She had gotten fresh flowers and there was also a bouquet from Steve. She said he was at the office and court with clients and that I should call when I got in. We took my things upstairs, I showered and changed and relaxed a few minutes and then my phone rang. Of course it was Steve. "Are you ok?" "I'm fine, just getting reorganized. I was just going to call you. Thank you for the flowers."

"I know you always love them."

"Yes I do and the love that comes with them."

"What are you going to do now?" "Right now I'm going to lie down for awhile and maybe sleep, I'm really tired." "Everyone at the restaurant wants to see you so are you up for dinner?"

"Of course. What time?"

"I should be there about 6:00." "Ok, fine. We can have a glass of wine and I can tell you about the business I did in NYC"

"For me there are more important things to talk about."

"I understand, we can do that too. See you later." So I rested and then got dressed and knew it would be another interesting but maybe difficult evening. I heard his protection shield was up. He was protecting himself as he should. I put on my black off the shoulder dress and some pearls and went to Maria for approval. She just smiled. Steve arrived, I gave him a hug and kiss as always but he was tense.

We sat on opposite couches and sipped a glass of wine. I started telling him about things in NYC and is initial response was "We have some other things to discuss." I just kept going about the wine and publishing company and he started to smile and relax. "How to I keep my pied piper with me."

"Constant love. I may be somewhat of a free spirit but I only want to be with you so you shouldn't worry. Just let me go sometime so I can smell the flowers and all will be fine. There's no other man nor do I want one."

He came to sit next to me, hugged and kissed me and said "I still have much to learn about you and from you."

"I told you you were stuck with me and you told me it wasn't being stuck, so?"

"Let's go for dinner so everyone will be happy and you can fill me in more on NYC. When are you going to take me there?"

"Soon, I hope."

The restaurant was busy but to my amazement when we walked in Hans and Jacque came quickly to hug and called to Joachim who came out of the kitchen with the biggest smile and also gave me a hug. And then things got livelier with music and clients greeting me, I didn't know what to think. Next thing I knew I was dancing with Steve with "Unforgettable" and then a fast one. They just had to keep pushing me around, I wasn't sure what was going on. I did go into the kitchen to offer my greetings and tell them of the meal I had prepared in NYC do to their help in teaching me. Finally we sat to have dinner and then Mom and Dad arrived so more greetings. They looked concerned but I said I was fine, I just went at the last minute to New York for business and started talking to Dad about the distributor and restaurants of Mr. Sanders. We would have to get together tomorrow to go over more details on the distribution. I had a present for Mom and Dad from NYC so she said I should go by and have some lunch. We dined then said goodnight and I would have to face the night with Steve if he wanted to talk. I just wanted to go back the way it was but knew we needed to talk but wasn't sure I was up to it. We got home and while sitting on the couch Steve began gently caressing my face then my arms and held me close. "Do you want me to stay?" Then I knew he was really hurting.

All I could do was to go to him and say, "You hurt me, but time heals things, I needed to show you something about me. When I'm hurt I can't always deal with it I just run like a horse. It isn't good or adult but that's what I do, plus I have my moody side where I have to be alone or go alone. I only ask you to understand that. If you can you may be able to deal with me and be happy with me."

All he did was pull me to him, hold me, and say, "I love you as you are. I will deal with everything. I just know I have no life without you and that's all I know. Once again I'm sorry for that morning, I didn't understand what I had been thinking for so long and couldn't stand the thought of you being intimate with someone else and here I might succumb."

"You once said to me that we all have our history, it's where we are now that counts."

"So where are we."

"We love each other and just need to trust each other and try to go ahead but right now I need some time alone." He cringed. I would let him no when I had made a final decision. I know that sounded tough but I had to sure of my direction.

I told him the editor from New York would be coming on Tuesday and I would have to get him settled at the hotel and then for the next couple of weeks I would be very busy with him working most of the day an some evenings on my novel. I wouldn't have time for much more. He said he understood and we would try to squeeze in visits and dinner when possible. He understood how important it was for me o do a good job on the book.

I had a lot to catch up on but that was good, progress. I was going to Dad and Mom's for lunch to talk about business and be together. I had to check in with Curt about the horses. I had some information I needed to put together for Paul so I could send it to him. And so it went. I talked to Curt about the wine delivery I needed to go to NYC so we organized that and it would go off the next day. Then we went through the new distribution organization we had set up so I could see how we could work with the distributor in NYC. It would work. We had to know our inventory and do our pricing well so the profit margin would guarantee our efforts. We decided we could do it and still meet our contracts in Switzerland.

Dad was very excited and even said maybe we should look at more land for the next year. I said well let's look. Mom just shook her head but I said it keeps him interested and happy so why not. But Mom said, "but there is no one to leave the Janee legacy to." I knew what she was saying so I tried to appease her by saying it is our legacy while we are here and we have to consider who it goes to after. Think about that. I was already perhaps thinking that Steve and I should adopt a child so that they would have the benefits, I wasn't sure. Of course I thought of Jacque.

Steve kept calling every couple of hours to see what was going on. He said he would take care of dinner so not to worry and I just said I'm not worried I'm not the hausfrau. He just laughed. I said there is always peanut butter and jelly. Then he said, "Monique, I'm so happy, I have my baby back again. I just have some concern that I may lose her from time to time."

"I only took a temporary leave out of my own necessity. I'm here, but you know I will always want to go to Vienna. To ease your mind I reiterated "There is no one else Steve nor do I want anyone else it's just my personal drive to do my creative things. I do have that bad side of sometimes wanting to be totally alone without having to deal with anyone close to me questioning or criticizing me for any way I act and to be myself with no qualifications except myself and I also can get moody. You see I walk the tight rope trying to do everything I enjoy and when my energy is gone I have to take a break, hopefully I reach the platform first. My only guarantee is there is no other man I want to be with, you are the ultimate."

"How do I deserve this?"

I jokingly said, "You don't, but enjoy." We were Americans so could talk in a certain way.

Steve came prepared to cook dinner which I was surprised, I knew he could but he was a bit apprehensive because of Chris and my background. Anything after my day was fine. So he did wonderful tortellini with marinara sauce, added mushrooms, some aubergine on the side with lots of parmisian cheese. We feasted and then had ice cream with melted lindt chocolate which was my favorite. We ate, drank, talked, laughed and then did clean up together. He had gotten a movie so we went upstairs just to stretch out and enjoy. (What movie?)But he went back to the condo.

The next day we got back into the swing of things, he at his office and court, me at the computer, the horses, etc. I went to visit Mom and Dad to do some more planning about the vineyard. He had so much knowledge and I had a lot to learn. It was nice to still be so close to them even with Chris gone.

Steve called to ask where I wanted dinner and I didn't know so he said he would surprise me.

I asked him if I could come to court when he was handling a case. He hesitated and said it might make him nervous. I told him I wouldn't be critical I just wanted to see what went on. So he said ok just check with Genvieve what the schedule is and then I won't know when you are there until after.

One day I was in my dark side where I just needed to be alone and be quiet. That meant I had expended all my energy reserves. So, as he always did, Steve called between appointments and I told him, "I'm just going to take it easy today, I have the fireplace on and a good book and I may nap."

"Are you feeling ok. Should I call Dr. Bovet?"

"No. I'm not sick it's just I need time to be alone to rejuvenate."

"Do you want me to come up during lunch time?"

"I won't be good company. Just let me relax and be quiet and I'll be ok when you come home this evening."

"Are you sure. Is Maria there?"

"I'm sure and yes Maria is here but she knows my moods and will do her own thing for the day. I'll be fine."

"Ok, but I'll call you after court. Do you want anything from the market or any other store?"

"No everything is here except some fresh flowers so please pick some up if your coming up. We'll figure out something for dinner. I don't want to go out I just want to be quiet. Remember I'm not a client you have to ask questions of, ok?"

"Whatever my baby needs. I'm just always concerned."

Later came a call from Dr. Bovet. "Are you feeling ok?"

"Yes doctor I'm just tired and need some quiet time."

"Are you taking the vitamins I prescribed?"

"Yes sir. Don't worry, I just go into these moods sometimes. Steve has to learn that."

"You call me if you need me to check on you."

"Of course I will, don't worry."

"Perhaps it's time for another check up, why don't you come to the office in a few days and we'll do another blood test and check all the vitals."

"Ok let's make an appointment, and so we did. Thank you for your concern I' ll b

"Everyone will be unhappy if you are not up to your usual energetic self."

"Ok Dr. I'll be in on Monday."

And so I went to see the doctor and all seemed ok accept for my anemia. He once again sent my blood work to Geneva for a more in depth study. They simply weren't able to determine what to do with me so I said fine as long as it isn't life threatening I'll just live with it. He insisted on a regular follow ups and that did make me worry a bit but self said, "Just take care and this too shall pass."

CHAPTER 24

So I did stay home and had a lovely day finally with self, reading, dozing, thinking. Steve kept calling through the day to see if I was ok and I said fine. Later in the day I came awake with the sounds of Nat King Cole, it was dream like. I went to the door and downstairs there was Steve with a Cheshire grin on his face, stretched out on one of the couches awaiting my "revelation. I just smiled and went down and of course we started to dance. He was trying to cheer me up, thinking I was depressed. I just danced and laughed and felt most pampered. (put in some of the song titles other than Unforgettable) Then he said, "let's change and take a walk" and of course he meant to the horses which he knew would always cheer me up, so we did. There is nothing better than the fresh air, the aroma of the barn, the nickers from the horses, the touch of their soft muzzles when you feed them treats to get you into perspective. Curt just stood there smiling. When we went back to the house I said, "ok let's see what I can whip up for dinner." Although Steve never had me do this every day which I had done years ago, he loved when I said that. It was something special to him a sort of gift which I wanted it to be. And so it was Monique's pseudo Chinese, lots of vegetables with some slivered chicken and then steamed rice. We did it together, chopping vegetables and chicken, talking about seasonings and then about books we were both reading comparing notes about our reactions. He was absolutely my best friend and beyond that my lover. What more could one want. I wondered when the next brick was coming, such a doubting soul was I.

Although it was early November, Maria and I went shopping to start getting some Christmas things. We had Thanksgiving to plan for but mainly dinner. I wanted Christmas very special so wanted to get started. I wanted lots of candle, ribbons, wrap, ornaments and maybe I would see some gifts for my long list. I wanted to get an idea of what she might like so best way was to take her with me. She loved being part of it especially when we bought some things for her apartment. She was such a friend I wanted to include her in everything. We got home with the trunk full and laughed while we dragged everything into the house and put it into the catering room. Jenny and Peter were coming on the 23rd and would stay in our guest room. For Steve's brother and family, Paul and Juliana I went to see Messieur Sartons, the hotel manager, and we blocked off two of the best rooms, the suites. I called the car company to be prepared for some reservations for airport transfers and cars to come to the house. I would let them know how many we would need. I talked with the florist to order lots of poinsettias of all sizes and wreaths once again. Mademoiselle organizer was on her way. I just wanted everyone to celebrate. May we all stay well.

One day the 1st of December I had another of myself days and needed to just be alone. Steve, I think, was accepting that in me and just stayed away. I did my normal thing of being quiet, reading, thinking and snoozing and then it past and I started again with Christmas plans.

December 19 we went to select the Christmas tree. Steve insisted he had to be part of the selection and he picked out an even taller tree than the last year. This time they had to deliver because Curt didn't think the truck would hold it. Curt, with a helper got the tree up and then Maria I directed him what lights and ornaments to put on the top level because Steve would have a fit if I climbed the ladder. Poor Curt but he kept smiling. Maria and I finished all the part we could reach and then turned on the lights to a glorious display. What joy. Out came the candles and ribbons for the mantel and then the florist arrived with all the poinsettias and wreathes including the ones for the stable doors. The horses couldn't be left out. Steve kept calling to see what was going on and I just said, "We're very busy, you'll see when you come home bring your things to stay."

"I was getting worried I never hear that from you, are you sure?"

"Absolutely."

When he got home tired and worn he just stopped in his tracks and had the look of a child in wonder. He wandered around looking at everything and then sat and just smiled. I don't think he had experienced this since he was a child or since last year. So we opened a bottle of champagne and sat and enjoyed the sight and of course eventually each other.

I still had not decided on a gift for Steve. What to get this man. We had lots of CD's, books, artwork. I wanted it something special, not the typical clothes but I couldn't figure it out. It was a bit selfish but I asked him to come see some sculpture pieces, one in particular I had my eye on, a tall, marble piece in abstract so finely and delicately shaped and polished and he loved it and of course said let's purchase it. I said, "Well let me cogitate a little more about it. I'm always around so much work, I want to be sure." He went back to the office, I called the artist. Now how to get it into the house but have it a surprise. The artist said he would put it on a dolly with wheels, cover it and we would once again put it on Curt to hide it is his apartment and he would roll it in Christmas Eve—done. I would figure out a few smaller things for him.

On the 23rd we went to Chez Janee since we would be having dinner on Christmas Eve and Christmas Day at the house. Joachim had produced a wonderful banquet table with a fantastic assortment of food, tables with fresh flowers and candles. The champagne started to flow, people began to eat and then the dancing began. About 8:30 we were able to get away with a small group while the remainder stayed to party so we could go to the house to enjoy all the Christmas atmosphere. We continued to celebrate until everyone started to get tired. Everyone gone, Steve carried me up the stairs and we just looked at each other amazed with joy of being with or friends who were like family. We were like brand new lovers until we both fell asleep and hoped we could sleep in the next morning. Our house guests new they had run of the house and grounds and would take care of themselves until we could get our act together.

We slept late but heard our guests moving around. Finally we got up to shower and dress and join everyone. They had already had some sort of breakfast so we just did our thing. We all relaxed, took a walk, talked, laughed and came home to recuperate and get ready for the Eve. I was going to be Mrs. Claus again and "dish out" the presents with the help of our vineyard manager's two children who helped the previous year. We sat on the floor and made a big "to do" about every present. Everyone seemed happy and in the Eve mood. Then I said I had a special present for Steve but he interrupted saying he should go first. He handed me my present and when I opened it there was an envelope with obvious travel documents—a cruise to South America which I had always wanted to do. He couldn't have made me happier. I yelled and danced and said I have to learn more about their music and dance so we can do it all. Now we had two trips, Portugal and South America, to fit into the schedule Everyone was clapping over my joy.

Then it was time for the last present, the one for Steve. I said, "May I do it now?" "Of course. Do I get a frying pan or what? he said jokingly. So Curt and I went to his place and wheeled the sculpture piece over through the back door. I had figured out that I only needed to cover it with a sheet and do a big bow, I couldn't wrap it. And then I asked Steve to do the unveiling. He did and the light in his eyes said all I needed to know. He touched it gently and said "It will go here right?" I answered, "yes", where we thought so it is for both of us for our home. We placed it and then he came to me with arms open and hugged me like never before. He was a bit overwhelmed. That was our personal gift, but the best gift still was the loving people that were with us. All Steve could do at that point was to get more champagne for everyone and stare at the sculpture and then go to it to touch it again and realize that an artist with so many personal experiences had created the abstraction. I just sat and watched in awe, this was my loving husband who was beginning to understand my longing for art and all personal expression.

Then of course I went to the piano so everyone could sing Christmas Carols and then to our surprise came carolers outside the house from a nearby village. I hadn't expected this but invited them in to see the tree and decorations and of course offered them refreshments. What an Eve, the kind I always dreamed of, but often didn't have. A "family" celebrating all of the bounty of God's earth, what more could we want no matter how rich or poor. With all the ups and downs we had a blessed life.

Suddenly it seemed that all of us were crashing at the same moment so I said good night to you all. I will do breakfast tomorrow at 11 am so be ready, before that you are on your own.

Christmas morning Steve and I were still in bed when we heard people moving about. So we finally got up and I went to the kitchen to start breakfast and there I found Joachim already making preparations. "Why are you not at home with your family?" I will be there later but his is my gift to you. I had told him something light and simple and he said of course. So what did I find him doing; locks with cream cheese, seafood croquets, tiny sausages, all the preparation for any omelete one would want plus eggs benedict and I knew that was for me. Hopefully everyone would want that so his work would not be so difficult, but to Joachim it was not work it was art in his fashion. I asked him about juice and he said of course Madame, orange, apricot, apple or wine.

We laughed and we hugged and I thanked him and then gave him a present from myself which was not his bonus which I had already given. I gave him two books on cooking which I knew he did not have but wanted. He grabbed me for a hug and then excused himself for his outburst and I said there is nothing to excuse, he was part of family. After our sumptuous breakfast we all took a walk around the property and then returned to the house and everyone was on their own to listen to music, watch tv, read, sleep, walk whatever they chose.

Everyone was ready for dinner, Jennie and Peter, Juliana and Paul, James and Susan with their children, Mom and Dad, Jochaim and his wife all smiling, laughing ooing and ahhing over the table. It continued a

For Christmas dinner Joachim left me all the directions for dinner with all the cooking times, etc. He had prepared a stuffed turkey for all but mainly for Steve and myself as Americans and a goose which we enjoyed also and all the typical trimmings the same as last year. I was on deck to do the cooking and serving, but of course I would enlist everyone to help especially with clean up. What a festive evening. With all different backgrounds, all different ideas, all different "classes", if you will accept that, celebrating together. Everyone was ready for dinner, Jennie and Peter, Juliana and Paul, James and Susan with their children, Mom and Dad, Jochaim and his wife all smiling, laughing and all said they were hungry. we gorged ourselves. I had done my best to have a wonderful Christmas last year, this one was surpassing in happiness.

At one point I just sat and looked until I saw Steve looking at me and then we just smiled. It was our home. The next step was to offer a child this experience—not our own, at my age we felt it was too dangerous to have our own child, we had already talked with the doctor about it. I thought perhaps we could find a young child to enjoy all that we could offer and who could teach us a lot and to whom we could teach our life experiences. Who would that child be? Of course I had my idea, my loving Jacque 2. We would soon know.

Jenny, Peter and my NY friends were leaving on the 27th so we had some time the next day to relax together, hike, sight see or whatever.

The tree would be up for a few more days, the decorations would be packed and we would look to the New Year and what would it bring, who knew. It was a circle that was wonderful, enlightened and brought people together to enjoy this part of the dance of life.

What I loved most was Steve's reaction to the holiday. A simple "thank you for making this so special, it was wonderful." I knew he had enjoyed everything and I did see him in the morning by the sculpture quietly viewing and drawing his own perspectives about what the artist had meant to express, he was my best student. I knew the gift was special and one we would keep on enjoying every day in our home.

Unfortunately everyone had to go home and with that comes the let down the holidays do, they lift one up and let one down. The adrenalin stops flowing and we start to do the day to day but we had enjoyed together and would not forget. It would be my life to be greeting and saying temporary good bys to friends and places, a new kind of life with lots of ups and downs but most satisfying. But everyone seemed happy. My Viennese friends would be returning later in the day and in some parts of me I wanted to go with them but one can't have everything so I sent them off with my love and promise I would be there soon and in between talk with them via phone or the infamous email. It would be my life to be greeting and saying temporary good bys to friends and places, a new kind of life with lots of ups and downs but most satisfying

New Year's of course was celebrated at the restaurant and Joachim would once again prepare a feast. I sometimes wondered how Joachim did this day and day out. The banquet was prepared, the decorations in place, the musicians were ready and so it went with the eating, drinking of wine and dancing. We did reach midnight and toasted with everyone and then Steve took me away to go home and I was thankful. We enjoyed our own special "toast". We slept late New Year's Day, everything was quiet and we were back to our peace.

And so our lives got organized to our daily activities. I told Steve that Paul had an exhibit opening mid February and I wanted to be there to participate. He was a bit reluctant but finally agreed to no more than three nights away. So I went and helped Paul, enjoyed Jennie and Peter's company and had constant calls from Steve so I could report in. I told him everything that was going on and he honestly said he wished he were there so he too could enjoy. I said next time he would come with me and we would enjoy it together.

Paul was having an exhibit of the work of an American artists so we would have to work hard for sales. This artist was from New York City and was a most sophisticated painter of oils in abstract expressionism. He was doing well in the States so had begun to build somewhat of a name and following so we hoped this would entice our European friends. We did more marketing by mail and email to our past clients and the new ones we constantly added to our data base. The opening evening was full of people and listening to the conversation, positive and excited about the work. We managed to sell 3 pieces and hoped this would continue however were always realistic about the possibilities that it had been to the emotions of the opening that pieces were sold.

We went out and celebrated as usual, it was still just as fun and exciting to me as it had been since I began with Paul. I had learned so much and felt proud of the assistance I had provided for him. And I loved Vienna even more. Each time there I made sure I went to a performance at the Opera House or the Kunstverien and of course visited with Gabrielle.

CHAPTER 25

When I returned I started looking for a child we might adopt. There was of course Jacque 2 my little love. He was still at the Catholic orphanage where I volunteered for music and other activities. I liked him very much because, although a bit too precocious, was very intelligent and seemed to respond to me. So I asked if he could come to the house for dinner so Steve could meet and get to know him. They hit it off with soccer, the horses, and even the legal system. So we invited him more often to come for whatever we were doing. Steve didn't know what I had in mind because I often had children in the house for music lessons or just to have fun. But I liked this child and thought if something happens to me Steve will have another purpose. I had a premonition which I couldn't share with Steve because he would be too upset or as we say "freak out" about my future health. The child was almost 8 and of Swiss nationality. His parents had been killed in a car accident and there were no other relatives that we could find so that was why he was in the orphanage. So I set out to see what adoption would entail. One night I approached Steve with the idea that perhaps since we couldn't have our own children because of my age we could possibly seek the adoption route. His first response was why, aren't we happy. I said of course we are but I am just looking to the future, will you think about it. And my wonderful Steve said, "of course I'll think about it." I asked him if he liked Jacque 2 and he said of course he seems like a great kid but do we need that. I think he was concerned that he would lose part of me and he wasn't willing to do that—he was the "kid" in the household.

Jacque 2 was so much fun. We had him for a weekend and let him join in on our activities and Steve warmed up very quickly. So one day Steve asked me, "You want to adopt this boy don't you?"

"I'm thinking about it but only if you agree. You know me I can spread myself out so no one is alone."

"I know but it will change our life."

"Of course to a degree but we'd be offering a future for him to take over the legacy."

"Is that important to you."

I said, "yes" but I wasn't up to it today.

"How are you now?" "I'm ok."

"Shall I call and go get him for dinner?"

I smiled and said, "fantastic, please do. I'll start whipping something up."

Then my very intuitive husband looked at me with a smile and said, "You set me up."

I sheepishly admitted, "Yes. I wanted to know if you really liked having him here."

"Of course I do, he adds another wonderful addition to our life. You should be an attorney, you would set everyone up."

"No, I wouldn't"

"I'll be back in a half an hour with what I think is going to be our new son." I just smiled and gave him a hug.

"Make sure they pack some PJs and some clothes for tomorrow, I don't have anything for his size."

"What I do for you."

"But it is for you too. You will have a son. I wish I could give you one but this is the next best I can do."

"I love you," is all Steve could say.

So Jacque 2 arrived back with Steve, laughing and talking about something. I had dinner prepared and when finished Jacque 2 was there to help clean the dishes and put things away and then to go to his bed. He was of course in awe of the guest room. I showed him where our room was and that he should leave his door open if he needed we were there.

The poor little man asked me what do I do now Madame Monique. I said you put on your pj's and go to bed and sleep well and know we are here so you have nothing to worry about. He asked me if he got scared in the night what should he do and I said you come to us our door is open to you but you must be respectful and knock before.

"Ok, I think I can do this."

"I know you can or you would not be in our home. Do you understand?"

"Yes Monique" Somehow he had forgotten the madame.

"Your parents are gone, do you want new parents" I asked.

"Yes I would love to have a home again and with someone like you."

I thought my heart would burst. "Ok then we will see that you have home again, here or somewhere.

"But I want it with you and Messiur Steve."

My heart went out again and I needed to be honest with this child, "We will see. For now you are here tonight and tomorrow we will have a wonderful day. Bon nuit my lamb, sweet dreams.

He took my hand and held it and said "I promise not to be a problem." Sweet child.

In the morning we had breakfast and went to the horses. Steve was showing Jacque 2 all the equipment and trying to explain everything to him. This is what I wanted for him to have some more family because I had a premonition that my time might be limited. I was feeling very tired again and knew I needed to go to the doctor to see about the anemia but had avoided it for myself and for Steve. Something was going on in my system. I wanted to be sure Steve had someone to be responsible for if I passed since he had always been responsible for my needs. These thoughts I couldn't share with him so I was "setting" it up but couldn't share that with him now.

When we had finished with the horses Jacque 2 asked about the vineyards. He knew of them but had never walked through them to see the plants and learn about where the grapes came from so we walked and tried to show him how it happens. It was too early for the grapes but we could get him started on learning.

We had an early dinner so Steve could take Jacque 2 back because he would go to school early with the nuns and needed to sleep. Jacque thanked us like a gentleman but of course hugged me and hopefully hugged Steve when he returned to the orphanage. We said goodbye until the next time and his eyes looked whistfully at me as he said, "I hope it is soon."

Again my heart; I would take them all in if I thought I had the capability.

Steve came home and looked at me, gave me a hug and said "What do you really think, can we do this.?"

"I will be nothing less to you, you are my love, but I would love to have this child here. It won't always be easy but it can be such a joy. Don't you enjoy him?"

"Yes, honestly I do and I would like to have him in our life if it makes you happy."

"No, it must be a twosome here that both of us are happy."

He thought for a few moments and said, "I decided long ago what makes you happy makes me happy so I'm all for it. We have to file the adoption papers and I can do that and we'll go from there."

"Oh Steve are you sure, it is another person in our life who needs us and I don't want to take anything away from what we have."

"It will make us even more of a family and I know that will make us both happy. I only wish we had met earlier so we could have our own child. "I'm afraid I might lose you if you became pregnant because of your health problems and being older."

"Well let's talk to the doctor and see what he thinks before we go any further. Are you willing to do that."

"Of course, for you anything." After that conversation you know where we were and it was as always wonderful. We could never seem to get enough of each other, what a wonderful "problem".

So we talked with Dr. Bovet and his answer was that it would be too much of a risk for me and the child. You can conceive if you wish but with your anemia the child might have some problems and you may have some in child birth with the blood loss. So Steve said he would not accept anything that put me at any kind of risk, we will adopt. I was so thankful that he made the decision. First he wanted me but he was open to adoption. If it didn't work, that was ok, we can't have everything. I just knew there were children out there that needed homes and we could offer so much, not in things, but in love and understanding. So we went home and looked at each other and Steve said let's talk with Father about it. I hugged him knowing how much this meant for him to accept this. I loved the child and knew I might not always be around to take care of Steve and wanted some more family for him. We made an appointment with Father Joseph with Jacque present so he too would have a say. We set it up and Sister Clara brought in Jacque with eyes as big as saucers. He saw us and gave a big smile but then said, "Father did I do something wrong, why am I here?"

"No son, the Gavin's want to talk to you about something and wanted me here to listen."

Steve started, "Son are you happy being with us."

"Oh yes, very much, both of you. You are so kind, generous and fun to be with."

I asked him if he missed his mother and father.

"Oh yes, although I was only 2 when they died in the crash I remember how loving they were."

"Do you like doing things with us hiking, riding reading?"

"Very much you always make me feel so welcome, I have so much fun with you and Shady of course."

"Would you consider having another mother and father?"

"Very much if they were like you or better if they were you."

"Jacque," father Joseph said, "Mr and Mrs Gavin have asked me about the possibility of adopting you."

He just looked back and forth at each of us for a few seconds, then jumped up and went behind the desk to hug Father Joseph and ask if it were true, could it be.

"Yes son it can be, but you must tell them that is what you want."

He grabbed both my hands and said, "Absolutely." and then began to babble that he would be respectful, and good. "I love you both you have done so much and we have fun together but I don't know why you chose me there are many children." I said simply that we had gotten to know him, loved him and wanted him to share our life. He went to Steve and did the same thing. "What happens now? What do we do?"

"I must prepare the adoption papers and make an appointment with a judge who will want to ask you some questions."

"A judge? What kind of questions? I think I'll be scared."

"No you needn't be scared, we will be together, she will just want to be sure you have decided you want this."

Steve excused himself and made a phone call to a judge friend who made an appointment at noon for the next day, great no delays. We told Jacque 2 and he said, "Sisters will get me ready." To our amazement Jacque 2 got up and literary did a jig singing out "I'm going to have a new home." He came back and kissed each of us on the cheek went flying out the door almost literally it seemed above the ground.

We thanked Father Joseph. Steve was going back to the office to do the paperwork and see clients. I said I was going shopping of course for Jacque 2. I bought casual and dress shirts, slacks and jeans, pajamas, robe, slippers and picked out 3 pairs of shoes for him to try. I also found a great wind breaker and a dressier coat. Tomorrow I would take him to the tailor to have the pants hemmed and measured for a couple of suits. We would also have to buy new blazers and pants, the type he wore at school as a uniform.

We went with Jacque 2 the next day to see the judge who asked Jacque 2 how he felt about us and going to a new home. He said he was so pleased and excited. She said it was a big responsibility for us and he should realize it was for him also. He said he understood and would be the best he could. She was a friend of Steve's and said to him that it was a big step. She asked Jacque how he did in school, what activities he liked and had he really thought what it would be with a family. "I'm a very good student which will make Madame Monique and Messieur happy, I love sports, I love the beauty of their home but most of all the love they show each other." Out of the mouths of babes. She okayed the adoption papers without hesitation. Jacque wanted to see what she stamp so she said. "Well Messieur Jacque 2 come around on this side and see what I do with the papers." She signed them and then showed him the official stamp she had to apply. "So it is final once Messieur Steve presents the papers in the proper office."

"That's all, it's so fast and easy. Will I change my last name?"

"That is for you and your new parents to decide. That will be another form."

We thanked her. Jacque 2 asked if he could visit her sometime and she said absolutely.

After Steve and I as well as Jacque 2 who wanted to see how the filing was done went right away to the court house. After Jacque 2 and I went shopping. I had purchased some pants as well as jeans for him but they needed to be shortened, I wanted him fit for a couple of dress suits plus he needed several pairs of shoes. His eyes were as wide as saucers throughout the process. The slacks were ready after we made the shoe purchases.

He wanted to know if he would have the same big room and I told him yes so he wanted to look again. Of course his room now had a desk with books, notebooks, maps, pencil, pens and his closet had many new clothes for school and recreation. But I did not want a spoiled child around so I laid down the parameters. He would do well in school or there would be trouble, he would be polite and kind to everyone, his room was to be taken care of by himself not with Maria or I doing everything, the kitchen would always be in good order and he would have some chores. Chores such as helping Curt in the stable, assisting Maria when he could, helping wash the cars any son of mine was going to be disciplined.

Jacque 2 learned to prepare certain things for breakfast and loved doing it for us, he helped with dinner when appropriate, he never got upset when we said we were going out for an evening. He was a pleasure but I tried to make sure that he didn't always have to please, he had his own mind and should speak up which as talkative as he was I knew would not be a problem. I wanted to give him his wings to find his way with guidance from us. One day he asked us what he should call us. I was a little dumfounded and at first said Madame Monique and Msr Steve. He looked at me and his smart mind said but you are now my parents, can't I call you Mother and Father or Mom and Dad. All we could say was of course, our new family. So there it was Mom and Dad and son.

He went back to the orphanage for one more night to talk with Father the sisters and his friends. He wanted to share the happiness he felt and hoped his friends would not be jealous about his adoption. I was to pick him up after school the next day and gather the meager things he had there.

We walked together a short way to the bus stop which took him directly to school. I wanted him to be independent and do as much as he could on his own. We both enjoyed him so much and I made sure it did not take away from Steve's and my relationship, that was too precious to me. So I spent a few more minutes in my day to keep it all aflot and well worth the effort. We had the best, we were offering something special to this child and he came to the fore. He wasn't perfect, no one is they would be boring. He tried so hard. We had our ups and downs because sometimes he became quite headstrong and thought he knew more than he did. But we managed to work it out and end up ok. Steve was the even one monitoring us as I would sometimes fly off the handle and get upset.

And so we went on with our days of activity but always with lots of laughter and joy. When a problem came up we took care of it together and we were a family with so much to share. Jacque 2 did his chores and his studies, sometimes had his problems at school mainly because of his intelligence and sometimes his stubbornness but I worked with the teachers and with him and he seemed to understand and slowly grow. He was always loving, I'm afraid a bit of a charmer. We spent hours at the piano and listening to music, he seemed to love it as I did. He also liked going with me to art exhibits and absorbed all I could teach him. So our days were full with valuable times and experiences.

I did have a problem, there was one thing that Steve could not seem to get over. One night when we were talking and getting ready for bed he again brought up something he seemed to not get over, that I had been with other men but most of all Chris, saying he couldn't stand that I had been intimate with them. Being tired fighting my illness I lost my cool, no more even head. "We all have a history. You do too but I never confront you with that. Why is it that men can do what they want but women are not in the same category. I'm sick of hearing about this. I love you, I haven't been with any other man since I committed to you, I hardly look, what more do you want? I love you and try to please you."

"I just get images of you with Chris or someone else and it drives me crazy."

"Well you have to deal with that. I can't do anymore."

"You're not being reasonable, we need to talk about this."

"No, no more. I am not one of your clients. I have nothing to confess that you don't already know. You make me feel like I'm a loose woman, a slut who moves from one bed to the other." By now we were yelling at each other.

"Now you're getting hysterical."

"No I'm just fed up with this constant cloud. I have nothing to be ashamed of don't make me feel like I should."

"Monique, quiet down."

"No I won't."

And we went on and on as people unreasonably argue, making no sense, only getting in deeper. I just took my robe, my purse and phone and said "goodnight. I will sleep in the guest room and don't come in to talk any more or anything else and I went angrily to bed saying to SELF enough is enough."

I awoke about 4 am and couldn't sleep so got up and left Jacque a note that I was going out for my alone time and not to worry. By now we was self sufficient as far as the day to day things of setting his alarm to get up in time to shower, dress have breakfast on his own. I tried not to let him have to do that very often but I knew he could and if had a problem would ask his Dad or Maria. I showered and then went down to the garage where I kept my riding clothes so put on some jeans, a shirt, my sneakers so that I didn't have to go to our room and wake Steve. I just wanted to get out and walk along the water and breathe. It was one of my quirks and Steve new it. Sometimes I just had to be alone without any input; it was like my oasis. I walked by the lake and then went to a small café for some café and a petit pain au chocolate hoping not to find anyone I knew that I would have to chat with. On the note I had told Jacque that I would pick him up at school at 2:30 pm so to wait and not take the bus. He was waiting as

I drove up and jumped in and asked right away, "Are you ok Mom."

I just smiled and said, "Better, I'm sorry I wasn't home for you this morning."

"That's ok. I think I understand. You and Dad had a big argument, was it about me, did I do something wrong?"

"Absolutely not. We both love you and it was not about anything you did. You do a great job with school and home. No it is something between him and I."

"It has something to do with Uncle Chris wasn't it."

Out of the mouths of babes, this child observed everything. "Yes, and other things."

"Did you think you would have married Uncle Chris?"

"Yes, I did once but it would have been wrong he as erratic the time before his accident. Your Dad was the right one for me. Don't worry we will work it out and all will be well. Sometimes things just take some talking and time so that there is an understanding."

"Like Suzanne, sometimes she just doesn't seem to get it when I say something. I guess males and females think a little differently sometimes but they can't do without each other."

"You are absolutely right and that is nothing that we've taught you, you just know that intuitively."

"Intuitively, hmm, I have to look that word up like you always have me do."

"You understand why I have you look up vocabulary words?"

"Yes, so I have more understanding."

"Exactly and so that you can write and talk with your God given intelligence."

"I love you Mom. Thank you for everything."

I thought my heart would burst once again. "And I love you. Let's go to the bookstore ok?"

"Great."

We bought a three different colored notebooks for his various projects and some highlighter pens he said he needed.

Then we went to see about some slacks and new shirts. He was starting to outgrow everything already. We left the slacks and jacket we found to be altered, I would pick up on Monday. I also found a new art book for Steve as he said he wanted to keep learning more about the contemporary art scene, I thought we could share that but we did have it wrapped as a present for him.

We got home and I said how about a ride, you on Serhalin and me on Sasha and his eyes lit up. So I said let's get our gear on and go see Curt and the horses. We saddled up and started out on the trail into fresh air and peace and quiet. Then my cell rang, it was Steve so I answered. He just asked, "How are you doing."

"Fine, we're out taking a ride to rest our souls." Then I passed the phone to Jacque 2.

"Hi Dad. We're out on the horses and it's wonderful to be so relaxed with Mom and looking out to the lake and over the land. What a joy to look from the hills, over the vineyards on the hills down to Montreux and out onto the lake. We are in a paradise."

"Enjoy son. She can teach you a lot about the horses and enjoying the beauty of the land."

"I know Dad, she is so special. Don't forget that."

"Son, I never forget that. Enjoy your time with her. What about homework?"

"After our ride will tackle that. I have lots of math problems to work on and I need help on an essay I need to write so will do that when we get back to the house. Of course we have to take care of the horses after the ride."

"Ok, let me talk to her again."

"How about pizza tonight at Daniels?"

"Ok, what time."

"My last appointment isn't until 5:30 so by the time I complete everything, let's say 7pm."

"Ok, we'll be there."

So we worked on math, did an outline for the essay and then showered and put on our finest jeans, shirts and sweaters and drove to the restaurant. Steve was already there waiting for us. Jacque 2 said hi and then disappeared to talk with the owner and cook about the pizza.

Steve just asked me if I was ok and I told him yes better. I had a lovely day with my alone time and then with Jacque 2,

Jacque 2 and Daniel appeared each with a pizza in hand. Jacque 2 showing off that he too could serve with his new friend. Steve had a present for Jacque 2 a cell phone but told him it was for calling us or Maria if he needed something or for emergencies, not for talking for hours with friends. He explained how to use it and about the minutes. If he needed to talk with friends he should use the house phone. Jacque was so excited that he had to call someone right away so we had him call his grandparents. We would have to watch the use of this but I did think it was a good idea since we were often in different places and he did have to come a ways to get home. Jacque 2 gave the book we had gotten for Steve. He was happy and said he would study it diligently. Then I got one. A leather bound journal book with Monique inscribed on the front with a beautiful pen attached. Steve told me the store had the record so I could always order more. Of course I immediately dated my first entry about the day and our evening.

Then dear Jacque 2 with his knowing self said, "Dad you haven't danced with Mom tonight. Would you please? Let's go to the restaurant I want to watch, you do it so beautifully. I thought to myself I did a good job choosing this child.

We both smiled and how could one say no so we did and everything felt so much better. Then I said to Jacque 2, "You must dance we me also or the evening won't be complete."

"Ok Mom you might have to lead me, sometimes I don't know where to go."

"We'll figure it out. Just listen to the music and enjoy." What fun. Now I had two men again. And so we went home all content.

The next day was Saturday so we could all sleep in, no school, no office, for me there was always something but I could fit it in. It was raining so we put on the fireplace and all got special books and just got comfy in the living room, soon I was taking a nap.

Steve wanted to take me for dinner that evening to the restaurant in Vevey which we both enjoyed. Jacque had a friend coming over to stay overnight so I said fine, let's do it.

We had been at the restaurant before, a small, intimate setting, with very good food. They often had my favorite bouillabaisse. Little did I know that he had ordered that ahead. He said he just wanted a romantic evening with his lady which every woman wants to hear every so often. They also had some local musicians on the weekends so there was dancing which of course we always loved. So we started with the wine and danced, and then started with dinner and for once I was very hungry so Steve loved it as I really finally ate my meal. Then he excused himself and went out and I wondered what he doing. He came back with a big smile and presented me with a package.

So I opened it and there was the most exquisite, gorgeous bracelet inside. It consisted of several strands of filigreed gold with the top setting in an abstract design of sapphires and diamonds. I had never seen anything like it. He put it on and it draped on my wrist, the style I liked so much. He looked at me apprehensively as if I wouldn't like it and all I could do was let tears come streaming down and say, "it is exquisite, gorgeous, a work of art." Then for whatever reason I said you don't have to ply me with gifts, you are my gift, don't you know that?

"I'm trying to be. I just want you know that and sometimes I just have to reiterate it with gifts."

The owner came over as did some of the other people whom we knew from the area and admired and asked what the occasion was. Steve just said simply, "love."

When we arrived home I still was admiring the bracelet. Our door was open so Jacque knew it was ok to ask if he could come in. He knew something was going on and he wasn't going to miss a thing. "May I come in? You don't need such a big bed you are always like one person so close together. Are you loving Mom, Dad?" Out of the mouths of babes.

"What are you doing up so late. Well we've been on the computer and watched a movie because we know we can sleep late tomorrow." When he saw the bracelet he used the same words, gorgeous, exquisite and just the style Mom likes. It is an art piece. Steve laid there amazed and said, "This is your son."

"Our son. You picked out the bracelet, he just used my words to describe it." God what joy. All was forgiven, the husband, the stubborn child, they were mine to love. "Now where do I wear this?"

"Anywhere you want. Our trips, to the market. Enjoy it. And you can wear it to a party we're invited to at Messieur Bolier a party to thank me for winning the case. James and Daphne, and several other people you know will be there and it will be smashing. He throws the best in the area."

So we go to the black tie dinner of Messieur Bollier. It was a fantastic mansion, which I wouldn't have wanted. It was extremely large and a bit pretentious. Steve had asked me which dress I would wear and I just said I wasn't sure, he didn't know that Gabrielle had sent me a new gown, fitted with the back open again and cut outs at the sides along my waist, in a soft blue, quiet sexy. Steve and Jacque were down stairs awaiting me and I got the oohs and ahhs from both. Sometimes it was like a fairy tale where I was the princess. The party was most enjoyable. I even admired his art collection which in most cases was quite excellent. I told him of Paul's gallery and he said he would like to see photos of the next exhibit's work so I kept moving on.

So we had home, family, business, a most comfortable life. We three were so close. Steve and I couldn't believe how the years were passing but we saw it in the growth of Jacque 2 with the passing of each school year. Soon it would be time to talk of the university.

At the beginning of May the fatigue started again, I was feeling more tired but tried to hide that. I finally went to Dr. Bovet and told him how I feeling and so he did another blood workup and said we'll see. It again anemia, but they found that it was a virus causing it and they would have to do some special drug therapy to try to arrest it. He would be in touch with a Dr Egger in Zurich. I hated drugs but I said for my family I would try anything to get well. I was on the drug program but also vitamins, iron and was to eat 6 times a day to try to build up my strength. My men came to my constant assistance and it brought them closer because they had a program, Mom. I started feeling better and could get on with some of my activities. We could go to the restaurant and do our dancing with Steve and now my other man Jacque 2 who had a great feel for music. I wanted to stay strong for them and would try my best.

Dr. Egger had been doing a lot of research and had a new, experimental, drug they would try for the virus. They were not sure of the side effects but I was willing to try anything that would improve my condition. They admitted me to the hospital in Geneva, for testing and therapy. The doctor there and Dr. Egger came to explain the therapy. They thought if they could rid me of the virus, they could then treat the anemia and with my efforts with diet, drug therapy and rest, I could get better. They admitted me to the hospital for the testing and therapy. Steve left James and Genevieve in charge of the office and came to stay with me at the hospital while they started the treatments. There were shots they had to administer and then I would go on a pill therapy. I would continue taking all the recommended vitamins, iron and I had to eat 6 times a day to build my stamina. They got me up to walk several times a day to keep muscle strength. Poor Steve stayed with me the whole time sleeping on a cot in my room only going to the hotel to shower and change. I asked for Jacque 2 so he ordered a car to bring him from Montreux to the hospital, gave him specific instructions as to where to meet and soon he too was with me. Finally the doctors were more positive because my temperature dropped, all the other vital signs were fine. When my temperature reached normal they said they would release me to go home under the care of my doctor and nurses when Steve could not be with me. Steve would not allow me to ride in the car and insisted on an ambulance to take me home with Jacque 2 riding with me. When we arrived he assisted and carried me up to our room. I felt like an invalid but thank heavens I had them all to assist as I felt so weak. I hated it, why me I asked SELF. SELF said it will in the end make you a stronger person. I hoped so. The weeks went by with me trying to do everything I was instructed to do and taking the injections of the new drug and soon started feeling better. Maybe there would be an end to this after all, I couldn't leave them alone. After the last blood test the doctors said they saw no sign of the virus so it was up to me to eat and rest. We often joke about wanting to just stay in bed when we're busy with life, well I wanted to get out of bed so I set my own regime. I would eat, rest, walk and try to work with the horses and get back to some normal state.

I soon was feeling much better so hopefully the drug therapy was fighting the virus. Steve was always loving and watching me carefully until I said stop already, I'm going to get well." He said I had to because there was no quality life for him without me so I tried harder.

But as I was trying to heal another virus or some type of disease arrived, one that hit a section of the vineyards. This was a tough one because if we didn't find a way to eradicate it it could take the entire crop out. Curt and Dad sent samples to the office for disease control and they sent out a man to take samples for testing. He was able to determine what it was and recommended not only a spray but a substance to put into the soil so we started that and then waited. More vines succumbed but soon it stopped and didn't go on to infect more vines. It looked like we had won the battle but now had to replenish the vines so the planting began. They would take several years to be producing. It was lucky Dad and I had bought the other property, we would be able to meet our future orders.

Life for us continued with me on a limited schedule which I hated but had to accept. We had gotten through the adolescent years with Jacque 2 and then it seemed suddenly he was ready for college. He surprised us by saying he wanted to go to Harvard in Boston, Steve's alma mater. We questioned him about his reasons and his point was that his parents were American and he needed to learn more about living there plus he had heard such great things about the school. He would be so far away, I was concerned but finally he won out and we agreed. And so the day came when he would be flying off and of course we were both apprehensive, that day we dropped the diminutive of 2 He was so excited one couldn't help but understand the beauty of youth. Both of us reminisced our entering the university and laughed at our naivete and our excuberance at new beginnings. I had felt the same when I left California for Vienna, it all was a new adventure.

Jacque settled in. He was always in contact with us and doing very well in school what more could we ask. Some of Steve's college friends lived in the area so Jacque had some friendly connections as well as those he made at school. We just missed him and his liveliness and precocious questions.

Jacque of course met a young lady at school, Christina and was totally in love at the age I wish I had met his father so we would have had so many more years together. He called us after his first year and said he wanted to come home to go to school in Geneva and he was bringing Christina. We said come home and bring whomever. Jacque arrived with his love and we were there with open arms for both. After both of us hugging Jacque he introduced us to Christina;

All I could say was, "Welcome, you are more beautiful than Jacque said. Let's take your things and get you settled in Jacque's room.

Jacque was my child again as he entered the room and looked around remembering the times he had enjoyed there. He turned and hugged me and said, "You kept it as I left it."

"Of course, it's your special room." I had fresh flowers for them and showed Christina all the things I had placed for them, notions, robes even PJ's if they needed them. I was not an old fashioned mother about understanding that they had been intimate. She suddenly came and hugged me saying you are just how Jacque has always described you and I know we will be friends."

"Of course we will. Get settled and come down we have lots to talk about." We did talk as we walked around the property in the fresh air. Chistina was amazed at the property, the house, the barn. "This is a paradise."

Jacque reiterated that he wanted to go to school in Geneva for a law degree while Christina would do studies in the arts. He wanted to be involved in the business. He had much to learn but was capable of doing that and we were pleased. He wanted to marry Christina and Steve in his way said, "But you are so young." Jacque hit him with "Wouldn't you have liked to be with Mom from the age we are? I've always known how close you have been mentally and physically and I want the same thing."

Steve just answered, "Absolutely, we would have had more wonderful years. Just be sure she is the one." "She is Dad."

"Only you can know if that is true. Then let's make the plans. When do you want this event? We can have it in the same chapel where we were married and Gabrielle can do her gown if you want that."

"As soon as we can put it all together. Anything with Mom's taste will be what I want she can plan with Christina. We'll need to find a place in Geneva and get settled long before school starts so I think we should set a date for the end of June or first of July only 3 or 4 weeks away." We had to move quickly.

"I can do it with your help Mom and Dad. I really want to carry on the legacy for both of you and grandma and grandpa. I will do my best. I want our home hear in Montreux after school."

"Is Christina aware of all of this."

"Of course. I asked her and she said yes but I've yet to chose the ring, I need Dad's help."

And so the next day we began making plans, I was as excited as Christina and made sure I included here in every decision. I contacted Gabrielle and she said she would do as she had done for me to send some design ideas and fabrics. The reception would be at the restaurant as in the past and all that part would be worked out with Joachim. In my heart I had only trepidation that they were only 19, so young but I did know that Jacque was always ahead of his age group quite mature for his yeas. I hoped he was a lover like his father so she would be as happy as I had been and was.

And so another wedding on July 1. Steve's parents and mom and dad Janee although up in age were to come as were Peter and Jennie, Paul and Guliana. They all had known and loved Jacque before and wanted to celebrate with them.

On the wedding day Chistina looked like an angel in her white Gabrielle gown, as Steve said I did, the flowers were delicate and perfect, the reception went off with great pleasure for all so now we had not only a son back with us but a daughter to enjoy. They would leave in a few days for Geneva where they both would be at the university. I had set up a trust fund through James for Jacque so he would have to monitor his money and be on his own to take care of his new wife. They found a small, charming apartment near the university and started their studies. Of course they would come home many weekends but that was fine. They had decided to marry so young but they needed to learn how to take care of everything. Jacque was studying law but also with some business and marketing classes. Christina was a right side of the brain person like myself and was studying music, art and literature. We had much to discuss when they were home, it was wonderful.

Unfortunately another brick came into the road. In August I started feeling weak again, it was a little over a year since my last episode. I checked in with Dr. Bovet. The original virus, as Dr.Egger referred to it, or another had returned in my system. I believe it was like a type of cancer, remission and then return. I started running high temperatures and was getting weaker. So we would have to go through some sort of sequence. Dr. Egger had been doing more research and had developed a new, but experimental drug. They did not yet know all the side effects but I decided they could go ahead He once again flew to Geneva from Zurich. This time they could not combat the virus with any drug no matter what they tried. I knew what the outcome was going to be and tried to console Steve. I went down hill quickly and knew I would leave him alone. But he now had Jacque and Chistina to live for but it would not be easy for him. He sat with me each day and we talked and tried to laugh. Via ambulance I was able to go home again and would be under the care of my doctor. But I knew that Dr. Egger would be coming on the weekend and would check on me again. He decided to stay at the hotel but would be coming to the house periodically. Steve met him at the restaurant to introduce him around and made sure he would have everything, then came back to the house with special goodies from Joachim. I was really feeling much better, had more energy and an appetite..

Steve told Dr.Egger will try anything that might help, I can't lose her vitality or more importantly her. She is my life and I don't know if I can survive without here.

We met at Dr. Bovet's office Saturday at 10:00 am and an exam began once again. Dr Egger of course drew blood, gave it to the technician asking for immediate response. He did ultrasound tests on intestinal and upper tracts of my body, then asked me lot of questions about fatigue, pain, discomfort of any kind. We waited for the tests to be completed. He reviewed everything, asked some more questions. Then he explained that he could try the new drug with a series of injections and then keep me on the vitamin B 12 complex, iron and food regime. He wanted me for the first week to come in each day for a B shot and then every other day. He would then do some more tests and see what the prognosis would be. I would have to cooperate in every way. He asked if I was willing to try an experimental drug he had develop. At my point what possibilities did I have of course. "Let's get started right away. So he came back within the hour and gave me the first injection and told me I must eat at least small portions 6 times a day. He addressed Steve, "See what she is hungry for and see that she eats it. With the rest of her vitals the type of food is not the issue, the issue is eating. I understand you are both gourmands having the restaurant in Montreux so go find something she enjoys and dine. He said he wanted to give me another shot of the end of the day and on Sunday before he left to return Zurich. He felt it would help stimulate me and start building my strength. Who knew what the side effects would be, they were experimenting with me, I wasn't going to worry about that right now.

So Steve asked me, "What are you hungry for? I'll go right now and find it."

"Corn beef on good rye bread with some mustard and lots of slaw. Oh and also a couple of big dill pickles.

"You've got it I'm on my way. Please don't go anywhere."

"I have new hope so I'm not going to my final sleep yet."

When he came back he had it all and we both devoured it. I couldn't believe I was so hungry. Some of the basic things are the very best and satisfy the most. We both laughed which we hadn't done for a few days, me the most seeing the pleasure on his face. Hope, may we always have it no matter what the circumstances. Dr. Eggert went back to Zurich where he intended to continue his research. Dr. Bouvet came every day with the round of injection of the new drug they had been processing. Asked what I had eaten and smiled. Tomorrow put in your order again to your husband for something else you like, it will help your system. What a blessing this man was, I really did trust him. If he was wrong at least he was giving it his all and trying to cure, my idea of what a doctor should have in his or her physic, the ultimate caring. I thought how once a horse of mine was suffering with lameness due to arthritis and old age and the veterinarian, Dr. Tyler, asked me "What do you want with this horse." I responded with, "The longest time we can share our rides and workouts together without he having undo pain." He smiled and responded with, "Then this means the Cadillac treatment." So he was placed on inflammatory medication and acupuncture and we had three more years together before he was retired. I told the story to Dr. Bovet who smiled and said, "This is the Cadillac treatment for you but you must do the plan I will prepare for you and you will enjoy many more years."

The nurse, I had one around the clock, was to be there for my needs while Dr, Bouvet would administer the shots Dr. Egger required. This was done about every 5-6 hours, aggressive but if it worked why not. Poor Steve was exhausted but tried to look strong. Dr. Bovet arrived one morning and administered the shot. He took my temperature and it had dropped already 2 points. He then asked me questions about any new symptoms that might be occurring from the drug. My answers were no, I slept, I was hungry, no pain. So he smiled at Steve and said," back to a restaurant or whatever for food." This time I wanted fresh fruit salad and a "good" quiche Lorraine. So Steve went in search of the banquet saying, "I wish Joachim were right here but I'll go to the restaurant." We had a wonderful lunch together.

Dr. Egger had returned as I was his experimental case but that was ok if he could achieve a positive response. He came to the house even though I had round the clock nurse care. He was monitoring be very carefully. One nurse helped me up to get me walking and then I insisted on taking a shower and doing my hair. All was done and I felt so much better and then took a nap while Steve went out to make calls to check on everything, clients, home, Jacque. When I got angry and said why is this happening I prayed and meditated to try to keep my spirits up. I did believe that your own inner attitude can help in healing.

Dr. Egger and Bovet arrived every day again to recheck temperature and take new blood samples and to be sure the shots were be administered as prescribed. They both were beaming saying the results were so positive they were thinking they were winning the fight. They thought I was much stronger and everything looked much better. Dr. Egger was keeping very specific records to judge the workings of the drugs. He said he believed he had finally gotten it to a level to help all anemia patients no matter the cause. I felt like a guinea pig for their experiments but if it was working and could help others I so of course was pleased.

So the next few weeks I felt stronger and started to work on my special projects and of course Steve was beaming. He insisted I do only what I wanted and to rest. The medication continued and I was pleased with the results although I had never been a fan of medication before, if it worked I would try.

So September, October, November and December seemed to go very well. We once again did a wonderful Christmas celebration with friends and family. Jenny and Peter were there with their grown children, Jacque and Christina of course, Paul and Juliana, James and Daphne, and many others. I couldn't do what I normally would have but everyone pitched in which was even better. It seemed I would have some time left.

By mid January again the fatigue came back and I knew the miracle might not occur, that I would live to a ripe old age and enjoy all it had to offer. We called Dr. Egger and he returned and said he wanted to try more injections so I said ok. They were new ones he kept working on. In my heart I knew he wanted it all to be positive.

Christina and Jacque wanted to come for weekend, of course that was find.

"Oh please do will have some fun and not dwell on illness.

Jacque and Christiana arrived with fresh flowers and after many hugs and kisses we sat and talked and tried to laugh. Our dear Joaquim came to prepare some dinner and we all tried, including Maria, to enjoy. Of course included was some delicious Janee/Gavin the wine from the vineyards that Jacque would take care of. Christina had shown interest in working on art projects with the gallery so I knew if I was to leave life they would carry on my dreams. I just thanked them for all the joy and fullness of life they had given me then they saw my fatigue and we went upstairs for me to go to bed. hand. I thanked them for all the joy and fullness of life they had given me and not to worry I was going to be fine. I also asked for some chocolate, Steve provided the box and joined me. Then I said, "some music, Nat King Cole.

Sunday we walked in the vineyards and Jacque and Chrisina went horseback riding I wasn't yet up to that. I went over some more of what I did with Paul and what she might consider doing, she seemed so excited. Then Jacque insisted on visiting with Father Bauer and the sisters and then go for dinner at the restaurant so he could visit with the rest of his family as he called them. They were over joyed to see him and that he would soon be living in Montreux. When they left that evening I was wistful but not unhappy.

In the morning Dr. Egger wanted me to go to the hospital to do an MRI and some other tests. He was determined he could beat this virus but wanted to be sure there weren't any other complications which of course my ears went up because of cancer. Steve of course went with me looking very worried. The tests were done and fortunately nothing else was found. He then administered yet another form of the drug he was researching. By the end of a 5 day stay I was doing better and begged to go home. Dr. Egger agreed but was staying on and would see me every day. By the end of 2 weeks I was coming around more to my own self. I began to think miracles can happen if you believe and stay positive enough.

Dr.Egger said I would have to remain on the drugs and curtail my usual schedule. "Let some of the others do more of the business so you can enjoy the things you love most."

I said I would and would follow the regime he set up for me. So in our late 50's since I didn't want to yet leave this life I believed I had more time. Steve and I agreed we would do only the most important things one of which was travel. We would build another apartment attached to the house and bring another lovely lady in as Maria was though well was often feeling her age and I did not want her to overdue. Jacque and Christna were graduating from the University in May so of course we were there. They would move to Montreux so we began to look for a house for them. They loved our land so much that they brought up building another house on the property just as Steve and I had discussed when we first married. We all decided it was a great idea I still had the plans from Jennie so I would in touch were if she had any new ideas for it. She answered only if I can come for a visit and of course you know my response. So in a couple of weeks she was there and we all were going over the plans making a few changes with her expert input. So in the meantime Jacque and Christina would stay in one our condos redoing it anyway they wanted and building would begin.

While Jennie was there we had long walks, went horseback riding, went ice skating laughing the whole time and of course shopping. We talked it seemed forever of life and it's direction and of our wonderful friendship, one of the most positive happenings in my life journey; Paul came several days later so the four of us kept enjoying each other. When they left I again felt wistful but was confident now that I would go again to Vienna many times in the next years especially taking Christina with me in the next many years until my cane appeared.

In the next few years even with the business we traveled again to France Paris and Provence, the United Kingdom, throughout Germany, Spain and Portugal, Greece and isles, Czech Republic, Hungary, Romania, the western part of Austria he had never seen Salzburg, rented a villa in Tuscany then went to Venice and Rome. We also did several cruises a long one to Japan and China, shorter ones to the Caribbean and a river boat from Amsterdam to Buapest. We loved every minute of it and always when we got home started planning the next ones still on our list like Australia and New Zealand and not to be left out the US the major cities and some of the countryside. We definitely had that on our list to do again. Jacque was now working with the vineyard and the other business while Christina was finding her way in design and art. We had the where-with-all and we took advantage of it. All the time with the drugs my health was good even if I did get more tired sometimes. God bless Dr. Egger and others like him who had a dream of a cure or at least a stabilization of a strange decease. I kept seeing him so he could continually check on my progress. To add to our happiness was the announcement from Jacque and Christina we would soon be grandparents and the family would continue. What a miracle that I would still be here for that joy.

So with all the concern I had of leaving this life prematurely I had been given an extra lease on life via Dr. Bouvet and the knowledge and persistence of Dr.Egger/

And so we continued our journey of excitement, adventure and loving. Whatever life brought us we had worked with it, life with its twist and turns, confusion, loss and pain had dealt us an excellent hand.

We were totally at peace with it and as always looking forward even to the time we took out our canes and knew we would still be part of the dance of life.